Pride Publishing books by Catherine Curzon and Eleanor Harkstead

Single Books
An Actor's Guide to Romance
A Late Summer Night's Dream
The Captain's Ghostly Gamble
The Captain's Cornish Christmas
The Captain's Flirty Fireworks

Captivating Captains
The Captain and the Cavalry Trooper
The Captain and the Cricketer
The Captain and the Theatrical

Pride Publishing books by Catherine Curzon

Anthology
I Need a Hero: The Angel on the Northern Line

Pride Publishing books by Eleanor Harkstead

Single Books
The Low Road

Captivating Captains

THE CAPTAIN AND THE CRICKETER

CATHERINE CURZON &
ELEANOR HARKSTEAD

The Captain and the Cricketer
ISBN # 978-1-913186-16-6
©Copyright Catherine Curzon and Eleanor Harkstead 2018
Cover Art by Cherith Vaughan ©Copyright July 2018
Interior text design by Claire Siemaszkiewicz
Pride Publishing

Published in 2019 by Pride Publishing, United Kingdom.

Pride Publishing is an imprint of Totally Entwined Group Limited.

THE CAPTAIN AND THE CRICKETER

Dedication

EH—For Charlotte, and our games of cricket in the park after school.
CC—To the epic, fabulous and never less than awesome Badass Bookworms—don't put this one in the jar!

Chapter One

What on earth are they feeding these babies?

Another ruddy-cheeked mother passed her enormous child to Henry. He balanced it on his hip, smiling politely as he jiggled it up and down.

"What a lovely boy!"

Puppies, kittens, foals, lambs, calves and piglets were more Henry Fitzwalter's style, the daily business of a countryside vet. He was at ease around them. But not human babies – they were strange and alien beasts indeed. The infant reached out its pudgy hand and tugged Henry on the nose, yanked Henry's neatly trimmed sideburn then grabbed a length of his hair and pulled.

Henry winced. "Certainly a strong 'un!"

"Daniel, you bad boy!" His mother at least had the grace to be contrite regarding her infant's outrageous thuggery, and wrestled the unfeasibly large child from Longley Parva's vet.

Nestled in the South Downs, Longley Parva had been the home of Henry's family for generations. And today, on this sunny Sunday afternoon, Longley Parva was closed for a street party to raise funds for the roof of the village hall.

Daniel was swapped for another child, who came accompanied by the odor of milk. Henry bounced the baby and it cooed at him. It appeared to be a little girl, judging by how frilly its outfit was, and although it was almost entirely bald, it was wearing a sequined Alice band.

A car tooted, an engine revved. A nearby shout of, "The road's closed for the party — what's the bloody matter with people?"

Women's Institute stalwart Mrs. Fortescue tutted. "Mind your language in front of the babies!"

Henry, ignoring the baby's grip on his knitted tie, stared from his vantage point at the top of the village's High Street toward the other end, where barriers and stalls were being shifted as a car approached.

A classic car in British racing green nosed its way toward him. He knew it, because it had been tootling around the village for Henry's whole life and for decades before that too. Everyone in England knew it, because this was the soft-top Jaguar of Captain George Standish-Brookes. This was the soft-top Jaguar that had transported its driver and his popular histories straight into the nation's hearts.

Henry clenched his jaw. *That bloody man.*

Cries of "It's Captain George!" filled the street, the Longley Parvans nudging one another and grinning, some even waving as the car wound its way along the crowded road. The final of the Bonny Baby Competition was forgotten.

George drove into the center of the village like the returning hero he was, classic Wayfarers hiding his eyes, the car horn blaring merrily and a crowd following as though the Red Sea had just parted.

George—Henry's childhood friend through thick and thin, until the day the Longley Parva Cup disappeared. George—the television historian with the knowing wink and dazzling smile. George, who sailed through life without a care in the world, waving now at the locals as he drove toward the podium with one hand on the steering wheel.

The handsome bastard.

Of course the road closure didn't apply to George, even though the vicar on his bicycle had been turned away and told to come back on foot. Rules *never* applied to Captain George Standish-Brookes. Not at school, not in his Bohemian home, and now, not at the village fête.

George made his own rules.

Unable to raise a hand in polite though grudging welcome without dropping the baby, Henry gave George a terse nod.

"Fitz!" George turned off the ignition and the car, somehow, came to rest at just the right angle for a classic car shoot. He pushed open the door and hopped out onto the green, a vision of easy, casual confidence in cricket sweater and chinos, his dark hair tousled just so, the sun glinting from the face of his watch.

Who still wears a watch these days, anyway?

Captain George did, because then he could wear a regimental watch strap too.

"What a welcome." George laughed, pushing the Wayfarers up into his hair. He looked around at the bunting and sausage rolls, the orange squash and bonny babies. "Have I crashed a party?"

Henry clenched his jaw. "I suppose those sunglasses prevented you from being able to read the sign at the top of the road, Captain George? *'Street party — strictly no entrance'*. You nearly mowed down half the village, you fool!"

He had forgotten that he was standing in front of a microphone. After a blast of feedback, his sarcastic reprimand echoed down the bustling street.

"Shut up, vet'n'ry!" someone shouted from the crowd.

"Yeah, you shut up! It's Captain George!" someone else chimed in. Within moments, the street was full of jeers aimed at Henry. Even the baby joined in, yanking Henry's tie so hard he nearly headbutted the microphone. George stepped up, his hands held in front of him in a call for calm. Naturally, *he* knew how to use a microphone, there was no wail of aggressive feedback to deafen *him*.

"Hello, Longley Parvans!" A chorus of greeting went up. "Sorry for nearly mowing you down — blame my enthusiasm to see this marvelous village once more. Some things, I notice" — he cast a long, comical look at Henry — "never change!"

Henry glared at the car and glared at George. "No, they don't, do they?"

The baby started to grizzle, its face turning tomato red. Henry bounced it more energetically on his hip, just as a hiccupping noise started up in its throat. He looked over his shoulder, wondering where its mother had got to. A reporter from the local paper had slipped in between the locals and had clambered onto the podium. "Give us a smile, Captain George! Can we get a few words for *The Bugle*?"

"I've just been around the world for my *Secret History of Magellan*, which you can watch this Christmas on the Beeb!" He winked, a twinkle in his eye that made at least one of the girls from the riding school fan her face. "And I *still* haven't found anywhere as beautiful as good old Longley Parva!"

Applause rippled through the crowd, along with enthusiastic nods. And — *for heaven's sake, was it really necessary?* — a cheer began.

"Hip-hip-hooray! Hip-hip-hooray! Hip-hip-hooray for Captain George!"

Mrs. Fortescue's shoes banged loudly across the podium as she approached their returning hero. "Captain, could I possibly ask you to assist with the Bonny Baby Competition?"

"The divine Mrs. F.!" George kissed her on both cheeks. "It would be a pleasure!"

Henry knew better than to cross Mrs. Fortescue. She took the frilly child from his arms and deposited it in George's embrace. Laughter echoed through the crowd, and the child's mother now appeared, beaming up at George. Henry could do nothing more than stand there as George bounced the baby more and more, the hiccupping noise now a rumble.

The baby opened its little mouth and ejected a vast stream of curdled milk.

All over the shoulder of Henry's tweed jacket.

"Brilliant!" The photographer tipped his head back, laughing. "What a great photo!"

"You can't print that!" Henry stared in horror from the mess on his shoulder into the hungry lens of the camera. He dug in his pocket to retrieve a handkerchief and began to mop at the sour-smelling deposit. If it wasn't enough that Longley Parva's animal population voided their bodily fluids over him on a near-daily basis, now the human residents had joined in as well.

"You're a poppet, aren't you?" George bounced the now empty baby, who gurgled happily at him. Then the mother, who was even more thrilled by the celebrity in their midst, slipped her arm through George's and grinned for the photographer.

"Would you mind just sort of utching up a bit?" The photographer gestured Henry to step to his right. "I need you out of frame, mate!"

Henry closed his lips in a tight line and nodded. "Of course. The local vet isn't as exciting as a *bona fide* TV historian, after all."

"And war hero," the photographer reminded him saucily.

Henry manfully resisted the urge to roll his eyes. Still dabbing at his jacket, he walked past Mrs. Fortescue, only delivering a tight smile of acknowledgment, and hopped down from the podium. Henry was supposed to be judging the jam-making competition in fifteen minutes, but he wondered if he would be ousted from that gig too.

At least jam couldn't vomit on your shoulder, though, there was that.

"God," the stable girl told her equally flushed friend as Henry passed, "he's even *more* gorgeous in the flesh than on the telly!"

Then she glanced at the sick-stained vet and touched her hair self-consciously. With a grimace, she murmured, "You missed some puke, Mr. Fitzwalter."

Henry indicated over his shoulder with a jab of his thumb. "Will you tell Miss Watson on the jam stall that I'm going home? I can't judge jam like this." Once more, he pressed his lips into a thin, disapproving line.

"But I'm certain that our resident celebrity will *relish* doing the honors."

Somewhat proud of his pun, Henry went on his way. Longley Parva Manor was but a short walk from the main road and Henry would go home, sit in the bath with a whiskey and hope George left again soon.

"Fitz!" George's voice again, full of laughter and carefree bonhomie, *smooth and easy as hot chocolate*, as one of his adoring Sunday newspaper critics once said. "I say, Fitz!"

Henry skidded to a halt on the gravel at the bottom of his driveway and turned to watch George approach. Behind him trailed a long line of smiling faces, the ladies who adored him and children who wanted to be him and men who wanted to buy him a pint. George the handsome, tan Pied Piper leading his faithful.

"What do *you*, of all people, want with *me?*"

"Mrs. F. tells me you're on jam duty." He slapped his hand down against Henry's clean shoulder. "When I was stung by a ray, did I let it put me off finishing my secret shipwrecks filming? No. When I broke my wrist wielding a war hammer, did I give up my location work for *Secrets of the Vikings*? I did not! Come on, Fitz, are you going to let a bit of baby sick defeat you?"

"Defeat me? I smell of vomit, Captain bloody George. I can't taste the jam with the tang of baby sick in my nostrils!"

"It's a jacket, Fitz." George laughed, a long, loud bray. "Take it off, man!"

"That's altogether too casual for a man of my position." Somehow, Henry had managed to speak though he had barely moved his lips. But his hand had already drifted to the top button of his jacket, as if

George had him mesmerized by the sheer force of his personality. "Very well, then."

Henry unfastened first the top button, then the second, his eyes never leaving George's.

Oh, come to your senses, you idiot.

Henry broke his gaze and focused on his remaining buttons. George turned back to his adoring fans and, caving in to the clamoring of some of the children in the crowd, took a pen from one of the blushing mothers and began happily signing autographs. Cameras clicked, children laughed and right there, all smiles in the summer sunshine, George Standish-Brookes no doubt sold a dozen or more books on that magnetic personality alone.

Jacket draped over his arm, Henry cleared his throat, trying to make his way through the crowd, back to his jam-judging duties. If only he was on television and had recklessly driven a classic sports car through a group of pedestrians, it would've been much easier.

He took his pocket watch from his waistcoat and checked the time.

"Excuse me — please — would you — mind your back, sorry, coming through."

"Jam-judging vet incoming!" George clapped his hands and the crowd parted ahead of Henry. "Thank you, my fellow Parvans!"

Henry looked back at George. As he raised his hand in a quick, small gesture of thanks, a smile edged onto his face. And that would never do.

He strode into the stripy gazebo, where there were trestle tables loaded with jars of jam. The jam makers' looks of pride exceeded those of the parents in the Bonny Baby Competition.

"Where have you been? Teaspoons at the ready, Mr. Fitzwalter!"

Mrs. Fortescue pressed a metal spoon into Henry's hand. He looked at his face upside down in its curved surface. Was there any point in him even beginning this, when George would surely arrive at any moment and charm everyone into submission? The jam was in neat, unlabeled pots, laid out side by side, just waiting to send him to an over-sweetened, sugary grave. And on the edge of his vision was George, still signing and posing, kissing cheeks and throwing babies aloft and ruffling the hair of adoring little children.

He probably makes bloody jam too.

"Greengage? Very good. Excellent." The fruit had just the right sharpness, just the right sweetness. It was the best jam Henry had tried. But he should've guessed who'd made it before he locked eyes on Steph, who was grinning at him from outside the tent, her bobbed hair shining in the sunlight like an advert for shampoo.

And if she was here, then Ed wasn't far away.

George *and* Ed — the most popular boy in school and the scourge of the common room together once more.

Can today could get any worse?

When Henry tried the next, sugarless, jam, he realized that he was wrong.

He couldn't spit it delicately into his handkerchief, which was now wet with baby curds. He couldn't see a paper napkin anywhere nearby. Henry would have to swallow it and nod politely, as he did with everything in his life.

Don't make a fuss.

Except, wasn't that just what he had done by rushing off from the Bonny Baby Competition?

"Now, Mr. Fitzwalter, is there a winner?"

Henry glanced toward Steph. She had, without doubt, made the best jam. But she couldn't win. Because for several years, more off than on, they had had what one might call a dalliance. An understanding. And she had finally broken it off and married Ed. Ed, who had made his millions in the City and had returned to Longley Parva to live in the world's most garish new-build faux-Georgian pile. The village gossips would have a field day if Henry awarded Steph the prize.

"I think it has to be the...the raspberry. This one." Henry held up the jar, which should've been awarded a highly commended second place.

Steph's grin faded and she wandered away.

Outside he heard George's voice on the microphone once more, something about letting children have their photos taken with the Jaguar, *television's most famous motor*. None of those children would be sick, Henry knew that already. Life just didn't work that way. There was always sugar in George's jam — the heavens were just aligned like that.

Henry shoved his hands into his pockets, his soiled jacket draped over his arm. He left the jam tent and paused, watching George. His erstwhile friend posed against his car, mugging for the cameras, arms around the shoulders of grinning children. It was so easy for him, the grin, the sparkling glance — he had never been any different. The most charming boy in the South Downs. And for some reason, George had been Henry's best friend. It seemed impossible now. Henry was boring and George glittered.

"Fitz!" George waved his hand as though Henry might not be able to see him. "Come and get a snap with your old chum!"

No escape route presented itself. Henry crunched across the road, his brogues carrying him inexorably onward to the man who had once been his friend. Until that very public spat. Until Henry's accusation. And everyone in the village knew. Perhaps, for appearance's sake, it was best to pretend that everything had been smoothed over. Even though it hadn't been and never would be.

"Captain George, old bean! Righty-ho, then."

Henry wondered who on earth would bother taking a photo of him, but Steph emerged from the crowd, her phone angled for a landscape shot.

"That's it, the invincible boys! Smile!"

Henry flinched as George's arm came around his shoulder in a matey gesture, but he pasted on a grin nonetheless.

"Guess what, Fitz?" George squeezed Henry's shoulders. "I'm here *all* summer. Isn't that marvelous?"

Henry fidgeted his hands in his pockets.

"Erm…yes, that's marvelous. Any particular reason why you're gracing us with your presence for so long?"

"I'm mugging up on the ancestors *and* delving into the mystery of the Longley Parva Cup!"

Henry was still smiling because now other residents of the village had decided, for reasons best known only to themselves, to photograph their local vet with their local television celebrity. But there was no smile in his voice.

"The mystery is why you've never owned up to stealing the damned thing."

"I didn't steal it." George's fingers tightened on his shoulder and he whispered through his grin, his tone as cold as his smile was warm, "You've got me all wrong."

"Don't be daft, of course it was you. But go on then —" There was a challenge in Henry's voice, the same tone he had used as a boy. *Bet you can't climb that tree, bet you can't hit this ball for six, bet you can't swim underwater all the way to the boathouse.* "Prove me wrong — I'd love to see you try."

"I shall! And I might even turn it into a program." George held up one hand as though writing in the air. "*The Secret History of Longley Parva!*"

Henry threw back his head and laughed. "You don't change, do you?"

"Neither do you, despite being covered in baby sick!" George looked at Henry, who was determined not to return his gaze. He wouldn't, he told himself, because if he did, George would wink and laugh and try to win him over. "Bit whiffy in this hot sun, Fitz."

"I'm a vet, I have a strong stomach. When did *you* last put your arm up a cow's backside?"

"Last year!" George released him to take a baby from a young mother, his face a photo-perfect smile as he struck a pose. "For *Comic Relief Does Farming*? Didn't you pledge a few pounds, old pal?"

"Only after you skidded over in a cowpat. Best laugh I'd had in ages."

George laughed and turned away to sign another autograph. He always laughed at himself, and it was one of his more annoying traits. The fellow was mostly impossible to rile. Not totally, but mostly.

"Righty-ho, I'll be off then." Henry was sure that George was too engrossed in his fan club to hear him. He could make his escape from the damn man unnoticed. But the devil had stolen his tongue and spoke for him. "You know where to find me."

"Fitzwalter!" Ed Belcher's bellow shattered the gentle sounds of the summer gathering. Its owner was striding across the crowded green toward Henry, incongruous in a pinstriped suit, his red tie caught over one shoulder and his slicked-down hair glistening in the sunlight.

Henry tried a polite smile but could only manage a grimace. "Ed, what can I do for you?"

"What's this business with Stephy? Broke her back over the Aga churning out that jam!" He stopped a couple of feet from Henry. "Come on, let's talk turkey. What was the deal?"

"The raspberry pipped the greengage to the post, I'm afraid." It was a weak pun, but Henry went with it, and smiled at his adversary.

"That's balls, Fitzwalter," Ed barked. "Raspberry balls!"

"Easy, old thing." George glanced back at them. "Women and children present!"

Henry took a step toward Ed and lowered his voice. "I could've given my ex-girlfriend first prize — and then all the gossips in Longley Parva *and* Magna would've done their worst. You need to remind yourself how village life works, Ed, because you'll find yourself in a jam if you don't."

Henry grinned at his own joke, but Ed only glowered.

"You always were a little squirt, Fitzwalter, and you still are. If I were Alan Sugar, you'd make sure my wife won that ribbon and we both know it!" He attempted a smile, showing sharp, white teeth. "And I'm not far behind him nowadays, you know!"

Henry the judger of jam was silent, but Henry Fitzwalter the vet didn't rest. He was fond of his patients, even if he wasn't always fond of their owners. "How's that pregnant mare of yours?"

"About to drop another winner for Epsom, I bloody hope!" He laughed, as though there was something hilarious about that statement. "Deal with many racehorses, do you? I thought you were a cow's arse sort of chap!"

"Women and children!" George reminded him, earning another scowl from Ed.

"Mine is the nearest veterinary practice for miles, so…up to you, isn't it?" Henry extended his hand to shake. Ed took it, gripping tightly enough to prove that he wasn't *only* manly, he was the *most* manly in the village. It was a stock exchange sort of grip, a grip that said, *I've made my millions, don't get in my way.*

"And you, Georgie-boy, you should be making a series about me! One of your things for the BBC — *Ed Belcher, Millionaire!*"

George's reply was a disinterested smile and Ed looked back at Henry, still pumping his hand. Henry began to wince. He had only meant to shake hands as a gesture of farewell, not a fight to the death.

"Righty-ho, Ed — time I was gone, they're announcing Guess How Many Sweets in the Jar in five minutes. Wouldn't want to miss that!"

Henry turned away from Ed and rubbed at his hand, trying to revive his circulation. He bit back his retort. *Stephy shouldn't enter competitions if she can't cope with losing.* He wandered toward George's car again, drawn there as if by a magnet. Its immaculate paintwork gleamed in the early summer sun.

Imagine going for a spin in it, roof down, wind in your hair, threading through the leafy Sussex lanes. Imagine how perfect that would be. Then imagine George sitting beside you.

Henry felt George's eye on him.

"I mean it, Fitz," George called in a mirthful tone. "I am not and never was the Longley Parva Bandit!"

"An elaborate double-bluff, Standish-Brookes!" Henry laughed. "What's your plan, then, to unmask the Bandit? If — *supposing* – it's not you? Because I never got to have the trophy, even though I won it, and I don't like to sound like a man who bears grudges, but — "

"Tonight!" George stooped to address the little boy whose T-shirt he had just signed and told him, "Spread the word, my young friend, George Standish-Brookes will be revealing his next big project at seven in the pub and the whole village is invited. Drinks are on me!"

The boy blinked up at him and asked, "Can we be on the telly?"

"If your mum says yes!" George scrubbed the child's hair. "Now go forth, spread the word!"

Henry took his fob watch out again. "What *are* you planning, Captain George?"

But Henry didn't wait for an answer and began to make his way to the tea tent. He couldn't face the evening without a stomach full of scones.

"Seven o'clock, Fitz," he heard George call cheerily. "I'll even buy you a drink, though I bet you won't accept it!"

Henry skidded to a halt. He turned back to face George and pushed a lock of his unruly hair from his forehead. "Mine's a pint of our local ale — if you can remember what it is!"

"Since I'm the face of Longley Spitfire, I have no trouble recalling it," the newcomer laughed. "You might even see my mug gracing the pumps by Christmas!"

And I'll take a marker pen and add comedy mustaches to them all.

"I'm sure I will!" Henry raised a hand in farewell and trudged toward the tea tent.

Chapter Two

In his best corduroy jacket, Henry headed to The Green Man. It was six-thirty by his fob watch — it was either that or arrive at seven-thirty, just to annoy George, and he was fairly sure that by arriving early he would rile George more. Henry pushed open the door into the pub. He should've known that the offer of free drinks from a TV personality would fill the building to bursting half an hour before kick-off. And George, of course, was already there.

The Green Man, usually brisk on a summer evening, was packed. There was barely room to move, let alone reach the bar, and the door to the lounge was propped open to allow the tightly wedged drinkers a chance at the celebrity whose presence had already filled the taproom.

George was at the center of the storm, standing beside the enormous stone hearth. One elbow rested on the carved wooden mantelpiece next to a signed photograph of him in the garb of a World War II fighter ace, a bottle of Longley Spitfire held in one hand. The photo was aged to look as though it were vintage and framed in a neat wooden frame with a cream mount. It was new, of course.

"There was no charge for the ads," George was telling the groundsman with that same benevolent TV smile. "One does what one can for one's village, and that includes shouting about their beer from the rooftops!"

No charge. Of course there was no charge, George wouldn't want money for an advertisement when he could be paid in adoration, would he?

Because you love your village so much, you stole the bloody Longley Parva Cup!

Henry pouted and went to the bar. Before he could order his drink, he had a farmer on one side of him talking about the best treatment for mastitis in dairy cows and a woman old enough to be Father Time's grandmother on his other flank, asking him about feline toothpaste. He nodded, listening to both of them, interjecting with the benefit of his learning and experience, all the while trying to catch the landlord's eye.

Bob was gazing with unconcealed admiration at George, and his attention wasn't easy to get. Henry cleared his throat, he tapped a bar mat meaningfully on the polished wooden surface, he raised his hand but, all the time, Bob watched the man who had brought a week's worth of trade to his pub in one night. George, however, *did* glance to the bar. With a nod he called, "Bob, old pal, you've got chaps waiting for service!"

Only then did Bob unfold his burly arms and grace Henry with this attention. "Pint of Spitfire, vet'n'ry?"

Henry only realized then that the beer mat he'd been holding was emblazoned with George's face. There was a sudden metallic taste in his mouth—he had gone off the idea of Spitfire, but it was his favorite ale.

"Yes, Bob—thanks."

Henry slipped the beer mat into his pocket.

"Getting a bit packed in here, isn't it?" George addressed the question to the entire bar, all of whom, with the exception of one, called out their agreement. "Shall we take it outside?"

And so, George, at the head of a snake of villagers, led the way into the beer garden. Henry planted his feet on the ground, determined not to be swept along with them, but the tide was unstoppable and it was all he could do not to spill his pint as he was pushed and pulled across the room toward the open door and the scent of a summer evening beyond.

The sun still shone, balmy and bright, and bees buzzed here and there among the potted flowers, dancing with butterflies while a cat watched from the fence, every kind of creature summoned to this cricket jumper-clad Snow White. Even Ed and Steph were there, already seated at a table beneath a parasol, no doubt bonding over the open packet of salted peanuts that lay between them.

George climbed up onto an empty table, a rabble of adoring children crowding one another to sit at his feet, and every eye in the garden turned on him, awaiting the celebrity's announcement.

"Fifteen years ago," he began, "two young cricket stars—no offense, Ed, but you weren't one of them... I believe your first and last crack at the eleven ended with you turning tail and running away from a particularly solid sixer!"

There was a ripple of polite laughter but Henry noticed that Ed's own effort to join the mirth left him looking as though he had just smelled a cowpat.

"Two young men, myself and good old Henry, of course, were engaged in a titanic struggle for victory in the Longley Parva Single Wicket Cup. At stake, the infamous Longley Parva cup."

The cup. More of a vase, in fact, stolen from the cricket pavilion fifteen years ago, and Henry knew who the villain was. George Standish-Brookes had taken the trophy rather than let his friend win it because George won *everything* and he couldn't bear to be beaten by Henry. Not at cricket, of all things, even though Henry was the best by far, and George was the falsest friend a boy could ever hope for.

"Now, quite rightly, Fitz won that tournament. He never received his cup and to this day, that cup – vase, really – remains missing, the thief at large. That summer, life changed. Fitz went into vetting, I went off to join the army and do the odd bit of telly."

The laughter was more than polite now, but appreciative. Oh, what a modest, handsome, rich, effortlessly successful war hero George was!

Oh, how Henry loathed him.

"Yet Fitz never forgave that injustice and still, to this very day, blames his old pal George for stealing that vase. From that day to this, no single wicket has been fought and Henry Fitzwalter's record stands." George raised his glass of beer toward Henry, eliciting a small round of applause for his former friend's sporting triumph. "This summer, I intend to bring back the Longley Parva Single Wicket! I've invited a few pals you might know to take part – they're better known as the England Cricket Team, and I'll be turning our village adventure into a doc for Auntie Beeb. They're keen for a book too – the interest should bring a nice bit of cash into the village hall fund!"

A roar of appreciation rose from the crowd. A book, money, TV, the England Cricket Team in Longley Parva.

Of course George couldn't let Henry's triumph in the tournament stand – he had to send in the entire England team to win it from him.

"So, this is where you come in, my fellow Parvans! I'm home at last and I'm making each and every one of you the star of my Christmas special *The Secret History of the Longley Parva Cup!*"

Only George could turn his own dark deed into Sunday evening family entertainment. And of course, once George stood in front of the cameras, blinking his long eyelashes at the lenses, a careless toss of the head, admitting after all these years, *Sorry, chaps, I'm the Longley Parva Bandit!* The entire village – the entire South Downs, damn it, the entire country, plus everyone watching on BBC America, would sigh over him. *What a rascal!*

What an utter bastard.

But as Henry watched George down a pint to rapturous applause without a drop spilled, he realized he couldn't ignore the sliver of himself that wished George would prove him wrong. Deep down, he wanted to believe, after all these years, that maybe it wasn't George who had stolen the cup. That the cricket jumper he had turned up in wasn't just George's way of rubbing it in.

And of course, out of honor, if George wasn't a thief, then Henry would be required to apologize. And that would be the most difficult thing of all.

"So let's raise a glass to Longley Parva, the Longley Parvans and the cup, wheresoever it may currently be. Hip hip, hooray!"

And the whole beer garden chorused with him, the sound as loud as a summer storm and just as annoying as Ed in childhood, dragging his nails down the school blackboard whenever the teacher left the room.

"Ooof!" Henry's ale sloshed over the rim of his glass and spilled onto his jacket. An elbow in the ribs from Tom Golding was never a gentle nudge.

"Remember that, don't you? When the cup disappeared! You two lads were the stars of my team that year. Bloody good all-rounder, you are, Henry! Bloody glad you moved back to the village, otherwise — truth be told — with the other players in this village, we'd be the laughingstock of every team from here to Dartmoor."

"Keeps me fit." Henry, for the second time that day, dabbed at his jacket with a clean handkerchief. He didn't want to think about it — that moment of rage that had cost him a friendship.

"If George is here for a while, we should get him to join the team, eh, Skipper? What do you say? He's dressed for the part, I'll give him that!"

Yes, he has, hasn't he?

"Captain George'll be too busy, Tom, what with all the camera crews and outside broadcast units he'll have to deal with. He'll be sat in his makeup trailer, zhushing up his hair — he won't have time for cricket and cucumber sandwiches."

Tom slapped Henry on the shoulder and waved across to their temporarily resident celebrity. "Nah, I'll ask him — oi, George!"

"Tom, you old devil!" George leaped down from his impromptu stage and ambled over to join them, greeting him with a matey slap on the back. "What can I do for you?"

"Seeing as you'll be around for the season, don't suppose you'd consider joining your old team again, eh?" Tom put his glass down on a nearby table and mimed an overarm bowl. "Like the good ol' days, when you bowled out every bloody man in that Didthorne Magna friendly?"

"Before I accept, I should give you fair warning that I'm bloody average at the batting crease." George laughed, leaning one elbow on Tom's shoulder. "And still a daydreamer when I'm in the outfield. If you can live with that, I'd love to bring my steam-powered shoulder back to bowl, if the skipper will allow it!"

Henry gritted his teeth and extended his hand to George. "*I'm* the skipper, in case you were wondering, Captain George."

George seized Henry's hand and shook it. This wasn't the battle of strength in Ed's handshake, though, but a warm and firm gesture that lasted *just* long enough.

"Looks like I'm out before I'm in!" George laughed and shrugged. "There's no way our Fitz is going to let the suspected Longley Parva Bandit onto the pitch!"

"I told Tom you'd be too busy. If you want to join, you'd be welcome, of course you would, but—"

"Splendid." George beamed and Tom patted him encouragingly on the shoulder. "Then I'm on the team!"

"Great!" Only after the word had left his mouth did Henry realize he had said it.

"Just like the old days," was the opinion of his Nemesis. "Though without you braining me with a bat, of course!"

Henry curled his lips into a grudging smile. "I seem to recall that you ducked."

"Afghanistan was like Disney World in comparison." George laughed, but Henry knew that was a lie, because Henry knew what George had faced in Afghanistan. Everyone knew — it was etched across the front pages, the Internet, the public consciousness. Courage under fire. The true meaning of a hero.

Without being entirely conscious that he was doing it, Henry gave George a gentle pat on the shoulder. Then he cleared his throat and took a deep swallow of his ale.

"Hope you chaps don't mind me asking the England lads along to perform fielding duties." George looked from Tom to Henry with a smile. "Should bring a fair few pennies into the village hall fund, though, not to mention make good telly."

"Will they knock about with the kids in the practice nets, do you think?" Tom laughed as he turned to Henry. "The England lads fielding, eh — you'd have your work cut out to defend your title then, Skip!"

Henry replied with a mirthless chuckle and swilled the remains of his ale from side to side in his glass. He was trying very hard not to look up at George. *Of course* George's intervention in the village would be good. But why did he have to be here, why did he have to keep appearing at Henry's elbow? Reminding him, with every smile, of what he had lost?

"We could lay on a bit of a meet and greet for the kids too. Photos, autographs, a morning coaching with the team before the tournament?" George suggested with a grin.

Catherine Curzon & Eleanor Harkstead

A long, low sigh escaped Henry. "Of course! Can't disappoint the kiddies. And why not fling in a buffet and a clown on a unicycle as well?"

He hadn't meant to sound so bitter, but there it was, he'd said what he'd said. The golden boy had returned, after all. So Henry upended his glass and finished the dregs.

"Right—well, things to do. See you about, Cap'n George—Tom, you too." Henry made a sarcastic salute, then shoved his hands into his pockets and made for the gate at the side of the beer garden.

Chapter Three

George Standish-Brookes, of course, was never the first to leave a party. Nor was he the last, for he knew the value in leaving people wanting more. He drank a little, laughed a lot, signed the requisite number of autographs on all manner of objects and posed for a week's worth of photos in a couple of hours. He smiled to think that he had even considered trying to make his return to Longley Parva low-key, for he wouldn't know how to do low-key if his life depended on it.

After the noise and bustle of London, the frantic pressure of the filmed circumnavigation, the weight of the deadlines that *must* be met, the quiet streets of his childhood village were indeed a balm to a soul that nobody would ever have guessed might have known a moment's unhappiness. He strolled across the green, his hands in his pockets, and paused before the war memorial, blinking as he read the inscription through the darkness.

Let those who come after see to it that their names are not forgotten.

Captain George Standish-Brookes, the most dashing officer in the Household Cavalry, bowed his head for a few seconds in recognition of that shared sacrifice. Then he lifted his gaze and looked up into the heavens, the Milky Way blazing bright, studding the ink-black sky.

And there was a shooting star, as if on cue.

What an opening this would make to the book.

With that thought, George set off once again toward the cottage where he had grown from a babe into a boy and from there into a young man, ready to go off and fight for the country he loved. Here his father had died and his mother had worked and now, with Alexandra Standish-Brookes — *call me Andie, darling* — off making pots in her commune in Marrakech, this ramshackle pink cottage, shielded by trees and roses, its lopsided windows glowing with lamplight, was his home once more, at least for the summer.

Just the place for a chap to unwind, not to mention make a village famous.

At the door of the cottage he stopped and breathed in the scent of the climbing roses that framed the entrance. To his right a hedgehog snuffled through the grass, to his left a nightingale sang and, somewhere in the darkness, he heard the cry of a fox.

This was a long way from London.

George unlocked the door and stooped beneath the heavy-beamed head jamb into the low light of the hallway. Standing among the bright paintings on either side, his feet muffled by the vivid woven rug on the flagstone floor, he was instantly catapulted back to childhood. Mrs. Linley had done a sterling job in keeping the place homely during his mother's travels, and even now he could hear the chaos of this house. There had always been children playing and the radio booming, Andie shaping her pots or baking disastrous bread and trying and failing to make jam.

Now the cottage carried the fragrance of the bright, freshly cut blooms on every windowsill and there was no sound at all. He couldn't quite decide if it was wonderful or unbearable.

Wonderful, he told himself. *And it'll be even better when the mystery is solved.*

Chapter Four

On Monday morning, Henry was halfway out of his front door when the post arrived, courtesy of Manjit. He was still chewing his toast and managed to smear an important-looking envelope in Tiptree Tawny marmalade. The envelope demanded his attention, but so did his day ahead, a diary full of appointments, farmers and distressed pet owners.

And now another complication.

"There's a man in your lake, by the way." Manjit nodded across the gardens toward a circle of bulrushes in a natural dip of the lawn by the driveway. She grinned as if this was not surprising in the least and hopped onto her bicycle, the bell trilling as she pedaled away.

A man, in the lake of Longley Parva Manor?

Henry stuffed the soiled envelope into the pocket of his fourth-best tweed suit and strode across the lawn.

People didn't *swim* in the lake and nor would they ever – it was ornamental, a thing to be looked at now and again and fretted about whenever a daring cat jumped on its frozen surface in the coldest winters. Of course, before he even admitted it to himself, Henry knew there was only one man who would dare to have trespassed so shamelessly on the family land. When he reached the edge of the lake and saw the sun glistening off George Standish-Brookes' broad shoulders a second before they disappeared beneath the surface, his worst fears were realized.

"Get out of my bloody lake, man! What the hell do you think you're doing?"

He had no idea if George could hear him under the water, but Henry couldn't stop the words as they escaped him in a shout. Perhaps George couldn't, he realized, as his former friend surfaced for a second then dived down again. Either that or he was simply ignoring the squire of Longley Parva Manor.

Henry yelled and waved his arms about. "George, for God's sake, you idiot!" No *Captain George* now, not even a sarcastic one. "The last thing I need today is a drowning in my sodding lake!"

Especially not the drowning of a beloved local celebrity.

"What's that, old chap?" George broke through the mirrored surface, beaming at Henry. He tossed his head back, a shower of water spraying from his hair in the sunlight. "Bit naughty, I know, but I remembered the lake and just couldn't resist!"

Another angered shout was ready on Henry's lips, but it died away at the sight of George's chest, partly visible above the water. Henry had seen it in the flesh before, of course, but on the body of a gangly youth. And, like everyone else, had seen the more mature, muscled version on television. Shocked audiences wrote to *Points of View* to complain if that toned chest and stomach weren't bared to the camera at least once per episode of George's television series.

"You'll — you'll catch your death." Henry pointed his toe toward George's discarded clothes.

"You're talking to an enthusiastic ice swimmer." George laughed. "Come on, jump in!"

Oh, yes, the ice swimming.

Henry had seen that episode. More than once.

"I don't have time! And — and *I* can't go swimming in a lake. It's full of reeds. You can't see the bottom. *And* you've probably disturbed my newts!"

But Henry had swum the lake as a boy, with his friend George. They'd dared each other, raced each other, dived and splashed and laughed until the sun had set.

What had happened to *that* Henry Fitzwalter? Was he still there somewhere under the tweeds and the corduroy and the sensible brogues?

Of course not. What a ludicrous notion. The boy had fled.

"Your newts are perfectly happy, Fitz!" George lifted his arms and slicked his hand back over his wet hair. "Now come on, like the good old days? The pre-cricket bat days?"

Henry twisted the top button of his jacket. Awkward, he swung his foot and peered over his shoulder at the driveway as if someone was watching them. He took out his fob watch.

"I'm going to be late."

"What's the verdict on the lake?" George's arms were gently scything the water now, keeping him afloat. "Any objections to me taking a morning swim like back in the day?"

The muscles in George's shoulders rippled with his movements. Henry looked away, glancing down at his toes, which were wet with the dew.

"Yes, I do mind! Get out of my bloody lake!"

He shoved his hands into his pockets, waiting for George to leave. His fingers touched the envelope. Henry fished it out and turned it over to look at the return address.

It was from a solicitor's, Pennycuick & Sons.

"I'm swimming," George informed him brightly. "Come on, Fitz, don't be such a bore!"

"You can't just dive into someone's lake like that, it's not on! And anyway, I've got a letter here from a bloody solicitor, and you titting about in my bloody lake is the last sodding straw! Get out before I fetch the bloody boat hook and drag you out!"

"Calm down, Fitz." George laughed in the way that a man with no worries was able to do. Then, at a leisurely pace, he began to swim toward the lakeshore. Henry watched his interloper crest through the reedy water like a sleek otter. But the letter was burning in Henry's hand. He looked away from the glistening water creature and opened the envelope carefully.

Henry read the letter through three times. He still didn't understand it, although its contents seemed to be a presentiment of doom. *Pertaining to the intestate... Copyhold property... Unsubstantiated claim by descent... Grossly immoral conduct of one William Fitzwalter Esq... Prior historical claim... Enclosures Act... On behalf of our client...*

"Our client Ed Belcher? What the devil—?"

Henry took one step then stumbled, his knees buckling under him. He knelt on the ground, the letter on the lawn beside him. Frowning at the clinical, typed text, he tried to understand the import of what he had just read.

"Bad news?" George's voice was concerned. Henry heard the sound of splashing as his friend left the lake and a shadow fell, telling him that George was standing just a few feet away. "Is there an' 'ole in t'op 'edge, vet'n'ry? Is tha' sheep worryin' tha' pigs?"

"What the bloody hell are you on about—was that supposed to be a Yorkshire accent? It sounded more like you've contracted lockjaw from swimming in the lake!" Henry flicked the back of his hand against the letter as if it were a particularly annoying fly.

"It's from Ed Belcher's lawyers. It—it sounds as if Ed is making a claim that Longley Parva Manor is by rights *his*. You know what happened, don't you? Napoleonic Wars, my hellraiser ancestor played a cricket match and—so they say—William Fitzwalter gambled the house. He was playing against Ed's ancestor, and *your* ancestor, Reverend Standish, umpired. And the silly sods were too drunk to know who won. And now Ed has chosen *this* moment to rake up a two-hundred-year-old family squabble—as if that bloody prat needed any more money!"

"Ed was a bully at school, he's a bully now." George shrugged, his hands resting on his hips where a pair of thankfully generous swimming shorts ended and his naked torso began. "Chuck it away, pop your hand up a cow's rear end and crack on with the day!"

Henry tried to look George in the eye. "What sort of— *Chuck it away?* It's a letter from a lawyer, you can't just *chuck it away!*"

"Of course you can!" George laughed, as though this was the silliest jape in the world. "Into the bin, on with the day. Really, Fitz, do you take everything in life so seriously?"

Henry pulled himself back up to his feet and carefully folded the letter into its envelope. He balled his fists onto his hips and glared at the near-naked television personality on his lawn.

"Longley Parva Manor is at stake — the very ground you're stood on is at risk of being snatched away by a City boy with gelled hair, and you're telling me I should just lob this letter into the nearest bin? What planet do you live on, George?"

"Bloody hell, Fitz." George plucked the letter from Henry's hand and cast his glance over it. "Remember that time he stole your lunch when we were nine and I bopped him on the nose? He's stealing your lunch again, get over there and bop him yourself!"

"When he stole my lunch, he didn't recruit the most ruthless firm of solicitors in Sussex as intermediaries. As much as I would dearly love to see him bopped on the nose again, I don't quite think this can be resolved as easily as a playground tussle."

Henry held out his hand, waiting for George to return the letter. George shrugged and placed it in Henry's hand with exaggerated care. Then he stooped to pick up his discarded clothes. Henry wondered how anyone so close to being naked could be so collected, not self-conscious and apologetic as was the British way. Strutting about as though he was in Saint-Tropez rather than Sussex, water trailing in rivulets down his —

No.

Not cricket at all.

What did they do in the Army to take the lanky youth Henry remembered and turn him into a broad-shouldered, muscular —

George had turned, his back facing Henry. And Henry saw, across those wide shoulders, scattered scars.

No one could have avoided the photograph. George was in the middle of the image, a massive corona of blasted earth exploding behind him, a child in his arms. It had been circulated far and wide, across newspapers and magazines and television screens, and had catapulted him to celebrity as a reluctant hero. But Henry had not realized that had also been the moment that had scarred him.

Because where else had those marks across George's back come from?

George suddenly spun on his bare feet and met Henry's gaze. He had seen the scars on TV, of course, because George was never shy about shedding his shirt in the pursuit of good television, but he didn't remember them being so clear. And Henry *would* have remembered, not that he had been looking, not at all.

Henry took a deep breath and looked down at the letter in his hand. "Best get on. And don't you dare let me catch you swimming in my lake again—I don't want outside broadcast units churning up my flowerbeds."

"I shall leave you to your letter." George sniffed. "And your lake, sir."

Chapter Five

Longley Parva Old Hall stood in all its brash glory on the edge of the village. Somehow, despite the intervention of Henry, the WI, the vicar, the parish council, the primary school, the Rotary Club and an MP, planning permission had been granted for the red brick monstrosity.

Ed Belcher had deliberately based his mighty edifice – the first building that anyone arriving at the village would see – on the Georgian façade of Henry's home. The choice of red brick was a modernization, however, not to mention an abomination. Try as Ed might, though, Henry's house was the real thing, with creaking wooden floorboards and, behind the stucco frontage and early nineteenth-century tinkering, a Tudor layout. Ed certainly didn't have a priest hole, but then again, Henry didn't have underfloor heating, reliable electrics or draught-proof windows.

A brick wall ran for some distance along the main road, and Henry finally reached the gates. He pressed the intercom and, from the crackling he heard, someone at the other end picked up.

"Hello, is Ed there? It's Henry—I need a word."

He'd begun to wish he'd rung ahead, but on his walk up he'd been on the phone to Jonathan, who ran the surgery with him. Poor Jonathan would now have a very busy morning indeed, but what could Henry do? Let Ed swipe his house out from underneath him?

"You've reached Mr. Belcher, who is this?" Ed's voice, cocksure and bluff.

"*Henry*. It's Henry Fitzwalter."

The intercom clicked off. Seconds later there was a dull mechanical *clunk* and the wicket gate swung open at a leisurely pace. In the turning circle Ed's red Ferrari was being waxed by one of his household staff, a young man wearing enormous headphones and a determined expression.

Henry gritted his teeth and headed off down the driveway. Young, spindly trees flanked the black tarmac, and straight ahead was Ed's front door. Henry knocked against the wood-effect panels. The studs in its surface were a medieval affectation at odds with the house's attempt at Palladian grandeur.

No one answered. The young man continued to wax the car that cost more than Henry made in a year, humming loudly to the music in his headphones. The wax cloth squeaked on the bonnet until he paused and lifted one earpiece, loud guitars blasting from it.

"Help you, mate?"

"Henry Fitzwalter, here to see Ed Belcher. He's just let me in through the gates—do you know why he's not answering the door?" Henry banged again, this time pounding his fist. From inside, Ed's pack of wolfhounds—the lord of the manor's gun dogs, of course — barked and howled, but still he didn't come to the door.

"He'll make you wait," the young man told him with a roll of his eyes. "Count to sixty in your head and the door'll open. Guarantee it."

Then he dropped the earpiece and went back to work.

One, two, three, four…

…fifty-eight, fifty-nine –

"Henry!" Ed pulled the door open. He was back in pinstripes, of course. "Just on my way into town to make a few more millions, blacken a few more balls. What can I do for you?"

Henry held out the letter. He stared at Ed, trying to assume a stance that would declare *Henry Fitzwalter is no pushover and will not stand for your shilly-shallying.*

"You might think this is a rib-tickler of a joke, Ed, but I don't. Care to explain?"

"It's not funny, Henry, for either of us. It's a bloody mess." He took a shiny, sleek phone from his pocket and glanced at the screen. "I don't have time to go over it now, but I think you might be living in my house! And your people have been living in my house for two hundred years. What a turn up *that* is, eh, Henry?"

"*My* family have been living in *my* house for six hundred years. And we've been in the village since 1066 — it's in the Domesday Book. A Norman married the daughter of a Saxon baron and they built the castle." Henry spoke slowly, trying very hard not to pepper his declaration with swearing.

Ed nodded but it was clear that he wasn't listening. He was still looking at the screen of the phone he held in his small hand. His thumb moved to tap out a reply and he said, "Tonight, eight o'clock, your house? Or should I say, the house that *might* be yours? We'll get it all sorted out, I'm sure!"

"Yes, *I'm* sure. The lord of the manor will be in attendance at his Manorial Court to hear your plaint."

"We'll have a Scotch, get our balls out and see who's bigger." He jerked his thumb at the man cleaning the car. "Get the pool sifted, I need the Ferrari!"

"What the hell has cricket—oh, not *those* kind of balls." Henry folded the letter away into its marmalade-garlanded envelope. Did he have time to find a competent property lawyer? How bloody expensive would one be, on an evening call in the rural back end of beyond?

"Eight. We'll talk serious turkey." Ed opened the door of the Ferrari and climbed behind the wheel. "It's not personal, Henry, it's strictly business."

If only I'd let Steph win the sodding jam contest.

"Of course!"

"Don't forget, bring your balls!" Ed pulled the door shut and turned the key. The engine gave a roar like a jet and, with a screech of tires, sped off along the driveway and through the gates with a millimeter to spare as they swung open.

Henry whispered under his breath, "I hope you sodding crash, you monumental turd." But then he felt guilty, because what if Ed really *did* crash? He sighed. It was time to go back to his patients.

"Keep an eye on him," the young man told Henry, the headphones now around his neck. "He's slippery."

Henry nodded. He knew all about the slipperiness of Ed Belcher.

Henry was only walking because his Land Rover was being fiddled about with at the garage in Longley Magna. At least it wasn't raining—although just as he observed this, the clouds began to roll in and a distinct moistness filled the atmosphere. Being caught in a deluge was *just* what he needed at that moment.

He turned up his collar and trudged on along the lane. It was so narrow that it had no pavement, and Henry had to stop every time he heard a vehicle coming so that it could pass him. It felt as if every car in the southeast of England was trying to drive along it and the longer Henry took to walk to the surgery, the wetter he would get.

Toot-toot!

That bloody noise, the tootling horn that always sounded at the very end of George's programs. Roll credits, up comes the production logo and *toot-toot!* Of course, he had only watched George on TV a handful of times, and it was *always* by accident. He wouldn't deliberately tune in, after all.

And a third *toot*.

"Fitz!" George wound down the window of the Jaguar. It had been in the family for six decades now, Henry knew, because every ten years the Standish-Brookes family threw it a birthday party. "Gosh, aren't you wet?"

"You've got a guest slot on the Weather Channel as well now?" Henry pulled the collar of his tweed jacket higher. Wool was naturally waterproof and he would be fine. Lovely and dry. No need to –

George leaned across and opened the passenger door.

"Climb on in, vet'n'ry, let's be 'aving you!"

Rain dripped off Henry's hair as he bent to peer into the car. "Aren't you busy solving a mystery or something? Except you know full well who stole that cup! Bloody hell – do you seriously think that a lift in the rain would somehow make me forget what you did? You're like Toad of Toad Hall pratting about in this bloody car. I'll give you *toot-toot,* you hopeless plonker! Sling your hook, Captain George!"

"Pride comes before a very wet walk, Fitz!" George pulled the door shut with a *clunk*. Then he *toot-tooted* that bloody horn and sped off, splashing Henry with a liberal dose of puddle water as he went.

Henry spent most of the day in the rain. He borrowed Jonathan's car and yet still got drenched, standing in farmyards and fields in the downpour. At lunchtime he had half an hour to run home through the rain, grab his baby-soiled jacket and run to the village shop where they would send it to a dry cleaner. It would take a fortnight.

That left for this evening his second- and third-best tweed, or his pinstripes. His linen suit was too casual and his fourth-best tweed suit was soaked through. He rarely wore pinstripes — there was little opportunity as a vet — but if Ed Belcher was going to 'talk turkey' with him, then an appropriate suit of armor was required.

In fact, Henry could have worn the suit of armor that stood to attention by his front door. But that might be going a bit far. Even if that hadn't stopped George from clanking about the house in it at Henry's seventeenth birthday party. *Silly sod.*

* * * *

By half-past seven the rain had stopped and the village shone clean and unblemished in the bright summer evening. Perhaps nothing bad could happen after all.

As if to prove Henry wrong, the jet-plane roar of a Ferrari could be heard heading up his driveway.

Cometh the hour, cometh the man. A cannonade of knocks assaulted Henry's front door.

Henry took a moment to compose himself, just as he did when confronted with a raging bullock. Then he rose from the armchair beneath the portrait of William Fitzwalter and strode through to his hallway.

He opened the door, filling the space with his height and breadth and determination.

"Yes?"

"I've made a million quid, closed down three failing businesses and bought a new Vanquish all in the last eight hours. You're looking at King Kong's balls!" Ed stood, hands on hips, his chest puffed out. "So let's talk houses, shall we?"

Henry folded his arms. "Go on, then."

"Let's chew this shit, you and me, get our balls out and see who's got the biggest." Ed nodded his approval. "Not going to invite me in, Henry?"

Why must Ed always go on about balls? This was not only the man who wanted to take his home, but the man who had married Steph. What on earth had Steph told him about their awkward encounters in the bedroom? Henry took a deep breath.

"No need—you won't be here long, Ed. So you can start by explaining just what the hell is going on." Henry pondered anew the man's gelled hair, which made it look as if he were wearing a wig combed from plastic.

"Okay, I'll shoot from the hip." He raised his hands and laughed that cold laugh, not like the boom of amusement Henry had heard at school when Ed had tripped him or pushed him or kicked him across the cloakroom. That had been *real* jollity, not this fake effort at friendship.

"I've been looking through the family papers and I found something pretty damned interesting. This cricket match our great, great, great-whatever grandads played back when Jane Austen was all the rage." He prodded Henry in the chest. "They gambled the manor. *Your* home."

Henry's throat tightened. William Fitzwalter was safe in his portrait above the fireplace in the lounge, resplendent in his immaculate white neckcloth and tailcoat. He had Henry's chin and Henry's eyes and Henry's breadth of chest. But William Fitzwalter had a sparkle in his glance that was extinguished in Henry's, a recklessness that had been expunged as his DNA had passed down the generations to the sensible, twenty-first-century tweed-wearing vet of Longley Parva. And it was that recklessness that might lose Henry his home.

"I know — I've heard all about it. They gambled and they were very drunk. The winner was never recorded. But considering that two hundred years' worth of my family have lived in this house since then, I rather think 'Bad Billy' Fitzwalter won."

"The papers of Octavius Belcher, Esquire, seem to disagree." Ed folded his arms, all the time holding Henry's gaze. "It seems that, once our two cricketing ancestors sobered up, Octavius thought he'd won by one run, but your man thought the victory was *his*. Standish couldn't remember where he'd put the score sheet in his drunken haze, so they took his word for it that the victory was Fitzwalter's."

Ed raised his eyebrows, as though that was an earth-shattering revelation. "Now, interesting thing is that Standish and Fitzwalter were thick as thieves as the years went by, close as brothers once they were widowed. Belcher's diary reckons that this friendship calls the result into question. He *and I* think that *he* won that cricket match, and Fitzwalter's best pal, Standish, cheated him out of his prize. That would make *your* house *mine*."

Henry tipped his head to one side, considering.

I really should've found a property lawyer.

"I know you've long had your eye on my house. Even trying to copy it in red brick." *Like a simpleton.* "Perhaps you'll show me this diary, then?"

"Happy to, Henry. It's with my lawyer, I'll have him send you a copy across."

"Good. I'll get my lawyer to look it over and write your lawyer a letter telling you to *sod off*."

Was a smidgen of the spirit of William Fitzwalter yet alive in Henry's veins? Henry clamped his mouth shut. Telling Ed to *sod off* was possibly not a good idea. And neither was it a good idea to claim that he had a lawyer when he didn't. Because now he would have to find one—fast.

"Funny, isn't it? The Standish-Brookes and the Fitzwalters in each other's pockets all those years and what was it you fell out over? The dishonesty of good old George, thieving *your* cricket cup." Ed smirked, sucking in his cheeks. "So what if Standish was just as shifty as his great, great, God-knows-how-many more great grandson is?"

"One would hope there's some difference between a man of the cloth and a bloody television celebrity." Henry bristled. "You have delighted us long enough, Ed Belcher. It's time for you to leave."

"Let's do this as friends." Ed smiled. "I'll pay you market value minus ten percent, how's that? Come on, better than having me drag you into court!"

"You—you want to *buy* this house? Good luck with that, because it's not for sale!" Was it there again, just a touch of William Fitzwalter's fire? Which, Henry reminded himself, had got him into this pickle to start with. "Get off my land."

"The offer's on the table. I'll knock five percent off for each week that passes. Trust me, it's still cheaper than a lawyer."

"I won't be bullied by you, Ed. Do you realize that?" Henry prodded his finger against Ed's chest, emphasizing each word. "I. Will. Not!"

"I blacked your eyes and bruised your balls in school, *Henrietta*, and I'll do it again in court." Ed pushed his face very close to Henry's. "Tell your pal to make a telly series about *that*."

"You were very fond of grabbing other boys' testicles at school, weren't you, *Edwina*."

"And I've squeezed enough to make myself a millionaire." Ed's hand shot out, closing around Henry's balls as though to demonstrate. "I'll squeeze a whole fucking house out of yours."

Henry stifled his surprised gasp and clenched his jaw. Ed's grip tightened and slowly twisted. Henry glared at his tormentor even while every pain receptor in his groin leaped and twanged. He grabbed Ed's wrist, trying to disengage his grip, but Ed only clamped on harder.

"Time to leave, Belcher! Now-*owww*, shit!"

Perhaps, Henry realized, he was losing consciousness, because he had to be hallucinating. In his fevered, gonad-squeezing-induced world of pain, George Standish-Brookes was strolling across the lawn from the direction of the lake, dressed once again in only those bloody swimming shorts that sat just so on his hips —

Not a time for a man's mind to wander.

The vision of George, tan, his hair wet, his body glistening, ambled toward the two men who were locked in combat. He was smiling that faintly amused smile, seemingly enjoying every second of Ed's terrible vengeance.

"I gatecrashed your lake again," George told Henry. Then he took Ed Belcher's left ear between his finger and thumb and walked away, threatening to tear off the millionaire's appendage unless he released his iron fist from Henry's balls.

"Come on now, Ed, time to go!" George beamed and Ed, spluttering and swearing, released his grip on Henry's gonads.

Henry exhaled raggedly and clutched the doorjamb to hold himself up. The sight of Ed, puce-faced and swearing in a most creative fashion, almost compensated for the extraordinary pain that he now found himself in.

"You'll be hearing from me!" Ed wagged his finger. "And, George, you can shag all the princesses you want, I'll always be richer than you!"

With that he climbed into his Ferrari and raced away, the sound of the engine fading into the distance.

"Lucky I *did* sneak along for a cheeky swim, or you'd be singing soprano now!" George was making his way back toward the door. "I thought you weren't at home!"

"What the—?" Henry dearly wanted to find an ice pack for his mangled groin, but now he had a television personality in naught but a pair of swim shorts to deal with. "George, I told you not to swim in my lake, and you've blithely carried on! I can't have near-naked men strutting about my grounds, splashing about in my bloody lake! What will people say? This *can't* go on, George—my poor newts will be traumatized!"

"I'm going to put you in my documentary." George said it as though it was a threat, his hands on his hips once more. "The grumpy old squire who accuses our hero of a crime he didn't commit!"

"Of course it was you!" In his exasperation, Henry's voice rose unfortunately high and reedy, as if Ed's hand was still clamped about his tender appendages. "You'd gone on and on and on about wanting to win the cup, and then *I* won it, and—it just vanished. How convenient! It must be in your cottage somewhere, hiding in plain sight amongst your mother's pottery. And don't for one minute think that just because the rest of Longley Parva hungers after your every glance and crumb of attention and witty joke that *I* will succumb to your charm. *Oh, ha ha, Captain George, for fifteen years you've cheated me out of my trophy, but you've just winked at me like you do on the telly, all is forgiven, what a lark, you loveable rogue!* Sod. That."

And *Britain's Favorite (and Sexiest!) Hero*, as the bloody *Daily Mail* termed him, blinked. Of course it wasn't a normal blink, a blink like Henry might have done, but a bat of long eyelashes over his green eyes, the sort that had commissioning editors reaching for their checkbooks.

"Stop being a baby," George said after a long pause, annoyance winning the battle with that *hail fellow, well met* façade despite how much he tried to keep a carefree smile on his face. "I'm surprised you had anything down there for Ed to grab, old chap!"

And that, clearly, was supposed to be the final word because George turned and strode away in the direction of the disputed lake.

Wincing with every step, Henry went in pursuit.

"A baby? *A baby!* I'm not the man who drifts about in a consequence-free bubble, twisting everyone around his finger because he's famous. For what? For taking your shirt off on telly and driving about in that bloody ridiculous car! You're an overgrown child, that's what you are! Me, I've got a business to run, employees to pay, animals to care for, an old house to look after, and you? You're just titting about, swimming in my lake, when I've already told you not to! Rules apply to you, Captain George, just as they apply to everyone else. And that includes theft!"

This time, to add insult to injury, it appeared that George's swim hadn't been a spur of the moment decision as he was passing, because he had brought a towel. *A towel!* A towel that the bloody queen's bloody shampoo and set had probably been bloody dried on too, or the Dalai Lama had blessed when he and George had their much-vaunted, award-winning, 'now an international bestseller' *Conversations on Peace* atop a mountain somewhere.

George stooped to scoop up a T-shirt and pull it on, draping the towel over his shoulders as though he was on the beach in Barbados. Then he looked Henry up and down and said, "I'm not surprised you're in a grump, wearing pinstripes in such beautiful weather."

Another final word!

And off he went, humming as only a man without a care in the world could.

"One doesn't prat about in shorts when one's home is under threat!" Not that Henry owned any shorts, but that was beside the point. A quick twitch at his gusset to rearrange his bruised fellows and Henry was off again, pursuing his former friend. "You can't just turn up in the village and—and take over, and swim in my lake, and wander about in the almost altogether, and call me a grump! You have no idea what my life has been like in this place since you sodded off, not a clue!"

"Are you going to chase me all the way home?" George, the former soldier, former fastest bowler on the village green, former thief, broke into a steady jog across the lawn toward the fence that divided Henry's land from the fields beyond. From there, the colorful garden of George's family home was visible and Henry knew now that this was the fox's tunnel, because they had run along this path countless times in boyhood, dashing between houses and games. Through the Standish-Brookes garden gate, into the meadow and it was a short excursion into Henry's own estate and, without any permission at all, into his lake.

George hopped over the fence and jogged on with a call of, "Keep up if you're still telling me off!"

Henry panted as he hurried, the pain in his groin not diminishing. On reaching the fence, he very carefully lifted his leg to climb over. He paused, wincing as he straddled the fence, and called across the meadow after the retreating figure of George.

"Well, no one else will do it, so as skipper of the cricket team, churchwarden and Clerk of the Parish Council, it is my responsibility to bring you into line— you louche bloody bastard!"

Henry shook his fist. There was no one to see, besides the Cabbage White butterflies that darted through the golden evening air.

They passed through the gate, the first time Henry had done so in fifteen years. Not the first time he had been in the garden in so long, of course, for *call-me-Andie* had often invited the village to the house for exotic drinks and an adoring rundown of her son's many achievements, but it was the first time he had been here with George in nearly half a lifetime. Only now did George cease his gentle barefoot jog and, with not a bead of sweat on his brow, turn to face Henry.

"If you stood up to Belcher the way you've persecuted me for the last fifteen years," he decided, "you might not be in this pickle now."

"Perhaps if you hadn't robbed me fifteen years ago, Belcher wouldn't think he has *carte blanche* to rob me now! But that's fine, I apparently have *doormat* written across my forehead anyway, so what's one more footprint on my face before I end up living in a cardboard box in a bus stop?"

"Right." George gave a single firm nod. "This has gone on long enough, Fitz. I'm going to have to ask you anyway for the program, so tell me, Henry Fitzwalter, Poirot, Miss Marple and Columbo all rolled into one, what, according to *you*, happened on that balmy day back when the world was a lot less bloody pinstriped than it is now?"

Chapter Six

Fifteen years earlier

Henry stood on the veranda of the cricket pavilion, looking out across the pitch. Tom Golding, floppy white sunhat wedged onto his head, was setting up the stumps for the Single Wicket match.

One year into his veterinary surgeon degree, Henry was home for the summer vac. Being the son of a vet, his vacation wasn't entirely relaxing, as he had to spend his days helping out at the surgery. But at least there was time for cricket.

Henry waved as a familiar face appeared from the other side of the practice nets. What luck, that George's leave should overlap with Henry's vac.

"Ready to surrender your crown?" George called and waved his hand in the air. "The Standish-Brookes are coming to whip the throne out from under the bottoms of the Fitzwalters at last!"

Henry folded his arms against the guardrail of the veranda and laughed.

"You're going to be very disappointed, Standish-Brookes — prepare to lose! That cup is going to be mine! It'll look jolly nice on the mantelpiece under Bad Billy's portrait."

"It'll look even better snuggled beneath Lady Georgina's proud, painted bosom!" George broke into a jog as he crossed the grass, no longer the gangly lad who had made his name as the finest bowler the village had seen in many a year. "My bowling arm's primed and my batting arm's newly trained — you're in for a proper walloping, Fitz!"

George suited a cricket jumper, it had to be said. Henry realized he was smiling at George in a manner that he really oughtn't. But George wouldn't notice, he was sure.

"You think you'll beat a Cambridge blue, do you, Standy-Bee? I think not!"

"I think it's all in the wrist, and I've got a hell of a wrist, young shaver!"

Henry bounded down the steps of the pavilion and caught George in a matey headlock, grabbing his thick hair and whirling the pair of them around in a circle. George grasped Henry around the waist. It was as if they were twelve again, laughing and hooting, dust kicking up around their feet. George tripped Henry up, and with their arms still locked around each other, they flew sprawling to the ground.

"Lads, come on, now!" Tom hauled them up by the collars of their shirts. "Neither of you'll win if you carry on with that caper. You were my two best players in the under-eighteens — you should set an example for the other boys."

"Your lot have had that trophy for two hundred bloody years, so it's our turn now!" George slapped his hand against Henry's back and laughed. "May the best man win, Fitz!"

"I will—so we'll have it for another two hundred more!"

Steph was sitting nearby with her friends, making a picnic of it by the side of the pavilion. They smiled and giggled at the players. Henry, fielding near George, rolled up his sleeves and flexed his forearm.

"Look at that, George, look at these muscles—large animal work, that is."

The sound of the girls' flirtatious laughter drifted toward them. George glanced over his shoulder at the young ladies and asked Henry, "Are you still chasing after Steph, then?"

Henry turned his back on the girls and lowered his voice. "Keep it under your hat, but I rather think she's chasing after me!"

"Will you let her catch you?"

I'll have to. Henry avoided George's eye. In less than a year, his friend had blossomed from lanky youth to handsome young man, and it hurt to look at him, knowing that—

"Dad's really fond of her. Said she'd suit the manor. I think even Bad Billy likes her—I'm sure his portrait winked at her when she popped round the other day."

"Well, you know, they say our gorgeous Georgina was no stranger to the bedchambers of LP." George winked. "And I *do* bear a striking resemblance to her portrait. Picture me in a powdered wig and rouge!"

What on earth was George implying? Henry stared at him. Surely not. Surely it was a joke. *But what if—?*

No. Ridiculous.

Henry suddenly felt rather warm. He gestured across to Mr. Dalrymple, who was tapping his bat in readiness, and trotted off to a more advantageous position. "Back to the game, eh? Silly sod always hits this way. I'll catch him out—just you watch!"

"All in the wrist, Fitz!" George wandered away, hands in pockets, not at all ready to field.

It wasn't innuendo, it couldn't be—cricket was all balls and wrists and creases and sticky wickets. That was just the game. *But my God, what if— ?*

Without even turning to see the ball as it arced up, Henry shot out one hand and caught it. He barely registered that he had done it, having merely acted on instinct. Enthusiastic applause rippled from the pavilion and loud cheers whooped from Steph and her friends. Henry turned and executed a courtly bow to his audience, before realizing it was his turn to bat.

George bounded over, leaving the crease to follow his best friend to the wicket. He put his hand in the small of Henry's back and leaned close to whisper, "Hell of a catch, Fitz. Well played, mate."

It was astonishing that George could inhabit such a manly frame and yet still have those long lashes and elegant green eyes. There was something pretty about how handsome he was, a delicate edge to —

"Come along, Henry, m' boy! Stop shilly-shallying about like a girl!" The booming voice of Henry's father carried across the cricket ground and over half of Longley Parva.

"Thanks, George." Henry patted him quickly on the shoulder, heart pounding. He looked up at the pavilion and watched his father sink a pint of ale, a cheese sandwich in his other hand. Steph, her head on one side, shielded her eyes with her hand as she smiled at Henry. Gulping, he kicked at the grass with his spiked soles. "Ready?"

George trotted across the grass to take up position, weighing the cricket ball in his hand. He turned and offered Henry a gentlemanly salute, softly brushing the ball against the weave of his jumper. Henry watched him, George's routine as established as his own, everything about his best friend utterly familiar to him. He watched the movement of the ball, the way George lowered his head slightly and, with his free hand, hitched the leg of his whites just a little.

He lifted his hand and ran it through his black hair, then touched it to his lips. Then, finally, George transferred the ball to his other palm and took his run, bowling with his customary, celebrated speed.

Henry swung his bat and with a smart *tock* sent the ball soaring over the boundary rope. A six. An easy-peasy six. The first six of the game.

"Got to try harder than that, George!"

It could almost just be the two of them out here, their gazes settled on each other, never shifting away. Someone whistled from the crowd. Henry ignored them and waited for George's next ball.

"Lulling you, old pal!" George went through his routine again, the polishing on the sweater, the hitch of the whites, the touch to the lips. Then there was the run again and the ball was flying at him.

Those lips, those full, soft lips, that Henry would never –

Again, Henry merely raised his bat a whisper and the ball flew through the summer air, almost out of sight, before coming down to land just outside the boundary. From the crowd Ed could be heard calling, "Another sixer!"

"If not for the sprained ankle, you'd be leaving us in the dust, eh, Ed?" George laughed, shaking his head as he retrieved the ball.

"I bloody would," Ed replied. "Not every man can claim he sprained his ankle falling out of a chopper after a Moët blowout!"

Henry raised his eyebrow. He wasn't going to engage Ed and risk losing his concentration. "Come on, George, as hard as you can!"

"That cup's coming home with me tonight," George replied cheerily, polishing the ball on his sweater. "I'm not a skinny lad anymore!"

Yes, I'd noticed.

A third six. The crowd roared its approval, none louder than George. He might be bowling, he might be Henry's closest rival for the cup this year, but he was a friend first and foremost. He leaped into the air, clapping his hands above his head and cried, "Go on, Fitz!"

Henry passed his tongue over his bottom lip and focused, blocking out everything else. His father shouting "Sissy!" when he got a four, a hot air balloon that decided to puff about in his peripheral vision for five minutes, the giggling gang of applauding girls, and Ed hobbling along the boundary until Tom ordered him away.

Once Henry passed his personal best of one-twenty, he at last noticed the sweat dampening his hair, and soreness in his shoulder and stiffness in his fingers. He was exhausted but exhilarated, and at one-thirty he was bowled out as a Longley Parva legend was born.

He threw aside his bat and he and George jogged toward each other, grinning.

Panting, Henry clapped George on his broad shoulder. "I'd like to see you beat *that*, Standy-Bee."

"After lunch, Fitz, I'm going to show you how to play cricket." George threw his arms around Henry, embracing him in a bear hug. "That was a hell of an innings, you've made me a proud pal!"

Henry closed his eyes for two seconds, enjoying the sensation of being in George's embrace. But he couldn't, not with everyone watching. He slowly disentangled himself from George's strong arms.

"Sorry, George—I'm all sweaty! Time for cucumber sandwiches."

"The lunch of champions." His arm still around Henry's shoulders, George steered his friend toward the pavilion and the adoration of his fellow Parvans.

Lunch passed in a blur of Scotch eggs, cucumber sandwiches, pork pies, prawn *vol au vents* and slices of Battenberg cake. Everyone in Longley Parva, it seemed, wanted to congratulate Henry, and at his side was George assuring all of them that he would easily beat Henry with one hundred and forty runs. Ed promised that next year, as long as he didn't have any further accidents involving helicopters and champagne, he would beat them both. And Steph lingered by the refreshments table, her mother saying loud enough for everyone to hear, "Well, the skipper's wife has to help arrange the tea, so it's good practice for you, darling."

After lunch, accompanied by the gentle applause of the spectators, the cricketers trotted back onto the pitch.

This time it was George's turn at the wicket, and though he cut a commanding, broad figure thanks to his time at Sandhurst, he was the first to announce, "I've got a fight on my hands. It might've been easier to just *steal* the trophy!"

Henry laughed as he prepared for his run-up.

"Good luck with that, George, someone might just notice!"

"Nip off for a cheeky cig, do a cheeky bit of thieving." He tapped the bat on the ground. "I jest, of course. Officers in the Household Cavalry would never do such a thing!"

"I wondered where you were going with that corgi hidden up your jumper!" Henry rubbed at his shoulder. A discreet belch escaped him thanks to the cucumber sandwiches, then his long, solid legs carried him effortlessly to the crease, where he delivered a perfect overarm bowl. George was ready, Henry knew that. He saw the strong shoulders square, the green eyes fix on him and, moments after the ball left his hand, he saw the wicket fall.

George turned, looking down in disbelief. Then he looked at the spectators, who erupted in a hail of cheers and a few cries of "Howzat!"

For a few seconds George appeared utterly bewildered then, with a loud cry of celebration, he threw down the bat and ran toward Henry.

Henry gaped at him. No, this wasn't right. George was going to get a century and go on and on — not lose. Not in front of the whole village, right after Henry's triumph.

"Bloody hell, George — what was that?"

"I was just—" He laughed, enfolding Henry in another bear hug. "I was watching you and then— I sort of drifted off, I suppose. You did it, old man, two hundred years in the Fitz family!"

Everyone was clapping for Henry, but the victor cheered for George.

"Drifted off?" Henry laughed affectionately. "Must've been a carb-crash after lunch!"

"Or maybe I was plotting how to pinch the Longley Parva Cup," George teased, finally releasing the hug. "What a fellow!"

"Wouldn't have happened if not for this ankle!" Even as he spoke, Ed was hobbling across the pitch on his ebony walking cane, his father standing at the boundary with his pinstripe-clad arms folded, shaking his head. "Next year, Henry, next year that cup is coming to the Belchers."

"If we can find a day when you're not half-cut on champers, then you're on!"

"Take cover!" Someone yelled the warning as large drops of water began to fall from the still-blue sky and spectators and players alike ran for cover toward the shelter of the pavilion. Henry ran too, even though his progress was delayed by every young lady and old boy in the village approaching to offer their congratulations on his feat.

Steph linked her arm in his, her cardigan held over her head like a canopy.

"I'll keep you dry—run!" She giggled as she tried to squire her squire to the pavilion, but, feeling her goosebumps against his arm, Henry looked around and wondered where on earth George had got to.

Poor sod must be utterly humiliated, even if he had put a brave face on it.

Henry waited on the veranda, Steph's arm still hooked through his. If only he could slip off and find his friend. But Steph was anchored to the spot, absorbing the praise that was aimed at Henry, while Fitzwalter Senior nodded at Steph and gave his son the thumbs up.

It was nothing more than a shower and, as the rain ceased, so did George appear once more. He bounded around from the back of the pavilion, calling to Henry and Steph, "Look at the lovebirds!"

"Just sheltering from the rain." How did one extract oneself politely from a grip like that? And really, everyone in Longley Parva seemed to think that Henry and Steph should be an item, all except one person.

And he'd just won the Longley Parva Cup.

"Come one, come all." Alan Belcher emerged from the pavilion with his hobbling son in pursuit, waving his arm. "Onto the pitch and let's get this cup presented. What're entrepreneurs for if not to give the trophy to yet *another* Fitzwalter?"

Henry's father appeared from the direction of the loos. His step was unsteady from a stream of celebratory Longley Spitfires. "A noble tradition, Belcher! Beat you to it myself, remember!"

"Thanks to a bit of weighting in the ball," Belcher decided. "But I'll let it pass since I was the first to make it to a million! Nobody cares about an old cricket vase when you've got a Maserati in the driveway!"

Mrs. Dalrymple, mayoress, carved a route through the crowd. She stood on the steps and clapped her hands, and everyone fell silent.

"And now, the presentation of the coveted Longley Parva Cup! The prize-giving will take place on the pitch!" She smiled at the trainee vet and skipper-in-waiting and guided the players and spectators across the springy grass. Henry slipped his bat under his arm, smiling, trying to appear humble even though inside a full firework display was going off.

Once everyone was assembled to her liking, Mrs. Dalrymple stared back toward the pavilion.

"What the devil is Tom up to?"

Henry turned. Tom was pantomiming his dismay. Shrugging, turning out his hands, pointing.

Mrs. Dalrymple cupped her sizeable hands about her mouth, turning them into a megaphone. Her voice could be heard halfway to Brighton as she shouted, "Tom, bring the bloody cup, you fool!"

Tom ran from the pavilion, his face ashen.

"Where's the cup?" Mrs. Dalrymple glared at him. "I can't award Henry the cup if you haven't got it. Where is it?"

He bent over and clutched his knees before looking up at the Parvans, his gaze settling on Henry. "It's gone."

A gasp of alarm rippled through the crowd.

"The back door of the office is open. I said we needed a new padlock, that one is rusted to buggery, and now look what's happened!"

"Henry Fitzwalter needs his cup." Mrs. Dalrymple settled her bunched fists on her hips. "Go and find it, Tom."

"I've just been looking for it, Gladys! For God's sake, someone must've nicked it!"

Not now.

Not at the moment of Henry's triumph, the cup that he'd dreamed of winning through his boyhood, that should've been in his hands, but was now — *Where was it? Who would nick it?*

Steph clung to his arm and George, with a devil-may-care laugh, announced, "It was the only way we Standish-Brookes were ever going to get it, after all!"

Henry was frozen with shock. *No. Not George.* Not his bloody best friend.

"You—you bloody took it? *My* trophy?"

"Well," Ed added, "he *did* throw the match for you, Henry. Maybe he changed his mind when he realized his people had lost. *Again*."

"Not now, Ed!" Henry gripped his bat's handle as if he was about to hit another six. "Where is it, George? This isn't funny, no one's laughing—where's my trophy?"

"*Me*?" George pressed his hand to his chest, all wounded innocence. "It was a *joke*, Fitz! Why would I take your trophy?"

Steph tightened her grip on Henry's arm. His whole world collapsed. George's green eyes and long lashes and full lips… He could never, ever have them. He couldn't bear it anymore.

"Because you're an idiot, because you're a reckless nightmare, because *you threw the match!*"

Henry swung the bat over his head, self-control entirely lost.

"This was my victory—but one last petty rivalry and—" He didn't stop, even when George ducked nimbly out of the path of the whirling bat. "I thought you were my friend! Don't you ever speak to me *ever again!*"

"Erm… Mr. Fitzwalter?" Mrs. Dalrymple appeared to be the only person brave enough to confront the cricket-bat-wielding maniac, and at last Henry blinked away his madness.

Through tears, he was dimly aware that the crowd who had come to see him receive his trophy were edging slowly back across the field. Shocked conversation whispered through them as they receded.

George was standing a few feet away, his mouth gaping and his horrified gaze fixed on Henry. Something was gripped in his hand but it wasn't a

Georgian vase, it was a cricket ball. He looked down at the ball, then up at Henry and finally down at the ball again. He threw it onto the pitch and turned. George walked away, his mother running after him in a clatter of wooden bracelets and a cloud of patchouli.

It was Ed who picked up the discarded cricket ball and looked at it. There on the red surface, whittled by George with a blade, was a scratched inscription.

HF – 130 – GSB

"He took it." Belcher sniffed, taking the ball from his son. "Thoroughly strange sort of family, that one."

He strolled away to the outfield and beyond, toward the dense copse in which Henry and George had learned to climb trees and had built their forts and hideaways each summer. Without a glance back, Belcher flung the ball overarm into the trees and shouted, "Six, Ed!"

"Henry, Henry!" Steph consoled him with her yielding embrace and the scent of her soft vanilla perfume.

At least, Henry assumed she was trying to. But nothing could ever console him now.

Chapter Seven

Henry passed his hand through his hair and sighed. That was his version of events—edited to avoid admitting to George that he had gazed at his lips and wished that he could—

"What happened to the ball from that match?" George stood at the back door to the cottage as he spoke, his arms folded tight across his chest. Rather muscular arms, Henry registered, while trying not to notice. The sort of arms that could probably give a hell of a hug if one were—

A thief's arms.

"As I told you—Belcher Senior threw it into the copse."

"Oh well, at least you're not accusing me of taking that too," George told him. "Chasing me across the field, shouting and carrying on. I came home for a peaceful summer, and you're *still* yammering on about that bloody vase!"

"Because we were such friends, and—and I couldn't look you in the eye anymore! But everywhere I go—

there you are! I switch on my television, *there's Captain George*, I flick through a newspaper, *there's Captain George*, I put on Radio 3 and *there's Captain George*, I watch *Comic Relief*, and *there's Captain George, Royal Command Performance? There's Captain George!* Bloody hell, a bus goes past me in Brighton, it's got an advert on it and who's that? *Doesn't he look rather familiar, because of course — it's Captain George.* And then — and then — I'm judging a Bonny Baby Contest, and you bloody turn up again! I can't get away from you!"

"It's a *vase*, Fitz." George laughed in disbelief. "It wasn't worth a friendship."

Henry pursed his lips. He was back on the crease again, swinging the cricket bat over his head, tears pricking his eyes. Henry mumbled, "Do you think I don't know that?"

"Shall we leave it there then? Agree to keep out of each other's way, and I won't ask you to be in the doc." George reached for the door handle. "I'll get someone to play you, give Dom a bell or someone like that."

Henry nodded. Once more, he felt defeated. As he was about to walk away, he paused and looked over his shoulder.

"Thanks for earlier. For sorting out Ed, when he was —" Henry grimaced and peered down at his groin. "I — I appreciate it."

"I'm still *your* friend." George quirked a smile. "Even if you can't stand me."

"It's not exactly easy to avoid you, old bean."

"You could always get rid of your TV? Otherwise, hold on until autumn and maybe I'll be on my travels again."

"Anywhere nice?"

"The Beeb wanted to film me visiting Darioush. He and his folks live in Sweden now." George shook his head, referring to the wide-eyed little boy in *that* photograph. Henry knew that Darioush wouldn't be *anywhere* now if not for George, of course, sheltering him from the blast with his own body. "I've already said *no thanks* to that, I'm not turning good people into a circus sideshow. Maybe something, I don't know, Amazonian? Bit of a gad through the Amazon Basin or something, I'll give it a think."

Captain George Standish-Brookes turning down an opportunity for television?

Henry sank his hands into his trouser pockets. The irritating, ubiquitous celebrity took on a new light. How many other things had George refused, and never trumpeted forth about?

He gave his erstwhile friend a firm nod.

"Jolly decent of you, George, refusing to do that filming with the little chap you saved."

"They're just a nice family living a peaceful life, they don't want to be a Christmas special." He shrugged, keeping up his self-deprecating act to the last. "Maybe I'll do a hot air balloon over the Andes, bit of fun like that. A chap gets tired of roaming sometimes, you know? I'm rather getting a taste for the sitting-at-home-writing-books side of history."

Henry came back to the door of the cottage and propped himself up against it.

"Do you know what'd make for an interesting book? Bad Billy Fitzwalter and Reverend Standish and bloody Belcher! Don't you think?" Henry forgot that half an hour earlier he'd been bellowing in fury at this man. Instead, he felt confiding. "Now, Ed let slip that he's got certain papers that belonged to his ancestor, even a diary, which sounds to me as if it's full of gossip about Bad Billy and the vicar. My grandfather deposited a load of papers relating to the manor in the county archive—Father said it was all boring stuff about who rented what field, but *I* heard that there's something rather salacious in those documents. I keep meaning to go and have a look, but...well...I'm a busy chap. Don't you think that would be fascinating? Georgian gents getting up to no good? *I'd* read it."

"I wonder." George frowned and let go of the door handle, turning back to Henry. "And not many vicars have a mum like Georgina, do they? Four husbands, a dozen children and all sorts of saucy rumors. You've got me wondering now, Fitz."

"Georgina was quite the one, wasn't she!" Henry chuckled. "Have you ever seen Bad Billy's will? I found it copied out in the back of a family Bible. From what I could make out, your Reverend was actually living at the manor—he left the rectory to the curate. Billy bequeathed him two rooms and the necessary furniture, and all the wood he needed! I mean—for lighting a fire. I mean...they were close friends."

"Merry widowers indeed." George laughed, for a moment taking on a very definite resemblance to the breast-baring Georgian minx who smiled out from an oil painting in the sitting room of the cottage. "And this would be when the Reverend Standish's boys had gone off to school? Paid for by their grandma Georgina's ill-gotten gains, I believe!"

"Yes, that's it! Loved to have been a fly on the wall of the manor in those days, eh? What were they getting up to? Bad Billy left his wine cellar to the Reverend—they must've had some amazing parties!"

Henry couldn't remember when he'd last had a party at the manor, let alone an *amazing* one. But it was enough that he and George were, strangely, standing at the cottage door laughing. How on earth had this come to pass?

George slapped his hand to Henry's arm and nodded to the garden with its rustic wooden bench, the bucolic duck pond and clouds of bees buzzing around bright-colored flowers.

"Let's have a little snifter, you and I, see the day out in the garden?" He opened the back door. "I'll grab a couple of G&Ts and we'll have a think about this Ed problem. I'm a criminal mastermind, after all!"

Henry swallowed. "I'd like that. I really would."

"Have you eaten?" He pushed the door open a little farther as he spoke, pottering into the cottage. "Come on in, Fitz, let's get some treats together for our picnic!"

"Now you come to mention it — haven't had anything apart from some toast for breakfast. And that feels like a long time ago."

As if he were an interloper, Henry left the balmy evening and entered George's cottage. Although the ceiling was low, the cottage wasn't dingy, thanks to the profusion of bright colors that glowed and sparkled within its ancient walls. Amber-covered cushions and turquoise drapes, ornate lanterns and curlicued candlesticks, mirrored wind-chimes and colored glass cluttered the space. It was the most bohemian house in the village, and Henry knew full well how ridiculous he was in this cottage — pinstripes against sequins, Old Spice against incense sticks.

So many fond memories rushed back to Henry that he almost forgot why he was there. The stairs that he and George had run up and down heading from one game to another, the mirror in the corridor that they had stood in front of, checking their hair before the school disco, the armchair that a very drunk George had draped a very drunk Henry over one New Year's Eve. A vision sparkled by him—George's mother, hands caked in drying clay, a chiffon scarf wound about her ebony hair, pressing a kiss to the top of Henry's head as she wafted off to her kiln.

The kitchen was just as Henry remembered it, with a large wooden table and a ramshackle collection of old kitchen cupboards. Corn dollies stood across the mantelpiece and bunches of dried herbs dangled from the laundry rack overhead, along with a rather old tea towel from Beaulieu Motor Museum.

"Chuck off your jacket, Fitz, I promise not to nick it." George busied himself mixing a couple of very generous gin and tonics, the glasses stuffed with ice and freshly cut slices of lemon. "So, 'orrible Ed's really after your house? I was listening to every word. It'd make a hell of a show, wouldn't it?"

"What? George, I'm going to lose my house because two hundred years ago our ancestors got drunk!" Henry sighed. "Closing scene—me, under a bridge in a soggy cardboard box, Ed's laughter echoing as he hops into his Ferrari. What great telly that would be—except I'd never see it as I *wouldn't have a house!*"

Toot-bloody-*toot.*

"Oh, don't be melodramatic!" George put one of the glasses in front of Henry, the ice tinkling merrily against the sides. "Get yourself a lawyer, laugh him out of court! I've got some treats, if you're feeling naughty."

Henry's stomach answered for him with a gurgling roar.

"I think that means I'm hungry…" He unbuttoned his jacket and sighed. "I wish I could get a lawyer, but you see, I can't, George, because I haven't the money. I've barely got the spondoolicks to get my Landy fixed up."

George opened the fridge and began to pull out the contents. There was fresh ham and cheeses, chicken and pâté, golden butter and crisp green salad. Bright red tomatoes joined the pile of treats, along with plump strawberries and quiche from the fête. He threw the food onto a tray, adding plates and cutlery before telling Henry, "Grab the bread, Fitz, we can sit on the grass—"

George paused before he spoke again.

"You don't want to sit on grass in that stunning suit. You can have the bench." He looked Henry up and down, though there was no sense of judgment, only consideration. "Old buildings, Fitz, they take a hell of a lot of upkeep."

"It's not just the house." Henry put his hand around the cold glass of gin and tonic. "It's the business."

George nodded, the casual mirth leaving his expression. "What's going on, Fitz?"

Henry took a large gulp of his drink, then passed the back of his hand across his mouth.

"It's nothing terrible, I don't mean to whinge. I'm— maybe I'm too soft. I didn't become a vet to turn away a sick animal just because the owner struggles to pay for treatment. I've got the wages for the nurses and the receptionists, and the surgery itself. I had the whole place refurbed a couple of years ago, after Dad retired—it's so swanky now—but that cost a packet. And the thing is—I'd get by, I would, but now I've got to find the money to fight off bloody Belcher, just to keep a roof over my head!"

"I've got a few bob I can lend you, don't fret about that." George reached out and patted Henry's hand. "And none of it was stolen, before you start telling me what a rotten sort I am."

Henry dropped his gaze from George's sparkling eyes.

"I'm not here with a begging bowl, George. I really wouldn't expect you to lend me money. How could I ask you for help, after I−? I shouldn't need to ask anyone. I'm a Fitzwalter, for heaven's sake!"

"Our families go back centuries, Fitz, and for a time…" He shrugged, his smile nostalgic. "Well, you and I were as close as a Fitzwalter and a Standish-Brookes ever were. Water under the bridge and all that. Boys can't be best friends forever, I suppose."

But I wanted to be. Henry took another slug of gin and attempted to ignore the ache inside him.

"I'm sorry. Do you know that I am, actually, sorry? For losing my rag at you. But when that trophy vanished, what else was I supposed to think? You'd gone on and on and on about wanting to win it, and then *I* won it and−it just vanished. And I can't undo any of it, how I behaved to you, how you must've felt in front of all those people, me accusing you like that, I−I know now that I was trying to push you away. I thought it'd make my life less complicated but all I did was end up lonely."

"I was very angry−bread, Fitz−because I *was* innocent. I *am* innocent." George stepped out into the garden. "But then I got shipped out to Afghanistan and realized that the world is full of much bigger injustices than a cricket vase in Longley Parva.

"And then I came back and the *Daily Mail* decided I was romancing a lady who is now a princess." George pottered across the lawn and set the food down beside the pond, close enough for Henry to sit on the bench and still be part of the picnic. He began to unload the tray, adding, "Now I hang out on mountaintops and make TV shows that annoy very learned gents like you, but a lot of people enjoy them, so I can live with the critics."

Henry carefully sat, his undercarriage still radiating pain.

"I've watched them all, your programs. I s'pose I can't hate them that much!"

"Bread?" George held out his hand and took the loaf from Henry, setting it on the tray before he dropped down to lounge on the grass, casting the towel aside. "Do you buy the books too?"

Without looking at George, Henry nodded. "I don't exactly go out of my way to avoid you." His voice was quiet.

George leaned back on the grass, propped on one elbow. His legs were crossed at the ankle and he looked over his shoulder, peering up at Henry from beneath *those* eyelashes.

"Would you like me to sign them for you?" He smiled. "And would you like some very nice quiche?"

"Yes to both."

His friend sat up and began assembling a mountainous selection of food on one of the plates, balancing each new item as though playing Jenga. Eventually he twisted his body to face Henry and, with great care, passed up the laden plate.

"*Please* don't drop this down that suit, or you'll fall out with me again." George similarly piled up his own supper. "I wonder if the Reverend and Squire F. ever sat out like this, boozing and eating and watching the ducks potter about…"

"I'm certain of it. *My dear, loving friend*, as Bad Billy referred to the Rev. in his will." Henry glanced away from George and forked some food into his mouth. "This quiche is good—a Mrs. Dalrymple special, I suspect. It's like being at the cricket."

The evening was still warm and Henry laid down his fork and finally shrugged off his jacket. He laid it neatly over the bench and unfastened the bottom two buttons of his waistcoat. As he placed his hand flat over his stomach, his fingers twitching at the third button, he realized that George had been watching.

"Go on, Fitz, live dangerously?" George lay back on the emerald grass and pillowed his hands behind his head. "*My dear, loving friend.*"

Henry laughed awkwardly. "Do you think I should? What will the papers say? *Wild scenes in Captain George's cottage garden as local vet strips off!*"

But even as he laughed, Henry unbuttoned his waistcoat. His gaze didn't leave George's until he turned to drape his removed garment on the bench. Then Henry wondered why he had he stared at George like that. They were just two old friends eating dinner in a garden. Even if one of them had extremely handsome, long-lashed eyes.

"What would it take to tempt you out of your tie, I wonder?" George reached over to the picnic and picked up the first thing he touched. He held it up for identification and said, "I'll give you this ripe strawberry if you'll take it off."

"A strawberry for my dignity!" Henry joked. "Go on, then."

He glanced at George, then looked down at his tie as he unknotted it, the silk rasping against his skin. He pulled it out from under his collar and dangled it on one finger.

"Am I supposed to twirl it above my head as well?"

"We'll need more gin for that." George sat up and held out the offering as though it were the most priceless treasure in the world. "Your strawberry, sir."

Henry chucked the tie aside and gratefully took the strawberry from George's hand. Juice spurted onto his immaculate white shirt as soon as he bit into it.

"Makes a change from baby vomit!" He laughed.

George, however, was on his feet in an instant and bolting for the cottage with a cry of, "We'll sort it, no need to panic!"

Henry *wasn't* panicking, and the fact that George had expected another eruption of temper was rather sobering. Still, he munched on the strawberry and watched the ducks performing their lazy laps of the pond until George re-emerged. He was carrying two more immense glasses of gin and tonic and slung over one shoulder was— What *was* it?

"Here you go, old pal. Your G"—George handed Henry the drink, then took the T-shirt from his shoulder and held it out—"and a T of a different sort. Pop it on and I'll get that shirt into the washer. Didn't want you to huff off home all because of a rogue strawberry!"

"Gosh. I haven't comported myself very well, have I?"

"Says the man who tried to brain me with a cricket bat?" He shrugged and nodded toward the T-shirt before teasing, "This shirt's been to war and everything, Fitz. I chose you a properly butch one."

Henry saluted him, grinning. "Thanks, Captain George."

He got to his feet, untwisting his cufflinks. Then he turned his back and took off his shirt, embarrassed that his body was a shambles compared to George's perfect, toned torso. He pulled the T-shirt on over his head and tugged it down.

"Can't remember the last time I wore a T-shirt." He grinned at George. The khaki didn't go so badly with pinstripes. "You'll have me swimming in the lake next!"

"Sorry about the newts, but they didn't seem to mind us splashing about for the *first* twenty years or so." He took the shirt from Henry. "I'll stick this in the washer. Pud?"

"It did come as rather a surprise—especially as the post lady saw you. Erm—but yes, pudding would be delightful."

"Sit tight, I'll be back!"

"Are you sure you don't need a hand?" But George had disappeared out of earshot, so Henry stretched out his legs and enjoyed the peace of the evening. He kicked off his brogues and wriggled his feet out of his socks. How pleasant the grass felt against his skin. Minutes passed before George returned once more, a plate in each hand.

"The fête's finest!" He handed one plate, piled with cakes and pastries, to Henry. Then George sat down to rest on the grass again, juggling his own laden plate as he went.

"See, you look more relaxed already."

"Good grief, George—what a haul! Did you need a wheelbarrow to cart all this home?"

"People sort of throw things at me," George admitted bashfully. "And I take them because it's rude not to, isn't it? In London it's not a problem, there are plenty of charities and places where you can pass the freebies along to people who need them, but here... Well, not many Longley Parvans are in need of charity."

Once again, the humble version of George hove into view. But Henry knew it wasn't an act. It was the George he'd been friends with as a boy, generous and kind to a fault. It was the George that Henry had loved, the George he had pushed away. The George who was now offering charity to Henry. Pursing his lips, Henry shoved aside the proud, stuffy voice within him that would declare, *'I don't need anyone's help, certainly not George's.'* What good had any of that blustery nonsense done?

"We're very lucky here." Henry closed his eyes, enjoying the sensation of the sun's warmth on his face. "There's the farms, and—dare I say it—Ed's racing stables, the riding school and the odd tourist who pops through and patronizes our tearooms. Keeps people in a job. We Parvans have got a lot to be thankful for, really."

"And they've all forgiven me for *not* stealing the cup." There was mirth in George's voice. "I think it was squiring the now-princess Eleanor that did it."

Henry nearly choked on his mouthful of cheesecake. The day after Steph had finally given up and moved on to Ed, that photo had appeared in the newspapers. *Everywhere.*

"How—how did that work out, George? I mean...did she marry the prince on a rebound from you? It all happened rather fast, didn't it? Weren't you upset?"

George looked at Henry and narrowed his eyes as though sizing him up. He lifted a jam tart to his mouth, bit it and said, "The papers told you that we had a brief fling and remained friends. Don't you believe them?"

"Forgive me, George, but she didn't really seem to be — your type."

Henry concentrated on jabbing his fork into a miniature lemon torte. This wasn't an area he should be drifting into, he knew, but sitting here in George's garden, wearing George's T-shirt, he could do nothing else but plunge haphazardly on.

"So…what *is* my type?"

Henry felt a warm blush rise up to his face. His stomach lurched and he put down his fork. All that gin on an empty stomach.

"Must I say, really? I was surprised, George, that you had been romantically linked to…"

Henry looked George in the eye. He was accusing him again.

But was he really? There'd been something in a gossipy celebrity magazine that he'd caught his receptionist reading once. Taken by telephoto lens, it showed George on location, shirtless of course, his arm around the waist of a soundman as they played about with his enormous boom microphone. And numerous times before George had gone off to the Army and Henry had left for vet school — a thousand small moments, glances, gazes. A brush of a hand, a press of the knee.

"A younger girl?" George helpfully asked. "Only four years, no scandal there."

Henry dropped his chin to his chest. Then he was wrong.

"No, I — it's nothing, I only thought, *gosh, George, with a woman?* Sorry. You were in the Army and everything, I mean, how ridiculous of me to think — " *To hope.* "That you might be more interested in...well...chaps."

"Oh." George's full lips pursed and he reclined on the grass once more. "Chaps."

"You know what I mean..." Henry tugged at the hem of the T-shirt. It suddenly felt too tight. "Gay. I mean... Blimey, I haven't offended you, have I? There's nothing wrong at all with that. *Nothing.*"

Unless you're a village stalwart and you're expected to put a woman in your manor house, and your father constantly jibed at you for not being man enough, and just to prove that you were, you went into a pen with a bull and got a horn in your belly for your trouble.

"If I *were* gay, and I'm not saying that I *am*, would you still be my chum?" George looked up at Henry from his spot on the grass. "Although we're not really chums now, are we? You like me now but tomorrow, without gin in you, you won't."

Henry put aside his plate. "In my job, one of the most important things I do is earn the trust of my patients. It can take so long, and sometimes I never manage it, but you know — that trust can be lost in a moment." Henry snapped his fingers. "Just one thing — a loud noise, a sudden movement, something which accidentally or unavoidably causes pain — and it's gone."

He couldn't look at George, at those big green eyes. Instead, he brought his knee up to his chest and watched his own bare toes as they gripped the edge of the bench.

"And it's the same with you, George. I've lost your trust. Shouting and carrying on like that, I know I have." Henry looked up and saw something soft in

George's expression. "I'd do anything to win it back. I would. Name it, George, and I promise you, I won't ever do anything to hurt you again."

"I didn't steal that vase and I'm not a reckless nightmare," George told him firmly, but there was a sadness in his tone too. "I was more proud than anybody when you smashed the batting record that day and I made a daft joke, but that's *all* it was. I disappeared because I had to run home and get my knife so I could scratch onto the ball and now—well, even *that* got lost. What a rotten bloody day it was."

"Oh, George!" Henry held his hand over his mouth. He wasn't going to cry, he wasn't. "Look, the cup's lost and the ball's lost, but—here's us two, sat here together. Being civil to one another. Having—having a jolly nice time. And I—earlier, when I ran after you, yelling, even though you'd just rescued me from Ed... It's probably best not to put much stock in the words of a man whose balls are on fire!"

A giggle rose up inside Henry, but he pushed it down as there was something he needed to say.

"And—George, if you're gay, it's—it's a good thing. What do you think I was doing in Brighton, the day I saw your face on the side of a bus?" Henry took a deep breath. He'd never admitted it before to anyone, barely to himself. "It'd be very nice indeed not to be the only gay chap in Longley Parva, even if it's just for a summer."

"Are you—" George blinked, his mouth opening and closing. "Well, I would never've guessed it, how marvelous! Are you all out and proud then? I always said you were too good for Steph, didn't I?"

"You did, and I should've listened, and no, I am very much not out, and not very proud either. Guess what I did in Brighton? Wandered about the prom in a linen suit, eating an ice cream. And I tried to get up the courage to go into a pub that had a big rainbow flag outside it, and I got one saucy raised eyebrow from a chap as I licked my ice cream — *lucky ice-cream*, he said — realized what it looked like I was doing to my Mr. Whippy, and dropped my Flake on the floor. And came home."

"So is there a significant other hiding somewhere?" George pushed himself up from the grass and met Henry's gaze. "I'd love to meet the chap who sets your heart aflutter."

Why was George so beautiful? It really wasn't fair. *Lucky bloody princess.*

"I'd love to meet him too!"

"Come on, Fitz, a good-looking boy like you? Nicely dressed, well-spoken, fetching chums like me?" He knocked his fist against Henry's shin. "We can find you a gent!"

"That's very kind of you, matchmaking like your ancestor Lady Georgina, but why would anyone want to go out with a curmudgeonly old fart like me?"

"Aside from trying to brain me, you're a fine catch." George beamed. "I *did* wonder, you know. You got a bit misty-eyed when we went along to collect my reggies that day. I thought it was just the uniform because you and Steph — "

So George was straight? Henry smiled at him. He could finally say it.

"You looked *gorgeous* in that uniform!"

"I look even better in it now, Fitz." His friend laughed. "Why didn't you tell me, instead of just... *gazing*?"

"What sort of eighteen-year-old boy wants to hear that from his best friend? *You're gorgeous and I wish you'd pinion me to the wall and kiss me?*" Henry laughed. What a relief, to finally admit it. How ridiculous to have held back for so long.

"You never know, I might have done it." George laughed, his head thrown back. *What a nice thing to have a straight mate who is so accepting,* Henry thought. *Who didn't seem bothered at all to have been the object of his affections.*

"That day, when I accused you of taking the cup... I was frightened of how I felt. Steph was there, and my father was there, and it all seemed so convenient. I could go out with her, and it would be fine, I could convince myself that I wouldn't be wondering, every time she kissed me, every time we — you know — went to bed, what would this be like with a man? I don't know how she put up with me. But that cup disappearing... I wanted to believe that you'd stolen it because I wanted to hate you. I wanted you to hate *me*. So bloody infantile. Because you didn't steal it, did you? Oh, God, I'm such a fool!"

There was a narrow slice of time during which Henry almost cried. But he didn't. Because he laughed, hysterically, with such volume that the ducks squawked and flew away across the pond.

"I was angry at you, but I never hated you!" George caught Henry's bare toes for a second, tugging them. "Why the devil would you want me to hate you?"

"Because — because if you hated me, I could stop loving you."

"You —" George swallowed, Henry saw the movement in his throat. "Did it work?"

Henry gazed at him. At that handsome face and the strong, tan neck and the suggestion of muscles under his T-shirt, at the thick, dark hair and what was visible of George's toned, bare legs. He didn't need that uniform to look gorgeous. Henry shoved aside all the weight of the unlived years, and wondered – if he told George the truth, what the hell would this super-heterosexual television celebrity do?

Make a documentary about closeted rural types, perhaps?

No, that wasn't the George that Henry had loved.

"George, I…" Henry pressed his palms together.

"Captain Standish-Brookes!" Standing in the meadow at the back gate was the entire Crawford family – husband, wife, five children under the age of seven and three large Labradors. The little boys and girls stood on tiptoe and peered over the hedge for a chance to see the celebrity and their father told George happily, "They're Robin Hood crazy thanks to you. Can we get a photo of you with the kids?"

"We'll continue this, Fitz," George murmured before he leaped to his feet, beaming at the children. "Of course, bring them in. I've probably got a couple of bowstrings somewhere if you want a souvenir, my little Merry Men and Women!"

The children cheered and George beckoned the family into his garden.

What the dickens am I still doing here?

Once the last of the Crawfords, including the dogs, had trooped into the cottage behind George, Henry dressed as fast as he could. He shoved his socks into his pocket along with his tie, pushed his feet back into his brogues and grabbed his discarded waistcoat and jacket from the bench. Then he was off, flying through the meadow, wondering how he could have been so unguarded, so bloody stupid.

You nearly told the straightest man on telly that you still hold a flame for him.

Henry didn't stop until he banged the front door of Longley Parva Manor shut behind him as if all the devils in hell were in pursuit. He threw his armful of clothes onto the old oaken chest in the hallway and wandered into the lounge, shoelaces trailing. Bad Billy Fitzwalter stared down at him from his frame on the chimney breast.

If Henry believed in such things, he would have sworn that his ancestor had quirked an eyebrow at him.

Chapter Eight

George didn't sleep well. This was new, for George *always* slept well, but his friend-turned-enemy-turned-friend-again had never professed love for him before.

Well, an old love, a flame burned out.

At three o'clock that morning he was in the sitting room with Georgina's portrait, asking that most notorious ancestor how one went about dealing with this. She, he knew, had slept with men and women alike. She'd gambled and drunk and died rich, happy and infamous but then, she hadn't had a TV career to contend with.

If only he had known, what a life they might have had, George and Fitz.

Life is full of what ifs, though, isn't it?

Lucky the man who won Henry's heart.

As the sun rose George went for a run, covering miles as he pounded through fields and along tracks and roads, head down, The Beach Boys pumping from his earphones. As he ran, as he sweated out the worries of the night and how to get the shirt back to Henry without making his friend even more uncomfortable, he formulated a plan. Henry might not want charity, but that didn't mean George couldn't intervene with 'orrible Ed Belcher on the sly.

He showered and breakfasted on jam tarts. Then he dressed casually in chinos and a shirt, relaxed but not too informal, before taking a steady stroll over to the Belcher monstrosity, the mansion and stud farm as much an eyesore today as they ever were. At the locked gate, George pressed the intercom and waited patiently.

"Hello? That my Bolly delivery from Ocado? If it's not, piss off!"

Ed Belcher, charming as ever.

"Hello, Mr. Ed, it's George! Got a mo?"

"You, is it? Television personality? Better not have a film crew with you, but if you *have,* I can get my PR team on the blower. What do you want?"

"Bit of a chat?"

"Not every day a *bona fide* celebrity turns up on my doorstep. Even one who nearly ripped my ear off—just a joke, eh? Eh?" A buzzer sounded somewhere and the gate unlocked. "Come on in!"

George pottered through the wicket gate and up the driveway toward the house. Outside was the Ferrari, one of the marks of Ed's success, along with the Aston and the yacht and the stable full of racehorses. Like his father, who now resided in Monaco, Ed Belcher was rich beyond George's imagining, but George wouldn't trade places with him for the world. He had been inside the Belcher house and it was all hard edges. Glass and marble and gold—there was no softness to be found in the mansion or the man who inhabited it.

And after three decades, the jury was still out on his bloody wife too.

Ed had opened the door and was lounging on the front step with a purple Ralph Lauren jumper around his shoulders. He waved, his heavy watch sliding down his arm as he raised his hand in greeting.

"George! Hello there, how are you? Welcome once again to Longley Parva Old Hall, eh? Buck's Fizz in the kitchen?"

"That's how you greet a visitor." George laughed as though Ed were his favorite person in the world. "Lead the way!"

"Steph!" Ed bellowed, his voice echoing off the shiny walls as he led his guest into the house. "Got that Buck's Fizz ready for our visitor yet?"

The kitchen was at the back of the house, with a huge window overlooking a flat lawn that appeared to have had all of its life tweezered out of it. As, apparently, had Steph, who was pouring champagne into tall glasses on the gray granite worktop.

"Captain George Standish-Brookes, to what do we owe this honor?" She pouted at George and held out a glass to him.

"Stephanie Belcher." George kissed her contoured cheek as he took the glass. "Sorry about the jam disappointment!"

Her face turned pale, then she rallied. "That's what happens if you wound someone's masculine pride, I have discovered."

She clinked her own glass against George's, but he was thinking about Henry again, in linen, in Brighton, licking—

Back to business.

"Fitz is a straight arrow." Not the best choice of words, he admonished himself. "And jam judging is anonymous after the Mrs. Knowles versus Mrs. Tanvir debacle—blood on the prize sponges and all that!"

He took a sip of the Buck's Fizz, which was rather more champagne than orange juice. *How the other half live*, George supposed.

Brighton, though, a hot summer day, a long summer night and—

No, that chance had flown fifteen years ago.

"What's this I've heard, Eddie old chap, about you making a play for Fitz's old country pile?" George laughed, every inch the hoo-ray even if it twisted his stomach into a knot. Here in this temple of sharp corners without an inch of comfort or a hint of chaos he saw nothing to enjoy, no color or life or living, yet he had a part to play. "You live in a bloody palace, Ed. Why would you want to move into a place that's leaking, sloping and generally creaking with age?"

"As the saying goes, *give unto Caesar that which is his.* It's my house by rights." The corner of Ed's mouth turned up in a sneer, revealing teeth stained with orange juice.

"You'll need a bloody good lawyer, mate!" George looked at Steph, composing his most irresistible smile. "What's your take on the feud that just won't die?"

She tucked her hair behind her ear in a studied manner and blinked her empty blue eyes at him.

"Isn't it all to do with that creepy man in the portrait above Henry's fireplace? His gaze follows you around the room. I begged Henry to turn it to the wall, and he refused!"

"Come on, Steph." George concentrated his efforts on her as he sipped at the cocktail. "Which would you rather have? A tumbledown bit of a stately dump or *this*? I know which I'd choose."

And it isn't Belcher Towers...

Steph tugged at the gold Versace chain around her neck. It left a red mark.

"Oh, this, of course! We've got a pool and a subterranean garage, helicopter pad and absolutely no draughts!"

"Home cinema," Ed added, puffing out his chest. "Games room, indoor pool, fully equipped gym." The millionaire patted his flat stomach. "And what that doesn't fix, the doctor will, eh?"

He nudged George, crowing with laughter, and George joined in, wondering what exactly Ed *meant*. Was Ed silicone and Botox? Could a stomach *be* silicone and Botox? *Who knew.*

"Why don't you come over one night, Captain George?" Steph lounged against the worktop, hand on her hip, bosom tilted forward. "Bring your documentaries with you, we can set them up in the home cinema. I'll make some nibbles, it'd be fun."

"Oh, God, you don't want to see my ugly mug blown up to thirty feet tall!" George grimaced, but threw Steph a glance anyway, just to show willing. She was looking at him in turn and, as their gazes met, she very slowly drew her tongue over her top lip. This village really *was* a hive of drama, George realized. Enough for a dozen Christmas specials!

"Old Brooky with his top off all over my cinema?" Ed scowled. "Not my idea of a good time, Steph!"

Steph glared at him over the rim of her glass as she gulped down the entirety of her Buck's Fizz. She clanged the empty glass down onto the worktop and put her hand in front of her mouth.

Surely she wasn't stifling a belch?

Then she poured some more.

"*Your* home cinema, Ed-babes?"

"*Ours*, Stephy-Steph."

With the tip of one manicured finger, Steph stroked a line down her husband's face, all the while pouting at George.

"That's better, Ed-babes."

"So this lawyer business," George said. "A good old jape, eh?"

Ed adjusted his cufflinks and grinned. "Of course not — I want my house. *My* house, that *my* family were cheated out of by Henry's ancestor and by yours — your drunken, profligate vicar ancestor."

"He was all of those things." He laughed. "But he lost the scores, he didn't fabricate them. A vicar's word can be trusted!"

"I find it very hard to believe that anyone related to you could possibly be trusted."

Steph rounded on her husband. "Ed-babes, Captain George is our guest."

"It's all right —" George began, but one look at Steph's annoyance silenced him. Here was a chink in the Belcher armor, he realized, a possible way in. He was in the media, after all — he knew all about exploiting his angles.

"Yes — Stephy-Steph, you're quite right. I did invite George in." Ed raised his glass to him, smiling, but his face rapidly assumed a stern frown. "But just so you know, George, I'm deadly serious. And I will keep squeezing your ex-friend's balls until I get my house back."

Steph, at least, winced just a little. But she turned a bright, beaming grin that was as fake as her nails on George.

"Just Ed-babes and his little joke!"

"Squeeze all you like for me, old man," George assured them. "You don't accuse *me* of being a thief and get away with it. Oh, I might smile for the fête, but that's as far as it goes."

"Ha! I knew it. What a shower that man is. Prances about in his tweeds, nearly brained his best friend with a cricket bat and clings on to his outdated idea of gentility. And" — Ed leaned toward George and added in a stage whisper, jabbing his finger toward his wife — "a crap shag by all accounts, too!"

"I'm sure George doesn't need to know about that, Ed-babes." Steph had the grace to look embarrassed. "Darling, I told you not to repeat that — I don't kiss and tell."

George glanced at Steph and gave the barest hint of a wink. "You've always had class, Steph."

She shrugged in a casual fashion and pouted again.

"Course she has, in spades — that's why I married her." Ed put his arm around her waist and drew her near to him. Then he stuck his tongue into her ear.

"Stop it, Ed-babes, not in front of Captain George!" Steph grinned at George with such a salacious look in her eye that George braced himself, hoping she wasn't about to invite him to a threesome over the kitchen counter.

"Look, Ed, Steph, balls out and all that." George leaned his arm on the worktop, lowering his eyelids just a little to give that flirtatious look that had led to a terrifying encounter with a *GMTV* presenter on the famous sofa. "I'm always looking to advance my career, and I can return the favor. Have you guys thought about TV?"

Steph nudged her husband and Ed looked up with a grunt.

"Yes, of course! Like *The Apprentice*. Think you could wangle that for me? I'd be great at that." He wagged his finger at Steph, and in a voice that sounded more suited for the bedroom than the boardroom, whispered to his wife, "*You're fired.*"

"I should have my own cookery program." Steph was back to tugging her gold chain, pulling just a little too tightly as she met George's eyes. "Footage of me out for a horse ride, then wandering about the stables in figure-hugging jods, and cut to me in the kitchen — I'd be a rural Nigella, steaming pans of prize-winning greengage jam everywhere!"

"I was thinking of something for the two of you," George agreed, having not thought of anything of the sort until this moment. "A real power couple, maybe choosing a power couple to follow in your footsteps? Steph judging the girls — who's more qualified, after all? — Ed judging the guys. Look at you both, you've got it all, I reckon people would gag for you."

Steph beamed, then squeaked as Ed pinched her bottom and nuzzled her neck. *The 1812 Overture* interrupted, bursting from an intercom on the wall. Ed groaned and went over to speak into the intercom. George looked at Steph as he took another sip from the glass. He lowered it, glanced over his shoulder at Ed and whispered, "I wouldn't tell Ed this, but I've a feeling I might be looking at the *real* star of the show."

Steph fluttered at him, simpering her oddly plump lips. She thrust forward her bosom again and lowered her voice.

"The offer still stands—swing by sometime and let's entertain ourselves in the home cinema."

"Balls!" Ed slammed his fist into his palm and came back to stand beside his wife. "Bloody balls! Got a cripple on our hands."

"Oh, that foal, Ed-babes? The one the vet's come down from London to look at?"

"The very same. Useless, limping thing. Bound for the bloody glue factory!"

George nodded a manly nod, squaring his jaw. He should let this go, he knew. He was here for the summer and only the summer, then off around the world again, he didn't need complications like vets and foals or—

"Never seen the stud, Ed. Any chance of a quick nose out there if you're going anyway?"

Ed gave George a matey slap on the shoulder. "Sure thing—if you're going to turn us into telly, then it's a good place to start."

George followed Ed out through a side door, along a path and finally into the stud. The smell of horses rose up around them, the business of the stables in full swing. Ed raised his hand to a man in Hunters who was waiting for them by one of the stalls.

"Most expensive equine guy in the country, Captain George—*in the country!* Now *there's* something for your program. Wouldn't find this fella in tweed trousers with his arm up a cow's arse at midnight, I can tell you that for nothing!"

George nodded approvingly, thinking once more of that chap in his pinstripe suit, that chap who had once loved him.

"What the hell is wrong with bloodlines, eh, George? Bloody good stallion, bloody good mare and what do I get—look over here, just look at this useless dog's breakfast." Ed gripped George's shoulder and piloted him to a split stable door. A plaque on the wall said FOAL 12.

George wondered now at the wisdom of this but it was too late to do anything more than just stand there and peer over the door at the inhabitant of the stable.

There, standing with one leg just slightly at an angle, as though making an effort to look absolutely normal, was Foal 12. The horse was black as a starless night, wide eyes shining with hope at the new arrivals, and George knew there and then that he would be leaving this house with a pet foal. What he would do after that he wasn't sure, but he couldn't leave the lanky little chap here.

Ed shrugged at George. "Bolt job, eh? Best thing for it. Put it out of its misery, and me out of mine—bloody packet this cripple's cost me. Can't race it like that, let alone ride it—look at its gammy leg! No room for passengers at my stables."

"What's his name?"

"Name?" Ed tipped his head back and laughed, saliva clinging to his teeth. "It doesn't have one. Other than— that." Ed knocked his knuckles against the plaque. "And when it's gone, there'll be another Foal 12. Hopefully a darned sight more useful than this *thing*."

"Think of the PR, Ed." George held up his hands as though framing a shot. "Millionaire Ed Belcher is the sort of man who *cares* about his foal and does all he can to re-home it even though it's about as much use as a chocolate fireguard. Let me take him, stick him in the doc, the powers that be will *love* it."

Rubbing his chin, Ed leaned against the stable door and Foal 12 stepped back from him.

"You—you really think so?" Ed met George's gaze. "I wouldn't want any of the gentlemen on the exchange to see it and think I'd lost my balls."

"I get that." He nodded thoughtfully. "So we say it's Steph's mothering instinct. Steel Ed, silken Steph? He's hard, but he knows how to keep his woman happy."

"You bet I do!" Ed clenched his fist and made a grotesque movement with his arm. "Right, well—if you take it off my hands, then I won't have to deal with the bolt fee or the disposal of the body, will I? Makes sense."

The man in Hunters had been standing nearby, arms folded. He advanced toward George, hand held out. "There's still my fee for the visit today, of course."

"Oh yes!" Ed slapped the man's shoulder and grinned. "You send it on to my friend Captain George here, seeing as this is now *his* horse. But, George, I won't charge you for the hire of the horsebox! What?" He laughed as if he had made the funniest joke known to humanity.

"Good man." George laughed and asked, "It's just a lame leg, yes? Otherwise sound?"

The man knocked his wellington against the concrete. "Yes, just the leg. In fine fettle otherwise."

"*Just* the leg? Could you drive a car that didn't have any wheels?" Ed guffawed. "You're welcome to it, mate, and if it's good telly, then go for it. Right—things to do, deals to make, balls to squeeze, you know how it is. See you around, Brookesy!"

Ed slapped George hard across the back and made off across the stable yard.

George had acquired a horse.

This was a turn-up for a man who was planning a jaunt up the Amazon.

Chapter Nine

Avoiding a village celebrity in a place the size of Longley Parva was quite a mission, but Henry had to. Staff at the surgery, patients' owners, Manjit with the morning post — everyone tried to plumb him for details about Captain George and their childhood friendship. And Henry would remember an appointment or claim that his phone was ringing with an important call — anything to save himself from the mortifying fact that he had, at last, come out — and to the man he had hurt all those years before.

Beside his bed, Henry put the Longley Spitfire beer mat bearing George's face next to the framed photo of himself and George, side by side, at George's passing out parade. George, handsome as could be in a khaki-green tunic with shiny buttons, his cap neatly tucked under his arm. Henry beside him, in his best tweeds. He had kept the photo in a cupboard, wrapped in tissue paper, too ashamed to look at it for fifteen years.

And now he touched his fingertip to it before going to sleep, and on rising in the morning. Each and every time, he wondered what on earth he could do. A crush on a straight man.

Pillock.

"What would you do, Billy, if you were me?"

Henry, in corduroy trousers and a grandad shirt with a fraying neck, peered up at the portrait of his ancestor. He had just come in from work and was polishing off a cup of tea.

"Hide from him, that's what *I'd* do. But you, Billy? No, you wouldn't. No one with a sparkle like that in your eye would hide. But he'll never love me back, and I can't bear to look at him. It breaks my heart. It's best if I hide. Then again, where *will* I hide if Ed takes the manor?"

And *could* he hide from George? He had avoided his phone calls since that night in the garden, and he knew that his old friend would give up sooner or later. After all, George had people queuing up to be his friend.

George would forget him.

As that horrible thought occurred to Henry, there came a heavy knock at the front door. It was a no-nonsense sort of knock, a property lawyer coming to take his house sort of knock.

Knock knock knock. There it was again, insistent and aggressive.

"It's all your fault, Billy. I ought to chuck your portrait on the fire, you improvident libertine. *That'd* serve you right."

Clutching his mug of tea as if it were his only source of courage, Henry shuffled into the hall. He paused by the suit of armor that had graced the field at Agincourt and imagined himself donning it to go into battle against Ed.

Fool.

Henry pulled back the bolts on the door and blinked into the sunlight at his visitor.

"Hello, Fitz!" George grinned and clapped his hand against Henry's shoulder. "Been avoiding me, old chap?"

Henry gulped.

"Oh—Captain George. Well—this is a surprise."

No, not you, anyone but you. Apart from Ed, perhaps.

"Busy, George, busy vetting about the place." Henry toyed with a shirt button, trying to look casual when *this man* was standing in front of him. The man he wanted to avoid but couldn't. "I'm sure you can imagine what that's like."

"Well, I've got someone for you to meet." George looked to his right and called, "C'mon, Jez!"

From the direction he had been looking, to Henry's surprise, a sleek, black foal appeared. It was limping a little, he immediately noticed, and came to George as obediently as a dog, receiving a gentle pat on the head by way of thanks.

"What a lovely little chap!" A horse. A *horse?* "Hang on—George, have you bought a horse? A horse with a limp? Or have you just borrowed him for the day?"

"I've been ringing and ringing, Fitz, but you wouldn't pick up the phone and little Jez wanted to meet you, so we had to come over." He scratched the foal's ears gently. "He's mine, because Ed was about to have him shot by *England's best vet* or some such rubbish."

"I dropped my phone in the bath," Henry lied in monotone. It was the best he could manage. "So you walked him here, from your cottage—or have you found a stable for him somewhere in the village?"

"He was in the kitchen for the first night, but he and I spent the day clearing out the shed, so now he has a place of his own while he's still a little fellow. Not sure what we'll do when he hits full-size, but for now, he's got a fine pad." George peered around Henry. "Can we come in, then, or have you dropped your house in the bath too?"

It would be rude to say no.

"Come in." Henry gestured into the hallway with his mug. "Just having a cuppa. There's some Earl Grey left in the pot if you want some."

"Come on, Jez," George urged the foal. "That okay, Fitz? He's into architecture, he'd love to see the manor."

"He—he could—" *Be tethered up outside on the lawn?* But there was something so childlike about George's enthusiasm for the foal that Henry couldn't bear to stop George from bringing it into his house. "Yes…why not? Come on in, Jez, welcome to Longley Parva Manor."

"Master Jeremy Standish-Brookes, meet Mr. Henry Fitzwalter. Mr. Fitzwalter, Master Standy-Bee."

Standy-Bee. There was a name he hadn't heard for a long time.

"The pleasure's all mine, Jez." Henry stroked the horse with the practiced hand of an expert. He bent down and gently touched the lame leg, wondering how he could help the creature to lose his limp.

George beamed at the sight. He leaned on the doorjamb to watch, casual in jeans and a polo shirt— the one he'd worn to play a match for the Queen's birthday, Henry noticed. That was the match at which he'd first been photographed with Eleanor Knight, later to marry one of that same monarch's grandsons.

"Jez and I have got lots in common," his friend said. "Same music, same films and he loves history. We both like jam tarts too."

Henry laughed. He regretted ignoring George's calls. They could be friends, and that would be enough. "Oh, George — please don't feed him jam tarts! Come on through to the lounge. The pot's in there and I'll grab you a mug."

"No tarts? Are you going to say no cream horns too?" George walked into the hallway, Jez following him at a sprightly enough pace despite his awkward leg. "Of course I wouldn't, vet'n'ry. I do know a thing or two about horses!"

"Can you — can you just keep him off the rugs? The parquet's easy enough to clean but the rugs... I have to send them to a specialist."

Henry went off to the kitchen to find a mug and the biscuit tin and rummaged in the vegetable box for a carrot. Balancing his hoard in his arms, Henry returned to find George sitting on the floor, the foal lying beside him with its head in his lap.

Just another day in Longley Parva. Nothing strange about this at all, nothing odd about leaving one's lounge for three minutes only to return to find television's George Standish-Brookes relaxing on the parquet with a foal.

And singing to it.

Singing *Yellow Submarine*, in fact.

George looked up at Henry and smiled, reaching the end of the verse. He stroked his hand through Jez's black mane and said, "Your phone's on the chair there, Fitz. It's not in the bath."

Henry turned his back to George as he poured the tea.

"I know, I should've answered your calls. Or at least sent you a text. I know how ill-mannered I must seem. But I was...overwhelmed. What I told you, about my — tastes. I've never told anyone before. And you're the straightest man alive, and I—I felt so embarrassed." Henry looked over his shoulder at his friend. "Milk?"

"Just as it comes, please." He heard George draw in a deep breath, as though he was about to confess some dreadful thing. "I've got something to tell you, Fitz, and I am so terribly, terribly sorry for what I'm about to say."

"It's all right." Henry spoke without conviction, his heart plummeting like a stone dropped down a well. "Just—say it."

"First, I'm very touched that you shared your secret with me but— You're going to go through the roof." Another deep breath and George launched. "Jez slept in the kitchen just that one night and he sort of, well, chewed your shirt up a little bit. It's beyond darning, Fitz, and I don't want you to be furious but you will be—"

"I'm a vet, for God's sake—I'm quite used to animals destroying my wardrobe. Heck—cut the shirt up and use it for dusters."

Henry placed a mug of tea beside George, careful that it wasn't too near the contented foal.

"Was that it?" Henry looked up at the portrait of Bad Billy, who seemed confused but ultimately charmed by the sight of the horse in his drawing room.

"I was right, wasn't I?" George shrugged, looking down at his fingers as they tangled in Jez's mane. "We were friends in the garden but once the gin wore off you wouldn't even take my calls. Do you really think I'd judge you for being gay, Fitz?"

"I panicked when the bloody Crawfords turned up." Henry scraped his hand through his hair. He'd hurt George again. Was he capable of nothing else? "I wanted to tell you… But you're straight, it's easy for you. At least, I imagine it is. I really wouldn't know."

"You should stop making assumptions. It's not easy for me at all."

Henry crouched down on the floor opposite George, the foal between them, and stroked Jez's neck.

"The media poking their noses in all the time? I s'pose that must be a bind. I know I wouldn't find it easy."

"It was me who introduced Eleanor to her prince—he and I've been friends since Afghanistan. You lot just assumed *I* was the boyfriend. Perfect for Eli, since it meant she got to fly under the radar into Kensington Palace." George smiled. "And I've built a whole career on a certain public persona, you know? A man's man, as you keep telling me. Straightest chap on TV, happy to throw off his shirt for the sake of historical accuracy."

"Are you—are you telling me…" *Henry, you dimwit.* "George, pardon my bluntness, but you are, aren't you? Like me. Not straight, I mean."

"I've always kept my private life private. There are some things that the public don't need to know and my sexual preference is one of them." George lifted his head, meeting Henry's gaze. "But I don't like you making assumptions about me, because you got it wrong. *Again.* I'm not a thief and I'm not straight, you just never asked."

"I'm sorry." There wasn't very much else that Henry could say. He stroked his hand down the foal's neck and brushed his fingers against George's. "I truly am sorry, George."

"And if you want to know—which you don't, but I want to tell you—I would've done anything for you, Fitz." George looked down again, his gaze fixing on Jez. "But you had Steph, so…"

The tears that Henry had managed to hold back for so long burst their banks with no warning. His head dipped with the force of them, and without meaning to, his bowed forehead came to rest against George's. Tears splashed over Henry's hand, over George's, over the foal's dark mane.

"Don't cry." He heard George's voice, soft and pleading. "I'm going to get Ed off your back and sort all of that out and you won't have anything to worry about, I promise."

"Thank you. You were always so kind — I couldn't help but love you."

"And I'm going to find you a hell of a boyfriend as well," he promised. "And he's going to be the luckiest man."

Henry brushed his hand against George's again. This time he didn't move it away, but laid it tenderly over George's. What was it that he saw in George's eyes, whenever they were turned to him? Was it affection, the sort that leads to —

"Do you have anyone, George — a boyfriend?"

"I've had a few flings over the years, not too many. *The Sun* got a long lenser of me with one of them, a sound guy?" He lifted his gaze, green eyes dancing with nostalgia. "And I managed to stay friends with all of them, so I'm not complaining, but I've been single for a while. I don't want my private life splashed over the tabloids."

Henry swallowed. Henry ran his tongue over his lip. Henry put down his mug of tea.

"Would it be weird… I suppose it must be, it's silly of me to suggest…ask, even… George, why don't we, you and I… Why don't we jolly well give it a go?"

"The thing is, what with me doing the telly and whatnot, I tend to be rather unsure about *coming out*. I was so in awe of what you told me the other night because you're shy and yet you're the one who — I can't just be *out*, you need to know that." George sighed deeply. "But would you really want to? With me?"

"*Yes!* Of course I would! Why else would I have suggested it? You're kind and lovely and too bloody handsome for your own good. It just depends if you can stand me. And the thing is — we can be discreet. No one will know. No one would even suspect that we were, you know, *boyfriends*."

The word was strange and exciting in Henry's mouth.

"Shall we give it a go? Our secret?" George's fingers caught Henry's. "And I *am* sorry about your shirt, honestly."

"It's just a shirt! Bloody hell, *this* is what matters — us two." Henry laughed gently, tightening his fingers around George's. "Captain George...would you do me the great honor of allowing me to kiss you?"

"I would *love* you to!"

Henry brought his free hand up to George's face. Was he really about to do this? He had wanted this for so long and never believed it could happen. He traced his fingertips across George's face, feeling the warmth of his skin under his touch, the contours of his cheekbones, the slight rasp of advancing stubble, then across those soft, full lips. He caressed the back of George's neck and finally brought their mouths together.

Just a light brush of the lips but Henry groaned, so much pent-up passion threatening to break free that he had to stop for a moment to breathe. Then he began again, tracing his lips against George's. He yielded to his tongue, slow and tender, exploring and tasting George as their kiss deepened.

He heard George's breath catch, felt George's fingers soft against his face, resting very gently on his cheek, the hand that held his own growing just a little tighter as the kiss went on.

George wanted him. It didn't seem possible.

Yet he *did*, it *was*, because this kiss told him all he needed to know. It wasn't tentative or nervous, but full of the enthusiasm that George seemed to pour into everything he did. And now he was pouring it into their kiss, and *Britain's Favourite (and Sexiest!) Hero*'s hand shifted to rest on Henry's shoulder, clinging to that frayed shirt.

Henry combed his fingers through George's thick, lustrous hair, sighing into the kiss at how good, how right, this felt. It was worth waiting fifteen years for.

Then a quiet whinny from the foal, and Henry moved his mouth from George's, his fingers tangling in the hair at the back of George's neck.

"Not in front of the children!" Henry joked.

George laughed softly. "I never thought I'd be your type, Fitz, not in a million years."

"You always were. I just didn't know what the hell to do. I only realized when... Do you remember that day we were walking back from the bus stop at Longley Magna, we'd been to Hove for the cricket, and you disappeared up into a tree? And you slipped and bounced off every branch and landed in the road?"

Henry rested his head on George's shoulder, his voice a confiding whisper. "I thought you were dead, and there was this rush in my stomach, and I knew then that I loved you, just at the moment I thought I'd lost you. I begged you not to die, and then you opened your eyes and grinned at me. I was so relieved—but so scared. Because I was eighteen and I loved my best friend. What's a chap to do?"

"I was hoping for mouth-to-mouth," George whispered impishly.

"Did you know? Could you see it?"

George shook his head and admitted, "You're possibly the straightest man I've ever met, then you got together with Steph and that was that."

"Stiff upper lip, old bean. Got me out of many a scrape. And into them, alas."

They sat in companionable silence, touching, caressing, until Henry said, "Shall we sort out dinner? Or do you need to dash off anywhere?"

"I'm just researching my doc, I'm in no rush to do anything," his—his *boyfriend*—said. He looked at his watch, fastened about his strong wrist with a weathered, well-loved regimental watchstrap. "Do you want something here or shall we wander down to the pub?"

"If we go to the pub, we'll have to be on our best behavior. No snogging in the snug."

But perhaps that would be a good exercise, to go about in public together, seen and yet unseen.

"We'll stick to the beer garden, so Jez can have some nice juicy grass." George combed his fingers through Henry's hair, caressing softly. "Sure you won't be too annoyed by my face on the beer mats?"

Henry grinned. "Promise you won't think I'm weird? I took one from the pub that day you arrived and put it on my bedside table."

"So we're already sharing a bedroom? Sounds good to me, darling."

The bedroom? Of course Henry had thought of that, had lain awake wondering what it would be like if his empty bed contained George beside him, but here, now, the reality of it— Henry pulled at the frayed collar of his shirt.

"I should go and change, really—if we're off out. Or do you not mind me looking like a farmhand?"

"You look perfect, I'm the permanent scruff!"

"I was half expecting you to wander into the pub topless, but…you do look nice in your polo shirt." Henry stroked his hand down George's chest and across his toned stomach. "It makes you look rather— ahem—sexy. I can say that now, can't I? Although perhaps not in front of Jez."

"I don't spend all my life topless. Good for box office, though!" George laughed and caught Henry's hand where it rested against his stomach. "People get rather annoyed if I don't, you know."

"Can I just say—full disclosure—I wrote *none* of those letters to *Points of View* to complain when you kept your top on in that one episode. I mean, you were in a mangrove swamp full of mosquitos—of course you weren't going to go topless! What the heck is wrong with some people?"

Henry became aware of something—someone— nudging his hip. But it couldn't be George, unless he'd grown a third hand. Henry laughed and reached into his pocket.

"Sorry, Jez—I didn't give you your carrot, did I!"

"I've only done nude the one time." George sat back a little so the foal had space to eat. "And then only the rear view, careening across the Norway tundra after a hell of a sauna. Did you see that one?"

Henry's gaze wandered toward the television on the other side of the room, and the stack of DVDs next to it. George would find out eventually — there was no way he could fib.

"I — I did see it, yes. I've got it on DVD, actually. Your bottom looked utterly splendid."

"You know, I'd be happy to sign it." George's smile was as impish now as it had been in childhood. "The DVD, not the arse."

"If you start signing your DVDs and books in this house, we won't get to the pub until breakfast." Henry laughed, but at his words George's smile grew even more impish and Henry realized what he'd said. "I mean — because there's lots for you to sign. I wouldn't presume — "

"First date, Fitz." He reached out to caress Henry's face with his fingertips. Very carefully and a little clumsily, Jez rose up to stand on his long, skinny legs, chewing the fresh carrot. George's gaze flitted across to watch the foal, his eyes shining with happiness.

Henry crouched on the edge of a tired sofa, retying the dangling laces on his decrepit desert boots. What on earth had changed? Had magnetic north shifted so far that this could happen? But it must have, unless he was dreaming, because George's soft murmurs to the foal were real.

"Come on then." George rose to his feet and held out his hand to Henry. "Let's have our date."

Chapter Ten

The last hour had not gone as George had expected, but far, far better. Hand in hand they strolled down the driveway with Jez following alongside, keeping close to his adoptive father. In all the years of acrimony, George had wondered when he would return to Longley Parva only to learn that Henry had married or moved away. He'd dreaded either bit of news, but somehow the former might have been worse. In a million years, though, he would never have expected that Henry Fitzwalter was gay, this manliest of men, solid and tweed-clad and so very, very straight.

Perhaps if he hadn't been on television, if he didn't have so many female fans and so much bound up with his military past, George might not have been so reticent about the private life that he kept *so* private, but what would happen if people knew? Would that be the end of the meteoric career trajectory of George Standish-Brookes?

Yet it hurt to release Henry's hand as they reached the end of the lane and came into the village where the early evening roads were dotted with dog walkers and horse riders. Now they were just two mates again, a couple of pals off for a pint or two at their local. With a horse.

Still they walked as close as they dared, and George was prouder than he had been of any BAFTA, any invitation to the palace, simply to stroll through their idyllic village with Henry at his side. They passed the village hall with its collapsing roof, the ivy-covered cottages, the medieval church with its bright blooms bursting in colorful clouds all over the churchyard, all of it soundtracked by a chorus of cheerily chirruping birds.

Henry gave George a rundown about all that had been happening in the village. Daft stories that usually involved locals' pets, but they throbbed with the import of international events. A dog running through traffic, a cat stuck up a telegraph pole, a mysterious theft of koi carp and the parrot that provided the clue to solve it, the primary school's hamster and its untimely death, a Labrador that arrived with the snow and vanished as soon as it melted.

And now, a television personality and his foal, heading into the pub garden.

"I wonder if they do tapas," George mused, even as he suspected that The Green Man hadn't quite moved into gastropub territory. He took his sunglasses from a pocket and slid them onto his nose. "Or a mezze?"

"A what-y? They do sharing platters—is that the same thing? When Bob introduced those, the Parvans nearly started a riot. *How modern, can't have that, where's me ploughman's lunch?* There are some people in this village who find a cod goujon a terrifying concept."

"Grab us a nice table, Fitz." George touched Henry's arm, noticing a small crowd of children haring over the beer garden toward them. He had a sixth sense for it now, spotting the keener fans a second before they spotted him. "I'll just let Jez meet his public then I'll be right with you."

He felt Henry's hand rest for a moment in the small of his back. To anyone else it would appear to be a friendly gesture, an *I'll get the beers in* signal, but George knew otherwise.

A little girl with pigtails and the remains of a lolly around her mouth hopped up and down and clapped. "Captain George, Captain George, can we ride your horsey?"

A little boy with grazed knees cheered. "Captain George, can I stroke his nose?"

A much smaller child, who quite possibly had no idea who George was, appeared in his line of sight, borne in on its mother's arms.

"Captain George, what a lovely horse!"

"What's his name?"

"Can he meet our donkey?"

"Do you like sheep, Captain George, do you?"

"Will you sign this beer mat?"

"Will you sign my arm, and I'll get it tattooed?"

"Wish he'd take his top off — shall we pin him down and whip it off?" This from a table of teenage girls, who perhaps hadn't meant him to hear.

Each approach was met with a smile, a joke, a photo or autograph when required. To the cheeky teens, however, George shot a pout of comical proportions as he told them, "It's my day off, ladies!"

"Boo!" they shouted.

"Sorry!" He laughed, signing one more arm before he finally retreated back to where Henry and the beer waited. Jez had already made his escape and was standing beside the shaded table, lazily chewing at a clump of juicy grass, his tail swishing happily.

"Grabbed a menu—and look!" Henry pushed a Longley Spitfire beer mat across the table to George. Someone had Biroed hearts around the photo on it of George as a flying ace. "Not guilty, m'lud!"

"Got a pen, Fitz?" George held out his hand, sure Henry was the sort of chap who would *always* have a pen. "I quite liked being RAF!"

Henry patted the pockets of the old suede jacket he'd flung on as they'd left for the pub. "Should have one— ah, here you go."

George scribbled something across the beer mat and passed it back to Henry. There, across his face, he'd written, *HF – 130 – GSB.*

"To make up for the cricket ball." He smiled. A small gesture, but one that felt like it meant something, as though it went a little way to mending the lost years.

Henry held it as carefully as he would have done a precious artifact.

"I'll kiss you my thanks later," he whispered.

"I think that's the least you can do." George looked down at the menu. "Fancy sharing something?"

"Go on, then! One of the controversial platters? I can't recommend any of them because I've never—well, not had anyone to share with before. I'm a steak-and-ale pie sort of chap. But teach me in your sophisticated ways, Captain George, do."

"Ladies!" George turned to address the still-giggling girls, not sure whether Henry was being sarcastic or not. Either way, it was adorable. "What do you recommend?"

The girls nominated one of their number to reply. "That Spanish one's nice, with the *chorizo*."

She said the Spanish word with a flourish, and her friends giggled all the more.

"Then *chorizo* it shall be!" George jumped up from his seat. "And I think another round of drinks for everyone!"

He stooped to kiss Jez's forelock and told him, "You behave."

Then George made his way into the cool shade of the pub. More autographs, more photos, more excitement when he put some cash behind the bar and finally the order was placed. He escaped back into the garden to see Henry gently stroking Jez, who looked utterly relaxed in the care of the *vet'n'ry*.

"I was thinking, Fitz, of those swimming pools for horses." George slipped back into his seat, just catching himself before he took Henry's hand. "Would that help my boy's leg, do you think?"

"Hydrotherapy, you mean? Although I do like the idea of a horse swimming pool—brings a whole new meaning to water polo!" Henry winked at him. "Well, it's worth a try. Has his leg been X-rayed, do you know? We need to find out if the lameness is muscular or skeletal."

"Ed's man said it was muscular. He reckoned Jez won't make a racehorse, but he could be a happy enough sort of chap." George reached out and stroked the foal's neck. "And a happy chap is good enough for me."

A little hesitant, Henry whispered, as if he shouldn't really say it but was determined to anyway, "*I'm* a happy chap." Then he spoke at normal volume, a vet talking through treatment options with a concerned owner. "It'll take time, and it'll take love, and maybe he'll need to go swimming, but not every horse can be a race winner, and it doesn't matter at all."

"I worry about him, though. If I want to go off to the Amazon or the Arctic or wherever, I can't really take Jez." George took a drink of beer and said casually, "I might have to hang around here instead and crack on with my next book."

Henry looked thoughtful, his blue eyes clouding over then clearing into a smile.

"Perhaps you should. And, don't forget, I've got plenty of space at the manor. There's the old stable block which I could get sorted out, and... Well, depending on how things pan out, of course."

"I was wondering if there might be a doc in Georgina, you know..." He watched Henry, studying that firm, strong jaw, the faint smile on his lips. *Are the rumors true, that sort of thing? Wonder what you'd find in the county archive? Lots of boring guff about tithe apportionments, or Georgian sex scandals!*

A teenage Parvan arrived at their table with their food. *Georgian sex scandals? Well done, George, that would give them something to discuss in the tap room.* The enormous plate was awash with meat and cheese, olive oil liberally sprinkled about and numerous, intriguing breaded objects which had apparently been deep-fried.

"How did I never know our village was capable of such a spread!" Henry blinked up at the sunshine. "Who needs to go on holiday? I'm in Spain!"

"Did a bit of rock climbing in Spain," George reminisced. "Broke an ankle. This is much less painful!"

Henry finished chewing his mouthful. "How on earth did you manage that? Did you fall off?"

"Nope, slipped on a sun-dried tomato after overindulging on sangria." George laughed, shaking his head. "That was just after I got out of the Army. I wrote the first book while I was laid up and the rest, as the cliché goes, is history."

And in all those adventures, seeing the world and all its wonders, not a single day had passed in which he hadn't thought of Henry.

"Perhaps it was just as well you broke your ankle, then!"

Henry balanced a slice of olive oil-drenched manchego on a slice of bread and wobbled the stack of food to his mouth. George watched him, his chin balanced on his hand. *Henry shouldn't wear pinstripes*, he decided. *He should be lazy in beer gardens forever.*

"You all right?" Henry grinned. Olive oil dribbled over his chin as he wedged the bread and cheese into his mouth. He wiped it off with a large cotton handkerchief, just as George felt the desert boot tap against his foot. It rested there, then nudged up the hem of George's jeans at the ankle.

"I'm just wondering why you pretend to be so buttoned-down and stuck up when you're really so bloody lovely," George murmured with a smile. He pushed his sunglasses up into his hair and fidgeted a little bashfully with the regimental strap of his watch. "I missed you a lot, Fitz."

"I missed you, too."

Henry brushed the crumbs from his hands and leaned against the table on his folded arms. His intent look told George he was about to confide again and George raised his finger in warning, glancing around the beer garden to check that they were unheard. They were being watched, but no one had approached, so George nodded.

Henry spoke quietly. "When Steph went off with Ed, I really thought about myself — about what I was doing. Hiding who I really was. I thought, *now, now's the time*, and for some daft reason, I wanted to tell you. But then you were in the newspapers with that posh woman, and I bottled it."

"I heard from Ma that the two of you hadn't worked out and she started nudging, *oh, Georgie, it's obvious how you feel, just tell him!*" He rolled his eyes. "But the thought of it, of how you might react. Ma knows everything, you can't get anything past her."

"I wonder if your mum realized that — well, I suppose you thought I might swing my cricket bat around again, didn't you? I'll never live that down, will I!" Henry shook his head and pronged one of the deep-fried objects with a fork. "Honestly, that whole interlude with Steph. She tried so hard to get me to — not that I should talk about this, but, you know, it was rather awkward in the bedroom. She put up with a lot, and she loved me, I know she did, but I let her go. It was for the best, really."

George thought of the odious couple at the enormous house of marble and glass, and a shiver ran through him. He recalled too well Ed's comment about Henry's bedroom prowess, and that had come from one person and one alone. Stephanie Belcher wasn't a lady by any stretch of the imagination, and Henry was too good for her, he always had been. She had been a spiteful little girl and a sarcastic young lady and had grown into a gorgon, yet somehow, only he could see it.

He painted on a smile and said, "Well, she's certainly met her soul mate now."

"I'm not entirely sure that Ed has a soul, though!" Henry laughed, a noise that veered dangerously toward the hysterical. Then he cleared his throat and held up his fork. "Interesting—deep-fried mashed potato and meat, all wrapped together in a tasty breadcrumb batter. Clever people, those Spanish."

"Well, she picked him!"

"She must see something in him that none of us can." Henry nodded, as if speaking a well-known truth. "I mean, he does love her. He made such a fuss when I didn't award her the jam prize. And maybe he has a point about the manor. If Bad Billy really did wager it, and lost, then by rights, as much as I'm loath to admit it, it must be Ed's."

"*What*?" That was loud enough to get the attentions of their fellow drinkers. Was Henry just going to make his bed in the road and let Ed drive his steamroller straight over him? Would Ed Belcher leave Henry flattened into the driveway of the manor? "How the *hell* can you, a sane man, even think that?"

"I can't afford a lawyer, George, you know that. I want to fight him, but I wonder if I'm on thin ice—we all know that Bad Billy was a bit of a one. What if I spend loads of money on a solicitor and discover that Ed's right? What's the gentlemanly thing to do, that's what I wonder—stand aside or fight?"

"You're talking to a former soldier. *Never* stand aside when injustice is about to happen, Fitz."

Henry reached across the table and squeezed George's hand. It was just on the right side of *intense conversation between two extremely heterosexual men.* George glanced down at their hands and, with an almost painfully apologetic look, reached to take another piece of food.

"You make me feel brave. I should fight him, shouldn't I? And not just grab his balls, but kick them into next week. Or…use a cricket bat." Henry gave him a sideways grin, and that foot—oh, that insubordinate foot—was nudging against George's again.

"We need to go through every inch of our houses, every piece of old paper, and find anything that even *mentions* their stupid bloody bet. A decent court'll lob it out, but the likes of Ed will tie you in legal knots." He popped a piece of tomato into his mouth. "The question I want answered is *why*? Why your house? Why now?"

"I can't work it out." Henry sighed, prodding at another deep-fried Spanish marvel. "Last year he was trying to buy the farm that backs onto his property. The farmer wouldn't sell up, there was argy-bargy, the farmer parked his pig transporter right outside Ed's gates, and finally he gave up! Then again, he said the smell of the pigs was upsetting his horses. But my house is on the other side of the village, so… Who knows?"

"What do you have from your side? Letters, diaries, *anything*?" George knew there were boxes of the stuff too in the attic of his cottage. "And did the Reverend leave anything among the manor papers? He lived there long eno—" George blinked. "Fitz, you don't think…?"

"A load of it went to the county archive, courtesy of my grandfather. But there might still be—what?" Henry stifled a laugh. "*My dear, loving friend*? You don't think—no! That they…?" Henry wafted his hand about, indicating the two of them. "In those days? Then again, I wouldn't put it past Billy, would you? Looked like quite the rascal!"

"A couple of respectable widowers, not even middle-aged?" George raised an eyebrow. "Wouldn't it be wonderful?"

"I always wondered why they didn't remarry. That was the usual thing, wasn't it, a wife to help them look after their children and their house, but instead the Reverend moved into the manor." Henry scratched his head, laughing again. "We've still got Bad Billy's bed! It's a bit wormy now, it's in a lumber room in the attic. But…maybe we should –"

"I'd love to know what the Rev. looked like, but no paintings, sadly!" George tutted. "Georgie said he took after her, though, which means he was a hell of a looker."

"The ravishing Reverend!"

"Who lost the bloody scorecard!"

"Toot-toot! Toot-*toot!*"

Their table was surrounded in seconds by drunk men in an assortment of rugby shirts and T-shirts, leaning into George's personal space and snapping selfies. Henry managed to move their nearly empty plate out of the way in time to stop it getting knocked onto the ground. George's first thought was for Jez, the little foal looking somewhat perturbed by this good-natured but loud invasion into his guardian's peaceful supper.

Without being asked, Henry took Jez's lead rein and led him into a farther corner of the beer garden, away from the noisy interlopers. George watched them both, then pasted on a smile for the fans. *Having people bellow toot-toot at you and mimic the horn of a Jaguar is a small price to pay for success*, he told himself as he posed and grinned and laughed and signed. Invitations to arm wrestle were politely declined and the men departed happily, leaving George to join his partner and the wide-eyed little horse. He stooped before Jez and whispered, "You all right, little man?"

"Maybe he needs a short walk before bedtime? It'd help his leg. We could take him through the woods — no marauding drunkards there, I hope!"

"Nor puckish boys falling out of trees?" George touched his hand to Henry's shoulder. "Let's go before we get pounced on again."

"Too right!"

As they made a move to go, the other occupants of the beer garden waved farewell to their local celebrity. George returned the gesture and called, "Drinks are on me, have a good night!"

Then he strolled away, toward the trees into which Alan Belcher had once hurled the cricket ball that had been intended for his best friend.

As they entered the cool, shady wood, Jez became calm and snuffled contentedly at the trees and the grasses. Everything was new to him.

Now that they were concealed by the trees, Henry and George were able to hold hands.

"You and I should go to Brighton next summer," George decided, realizing that perhaps meant he would still be here by then. Brighton was a long way from the Amazon, after all. He turned to look at Henry, that face he had known all his life, whose family had been there when his own father died, who knew him as no one else ever had. "And take Jez too."

"Are you going to gallop him along the beach at sunset? But yes, we *should* go to Brighton. It's only an hour in the car. Although — might take longer with a horsebox!" Henry smiled and ruffled his hand through George's hair.

"The Jag won't pull a horsebox. If only I knew a big, strong vet who had his own Land Rover." George pulled a comically thoughtful face. "I'd be so grateful, I'd push him up against the nearest tree and give him the biggest kiss…"

"The Landy is at your command."

"At my command-y?"

"If you give me a kiss-y."

George laughed, in so much of a hurry to get to the kissing that he forgot the pushing up against a tree part of the deal. Instead he slipped his arm around Henry's waist and pulled their bodies together, his lips tender and soft against his friend's. Henry's arms were tight around him, a slight tremble in his kiss as he ruffled George's hair again, his other hand settling in the small of George's back, holding him firm against him.

These were the sort of arms that George could happily imagine melting into, the sort of broad chest where he would rest his head as he slept. And it didn't matter that the world couldn't know, because Henry wasn't the sort of man to make a show of them. Henry was private and quiet and — wonderful. He wondered vaguely if would be possible to reawaken the love that Henry had spoken of but pushed the thought away. Such lofty ambitions were not for this evening.

The hand on George's back slipped lower, stroking over the curve of George's buttocks — that famous bottom that he had displayed for all to see on television screens across the nation. George noticed that there was something in Henry's trousers, and it was unlikely to be another carrot. He wouldn't draw attention to it, George decided. Who knew how experienced Henry was, after all, and the last thing he wanted was to scare Henry off.

Henry nudged his knee between George's legs, his hand coming to rest on George's waist as he walked them backward against a tree. George, however, broke the kiss to check that Jez was still happy with his lot. Seeing the foal chewing the grass, he allowed himself to be distracted by Henry once more.

Henry whispered as he ran his mouth over George's face. "I want to touch you, George. But does one *touch* on a first date?"

Perhaps he was more experienced than George had guessed, in that case. And the woods weren't the *wrong* place, were they, but would Henry look back at this and think they had been too quick? George, however, managed a gasp of, "Would you like to?"

Henry's blue eyes gazed into George's as he found his way to the front of George's jeans and cupped George's erection. Nimble fingers unbuckled his belt, then unfastened the top button. Henry slid his hand down inside the elastic of George's boxer shorts as Henry's panting mouth fell back to George's in a deep, sloppy kiss. Henry's other hand tugged down the zip and George groaned as Henry at last had him in his strong hand.

George pressed his back against the tree and closed his eyes, surrendering to Henry's touch and that irresistible kiss. He heard a slight, merry whinny from Jez, but it wasn't a sound to cause concern, he knew. Nobody would see them here.

"It's all in the wrist, that's what you always told me." Henry nipped at George's earlobe as he moved his hand back and forth. George replied with a soft moan of pleasure that turned into a cry of surprised pain when something hard dropped onto his foot, seemingly out of nowhere.

"What the —" The moment shattered. George's head snapped to the right where Jez stood a few inches away, peering at him. Then he looked down, past the intoxicating sight of Henry's hand on him, and saw —

"Bloody hell!" As George spoke, Henry released him. He quickly fastened his jeans before stooping to retrieve an object the size of an apple, caked in mud and moss, but beneath the foliage he could just see the hint of red. *It can't be* the *cricket ball*, George told himself, but still he scraped at the caked-on dirt of fifteen years and there beneath it, revealed as slowly as the inscription on a forgotten tomb, was the tribute he had etched more than half a lifetime ago.

HF – 130 – GSB

"It can't... Blimey, it is!" Henry put his arm around George's waist. "You know what this is, dear old Standy-Bee? It's a sign. Together, you and I, we can defeat the Belchers. Knock 'em for six!"

"Just like you've knocked me for six?" George pressed his lips to Henry's hair. For a second, no more, he *almost* told Henry about his plan to infiltrate the Belchers and put a stop to their schemes through money or charm, but he could already hear Henry telling him not to do anything silly. Instead, he told him, "When I was in Afghanistan, and it was all a bit nuts and things were blowing up and — I kept thinking of this bloody cricket ball and you and wondering, *does he think about me?*"

"Of course I did. Every day." Henry danced his fingertips across George's face, his lips brushing over his skin. "Your mum told me when you were deployed. You were in my thoughts all the time you were out there. And I had no right to, not after— Every day I'd look up at the sky and say, *keep him safe*. Then you were injured, and the first I knew of it was when I saw your mum loading a suitcase into that car of yours. She told me. That was before the photo was everywhere. I couldn't— My selfless, brave Captain George."

"I hate that photo," was his whispered confession. He had never said it before. Instead he went on chat shows and spoke of the horrors of war and the reward of knowing he'd done a good thing, that a child got a second chance because of him, but really, if he could wave a wand and have that picture disappear forever, he'd do it. It had defined him just as it had Darioush, the little boy he had carried to safety, whom George had sheltered from razors of shrapnel with his own body, and it had turned George Standish-Brookes from an officer with the Household Cavalry into a symbol for a hundred different causes. Those who wanted war, those who hated war, hawks and doves alike, he was suddenly used by them all to promote this agenda or that cause, when all he really wanted was to get on. Let the photographer have her moment and win the prizes, for he wanted none of them.

"I always wondered what you made of all that." Henry didn't say anything else, but traced his fingers over the inscription that George had carved into the ball. "Just think, all that has happened and that ball has been here all along. It'll look nice on your mantelpiece, with Georgina to watch over it so it never gets lost again."

"I didn't win it, Fitz, you did."

"No, because I lost my claim to it when I accused you. And after all" — Henry swept his hand toward the foal — "Jez did give it to you!"

"Only because he doesn't know our story yet, so he wouldn't have recognized it as yours." George weighed the cricket ball in his hand. "I want you to have it. I mean, if you'd rather not have a ball that's been stuck in a wood for fifteen years, that's fair enough, of course!"

"All right. I'll put it on *my* mantelpiece and Bad Billy can keep an eye on it. Though he might take one look at the ball and initiate another cricket wager, and God knows what he'll bet on this time."

"No more gambles, Fitz, you're too sensible for that!"

"Not for me — the closest I get is the tombola at the summer fête."

"I hope," George murmured, looping his arms around Henry's neck, "that crazy old Billy approves of soldiers."

"He had something to do with the Sussex Militia. His sword's in the attic somewhere. So yes, I'm sure he does approve!"

George smiled, sure that Reverend Standish would, too. Something was nagging at him, though, the thought that they might move too fast and miss something or, even worse, burn out the fire that had smoldered for so long.

"Would you mind if we slowed things down a bit? I want to enjoy courting my Fitz. I feel as though we've waited so long for each other, and — " He laughed, feeling his face flush. "It's important to me that we give ourselves a chance. I don't want this to be a fling."

"Of course, George." Did a blind come down over Henry's face then? George wasn't sure. A veneer of gentlemanly reserve, perhaps. "Maybe I shouldn't have put my— I could get rather carried away."

"No, no, it's not you, honestly!" Ridiculous, really, but he had the distinct impression he had punctured the mood of the evening. "I'm rather public property sometimes, you must've noticed. I want this to be romantic, old-fashioned, I suppose. Silly of me, I know."

"Not at all—it's sweet. It's better than a"—Henry looked down at the ground—"a quick grope. And I'm not saying that's what this is. Far from it. *Very* far from it. We should have a courtship."

When Henry looked up again, he was smiling. He looked, weirdly, five or even ten years younger than he had when George had first clapped eyes on him at the Bonny Baby Competition. Maybe it was that grin of his, that distinctly boyish grin.

"A romance," George concluded. "I'm so glad I came home."

"Me too. Let me help you get Jez to bed, and then— we can arrange our second date. What do you say to that?"

"I say yes. I've got my producer over tomorrow, but why don't we open a bottle of something in the evening and have a look through Billy's papers? I can throw us some supper together if you like." What would Henry eat? Sensible food, George imagined, even as he pictured some exotic Middle Eastern tagine tempting Henry from his Sunday roast.

They were off again, leading Jez through the evening woodland. Birds flew overhead, swooping to their roosts, and the dew began to fall.

"Your place or mine tomorrow?" Henry asked. He patted Jez's shoulder as George opened the garden gate.

"Let's make it mine, I'll cook something really special for you and we can sit out by the pond and find out what our two Regency bucks got up to." He watched Jez amble past, seemingly untroubled by his lame leg. "And Jez can chill out with the ducks."

"That will be lovely."

"It's still early, Fitz. Fancy a G&T?" George closed the gate and turned to take Henry's fingers in his own for a brief moment.

"Go on, then. And I promise to behave."

Henry brought their linked hands to his mouth and kissed them. George darted a look over Henry's shoulder then returned the gesture, pressing a kiss of his own to their entwined fingers. He smiled gently and told Henry, "Let's have a snuggle in the sitting room. Jez can come in for half an hour without causing too much drama. It's not as if Ma will find out there was a horse in her house!"

"Unless one swish of his tail destroys all her pottery."

"Jez is a horse of taste." George unlocked the cottage door and ushered Henry into the bright interior. "He likes his gran's work."

The young horse trotted into the cool hallway and George closed the door behind them. Henry glanced about, then took off his jacket and hung it on the newel post.

Now they were alone, and George found himself reaching for Henry's hand again, pulling him back for another kiss.

They were taking things slowly, George reminded himself, even as he recalled the touch of Henry's strong hand on his body. The name of the game was courtship and romance, even if Henry *had* filled his dreams for years. As they kissed again, he thought happily of how he, TV star, darling of every echelon of society, would use the charm and bravado that had served him so well to save Henry's house. How hard could it be, after all? No harder than finding a cricket ball that had been lost for fifteen years.

Twining their fingers together, Henry broke from the kiss. George found himself fixed to the spot by Henry's usually gentle blue eyes. There was a touch of fire in them now that George hadn't seen before. Henry combed his fingers through George's hair and swallowed before he spoke.

"I'm going to behave myself, dear old George."

"We've known each other thirty years," he murmured in reply, reaching his hand up to Henry's face. It was warm, the soft skin betraying the slightest hint of stubble beneath his palm. "I'm sure no one would object to a few more kisses?"

"Oh, yes — there's room to be a little naughty. Come here, Captain Standy-Bee. I have fifteen years of kisses for you."

"Let's go into the sitting room," George suggested between increasingly heated kisses. "There's a *very* comfortable sofa in there."

"An admirable suggestion."

They staggered in each other's arms into the lounge and collapsed onto the sofa. It gave a comical creak as they settled onto it, lying on their sides in a mountain of tie-dyed cushions. Henry's strong hands cupped George's buttocks again, pushing their hips together as they kissed deeply. George wandered his hand up the back of Henry's shirt, trailing his fingertips against his warm, firm skin.

"Where's your ball?" George's voice was all innocence, his eyelids batting. "I hope you put it somewhere safe."

"It's in my jacket pocket. That's not the cricket ball you can feel now."

"Oh, Fitz, now you've really got my hopes up!" George laughed, burying his face against Henry's shoulder.

"Gosh, George, that's my wallet, what else could it possibly be?"

"If I weren't a well-schooled gent who has squired members of the ruling house at Goodwood on more than one occasion," George told him, "I'd say I hoped it was your big, hard cock."

A grunt escaped Henry's throat, a suggestion of a buck in his hips. His breath was hot against George's neck as he spoke.

"I would ask you to unzip me and find out, but...we *are* courting. So the mystery of my trousers will have to linger on a while."

"Does courting mean my shirt has to stay on?" It was nothing Henry hadn't seen before, of course, but never quite so intimately.

Henry moved his large hands up from George's bottom and slid them under his polo shirt, stroking George's skin with strong sweeps.

He assumed a comedy *Disgusted of Basingstoke* voice, albeit rather breathless. "Dear Auntie Beeb, I must remonstrate in the strongest terms. I was romping on the sofa with television's Captain George Standish-Brookes and he kept his shirt on the whole time. What do I pay my license fee for, if not to gaze uninterrupted upon that finest of torsos? Yours, hoping to see that shirt flung onto the floor at Captain Standish-Brookes' earliest convenience, Mr. Henry Fitzwalter, RCVS."

"I would love to, but my hands are rather enjoying themselves already." He stroked his palms over Henry's back. "Might you do the honors?"

Henry grinned at him. George felt that smile like a caress.

"And have half the country jealous of me?" Henry started to edge the shirt up, inch by tantalizing inch. "I won't apologize for not rushing. I want to remember this forever."

"Take all the time you need, Fitz." George watched him, his breath quickening. "I'm going nowhere."

Were Henry's hands shaking? Just a tremble?

"Bloody hell, George — this is better than on telly!" Henry swept his palms over each inch of skin as it was exposed, until he had pushed the polo shirt up to George's armpits and could brush his fingertips over George's nipples.

The touch sent a jolt of pleasure through George and he arched his back, urging Henry not to stop. With a flex of his arms, he dragged the shirt over his head and tossed it aside.

"How do I measure up to the chap on the telly?"

Propping himself up on one arm, Henry passed his eyes up and down George.

"Not bad, I'd say." The hitch in Henry's voice as he spoke betrayed his admiration. George was no stranger to being gaped at appreciatively, but the — it was, wasn't it, or was he only imagining it? — adoring gaze of Henry Fitzwalter was the most precious look he had ever received.

Henry's voice was barely above a whisper. "Lie on your back, George, let me kiss your tummy."

It was somehow the most erotic thing George had ever heard and he shifted onto his back, unable to tear his gaze from Henry.

Henry pressed his mouth to George's, then snaked his tongue the length of George's neck. Once he reached the planes of George's chest, Henry kissed and nibbled his way across, teeth gently grazing his nipples. All the while, those fathomless blue eyes peered up at George. George sank his fingers into Henry's hair as that soft mouth moved ever lower.

With one hand on George's hip, the other tangling the fingers of George's free hand, Henry bathed television's most famous stomach with lips and tongue. The steadying hand on George's hip anchored him to the sofa even as he arched toward Henry's mouth.

Courting Standy-Bee, he reminded himself. *Courting and behaving and not tearing the chap's clothes off and rolling around in the rugs until the next day dawns.*

By God, though, he is a hard chap to resist.

The tender brush of Henry's tongue over George's navel had George moaning, and at last, and unfortunately, Henry raised his head. He placed his palm flat on George's stomach, while it was still wet from his kisses. Kneeling with George's legs pressed between his own, Henry panted and passed his hand through his hair.

"George... I'm sorry, I have to stop. I was seconds from undoing your jeans and—we're courting, right? Aren't we?"

"You're really very"—George smiled, combing his hand over Henry's soft hair—"lovely. You're lovely."

"Another day, though, I promise you that. Those jeans are coming off, and I'm going to keep kissing, *all* the way down." Henry winked. "But not on a first date, eh?"

"I don't—" George felt oddly thrown off kilter by that. "I'm not a tart, Fitz, don't think that. I just got a bit carried away. Sorry, I wouldn't want—"

He tutted, annoyed at himself and his own enthusiasm. *What must Henry think now?*

"If anything, *I'm* the tart." Henry danced his fingertips across George's stomach. Then, so light that he barely touched him, rested them on the bulge of George's erection. "You have such a beautiful cock. I want to pleasure you, George—I want to taste you."

"Oh, Fitz," George gasped. "How did we ever get by as enemies?"

Henry stroked George's hardness through his trousers. "Because somehow we knew that making up would be amazing?"

"I wouldn't have wanted..." He sighed, not sure *how* to say it. "The lads who left someone back home, I was always glad I wasn't one of them. I couldn't have gone out there if it meant leaving you."

Henry returned to lying on his side and curled his leg over George's. Linking their hands again, George was caught by those ridiculous blue eyes once more.

"You were in my thoughts—in my heart—every day," Henry said. "You still are, because I couldn't stop loving you."

"You—" He must have misunderstood surely, or was that— "I thought you hated me."

"I lied to myself. I wanted everyone to think I hated you—I wanted to stop loving you, because it scared me. There. That's the truth." Henry brought their linked hands to rest over his heart. "I don't expect anything, but I just hope you can at least forgive me."

"I forgave you the first time an IED went off next to our Scimitar." George fell silent for a few seconds, feeling Henry's heart pounding beneath his palm. Longley Parva had never seemed so far away as it had on that unremarkable Tuesday afternoon when the world had looked like it might end. "I phoned you that night but I got your voicemail... I didn't know what to say, so I never dared try again."

Henry's kiss was soft on George's cheek. "We're together now, George. I know thousands love television's Captain George Standish-Brookes, but *I* love my Standy-Bee."

"I love you, Fitz." George tried the words out, the words he had readied years earlier at the end of an unreliable phone line from the desert. He had never expected to hear his own voice saying them, yet here they were, and Henry didn't look at all perturbed. In fact, he looked happy, as happy as George felt.

"Thank goodness for that!" Henry chuckled, and George found himself pulled into his boyfriend's — his lover's — embrace. "I'm not going to let you go ever again, my dear old George."

"Also known as the luckiest man alive!" He laughed, clinging to Henry's waist. Maybe the Amazon could wait after all, since he now had a horse *and* a vet to look after.

"No, no, *I'm* the luckiest man alive!" Henry ruffled George's hair energetically.

They kissed again, deep, passionate kisses, echoed by strong, loving caresses. George slid his hand down to rest on Henry's bottom, holding their hips tight together as he felt his lover's erection pressing against him. This felt like more than courtship but he wasn't about to complain or even think, too caught in the feeling of loving and being loved in turn.

"You can stay tonight if you'd like to," he whispered, hearing Jez's hooves clipping into the kitchen in the silence that followed. "There's no pressure."

"Like to? I'd love to!" Henry stroked George's chin and kissed him, before adding, "Only thing is, I don't have my jim-jams with me."

"I'm hoping you won't need them, Fitz."

A hesitant look crossed Henry's face. He put his hand over his stomach, still clothed in his frayed top, then moved it away, grinning, all demurral gone.

"I hope so too."

"Before we get too carried away, let's put Jez to bed? Then the night's ours, Fitz."

Just as they disentangled themselves, George was struck with a moment of nostalgia. Sunday evenings at Longley Parva Manor with mugs of cocoa, toasting crumpets over the fire beneath Bad Billy's regard, Henry's father holding forth as they watched *All Creatures Great and Small*.

What could possibly have made him think of that?

Henry groaned. "Oh, bloody hell! That's my phone going off. Do you like the ringtone? Couldn't resist the theme tune of our favorite thing on telly!"

"It's very you, darling!"

George rolled down from the sofa and landed on his knees just in time to hear a clatter from the kitchen. Leaving Henry to answer the phone, he hurried through to the kitchen where Jez was finishing the last of half a dozen fresh apples, the wooden bowl still rocking back and forth on the ground. Jez's punishment was a cuddle from his owner and a fresh carrot for dessert. What was a boy for if not indulging, after all?

"Uncle Fitz is staying over," George confided to Jez in a whisper. "He loves me!"

George turned at the sound of a soft knock on the kitchen door, followed by a frustrated sigh.

"So sorry about this, dear old George. I've been summoned. Mrs. McKenna's cat has been hit by a car. It's still alive—it must be in a lot of pain. I can't leave it, George, I've got to go. I'd much rather stay with you than decide life or death over someone's pet, but... I've got to hurry."

"Oh God, did you get the Land Rover back?" George tried to recall Mrs. McKenna. Was she walking distance?

"Yes—it's only a couple of minutes to the surgery. They're waiting for me there. Look, let's do this again." Henry had already put on his jacket and was holding his car keys.

"Tomorrow night, remember? I'll cook?"

"Deal!" George received a quick kiss to his forehead, and as Henry ran through the hallway, he shouted, "I bloody love you, George—don't forget that!"

Chapter Eleven

The following morning Longley Parva slumbered, but the world of global business never slept. And nor did Steph Belcher. Across the Belcher bedroom with its planes of glass and marble, its mirrors and chandeliers and neutral colors, the chirrup of a Skype ringtone sounded. It rang out of a sleek silver laptop, echoing through the house.

A moment later, the ringtone bellowed out from another computer in the office, from Ed's phone and two tablets, providing a blaring wake-up call for the village's resident millionaire.

Steph tied on her pearl-gray silk dressing gown. She nudged her half-asleep husband. Not getting a swift response from the *baddest ball-breaker on the exchange*, she lifted his eye mask off his face and held the elastic at such a stretch that her husband would know she'd ping it back on him if he ignored her.

"Ed-babes? A call's coming through."

"Tell them to piss off." He yawned.

She let go of the mask and it snapped against Ed's face.

"Up!"

Ed let out a howl and bolted upright, his hand shooting out to seize the phone and hold it up.

"No contacts in, smart-arse," he barked, waving the screen at her. "Who is it?"

Steph swept up one of the tablets and dashed her fingertip across the screen. She flicked back her hair and flashed her porcelain-veneered teeth at the tiny black dot of the camera.

"Randy Cheese! What can we do for you? Must be the middle of the night over there!"

Her Saint-Tropez-tan legs carried her back to the bed and its satin sheets. She propped herself up in front of Ed so that he appeared like a second, miniature head attached to her shoulder.

"It's always office hours in the Cheese Tower," the New York billionaire told her as soon as his image appeared. His orange face filled the screen, face plump and cheeks ruddy atop a too-tight collar and tie. Cheese's boot-black hair was a slicked shadow and he peered more closely into the camera. "What the hell's going on, Belcher? You sleeping when you should be working?"

"Ed-babes was having a power nap." Steph pouted at the screen. "I was just waking him up – in the best way a woman can."

"So, what's the verdict on the crazy squire's house? How much does he want?"

Steph rolled her eyes and turned to glare at her husband, gesturing toward the screen. "*You* can tell him."

"Our local vet's nutty as a fruitcake, Mr. Cheese." Ed was a minute away from touching his forelock, it seemed. "He says he won't sell for any amount, not to an American."

Steph nodded, running her finger down from her collarbone to the V of her dressing gown. "Ed's quite right about that."

The kind vet who had tried to please her with nice words – the kind vet who had spent all his money on his business and not on Steph.

"But me and Steph have got a plan." Ed beamed. Steph tensed, not sure he fully *understood* the scheme or his part in it. Would he say the right thing? "And he can't go on forever, the place is going to run him into an early grave. So we're going to make an offer to buy the house off him and preserve it for the village, then give it to you for a nominal fee."

A huge fee, of course.

"And we can promise you that the planning go-ahead for Cheese Acres Golf and Resort is going to be a piece of cake," Ed went on. "Isn't that right, Stephy-boo?"

"Oh, yes."

Oh yes, it would, because her friend was having an affair with someone on the planning committee at the council, and Steph had casually let it be known that she would tell his wife about his dalliance if he didn't do all he could to ensure planning permission went through. And damn the bloody Parvans.

Steph smiled across thousands of miles at Randy Cheese. "I've been networking."

"Good girl." Cheese pointed one finger at the camera. "She's a good girl, hang on to that one. So, what's this nominal fee? Don't try to cross me, Belcher. I'll buy you, eat you, shit you out and sell you at a profit!"

Steph winced as Ed made a strangled noise. Below the line of the camera, she stabbed her fingernails into his wrist to bring him back into line.

"What we pay plus a finder's fee of ten percent?" Ed trotted out his line, Steph knowing that his lawyer would put whatever price on the document she told him to, even if they got the house for free thanks to that ancient cricketing wager. After all, Steph knew everybody, and when she'd mentioned to that same lawyer that she had noticed his young secretary's newborn mysteriously seemed to have no father on the scene, he had gone white as milk.

Yes, I'm a useful sort of wife.

She tipped her head to one side, twirling a length of her blonde hair about her finger. Rather like she did her men.

"So — I hope that's agreeable, Mr. Cheese? We're looking forward to your visit. *I'll* be providing the entertainment, by the way."

"When the bulldozers move in and get rid of that damned old eyesore of a manor, *then* I'll enjoy the entertainment," Cheese told her coolly. "And when Cheese Acres Golf and Resort opens in Pavley Longa, you and I can share a hole or two, Stephanie."

"Or three," she purred.

"I've got my handicap down to fourteen," Ed added, completely missing the innuendo. "So I'll be enjoying those holes too!"

"Stephanie, we'll talk again," Cheese told her. "Belcher, get on that goddamned house. Cheese out!"

"Goodbye, Randy!" Steph blew him a kiss and wriggled her long-nailed fingers at him.

"Bye," Ed called a moment after the call ended. Then he looked at Steph and told her, "He knows we're cheating him, he's going to have us whacked! We'll be in concrete boots!"

"How could he know? And a bit of good-natured cheating between businessmen—that's how the world turns, Ed-babes. You know that more than anyone."

"If he finds out we're trying to get the house for free…you'll need more than your tits to save us!"

Steph pulled her dressing gown tight around her, her cleavage disappearing from view. She was quiet for a moment, tapping her finger against her lips in thought.

"We have a trump card, though—television's Captain George. Henry might have blustered about in a rage when he turned up the other day, but I know that Henry still has little mementos of George stashed about his house. Photos of them as lads, vet novels that George bought him for Christmas yonks ago. George can't stand him, that much is obvious—his opening gambit, defending his old chum, was so fake! He's probably trying to shit-stir for this documentary of his, bit of pretend peril makes for good telly. And that documentary, remember, will star *us*. Now, imagine— what if we could persuade George to help us? We don't have to tell him exactly what our plans are, but he can help us get what we want. Can't he?"

Ed narrowed his eyes and nodded slowly. He looked Steph up and down, a leer on his thin lips.

"Old George's always been one for the birds, hasn't he? Banged a princess and all that? He won't pass up the chance to charter *your* territory, Steph." He patted her knee. "After all, he doesn't know what a dried-up old carrot you are! You know the rules, though—you can touch it, but he isn't sticking it in anywhere."

Dried-up old carrot? You shrivelly dicked bastard.

Steph pouted at her husband. "Ed-babes, you're the best lover I've ever had — you don't need to worry. One hand job from me and he'll give us Henry on a platter."

She hoped she sounded sincere, because she had that episode of George in the sauna on DVD and she liked to watch it alone when Ed was away on business. The thought of that delightful bottom hurrying away across the tundra had kept her from loneliness on several occasions.

"Here you are." He reached across to the marble bedside table and picked up his wallet. It bulged with cash but Ed's plump fingers plucked out the black credit card. The only credit card worth a damn. "Get yourself something nice. Something that'll give old Georgie a thrill?"

"Can I take the Ferrari?"

"Don't forget where you parked it this time, you daft cow." Ed smiled benevolently. "And remember, anything being poked where it shouldn't and there'll be a hell of a rumpus."

"Oh, Ed-babes, you silly billy!" She kissed the top of his head. "To the shops! And to gullible celebrities!"

Chapter Twelve

Henry paused at the garden gate. He saw the foal first, cropping at the lush green lawn. Then he saw the man, whose gaze had settled on the small horse and hadn't wandered from it. A surge of love washed through Henry. George, clad in nothing but a pair of loose black pajama bottoms, was balancing on the old stone step at the back door of his cottage. He was blinking against the daylight and Henry wondered — had George, like Henry, lain awake half the night, capable of nothing more than smiling at the dark ceiling above him?

George held a steaming mug in one hand. He raised it to his mouth and took a tentative sip. Then he balled his free hand into a fist and stretched his arm high above his head, causing the pajamas to edge just a little lower on his hips.

Beginning to feel like a peeping Tom, Henry decided to make his presence known.

He pretended he had only arrived at that exact moment, greeting them in cheery fashion as he pushed open the gate.

"Morning, George! Morning, Jez! I'm just on my way to the surgery, thought I'd pop by and say hello."

George's green eyes settled on his visitor and Henry saw the bright spark of affection flare there before he turned and put the mug on the windowsill. Then he stepped down onto the dewy grass and strolled over to greet him.

"I was just thinking about you." He smiled. "Good morning, Mr. Fitz."

"Good morning, Mr. Standy-Bee." Henry caught him around the waist and planted a big kiss on George's mouth. "I still love you, by the way. I thought you might like to know."

"That's a nice start to the day." George looped his arms around Henry's neck. "And I still love you, in case you were wondering."

"My dear old George." Henry rested his lips against George's ear and dropped his voice to a whisper. "I have half an hour, by the way."

"Cuppa?"

"Just had one." Henry tightened his arms around George—boyfriend, lover, whatever they were. "I'd rather have a kiss, should one be in the offing?"

"How was the cat?" George nuzzled Henry's neck. "I didn't like to phone last night in case the news was bad."

"Bilbo has used up one of her nine lives, is on a heroic dose of pain relief and now has an iron rod in her leg, but other than that, she's fine." Henry nipped at George's earlobe and pulled gently. "And if I ever find the bastard who hit her and did nothing to trace her owners, I will put their balls in a vise."

"You're a hero," he heard George whisper. "And I love you for it."

Henry laughed gently and rested his head on George's shoulder.

"I'm really not. It was me and Jonathan, in a well-equipped surgery, doing what we're trained to do. And now the mice and birds and bats of Longley Parva will continue to be terrorized by Bilbo. Somewhat stiffly, at least!"

"And how did my man sleep? I know I look bloody awful, I was up half the night like a giddy girl!"

"I couldn't sleep because I was so excited—about us—and when I did sleep, all I could do was dream of you."

"Funny you should say that." George's lips dotted a line of kisses to Henry's ear, the tip of his tongue sliding over the lobe. "I had a very nice dream about me, you and that out-of-bounds lake."

Henry stroked George's face, a rasp of unshaven cheek under his touch.

"When I walked past it this morning, I was so annoyed with myself for ever telling you off for swimming there—I was disappointed not to see you, dripping wet and almost naked in my garden."

"Does that mean I'd be welcome to come back in the morning?" He nipped at Henry's ear. "I promise to be dripping wet and almost naked whenever my Fitz requires it."

"You can swim in my lake anytime you like." Henry knew his body was responding to the closeness of George, the touch and the scent of him. But he wasn't ashamed. Because he could feel George's body react against him in the same way through their clothes. "Almost — or completely — naked, as you wish."

"I only put the PJs on to come out and see Jez," George whispered, his tongue darting into Henry's ear. "Five minutes earlier and you'd have found me naked, thinking of my Fitz."

Henry didn't know where the voice came from, but he spoke anyway, hoarse and urgent. "Take them off."

George affected a shocked voice to ask, "In the garden?"

"Who will see? Other than me and your little horse." *And dog walkers in the meadow, and ramblers and God knows who else.* Henry slid his hand down inside George's pajamas, tantalizing his lover with the lightest of touches against his erection. "Maybe in the kitchen, perhaps?"

"That would be up to Jez, vet'n'ry. If he's happy to chill out here, then I shall accompany you into that kitchen and give you a glimpse of the Household Cavalry's finest asset."

Henry looked across at the foal, who went on chewing at the lawn, indifferent to the canoodling that was happening right in front of him.

"He seems happy enough, does young Jez."

George smiled that impish smile of his and kissed Henry's cheek. "The kitchen it is, then!"

He took Henry's hand in his and they went up the step into the kitchen. Henry noticed that some of the herbs on the laundry rack were somewhat more nibbled since he'd last been in here, but his gaze soon returned to George.

"Come on, then, sexiest man in the universe — pajamas off and get over here to your lover!"

George laughed and withdrew his hand from Henry's. His fingers moved to the waistband of the slouchy black trousers, resting there for a few moments just above the shameless outline of his erection. These were the most stylish pajamas Henry had ever seen. Indeed, he wouldn't have guessed such a garment actually existed, sharing the world with his own sensible striped cottons.

With a tempting slowness George lazily stretched his arms above his head, the muscles in his body taut, displayed for his lover. Then he reached behind his head and crossed his arms, affording Henry one of the most brazen displays of peacocking he had ever seen, even from Standy-Bee, whom every camera loved.

A soft smile touched George's face and Henry challenged himself to meet his gaze rather than marvel at the physique he had longed for so many times. It was a battle he couldn't hope to win. Now George's hands were sliding down his tan, muscular chest, over the toned flatness of his stomach to the waistband of the pajamas.

As Henry watched, George nimbly unpicked the loose knot in the black tie that fastened the trousers. Then, finally, he drew them down, revealing the body that had filled so many of Henry's dreams. And he wanted Henry too, there was no doubt about that—and if there had been, the perky erection that now offered itself was more than proof.

"I'm all yours," George told him as he kicked the pajamas aside. "Think of me as your wake-up call."

Henry slipped one arm about George's waist and took the erection in his other hand. He gripped it tenderly, almost with reverence, then saw such heat in George's eyes that he began to stroke it. Good, firm, swift strokes for the handsome, naked man who was sighing against him.

"Sure you've only got half an hour?" George's voice was a tempting, low purr. "I'm usually good for a *lot* longer than that."

"All day?" Henry kissed his way to George's ear, whispering. "And all night as well? By God, your cock is magnificent. A stand-up member of the local community."

"Ahem!"

Henry interposed himself between his naked, aroused lover and the woman who was leaning in at the back door. A pashmina was draped over her cream-colored blouse and her gunmetal-gray trousers had the sort of sharp pleats in them that could slice bread.

"Who are—?" Henry blinked in surprise. She wasn't a local and Henry had absolutely no idea who she was.

"Am I interrupting, gentlemen? George, I tried ringing. And—the back door *was* open."

"Tabby!" George peered over Henry's shoulder at the new arrival. "Darling, you're at least two hours early!"

She glanced at the face of her enormous watch.

"Yes, I am. Felicity was off on a school trip, so I was up with the lark and I thought—why not drop by with croissants and have a breakfast meeting? Only I wasn't expecting to see your bottom on my arrival, nice as it is, lovey."

"Fitz, this is Tabitha Shakespeare, the lady who came up with the idea to take my shirt off and started *that* ball rolling." George seemed utterly at ease with this odd situation, and Henry found himself wondering at the ways of people *in the media*. "Tabby, this is Fitz, the chap with the cricket bat!"

Henry blushed as he realized her gaze had dropped to his trousers, her eyebrow rising. Then she grinned.

"Oh, *that* cricket bat! Lifelong friends turned lifelong enemies, turned — well. That would certainly make for good telly. Edited for pre-watershed of course." Tabitha took a step into the room, her kitten heels tapping on the quarry-tiled floor. "I'm Tabby, George's producer. I'm sure you won't be offended if I don't shake hands."

Henry shoved his hands into his pockets, to save them both the etiquette nightmare that they were now faced with.

"I'm Henry. I'm a vet."

"Chuck us my trousers, Tab, be a love?"

Putting her hand over her eyes like a visor, Tabitha grabbed for the pajama bottoms and held them out at arm's length. George took them and, with a *very* impish wink for Henry, made himself decent again. Or as decent as a man wearing nothing but a pair of oddly decadent pajama trousers could be.

"Lovely village, I must say. And an utterly bewitching little cottage, George! You must give me the name of your interior designer, it's beautiful! Ha ha, that tea towel with the cars on it, isn't it precious! Looks like it's up there by accident! Wonderful! That'll make such a lovely shot."

"Her name's *Ma*," George told her, leaning his chin on Henry's shoulder. "You'll stay for brekky, Fitz?"

With the woman who saw me — What did she see? Other than the mesmerizing sight of George's behind?

"Look, I'm — I'm not really a media sort of person. I'm not sure I — "

"You absolutely should stay!" Tabitha gripped Henry's biceps and squeezed as if she was testing the ripeness of the melons in Waitrose. "Gosh, have you done *Countryfile*? You'd be fantastic!"

Henry grinned awkwardly at George.

"He's the one who does the telly. I'm the one who does the—" *Hand jobs?* "I'm a handy person to know." *Oh, bloody hell.*

"Joking aside, Fitz, you've got the right look." George patted his own hand on top of Tabitha's. "Sort of real-life *All Creatures*?"

"Hasn't he just!" Tabitha's amber eyes glowed. "Oh, my goodness, I can see it now. You could drive around Sussex in George's car. *Wouldn't* that be perfect? Fly-on-the-wall doc, get you on *Springwatch*, you'd have a tie-in book, and can you imagine the calendar? You could take off your top and hold a baby lamb for March!"

"No—I really can't do that. Honestly, I couldn't. I'm just Henry, I'm thoroughly boring, really. I'm sure no one would want to see me giving a cat its annual jabs and humiliating it in the scales because it weighs the same as a small car. I honestly—no, I couldn't."

"Such lovely eyes, George, hasn't he? They'd be great on camera. Can you do *sympathetic*? You know, when you're breaking bad news? Make all the viewers tear up? Oh, and we'd get that shirt off you in a jiffy. Second episode, of course, a mere hint of it at the end of the first, just to keep the viewers hanging on. This could really work, Georgie—don't you think? Unless you'd rather I didn't commandeer your boyfriend!"

Henry blinked. "You two get on, I'll just—"

"He's gorgeous, isn't he?" George kissed Henry's cheek, looping one arm around his waist. "But I'll leave it up to Fitz to decide if he fancies prime time on Sunday night."

So presumably Tabitha knew about George's tastes and wasn't shocked by them at all. But then again, while television people probably weren't shocked, people in rural backwaters probably were. And fathers like Henry's—where did one even begin?

"Tabitha, whatever you may have seen, or not seen but assumed you saw, could you just..." Henry glanced toward the open back door as if the entire population of Longleys Parva and Magna were queuing up outside. "You see—I don't think our village is quite ready for a gay vet."

Tabitha dropped her large handbag on the kitchen table and started to take out a bag of croissants.

"Darling! I'm not going to out you. George keeps his private life private, don't you, lovey?" Tabitha tapped her finger against the side of her nose. "So don't worry, my lips are sealed. It's a shame, though, because you do make a *gorgeous* couple."

George offered Henry a winning smile, as though that alone might be enough to vouch for her. He trusted her, that much was clear, so there had to be something to say for that.

"Don't forget about tonight," he told Henry. "I'll make us something suitably spicy and we'll find out what the Rev. and his lordship *really* got up to."

"As long as the animals of Longley Parva remain in good health, then it's a date!"

Henry turned to Tabitha. He had just said *date*, in front of someone other than George. But Tabitha barely registered it.

"Butter and jam, Georgie? In the fridge?"

"From the village fête, no less. *Award-winning*, Tab." George pulled out a seat at the table and steered Henry into it. Then he crossed to the back door and called, "Jez, I've got an apple for you if you fancy it!"

The cottage, already somewhat unusual, seemed to have reached a new level of eccentricity. George busied himself brewing tea and Jez wandered happily in to join them as though this was all perfectly normal.

"This will make such wonderful television!" Tabby laughed. "A horse, in the kitchen! And Captain George with his top off, too. Bonkers rural with a bit of sex sells *so well*. Village fête, did you say, George? Don't suppose there's any more coming up soon, or could we just set one up, get the locals to pretend? Or — if there's one happening in a nearby village, we could always use that and just say it's Longley Parva. It's not like anyone'll know."

Henry peeled the greaseproof paper lid from the jam jar. "But the people of Longley Parva will."

"We don't need to fake it up, Tab, because there's a big push to buy a new thatch for the village hall," George told her. "And I've talked the England lads into coming over and playing a single wicket match with the locals. The story of the Longley Parva Cup and all that, Fitz here is sort of the villain in that one! Ideally I'd like to unmask the thief at the end but if we can't, well, we'll still have a big pot of rural eccentrics to spoon from!"

Henry looked from Tabitha to George. *Rural eccentrics?* His neighbors, customers, perhaps even Henry himself? He really didn't want to cause a rumpus, but the village was his home. George might have gone gadding off about the planet but Henry hadn't, and he wasn't going to see Longley Parva turned into a mockery just for television.

"George—what on earth are you...? You're not going to make fun of people, are you?"

"Do you think, Tab, just to give the doc a nice ending, I should find out if anyone is willing to stand up and say, I *nicked it*?" George scrubbed Henry's hair. "I mean, they don't have to be the *actual* thief, just someone suitably wild-eyed who's happy to pretend they were to blame? Nobody likes a mystery without a solution, do they?"

"Ooh! Oooh! I *like* it, George, I like it. Who do you suggest from your cast of hairy-palmed locals? Someone with an extra finger would be wonderful!" Tabby leaned back in her chair and laughed, smiling at Henry as if she expected him to join in.

George laughed and shook his head, still busy at the kettle. Yet he didn't say no, Henry noted. He didn't resolutely refuse to make the village look absurd.

"Because people in villages are all inbred and stupid?" Henry bit out the words. What the hell was wrong with George? Where had this side to him come from?

Tabitha hooted, a 'champagne bar at Cowes Week' laugh. "And you're saying they're not?"

Henry folded his arms. "But what if the papers got hold of them? Called them Thieving Keith or something? Made their life a misery turning up on their doorstep all the time, demanding to know why they stole the cup?"

"They'd be paid!" Tabitha grinned. "George, how are you getting on with that tea, lovey?"

"On its way!" George turned back to look at the table and reached out to stroke his hand over Jez's mane. "Or would it be better if I said I *did* do it? The lovable rogue after all, or is that taking a risk with the Standish-

Brookes brand? Fitz, can you introduce me to this Thieving Keith of yours, darling?"

"I just made him up. It was an example. It could be Robbing Roberta for all I know. Criminal Christopher. Jailbird Jenny. Purloining Paul." Henry narrowed his eyes as he sawed his croissant lengthways, the words bitter on his tongue. "Stealing Steph."

"Filching Fitz?" George put a teapot in the middle of the table and doled out mugs before he took his seat. "Don't look so worried, darling, it's a fun thing to be shown on Boxing Day. A perfect village, me in my regimental polo shirt, everyone looking a bit eccentric and terribly English. It's not *Big Brother!*"

"George—you've sold the idea to me, anyway!" Tabitha poured tea into each mug and lifted hers in salute. "Cheers!"

Henry lifted his cup. It was only polite, after all. Even if his voice was devoid of enthusiasm.

"Cheers." He patted George's thigh under the table. "But just don't— This village was your home once, George. Your mother still lives here. Don't make fun of the place, don't ridicule it just to churn out a television program. Because you're not just mocking Longley Parva—you're mocking *me*."

"Does it *sound* as though I'm mocking the place?" George still smiled, but Henry could hear the annoyance in his voice. "I'm just trying to make good telly. I'm not going to televise a hanging, for God's sake!"

"Fine. Make your documentary. Make us look like idiots because we're not all sophisticated and urban like you. And watch what happens the next time you set foot in The Green Man. You won't be the face of Longley Spitfire anymore. And you can leave all the money you like behind the bar, but not one of the locals will want to drink it. Anyway, I've said my piece. This croissant is very nice, Tabitha, thank you."

Henry managed to pronounce croissant without a trace of a French accent. Tabitha's eyebrows shot upward, then she grinned at Henry.

"Hold a village meeting, that's what you rural types do, isn't it? Let the locals decide." Chewing into the croissant, she lifted her eyes to George. "That in itself would make for good telly, wouldn't it, George—like that thing you did with the Icelandic sheep-shearers."

"No need to be precious, Fitz." He'd seen George's face fall before he spoke, though, betraying *something*. "I did live here for a long time, you know. I'm not one of your loathed London incomers!"

Tabitha reached across the table to touch Henry's hand.

"There you are, Mr. *All Creatures Great and Small*— George is an insider. And—it is *so* adorable how protective you are of the village. It'd make—"

Maybe he was being silly. Overreacting. Maybe it was just lingering embarrassment from having been caught out by a stranger.

"Great telly? Well, I'm glad my sincerity is useful for something."

"There, that's the spirit! And people love that, you know. Noble, upstanding member of the community." Tabitha beamed at him and Henry found his resistance melting like butter left out in the sun. Yet George was still looking at him with that unreadable expression, as though he had left a sentence unfinished, as though they had argued.

We haven't argued, have we?

Chapter Thirteen

"George!" Steph air-kissed him first on one cheek, then the other. "Darling! Thanks so much for coming. I thought you'd say no, what with it being short notice, but I came from London with all these macarons, and I thought—I bet an urbanite like George is *dying* for a macaron, it's not like you can get them anywhere around here, is it?"

She led her special guest out onto the patio, where a table was set for afternoon tea.

For two.

"Lil Dalrymple took Jez for the afternoon, or I would have had to ask if you allow horses in your back garden." George lifted his sunglasses a little and peered out across the ornamental grounds, which were made considerably *more* ornamental now that they contained a TV personality in cargo shorts and a very billowy shirt indeed. "But I don't turn down cake as a rule."

Steph raked her gaze up and down George's body, making no secret of her admiration. "Really—and yet you have an amazing figure like that? How do you do it? Lots of exercise, I bet!"

Strenuous, hopefully sweaty. Steph fanned her hand before her face and indicated a chair for him at the cast-iron table.

"You're great for a chap's ego, Steph!" George took the seat she offered and nodded toward the still waters of the enormous pool, a mosaic of Steph and Ed in the tiles at the bottom. "I swim a lot, run a bit. Then eat too much and have to do it all again."

"Bet you've got fantastic stamina!"

As this was phase one of the seduction, Steph was wearing the first of her outfits. A neat white blouse, tied at the waist, unbuttoned just enough for a quantity of bronzed cleavage to show. A full skirt in pastel pink. White lace espadrilles. It wasn't raunchy but wasn't quite demure — it had just the right amount of sexually frustrated trophy wife about it for her plans.

"Yeah, I do all right." He nodded. "You have to in my line of work, all the climbing and riding and whatnot."

Riding. Steph touched her fingertips to her neck and slowly met George's eyes.

"Yes...yes. All those rugged things you get up to."

"When I'm not eating macarons with the wife of a millionaire." He leaned forward and dropped his voice. "Where *is* Ed, by the way?"

"Canary Wharf — meeting with some banking person. Very boring stuff, of course! Won't be back until, oh, at least eight."

George glanced at his watch. It was a big, impressive-looking thing with an array of dials fastened onto a thick strap of deep blue and red. She'd seen something he'd done in which that watch strap had played a part, something military. Ed liked the tanks, but Steph was rather more interested in the scenes of the host hiking in the desert, sweating manfully.

"You must get bored when he's away," her companion said.

"A woman has ways of entertaining herself." She held a plate out toward George, pulling her shoulders together just enough to give her cleavage a boost. "Cream meringue?"

He took one, looking out at the pool and grounds once more. Three peacocks wandered past as though on cue, though their brightest feathers remained hidden. *Typical.*

"It's so lovely having you back in the village, Georgie—sorry, Captain George! Like the old days! Well—almost. I do hope you won't be a stranger. Don't vanish off for another fifteen years, will you?"

"I've been back two dozen times and you were always off somewhere being busy." George laughed and pushed his sunglasses up into his dark hair. His green eyes danced with mirth, meeting hers. "Either caravanning with Fitz or in Monte Carlo with Ed or just out buying all these gorgeous togs of yours. You're a hard girl to get hold of."

"I rather think Henry timed those dreadful caravan holidays to coincide with your visits." Steph batted her eyelashes as if fighting back the tears of a martyr. "You cannot imagine how much I suffered with those chemical toilets, and the rain—oh, God, the rain! And he could've afforded the French Riviera. Hasn't a clue about how to show a girl a good time."

"Old Fitz is a good bloke!" He took a bite of the meringue, merriment still showing in his gaze. "He'd have had the sun shine if he could, Steph, I reckon."

"You didn't go out with him, George. You have no idea what I endured. And the things he used to say about you—oh, it was awful! If you were on the television, he'd fly into a temper. He absolutely refused to watch it, bellowed at his father when he bought him one of your books for Christmas—he might appear to be all nicey-nicey Mr. Tweedy Squire, but he doesn't deserve your friendship, George. Oh, that he does *not*."

"He's not a fan then?"

Steph shook her head. "Not at all. Why, has he told you that he *is*?"

"Each to their own, I wouldn't ask." George smiled again and slid his glasses down to hide his eyes. "You can't win 'em all, Steph."

And Henry won't win against Ed.

She smiled her broadest smile, her head tipped to one side. George mirrored the gesture, teasing her, just as they would do to each other in childhood. Then he asked, "How old's your little monster now, anyway? Is it a school day?"

"The nanny deals with all that sort of thing." Steph nodded. "I just don't have the time to look after Sapphire. I'm sure you can imagine—I have *so* much to do. Pilates, nails, lunch here, lunch there, meetings with this lot of ladies, meetings with the other. Hairdresser once a fortnight—that's *very* important. Riding when I can, of course—keeps me supple, firms my thighs."

"Mine too!" George laughed, slapping the palm of his hand against one of his thighs and leaving it there, lingering against the annoyingly too-long-for-Steph shorts. "But come on, old girl, you're too busy for TV, you should've said—I was way too pushy with you and Ed!"

"Oh, no, I can make time, move a few lunches back until filming is over. That sort of thing. Easy-peasy! Would hate to let you down now that we've committed to you, Captain George. Wouldn't want to fall out of your good favor."

Steph crept her hand over the table and snared George's beneath it.

"So old Fitz hates me, eh?" George lowered his head and peered over the dark-lensed Wayfarers. When he spoke again, his voice was a low murmur. "Do he and Ed not get on either?"

"He doesn't get on with anybody in the village. I really stuck my neck out being his girlfriend for so long. He lurks about in that creepy old house of his like he's in *Beauty and the Beast*, except he'll never turn into a handsome prince. He'll always be a curmudgeonly old git — and to think I gave him the best years of my *life*!"

Steph stretched the last word out as long as she could, until it evolved into a wail of despair and agony that echoed around the garden. If she blinked just a little more, she would eke out a tear. Until — triumph! — there it was! An Oscar for Stephanie Belcher, tragic heroine.

"Hey, come on!" George turned his hand and caught her fingers in his own. "Don't let him get to you now, you've got Ed and little Sapphire to think about!"

"I know — I know! I cling onto that. I *do*." She gave George her best sweetly suffering smile, just as the lion's head fountain came to life and spat into the swimming pool. "I'm so glad I married Ed. Really. Even if sometimes I do get..." She had half-turned away from George, and threw a coy looked at him over her shoulder. "Terribly lonely."

"It's a big old house for just you, Saph and the nanny," George commiserated. "And if you get the old

Fitzwalter pile, you'll be rattling round even more. Stay put, Steph, I might even pop over and use your pool if you'll let me."

Captain George Standish-Brookes, in my pool, nearly naked? Steph's anonymous letters to *Points of View* had not been in vain if the man was willing to turn up at her own home and strip off.

"Of course! Feel free!"

She hadn't quite prepared for this. Her silver, high-leg bikini was upstairs in the bedroom.

Do I have time to hop in with him, or – no, that was phase two.

"I'll slip off these shoes and dangle my feet in, Georgie, if you don't mind?"

"Right now?" He sounded surprised but looked toward the water with a torn expression. "You invited me over for afternoon tea, I can't take liberties with you, Steph, it wouldn't be right."

"Why not? All this beautiful sunshine, I feel rather hot myself. Go on, have a dip!"

"Fitz *did* chase me away from his lake last time I stripped off without asking." She could see he was weakening, a combination of her womanly charms and the cool waters proving irresistible. "I'll finish my meringue, then I might treat myself to a quick splash about, if you really don't mind."

"Unlike Henry, I don't mind people having fun. Eat up and swim and just do whatever you like."

"So" – he took another bite of the meringue – "go on, tell me about this house deal. What's the real craic?"

Steph bit carefully into her macaron to avoid smudging her coral lip gloss. She took her time chewing as she built up to another mournful gaze.

"We need the house, George. How else can I explain it to you? It's a matter of pride to my husband, that his ancestors have been conned out of their birthright." She took the gold locket from around her neck and opened it to show George the photograph of the blonde-haired little girl it contained. "It should by rights be Sapphire's one day — think of her! The good name of Belcher has been done a great injustice by what can only be described as a swindling."

"This lawyer must be costing you chaps a packet, though, just to prove a point?"

"It's not a *point*, George! This is about integrity, family pride! They have no price. And, of course, Henry wouldn't know integrity if it hit him right in the middle of his pudgy face."

"It *is* a point, Steph, and life's too short to squabble over some drunken wager two hundred years ago." George pushed back his seat and stood. He put his sunglasses down on the table and looked to the pool. This was the moment, Steph realized. Here, in her garden, Captain George Standish-Brookes was going to strip.

How far, though?

Everything?

"Believe me, life's for laughing, swimming and loving. It's not for lawyering."

Steph sniffed. He'd forgotten to list golfing. Which was probably just as well. *He doesn't have a clue, does he?* This was going to be so easy, and she would even enjoy doing it.

"Sure you don't mind?" His hands were at the shirt, about to discard it. "You're being a jolly good sport, Steph."

"I don't mind at all." She fixed her eyes on him as she untied the ribbons on her shoes. The pedicure had cost enough—he was a lucky man to get a view of her bare feet.

She went over to the pool and posed on the side, like a clothed version of the Little Mermaid in Copenhagen, and swung one foot into the cool water, splashing her hand to and fro. A little bit of water dampening her blouse was all to the good.

Like the practiced seductress that she was, Steph glanced back over her shoulder as George drew the shirt up over his head and dropped it onto the chair. And there it was, that famous body, still tan from his round-the-world trip, toned in a way that Ed had never been. And it was in her garden.

Steph pouted her lips just enough. "Did you bring trunks, Captain? What will people say if they find you splashing about nude in my pool?"

"Don't worry, Steph, I'll spare you that." George laughed, walking toward her through the sunlight. "I'll be keeping my shorts on!"

Bugger.

"That's fine, George…you go ahead."

At least there was the chest to gaze at. And phase two—that was when those pesky shorts would drop. Steph would make sure of it.

"You're a happily married girl, I have to behave!" He walked around the pool and executed a perfect dive into the deep end, the waves lapping out to swish gently against her bare feet as the thrice-winner of Rear of the Year did a length of the pool and surfaced right beside her. George threw his head back and slicked his hands over his hair. Then he rested his forearms on the edge of the pool and told her, "This is much more fun than lawyering, eh?"

"Absolutely!"

Steph stroked her hand down her neck and undid a button on her blouse. George was watching and she threw back her head and laughed.

There were many ways to keep a man happy – Steph was well aware of that. Sometimes it might require her to disrobe, but other times she need only lend him her pool.

"Swimming, laughing and loving," George reminded her. "And two out of three ain't bad in one afternoon!"

He disappeared beneath the surface again, his arms before him as he cut a sleek, smooth arrow down the length of the pool. Steph watched, for the first time wondering if there *might* be a life beyond Ed. George couldn't be as rich, of course, but he was far from being poor either. And physically, he was far more impressive than the waste of space who shared her bed.

She was very much looking forward to phase two. Just imagine – there'd be the money from the manor as well as Old Hall and the golf course. The prenup was more than favorable – it had already come in handy when she had found out about Ed and that girl he was shagging. *'Remember the prenup'* and a mimed squeeze of a small pair of testicles had been enough to remind Ed where his loyalties should lie.

Steph had everything to play for.

"I need a pool," George exclaimed as he surfaced again. "But I don't think Ma'd be happy with my looking-after-the-cottage skills if I dug up the garden for a pool – and where would Jez hang out if I did that?"

Steph lowered her lashes, swirling the water with her hand. "You can use our pool whenever you like, Georgie."

"You're a good pal, Steph." He caught her fingers as they skimmed the water and dotted a kiss to the back of her hand. "So, if a chap was making a show about Longley P, what should he be sure not to miss? Apart from the lady of the mansion, of course?"

"Well...the boring old fart at the manor, but there's no point bothering him about being in it, because he'll only chase you out of his garden again. Erm...the cricket club, I suppose? Ed's stables, of course. The tea shop. The grave in the churchyard of that fool who died fighting a duel. The remains of the castle — are they worth including? It is just a pile of earth with lots of trees all over it, though. But it would give you the chance to dress up as a knight, perhaps. Mrs. Dalrymple — now, she knows all the old stories. Her mother took in evacuees, and there were the land girls, and a German plane crashed into the side of the hill over there. You could re-enact that! But of course, the real heart of the village now is the stables here, and Ed and I. You could call us Mr. and Mrs. Longley Parva, really."

Steph gave George's hand a squeeze. "Although Ed is so infrequently here, so in all honesty, the village is basically *me*."

"So you must be involved with this 1940s evening I've seen posters for? For the village hall fund?" George released Steph's hand. "We're going to be getting some footage of that. I *might* be putting in an appearance!"

Steph blinked, bashfully modest. "Oh, yes, I have been involved somewhat. Getting the bunting ready, making greengage jam — which some people *do* actually like—sourcing the music, helping with the catering arrangements…"

But of course, she wasn't about to tell George that it was Ed's PA who had ordered the bunting online, sourced a specialist 1940s DJ and hired a catering company. That said, the greengage jam really was going to emerge from the Old Hall kitchen, but, as with the jam that should have won at the fête, Sapphire's nanny had made it.

"I've got a wonderful dress as well, George. I'm getting my hair done at a salon in London especially. Your cameras will *love* it!"

"Save a dance for me?"

"Of course, George, I shall leave my dance card clear for you."

And the producer would see how good they looked in each other's arms. She'd get most of the screen time, she knew it. They'd jet off to America and Randy Cheese would love George and how he worked the media. Steph and George were the perfect pair—a power couple from a sleepy little village who could take over the world.

He glanced at his watch again and Steph smiled, thinking it rather sweet how keen he was to spend his time with her. And the pool had never looked better than it did right now.

"Shall I crack open a bottle, George, if you're staying for more than tea?"

"I need to be back for Jez in about forty-five minutes." He looked at his watch once more. "But I could probably have a glass of something if you fancy it? I could get used to the millionaire lifestyle!"

That bloody horse.

"Forty-five minutes? There's time for a quick glass, isn't there?"

"At least one!"

How many glasses would it take for him to forget she was a married woman? She gave George a fleeting glance of cleavage as she got to her feet. He smiled — the plan was definitely working.

"I'll be back in a tic."

Steph was gone slightly longer than it took to collect a bottle of wine and two glasses, but when she stepped out into the garden again, she was resplendent in a flowing wrap-dress that barely covered the silver bikini. Because why not? George was off home shortly, but one look at her in this and he would be back at Longley Parva Old Hall in no time.

She poured the drinks, enjoying the wide-eyed look on George's face as he stared at her.

"Here you are — a *very* expensive Pinot." Steph wandered back to the poolside. "Which I'm sure someone like you is more than accustomed to drinking. Old Hall has the finest wine cellar in the South Downs."

George reached up, the water rolling down his tan, toned arm as he took the glass from her. "Cheers, Mrs. Belcher."

Steph leaned down to the handsome swimmer, chinking her plastic glass against his. She was slow to move away, to ensure that he saw as much of her bikini-clad body at close quarters as was possible.

"Cheers, Captain!"

He took a long drink, a lingering smile on his lips when he lowered the glass and asked, "Do you *really* want to leave this behind for that old dump of Henry's?"

"It is a dump, isn't it!" Steph almost roared with laughter, but realizing that wasn't exactly alluring, she pressed her fingertips to her lips. She looked down at her glass. "But it's what Ed wants. And as I'm Mrs. Longley Parva, I should have the manor to go with it. Even if we bulldoze it and replace it with something new."

"Bulldoze it?" He took another drink. "Good luck on the planning applications, rather Ed than me!"

"Oh, we don't need to worry about a silly thing like that. I'm sure it's unsafe. Half of it's made of medieval cowpats, as Henry was proud of telling everyone who visited. What an embarrassing thing to announce at a dinner party—the man has no social graces whatsoever. Is he Stig of the Dump, living in a hole like that in *this* day and age?"

"You liked him well enough when he was your first love." George knocked her bare knee with his knuckle. "I remember it well!"

Steph gazed away, over George's head, over the garden, over to the rolling hills far off in the distance. Her voice was soft with the nostalgic memories of times past and worlds lost.

"That was then, George."

"For the sake of then, Steph. For when we were kids and climbing trees and, if you're me, falling out of them...let the guy keep his house?" He smiled. "Who wants a place made of cowpats anyway?"

Steph sighed. Such pretty words, but television presenters came out with all sorts of nonsense that half the time they didn't believe. Leave him dangling, though—if George did have some lingering sense of honor for the world of their youth, then he would definitely come back for a second visit.

"Let me think about it, George? I'll see if I can convince Ed. I can't promise, though — you realize that, don't you?"

"Mrs. Longley Parva, you're *still* a hell of a girl." He beamed up at her from the pool.

Steph kissed her fingertips and blew him a kiss.

"That was even better than this *amazing* wine!"

Oh, you won't escape my plans now, television's Captain George.

George put his glass on the edge of the pool and pushed off to swim another length. Steph watched him go with a smile that she knew was beautiful. She could do innocent, she could do sexy and, best of all, she could combine the two to devastating effect. She had ensnared vets, lawyers and millionaires. A TV presenter would be no challenge at all.

Chapter Fourteen

Everyone always went on about Henry's tweeds. They had become his trademark, which, he knew, meant he had become his own cliché. He was very fond of tweed, *but the best thing to do with a stale and predictable wardrobe* — so he had read in a magazine left at his surgery by one of the nurses — *is mix things up a little.*

So Henry decided to wear corduroy trousers and a checked shirt with rolled-up sleeves. He only ever dressed like that to loaf about at home, knowing that no one would see. But this was the new Henry, the Henry who was in love. And this was as casual as he got.

He arrived at the cottage gate to see George cradling Jez's head, whispering to him, and a surge of love sang through Henry's blood again. George looked up just as Henry pushed open the gate.

"George! Good evening."

"Fitz!" George's face lit up with his smile of welcome. "I've missed you, is that silly?"

Henry hurried into the garden and took George's hand.

"No, not at all—I missed you!"

Jez nuzzled a welcome against Henry's side as George put his arms around him, his head falling to rest against Henry's shoulder. George's embrace was tight, as though they had been parted for weeks.

Henry dropped his bag to the floor and held him. George's hair was slightly damp, as if he'd just got out of a shower.

How sweet of George to spruce up before our date.

All Henry had had time for was a quick spray of cologne to disguise the lingering smell of farmyards. Still his lover clung to him, George *and* the horse snuggled tight to Henry.

"I never thought I'd ever feel like this," Henry whispered into George's hair.

"I love you." George lifted his face to look at Henry. "I love you and your tweed and your house made of cowpats and your everything."

"My house made of—? Oh, yes! It's quite the conversation starter, that is! We're going to save my house, aren't we? I raided the library at home. I've got an old almanac that Bad Billy hid some letters in, and an estate diary and the Bible that his will was copied into. There must be something in all that which refers to the bloody cricket match!"

"Nobody's taking your house, Fitz, no matter what they think. And this morning... I wouldn't make this village look stupid, I love it here." He let his head fall again. "It's been bothering me all day that you think I'd do that."

Should Henry broach the question he had pondered all day—had they had their first argument? At least, their first since becoming a couple. But it was probably best not to say anything. It might only stir it up again, and it was safer left unremarked on. That seemed the healthiest thing to do.

"Sorry if I said the wrong thing in front of Tabitha. Bit defensive about old Parvy, I'm afraid, old chap."

"But is that what you think of me, that I'd rock up here, mock the place, mock *you* and then disappear again?" There was genuine hurt in George's tone, Henry realized. Had he really been thinking about this all day? "I do have feelings, you know. I'm not just someone on the TV who gets put into a box when they finish filming. Today, some old dear in the post office actually *patted my arse*, then this girl in the shop offered me fifty quid for my bloody shirt! Is this what it's like being a woman, do you think?"

"It was just…Tabitha going on about hairy palms. It set me off, I'm afraid. Sorry. There are some bloody weird people around here, but even so, one doesn't like to actually point it out. And as to your harassment at the hands, hairy of palm or otherwise, of the locals — they'll get bored of you soon enough. Perhaps!" Henry slid his hand down from George's waist to his bottom. Adopting a saucy tone, he asked, "Am I allowed to pat it, though?"

"And *only* you." He smiled. "You don't think I'd do that to Longley P., Fitz, do you? Not really?"

"Not you — but what about those media people you know? You would stop them, wouldn't you, if you thought they were going to mock us? Is there some clause you could put in somewhere? In — in your contract or whatever it is you have."

"I'm not just a pretty face." He was teasing now, the hurt gone. "Tab's exec producer, but I've produced all my own TV ever since the *gaucho* special. Even *I* got sick of looking at myself topless in that one. Nothing gets made unless I sign it off."

Henry gave George's bottom a firm pat. "Good. That's what I wanted to hear."

"I bet *you* loved the *gaucho* show." George squeezed Henry's bottom in turn. "Were you having a good old ogle?"

"Gosh, yes! All that horse riding and lassoing, the bit when you went under that waterfall, and your thighs tensing—" Henry stopped before he gave himself and his television viewing habits away. "Yes. I must say, it's a particular favorite of mine, that series."

"When they reviewed the tie-in book in *The Guardian*, do you know what they said? *'Shameless pin-ups thinly disguised as cultural history—an essential buy'.*" He laughed, slapping Henry's bottom lightly. "Still my favorite review, because it was honest *and* kind!"

"It does rather sum it up, doesn't it! I mean, not that I—well, all right I did. The pull-out poster was— Anyway, what's that delicious smell? Have you cooked us something lovely for dinner?"

"I have indeed! I know you're a beef and Yorkshires sort of a chap, so I've completely ignored that and prepared a Moroccan lamb tagine and couscous. Try it before you decide you don't like it, Fitz?"

"It certainly smells tasty. And if I can manage Spanish tapas one evening, then why not change continents and go Moroccan the next!"

George nodded with enthusiasm and stepped back, though he kept Henry's hand in his own. For a long moment they looked at each other, then kissed again, the touch soft and tender. The world was silent save the gentle sounds of the garden, the lap of the pond, Jez softly chewing the grass and, above, cheery birds passing over.

"I've been up in the attic, pulled down boxes full of stuff," George confided as he drew back slightly. "I thought we could snuggle down in the sitting room after supper with a few glasses of something nice and start reading?"

He blinked, his brow furrowing with thought that became a bright smile. "Isn't it funny? There's old Georgina, my scandalous grandmother many times removed, hanging over the fireplace with her bosoms on show and here's me, nearly three hundred years later, and everyone wants me to take my shirt off even when I'm just out buying bread!"

"She'd be proud, I'm sure."

George dotted a kiss to Henry's cheek. "Dinner?"

Chapter Fifteen

As the night drew on and the sitting room rug disappeared under receipts and household accounts and ink-blotted sermons, George lit some candles on the mantelpiece and came to sit beside Henry on the sofa, the same one that they had enjoyed so much yesterday. Henry laid his haul out on the blanket box that served as a coffee table and eyed the dusty crate that George had found in the loft.

"Where the heck do we look now, George?"

"What do you reckon, Georgie?" He looked at the painting above the fireplace, Lady Georgina smiling her knowing, ruby-red smile, a slash of color on her fashionably pale face. The same red made a flame of the feather in her powdered hair and for several seconds Henry watched as George stared at his namesake, her painted green eyes meeting his own.

Then he leaned forward and scooped into the box that had lain undisturbed in the cottage's attic for decades.

"Lady G. says we should have a look in here next."

George handed a bundle of papers to Henry, the pages

held tight with a ribbon of deep red. "Jez seemed happy in his stable, didn't he? He's settled in, just like his dad."

"It does look very cozy — I'm surprised you haven't moved in with him. I'm glad you've given him a home." Henry was very tempted to kiss George at that moment, but pushed the feeling aside. There were still all these documents to get through. "These look like laundry lists — shirts, petticoats, an extra fee for darning someone's woolen stockings, ironing a lace collar... Hmm, possibly not what we're looking for."

"I was thinking, though, it's funny how things work out." He pulled at the end of the ribbon, freeing the papers Henry held. "Because I've got Jez, and Reverend Tobias Standish, he had Rupert. So we Standy-Bees must have always liked keeping unorthodox pets!"

"Wasn't Rupert his horse? As far as I know, Bad Billy just had dogs. Very boring! He could at least have had a pet bear like Byron."

"Rupert was his goat! Ma found a mention of him in a parish meeting note, something to do with *Reverend Standish insisted on bringing his goat into the meeting*, that sort of thing. Po-faced as ever!"

Henry snorted with laughter, which unfortunately led to a quantity of dust from the untied documents shooting up his nostrils. With one sneeze of alarming velocity, the papers were scattered onto the floor.

"Damn and bloody hell." Henry got on his hands and knees to collect them up. "Receipt from the market — over two hundred years ago, someone bought pigs and sold sheep at Chipping Stedford. Look at this — household inventory for some poor chap who died — *a very old copper pot*. Well, that's jolly interesting. Ooh, a letter — *For the execution of the will, my expenses are heretofore attached."* Henry turned the page. "He's included the cost of pipes and tobacco from when he took some farmers round to price up the cattle! Imagine doing that now. Blimey."

Among the documents was a folded piece of what looked like vellum, creased and dirty with age, still waxy to the touch. "Oh, hello."

"Hello back." George laughed and cracked a sharp smack to Henry's bottom.

Henry grinned over his shoulder as he winced. "Did that sound a bit camp?"

"I'll let you decide that." George peered over his shoulder at the vellum. "What've you got?"

"It says *Tithe apportionment* on it. That's not going to be any use."

"Maybe there's nothing exciting *to* find." He yawned, leaning over to root through the box again. Long minutes passed with only the sound of shuffling papers to disturb the silence, George tying ribbons on discarded packets as they went along, keeping everything tidy as was his occasional way. It was toward the bottom of the box that George reached down and drew out a fresh bundle, laughing heartily as he did.

"Fitz, look!" He showed the bundled papers to Henry. A flamboyant hand had written *Rupert* and, beneath it, sketched an image of a fearsome-looking goat. A solid, black animal with horns dramatic enough to take on any storybook troll. "It's Rupert Standish, Jez's ancestor in spirit!"

Henry laughed. "Hope he doesn't grow horns like that!"

"I bet the Rev. missed old Rupert when he passed away. He raised him from a little goat. You've heard all the silly stories about him sitting in the front pew during sermons, eating from the collection plate?" George rested his head on Henry's shoulder for a second. "Jez is upholding a fine tradition."

"Indeed so!"

"This is going to be years of observations about a goat, isn't it? Feed bills, hoof care and—" George fell silent as he untied the deep blue ribbon and something far more solid than paper tumbled down into the cushions between them.

Henry gently plucked it free and held the silver oval on his palm. He carefully opened it, wondering what it could be as it was too large and not dainty enough to be a locket. On the right-hand side was a painted oval depicting two sitters and on the left, beneath glass, a slender plait of jet-black and chestnut hair.

"Isn't that—that's my Billy, isn't it? With—an ecclesiastical gentleman. It's not—?"

Henry looked from the man of the cloth in the miniature to the television man of action beside him. Apart from the preaching bands and the hair that had been brushed forward around his face, the sitter could have been George. George, in historical costume for his latest program about—*about Regency goat husbandry?*

"Well, if that's old Rev. Standish, I'm pleased to see he was quite a looker!" George peered closer. "That's definitely your Billy, isn't it?"

He brought his fingertip to touch the surface of the portrait very gently, snuggling against Henry as he did. It could have been the two of them, Henry knew, George and Fitz, Fitz and George, captured for posterity two hundred years ago.

"This really is the most amazing find." Henry put his arm around George's shoulder. "Unless they were very good friends, but... George, they must've been a couple."

There seemed something rather melancholy now about Bad Billy in his portrait above the manor's mantelpiece. Alone, with a dark, dramatic swirl of storm cloud behind him, eyes flashing—with all the forbidden desire he had for Tobias Standish. He couldn't share that huge portrait with his lover, they could only share a discreet miniature. But what an exquisite gem it was.

"I wonder how old this is? Is there a date on it?" Henry carefully closed it and turned it over. Engraved on the back was *TS – 7 Aug. 1812 – WF*. "Hold this a second—I just need to check something."

Henry felt like a detective and opened the cover of the Bible. A variety of hands over the decades had added the births, marriages and deaths of numerous Fitzwalters to the inside of the cover. Henry's birth had been recorded on the following page, in the margin beside a terrifying image of the Red Sea closing over the Egyptians.

"I thought as much—Billy's wife had died about a year before. When did Tobias lose his wife?"

"Oh, now you're asking." George narrowed his eyes and clicked his tongue. "Year before the Prince Re—1809?"

"So they were both widowers by 1812. I wonder if this miniature was to commemorate them, you know, moving in together. Or whatever they would have called it then?" Henry suddenly had an idea. "Wait, those laundry lists!"

"Look—here we are, just the laundry for some chap living by himself, with some servants." Henry rifled through the stack of old paper, running his finger over the dates. "And then—this is the first list after the date on the portrait. Bloody hell, look what's on it, George—a surplice! And look—there's one on the next list, and a fee for starching preaching bands."

"Oh, hang on..." George's lips parted and Henry could almost *see* him thinking. Then he delved back into the pile of papers. "Have a dig through, I bet you there's the shopping list from hell in there somewhere. Among those laundry papers and what have you, I suspect they kept it all together, if you get me."

"It would be sensible." Henry leafed through the laundry lists until, folded in half near the bottom, he found a receipt. "Well, they certainly splashed out, didn't they? This is a receipt from bloody Fortnum's—pickled quail's eggs, and game pie, and bonbons and a fruitcake! Oh, and what a surprise—look at the date."

Two days before the date on the miniature.

"It's a little wedding feast, Fitz." George blinked and looked at Henry, as though the enormity of the discovery had silenced him. He pressed a soft kiss to his lover's lips and whispered, "They were just like us."

"How brave they must've been. Back then. If anyone had found out that they were lovers—but if you look at the memorial tablets in the church, they died in old age, within days of each other. And were buried side by side."

Henry put the papers down so that he could hold George tightly to him.

"I hope that was a comfort to Toby when Rupert bleated his last," George murmured mischievously.

"He wasn't entirely alone in the world, because he still had his bad, blue-eyed squire!" Henry ruffled his hand through George's hair and kissed him, but before it could turn into a deeper embrace, he had a thought.

"Rupert was buried in the grounds at the manor, that's what I heard — my grandad said something about the grave of *the vicar's pet*. There's supposed to be a headstone somewhere, but I've never seen it."

"I thought you knew that place inside out. I want to lay flowers on Rupert's grave."

"There's overgrown corners that I've never ventured into. Brambles taller than a house, like Sleeping Beauty! I'll borrow a chainsaw maybe and cut it back — and then we can find Rupert's last resting place."

"I never even imagined — did you?" George kissed him again. "But this gives the Reverend motive for *losing* the score sheet, doesn't it?"

"Sadly, it does." Henry sighed, taking in the disordered piles of paper. "Maybe he chucked it on a fire or, if he didn't destroy it, it could be anywhere amongst this mess! We can't let Belcher get the house, though — because it's not just my family pile, is it? It's where two men lived together and loved when they shouldn't have. Longley Parva Manor is a piece of history."

"Part of me wants to make *this* the documentary, and nobody would dare *touch* the house." Henry felt George's sigh against his skin. "But another part says, *let them keep their secret*."

"And ours?"

"I'm sorry," he whispered. "I just can't — I mean, I don't want the press banging on our doors and I don't know — do you think it'd be a big deal for viewers?"

Henry caressed his hand across George's shoulders, feeling the strength in him.

"Do it when it feels right, George. And if it never does, we'll be like the squire and the vicar — but with a horse in the lounge rather than a goat in the drawing room."

"I hope their wedding day was perfect, Fitz. They deserved it to be."

"I'm sure it was, Standy-Bee."

Chapter Sixteen

"I'll help you tidy all this up, George. Papers flung about all over the damned place — sorry, I've turned up at your cottage and caused merry havoc!"

George, however, was still gazing at the image in the miniature as though hypnotized, his face showing a nostalgic smile. He pressed his fingertip to the glass, the plaited hair beneath, and told Henry, "This is their anniversary. We were meant to find this."

Henry glanced up at the portrait of Lady Georgina. The dancing candle flames imbued her face with life. She was smiling on them, just as she had smiled upon her son, Tobias, and his husband.

"I'm not superstitious, but even so — when was the last time anyone saw this?" Henry rested his head on George's shoulder. He was so comfortable there, as if the two of them had been molded specifically to slot together. "Tobias, once his husband had breathed his last, and he wanted one more glance at their faces as younger men, with all their lives ahead of them? Then he hid it away. Didn't destroy it—perhaps he couldn't bear to."

"He barely had time to do anything, did he? Passed away a day later or so." George stroked Henry's hair. "And said in his will that no man would die happier than he. He wanted us to see this—*they* chose *us* to share their secret."

"It's a precious secret to hold. And I suppose—the Reverend trusted us to do what was best. In their memory. All that time they lived together—did they keep it from the servants, or did they just pay them for their silence? Or did the staff respect them and never told? What did their children make of it! Such an extraordinary story."

"And it's one more reason for me to promise again that I would *never* make this village a joke. It's a place that's not quite— Well, I've been all over the world and I've never known anywhere like it."

If only Henry had seen more of the world than the occasional caravanning trip to Devon.

"Really? I'm biased, perhaps, but—isn't Longley Parva not *that* different from any other English village?"

"You're probably right, but...well, maybe I just care more about this one."

"All those places you've been to, and Longley Parva still your home. You still came back. Like—like a..." Henry, overwhelmed by their earlier discovery, was struggling for similes. "A salmon!"

"I hope that isn't a comment on my personal hygiene!"

Henry tweaked his nose and grinned. "Well, you do like splashing about in the water! Perhaps I should check to see if you have a tail?"

"And I thought you were a quiet sort of boy." He laughed. "But you're just sex mad, Fitz!"

"Me? Innocent old Henry?" He tickled his way under George's shirt and whispered, "I've brought my toothbrush, by the way."

He felt George's smile against his lips before they kissed, his lover's elegant fingers twining gently in his hair. George shifted in his seat to straddle Henry's lap, his other hand already working at the buttons of Henry's shirt.

"I *like* courting," he whispered.

Henry caught George's hand. He had to warn the fellow. It wasn't fair to subject him to his body without warning. Perhaps he should've told him earlier, before it was too late and they'd fallen in love.

"George—hang on. There's something I should tell you. It's embarrassing. You're so perfect, and I'm…not."

"I'm not perfect!" George laughed, perhaps suspecting some innocent bit of shyness. "I've got a hell of a shrapnel sprinkling across my shoulders for a start. I just know my best angles, that's all."

"But you got that from being heroic. And I—" Henry hung his head. He squeezed his eyes shut, trying to push back the horrible memories that came to him whenever he remembered that day, his father leaning over the fence, laughing—until his face had turned as pale as the whitewashed wall behind him.

"What's wrong?" George took a gentle hold of Henry's chin and tilted his face up. In the green eyes that met his own, Henry saw such tenderness that it almost undid him, and George whispered, "Whatever it is, tell me?"

Henry took a deep breath. The scar was ugly, he'd been told enough times. Perhaps if they kept the lights off, it wouldn't matter too much?

"Righty-ho, I'll tell you, then. It was a few years ago now, before Dad retired. We went out to Chibcombe Farm to examine a bull. Dad was going, *'Bloody useless vet you are, Henry, too much of a sissy to hold a sheep between your thighs, let alone a bull! Go and live in a city, hamsters are about your limit!'* And usually, I'd just nod, but that time..." Henry swallowed. A shiver started up in him. "Oh, it's horrible. I thought, *I'll show you!* As soon as we arrived, I got out of the Landy and ran over to the pen. Climbed over the gate. Dad was watching. *'Go on, my son! That's my boy!'* And I thought, *Blimey, I think he might be proud of me.* The bull was tethered, but I—I looked over at Dad and waved. Waved! And didn't notice that the rope was longer than I realized. The bloody bull came straight at me and got me right in the stomach with its horns."

"My God." George whispered the words. "Were you—you could've been killed."

"Yeah. Out of my own stupidity. Why do you think I couldn't summon up the courage to find a boyfriend? I didn't want to see the disgust on their face. I'd already seen it on— Well, I'd already seen it on *someone's* face. So I tended to keep my vest on."

Steph. Who hadn't visited him in the hospital and had laughed with Henry's father when she came to see him once he had been brought home. And who had told Henry that she was doing him a great favor by continuing to go out with him after he had been so disfigured.

"Whoever that was, they're not someone you want in your life." George's voice was firm, his gaze refusing to let Henry's skitter away again. "But I won't push you—this is at your pace, not mine. I love you, though, Fitz, whether your vest is on or off."

George's words made Henry feel brave. He wanted more than anything to feel George's skin against his own. And what about George's scars? They didn't seem to bother him at all.

"Shall I show you, then?" Henry would look away. He could avoid George's reaction if he looked away.

"If you're ready to, that's all that matters."

Henry guided George's hand back to the buttons on his shirt. He held George around the waist with his other hand. "Will you undo me? I mean, you already have! But—"

George smiled and put both his hands to work on the buttons, kissing Henry again as he carefully unfastened his shirt. There was no going back now. Would George laugh or recoil or, worse than either, give pitying looks and brave smiles?

In fact he did neither. Instead he parted Henry's shirt without breaking the kiss and the softness of his polo shirt with its vivid regimental colors settled against Henry's bare skin.

Henry sighed and held him close. It was going to be all right. George seemed to understand. Surely even Captain George must've had his moments when the scars he bore were too much, when the memories that came with them were overwhelming. And yet George was held up as a handsome heartthrob—a line of puckered skin would hold no horrors for him.

"I love you," George whispered, sliding his hands down Henry's chest, the touch caressing. "My Fitz."

It had been so long since anyone had touched Henry there—at least, anyone other than the doctor and his stethoscope. He gasped at the contact of another human being and the love that he felt in his touch. George drew back just as long as it took him to drag the polo shirt over his head and cast it aside, then he pressed his naked torso to Henry's, grinding his hips down as he did.

Henry tipped his head back against the sofa and ran his hands up and down George's back, from his shoulders all the way down to cup his buttocks, then back again. A soft grunt escaped his mouth at the hardness of those nipples pressing against him and those exquisite, perfect muscles that Henry could feel tensing with each of George's movements.

George's lips were warm against Henry's throat, his tongue tracing sinuous shapes where his kisses landed. He didn't seem interested in looking at the scar at all, but instead was devoting himself to his lover's pleasure, his palms sliding softly down Henry's back as his lips moved lower on his chest.

Goodness me.

"My dear old George—I love you!" Henry combed his fingers through George's hair, capable of little else as George bathed his untouched body with bold, loving kisses. Henry wondered how could he ever have been nervous about showing himself to this man.

George didn't seem to be stopping, though, and he continued to kiss his way down Henry's body. He drew Henry's nipple between his lips, teasing it with his tongue as he unfastened his lover's trusty old leather belt, then the unbreached button of his corduroys and finally the zip beneath it. All the time he was working at that stiffened nipple, drawing soft gasps from Henry's parted lips.

Henry reached one hand behind his head, clutching the back of the sofa, clutching anything, because this felt so good, and if George was headed where he seemed to be, then Henry was rather worried that he might fling himself off the sofa at the first brush of George's—hand? tongue?—against him. The thought of it was enough for a jolt to shoot through Henry's groin and his hips tried to lift from the cushion.

And did George remember that comment earlier about his *thighs tensing*? Perhaps, because that was precisely what he did in response, the slightest tightening of his muscles pushing Henry's hips back down. He took the prompting, though, and continued to kiss his way lower until he was sliding from Henry's lap to kneel on the floor between his legs. He was close to the scars now, but there was no change in the heated tenderness of his lips as the next kiss landed on the scarred skin that caused Henry so much pain.

A silver line, starting just under his ribs, cutting diagonally across him until it reached to the top of his leg.

'I don't want to see it, it's ugly.'

Henry shook his head, forcing those words and that voice out of his mind. It wasn't ugly. He could've died and he hadn't, and the reason for him receiving the wound didn't matter. Because he'd survived it—so that he could meet George once again. Because, at the moment he had realized that he could not escape the onslaught of the bull, it had been George he had thought of, and only him.

"My beautiful man," George murmured as he lifted his hand to ease Henry's boxers lower and free his erection. He shifted his gaze to meet Henry's and in one slow, sinuous movement, drew his tongue from the base of his cock to the tip, his eyes sparkling.

Was it polite to watch? Would it put George off?

But as Henry's eyes stayed locked on George's, it was evident that George was certainly not discouraged by his audience. If anything, those green eyes glittered all the more.

Henry gave himself over to George, a willing receiver of pleasure as George licked his length again. His erection twitched at the contact and Henry giggled – it was so intimate and loving and happy.

And really bloody good.

One last flick from that tongue then George parted his lips and slowly took Henry's cock into his mouth. He eased down, taking an inch at a time, holding Henry's hips against the sofa no matter how much they tried to rise.

Not that he would admit it right away, but Henry had dreamed of this moment. Both asleep and waking. *Wondering.* What would it feel like, the warm softness of George's mouth? But he had told himself so often that he shouldn't want it, shouldn't even wonder, and now the forbidden was his. And the forbidden was amazing, it had to be said.

He knew he was shouting something – George's name or words that sounded like it. He couldn't watch anymore, because he was poleaxed by pleasure, helpless as he lay against the sofa, George rising and falling on him. He was aware of nothing else, no cares or fears or the memory of anything bad ever having happened to him before.

Only this moment, this furnace of bliss that he had somehow tumbled into.

And George's pace increased, his lips growing tighter and his tongue caressing Henry's cock with each movement. He heard soft moans of encouragement in George's throat, urging him on.

Henry crossed his arm over his face. *Let go, just let go. Let go of the tweed and the fear and the cantankerousness.*

Let go of all that, Henry—was it Bad Billy whispering to him?—*let go, my lad, and live.*

A jumbled mess of words fell from Henry's mouth as a shudder took over his limbs. At the last moment before his orgasm slayed him, he gripped George's hair. Even with George trying to hold him down, Henry's hips bucked up from the sofa. He shook then fell still, exhaling all the breath he had in him as he sagged into a wanton yet satiated heap.

George slowed his pace, easing Henry down from his pleasure before he rocked back on his knees. There was something rather dainty about the way he touched his fingers to his lips and whispered, "I love you, darling, so bloody much."

"Thank you," Henry whispered to him. "Thank you for loving me."

"You look tired and happy." George reached out and took Henry's hand. "Even happier than Kermit. I never had you down as a Muppets boxers sort of chap."

"They were a Christmas present." Was Henry blushing? Quite possibly. Were these the underpants of a television celebrity's boyfriend? Possibly not. "I'm a vet—what else could I want other than a pair of pants with a cartoon frog on them?"

"Kermit isn't a cartoon, he's *real.*" George shook his head disapprovingly. "And if he wasn't real, he still wouldn't be a cartoon. He'd be a puppet."

"Yes — silly me, he's real, George, he lives in a swamp! Maybe you've even met him in your travels?"

"A hundred times, Fitz. Miss Piggy's a fan of mine." George rose to his feet and held out his hand. "Come to bed?"

Henry took George's hand and let him help him up to his feet — his legs were very far from steady. He pulled up his trousers and the embarrassing underpants with one hand. But the shirt Henry left undone, leaving his chest and his stomach on show. And the scar, too, but he didn't mind it because George didn't. And, he realized, neither should he.

Ever the gentleman, George scooped up Henry's overnight bag and slung it effortlessly over his shoulder. Then he looked to the portrait and said, "Goodnight, Georgie."

"Do you always say goodnight to her?"

"No." He laughed and admitted, "Yes."

"I will too, then." Henry paused in the doorway and raised his hand. "Goodnight, madam! Tell your son to give Billy Fitzwalter a hug from me."

George led Henry up the creaky old stairs, and Henry grinned at the photos covering the walls. George as a baby, as a small boy, George and his friend Henry.

"Do you still have that poster of David Gower on your bedroom wall?"

"He still has to share space with Darren Gough. Fancy you remembering that, my cricket idols." George laughed. "But I've outgrown my single bed, so I've moved into the master. Darren and David get to hang out in my old digs."

"Your mum's room?" Henry hesitated as they reached the landing. "Is that — I mean, will it feel a bit weird?"

"Oh, she hasn't slept in here for *years*," George assured him. "She turned the third bedroom into a meditation, yoga temple thing. She sleeps in there, surrounded by crystals and singing bowls. The master became the guest room, and now it's mine."

He pushed open the bedroom door and said, "After you, Mr. Fitz!"

Henry had been in this room a very long time ago. He and George had dared each other to go in and steal something—a lipstick, or a comb, or, as Henry had, a single leather sandal. And once they had performed their raid, they'd felt guilty and confessed their transgression to George's mum, who'd hugged them and forgiven them and made them eat carob biscuits.

Which was a punishment, even if George's mum hadn't thought so.

The room was still dominated by a huge old four-poster bed with red and gold brocaded curtains. The bed must've been as old as the house—generations of Brookeses had slept in it, so it was said. Slept in it and done other things too. George had flicked on the lamp and its soft glow made the room cozy and inviting.

"It's a beautiful room for a beautiful man," Henry decided.

"Look." George pointed proudly to the table beside the bed. There, just as it was in Henry's house, was that photo of the two of them at Sandhurst, celebrating the passing out parade. "The first thing I unpacked."

Henry crossed his arms over his bare chest and nudged his head against George's shoulder. Why had he let his muddled feelings nearly destroy their friendship, their love?

"It's next to my bed as well. You looked so handsome that day, Captain George."

"I had this silly idea that you'd see me in my uniform and forget that daft, lanky lad who'd been your friend in favor of his *manly* chap I thought I'd become, which I hadn't, of course." He laughed, looping his arms around Henry's waist. "I was still that silly boy in the cricket jumper who fell out of the tree in your eyes, and I hope I always will be."

Smiling at George, Henry brushed his lips over George's face, and settled on his mouth. They kissed tenderly, dropping away the last of their clothes until, naked, George dragged back the corner of the covers and they slid under. There, beneath the canopy that had sheltered his family for generations, George drew Henry into his embrace and held him in contented silence.

Chapter Seventeen

Had the sun been peering in for long around the curtains? Not that its beams would've settled upon anything untoward, besides two men, curled up asleep around each other. Henry yawned. They had fallen asleep almost as soon as they had got into bed, and Henry hadn't slept so well in ages. And now he was rested and loved, and it was Saturday morning. So he wasn't even late for work.

Henry pulled on his clothes, buttoning his shirt as he padded barefoot down the stairs.

"George? Good morning!"

Where was his host? Henry followed the music coming from the lounge.

George was sat — no, sprawled — among a pile of cushions in a large armchair before the window, one leg flung over the arm. He wore a cricket jersey trimmed in the colors of his regiment and casually creased chinos, and spread across his lap was the red regimental mess jacket of his officer's uniform. He held a cloth and was vigorously polishing the bright brass buttons while

Tabitha perched on the sofa, holding a steaming mug of tea.

"Fitz, darling, grab a cuppa and join us!" George beamed and waved the cloth. "We're talking inspiration!"

Inspiration?

That was certainly one word for it. Henry stared dumbly at the sight before him. George, impossibly handsome, the louche bastard — and that jacket, that damn jacket! Wind seemed to rush past his ears as he sped through a time-tunnel that spat him out at the military uniform shop. All that time ago, when George had swished back the changing room curtain and stepped out in that jacket. The gold buttons. The tantalizing gold buttons that Henry had longed to feel pressed against him, that he had longed to unfasten.

Henry returned to the now.

"Golly, that jacket…"

No other words were possible.

"Polishing my buttons ready for the 1940s evening. You *are* coming, Fitz?" George beckoned him over and lifted out of the chair just enough to kiss Henry's cheek before he returned to his lounging position.

Henry remembered to nod a good morning to Tabitha.

"I'm supposed to be going, but I don't have a 1940s costume. I don't know what to wear."

"Tweed, darling, and you're laughing!"

"Is it that simple?" Henry grinned, but then wondered why Tabitha was laughing. "It's a classic look. Especially for a vet."

"And I've told Tab that it's a no to anything that might make LP look like a sideshow, haven't I, Tab?" George looked to his immaculate producer. "So we're focusing on cricket and, I don't know, jam or something."

"Jam — oh, you can't possibly object to jam, Henry?" Tabitha put her cup down on the table. George had apparently cleared away all the documents that had filled the lounge only a few hours before. "Jam is uncontroversial."

"Well —" Bloody Steph and Bloody Ed and the bloody greengage jam. But at the sight of George and his gentle smile, Henry didn't care. Let the Belchers turn the jam contest into a drama if they chose — they were the ones who looked petty, not Henry. "Quite. Not controversial in the least."

"Tab." George looked suddenly inspired. "The Women's Institute?"

"Yes!" Tabitha clapped her hands. "The WI is very hot at the moment. Have your lot posed naked for a charity calendar?"

Henry thought his eyes would burst out of his skull.

"No, they bloody haven't! Longley Parva isn't some sort of weird hub of wild sex, you know!"

Tabitha giggled. "That's not the impression I got when I arrived here yesterday morning, Henry, but I'll take your word for it."

Henry was certain he was blushing.

"I could talk to Mrs. Dalrymple about a calendar," George offered. "It'd make a brilliant Christmas show, wouldn't it? And I could keep my clothes on for once!"

"Why not focus on her baking? Those are the sort of WI baps we should see, not — erm..."

"Baking, you say?" Tabitha swished her pashmina over her shoulder, brow furrowed in thought. "Baking is *very* hot."

"Certainly is." Here was a subject Henry knew something about. "You have to get the oven to just the right temperature, and if you spend all day in the kitchen, it gets very hot indeed."

"Mrs. Dalrymple might be an older woman, but she's still a *woman*," George pressed on, intent on defending his new best pal. "If she wants to pose in nothing but an apron and a smile, I say why not?"

He blinked up at Henry. "Do you bake, Fitz? This is a side of you I haven't seen. Will you make me a chocolate cake?"

Henry looked over at Tabitha. He could see her brain working. *A vet who can bake.*

"I dabble." He shrugged. "There's cake stalls at every event that happens in this village. Aside from eating the cake, I see it as a nice way to serve the community. Rock buns are my speciality. Sponge cakes with buttercream and homemade raspberry jam. That's a popular one, actually. The very occasional coffee square, from my gran's 1970s cookbook. I've tried bread, now and again. Not so good at that, though."

Tabitha clasped her hands around her knees, beaming. "How very English you are, Henry, if you don't mind me saying so. Are you certain you don't want to do television? A rural vet, clad in tweed, who bakes classic cakes?"

"But I—" It was hardly a lifestyle option. It was just how Henry was. "I don't think anyone needs to see me sweating in my kitchen, covered in butter and flour!"

"You forgot to mention that Henry is also gorgeous, Tab, which would do his prospects no harm." George laughed, then he gave Tabitha a stern look. "I can see it now, handsome vet saves puppy from tree, then unwinds by baking jam tarts over the closing credits."

Wafting her hand as if she'd forgotten there was no cigarette between her fingers, Tabitha nodded in agreement. "They'd love Henry on the weekend cookery chat shows, lovey. *There's* a chunk of promo right away!"

"The main thing is, Tabs, I want to concentrate a bit of time on old Lady G.'s bio and think about projects related to that for next year." This was news to Henry, though George was looking determined. "So for the Christmas show, I'd rather feature, as opposed to being the whole show. What do you think? GSB's cricketing, WI-ing summer sort of thing?"

"Anything that features bunting is hot, lovey, of course. But obscure, dusty aristos? Darling, what about the Amazon?" Tabitha's face looked rather pinched. She glanced at Henry, then turned to George. "The Brazilian government are lining up to accommodate us for the shoot. What about those endangered monkeys you were going to visit?"

"She had a clutch of husbands, an even bigger clutch of girlfriends, and her son kept a pet goat," he told her hopefully. "Does that not tempt you in?"

"An eccentric was he, her son?"

Good lord. Was he going to do it? Admit to his not-very-straight ancestors? George earned himself a wide grin from Henry.

But would he or George ever admit to the public that they were very far from straight themselves?

"He had his moments, but I think the focus would be on Georgina. After all, she was a trailblazer for her gender. Politics, business and all of it better than any man." George laughed and offered, "If it helps, I'll drag up and float about LP myself!"

"*Brava!*" Tabitha leaped to her feet. "My god, that would be amazing! And everyone would bang on about how *brave* it is of you, to go about in drag. Manly man in a corset, that sort of thing. But we must make sure you can pass, darling. We don't want *panto dame*, do we?"

Henry was aware of the fact that, once again, his jaw was hanging open. *George, in drag? George, in a corset?* His legs had turned to jelly.

"Sorry, I need to get that cup of tea, I think."

"And she dressed as a chap and went into London to scandalize the fellows in the city when they scoffed at a woman doing business," George told her, full of enthusiasm. "She squired Mrs. Armistead to the theater in full gentleman's dress so for me to do the odd scene reversing the drag— I'm sick of taking my top off, so let me put a corset *on* and see if we can make it fly?"

Henry didn't hear or see anything else. Until he blinked open his eyes and realized that he was lying on the floor, staring up at George and Tabitha.

"You all right, Fitz?" George went down on one knee and fanned him with the sleeve of his regimental jacket. "Horrified at the thought of me in a frock, eh?"

Henry grasped George's hand. "No, not at all — quite the contrary, in fact!"

Tabitha snorted loudly. "That idea passes muster with the gay community at least!"

"I wouldn't say I'm representative." But Henry wasn't looking at Tabitha as he addressed her. The sight of the regimental jacket was making him lightheaded again. "Must get a cuppa, eh?"

"What do you think, Fitz?" George stood beside the portrait and approximated Georgina's pose and expression. "Could I be Georgie with a cincher and some slap?"

"Mmmm… Yes. I mean, I'm not an expert on ladies, but—yes. You have her eyes." Henry looked toward George. "And so did her son."

George met his gaze and smiled, his expression one of undisguised adoration. Still looking to Henry, he told Tabitha, "I'm aiming for the *super feminine woman dresses as a chap* angle by playing the opposite *ex-soldier dresses as a girl* version? I'm not thinking of a whole six-parter in drag, just the odd scene here and there. I might even get into the full naval rig again too, I love the brocade."

"I don't think anyone would mind." Tabitha's voice became extra fruity, like a head girl who has spotted the nearby boys' school out on the field in their rugger gear again. "Ex-soldier does drag is hardly front-page news, darling—my cousin's a brigadier, I know all about what *you* chaps get up to!"

George, however, looked at her rather darkly and said, "What, apart from fighting wars, Tab?"

"Oh, darling…!" Tabitha pouted and crossed the room to George in a waft of strong-smelling perfume.

Henry darted aside to avoid her outstretched arms as she sallied forth. He could still remember the feel of the pitted skin across George's back as they had fallen asleep in each other's arms. George, however, maintained that very professional look he had assumed and asked, "And this year, are we on for the *cricketing, WI, English villages are lovely* special? I'll throw in a sunset dip in Fitz's lake to sweeten the deal if he says I can. Complete with lingering close-ups of me mid-dive?"

"Definitely!" Tabitha was already tapping at her phone. She looked up at George—and sparingly at Henry—with a somewhat equine, toothy grin.

"Now if you'll excuse me, Tabby, I must get my hard-working, handsome boyfriend a cup of tea and check Jez is happy with his breakfast." He kissed her cheek and laid his mess jacket down over the chair. "I'll be two minutes."

Henry followed George into the kitchen.

"Sorry about fainting, old bean."

"You had me worried!" George pulled Henry into his arms. "I didn't want to wake you, you were sleeping so deeply."

"It's a very comfortable bed! And you were very nice to hug all night." How lovely George smelled. Clean and yet spicy, warm, familiar and exciting. But there was a question Henry needed to ask. "I thought you wanted to go to the Amazon?"

"I've been to the Amazon a couple of times already." He shrugged as though it were just a trip to Sainsbury's. "Being with you, raising little Jez... That's my next adventure."

"Do you—do you really mean that?" Henry circled his thumb against George's jaw. "You're going to stay in the village?"

He nodded. "In a little cottage of my own. Ma'll be back by Christmas and much as I adore Andie, I wouldn't want to live with her and her panpipes."

"They are a bit of a chore. Depending on which way the wind's blowing in summer, I sometimes have to shut my windows. The noise drifts over the meadow, you see."

If only Henry could offer him something. But he might not even have a home of his own soon. Maybe

Henry would be the next inhabitant of Andie Standish-Brookes' shed. George was looking at him again, that same close look that made Henry feel as though he would never be able to keep a secret from him.

"Since it's your day off, shall we take Jez and Tabs down to the pub and let her have a look at the village? We could try another of those highly controversial platters if you like?" George pulled a scandalized face and added, "Or is that too London for you rural folk?"

"Well, I enjoyed it. Do you think we should get her a jacket potato with baked beans and cheese? She might not want to film here if she finds out we have such outré things as tapas sharing platters in Longley Parva. Saveloy rather than *chorizo*?"

"We'll get her a steak and Spitfire pie," George decided. "But I won't dress as an airman while she eats it."

Henry's mouth quirked up into a smile. "Pity..."

"Wait until the 1940s bash. I hope you'll approve of my choice of togs."

"Dressing up as an airman for that? Will the fake mustache tickle when we have a big snog in the car park and you give me a pair of nylons?"

"I'll take you for a spin in the Jag." George, always plummy, was now the epitome of the upper officer class. "And we'll enjoy a victory roll in the hay if you're lucky."

"Up, up and away!" Henry rushed his mouth to George's, forgetting that they were standing by the window, forgetting that George had a guest. Forgetting everything, because he was in love.

The gentle nuzzling of Jez's nose against Henry's back brought him to his senses and out of their kiss.

"Someone's ready to go and meet his fans." George put his arm around Jez's neck. "Tabs, grab your handbag, we're going into the village!"

Chapter Eighteen

It wasn't unusual for Henry to be drafted in as village tour guide. As lord of the manor, he was a splendid historical artifact, a coelacanth in tweeds.

Although this morning he was in corduroy.

Tabitha cooed with each fact that Henry related, snapping photos on her phone.

"...and in 1623, one poor chap died when the bell fell out of the tower in a storm and crushed him." The clock on the church steeple chose that moment to chime somewhat sarcastically as they passed by the churchyard's low stone wall. "Over here, we have the grave of Nehemiah Belcher, killed in a duel over Lady Georgina — at least, so they say. He was probably just cleaning his gun and it went off by accident. Now, the large stone cross on our right — "

"*Our* family always said that it was Lady G. who fired the fatal shot whilst dressed in her best suit but..." George shrugged. "We've always liked a tall tale, we Standy-Bees, but nobody else came forward to claim it!"

Tabitha pushed her sunglasses onto the top of her head.

"I'm liking this idea more and more! What a scene to re-enact—who would we get to play that Belcher chap? Does he have descendants in the village?"

"Enjoy the history for now, Tabs, we'll talk names later."

Henry pointed across the lane and continued with the tour.

"Just on the other side of the High Street, you can see what looks like a hill, covered in trees. That is nothing less than our castle! The hill is in fact the motte, where a wooden fortification would have stood—it's where the first Fitzwalters lived when they arrived in Longley Parva."

"King Fitz." George ruffled his lover's hair. "Ruler of all he surveyed."

Henry placed his hands on his hips, feet spread, and realized he'd posed like Henry VIII as painted by Holbein.

"And over here, the tearooms, which were apparently at one point home to a wizard..."

"Not a shirtless wizard, Tab," George teased. "Though I could daub myself in woad and yell at the night a bit if it'd look suitably savage on camera? Bare-arsed, every muscle tensed, all fire and brimstone? More Sauron than Gandalf?"

Henry stared. Tabitha stared. Mrs. Tanvir, who had just appeared at her front door with her tartan shopping trolley, stared.

"Hello, Mrs. T.!" George called cheerily, waving his hand. "Do you think I'd make a good naked wizard?"

"Erm—possibly?" She looked from George to Henry and her gaze settled on Tabitha. A smile came to her face and she nodded. "Morning to you! What do you think of our little village?"

"It's charming!"

"Mrs. Tanvir makes excellent jam," Henry offered.

The lady in question fluttered at Henry's praise. "You're very kind, Henry!" She raised her hand and rolled her trolley off toward the bus stop.

"All this marvelous jam in the village." Tabitha was tapping on her phone again. "We've had *Bake Off*, why not — *Jam Off*? Wait — I have it! The Village Green Self-*Preserves* Society! Classic 1960s pop on the theme tune, bunting — " Tabitha stretched her arm in an arc from one side of the road to the other. "A balloon arch! Oh, can you see it? I can!"

"Aaaaand this is what I'm trying to tell you, Tabby." George laughed. "I just offered the holy televisual grail, the Standy-Bee bum, and you were more interested in bunting, because this village is bloody perfect!"

"The bum *and* the jam, though — that would work. Although possibly not smeared in the jam. Then again..."

George rolled his eyes and ambled on with Jez at his side, giving Mrs. Tanvir a polite bow as they went. He called over his shoulder, "*Secret History of an English Village*. It fits my brand perfectly *and* it can only help keep the village hall standing!"

Henry swept his hand toward the unassuming building. *Hall* was a rather grand word for it — hut would've been better.

"And here it is! Formerly farm buildings, requisitioned in the early twentieth century for the village. All sorts of things go on here. It can turn into a theater for am-dram, a polling station during elections, a clinic for baby weigh-ins — then there's the parish council meetings, playgroup, keep fit classes, Brownies, Guides, Scouts, Cubs, St. John's Ambulance, youth club... You name it, it goes on here. And unfortunately" — Henry pointed toward the thatch — "the roof's knackered. When it rains, the kids have to run around fifteen different buckets, like an obstacle course."

Henry knew it was hardly the most visually appealing of buildings. It still had its workaday farmyard appearance, and over the years it had been inexpertly patched up. Part of its wall was made from corrugated iron, another part was made from vivid red modern bricks, and exterior lights clung to its pebble-dash like barnacles.

"For reasons which are mysterious to me, we can't get rid of the thatch and have tiles instead, even though it has to be replaced every few years. It's expensive, and...well..." If the village was going to be on telly, then Henry may as well make sure it was worth Longley Parva's while. "Hence all the fundraising that goes on."

"Very interesting." Tabitha nodded slowly. "You could build a new hall, of course?"

"Which would cost a great deal of money." Henry whistled through his teeth and realized too late that he sounded like a mechanic assessing the cost to repair a car.

"Tab, what Henry isn't telling you is that I'm going to be donating a portion of my profits from the tie-in book to the village hall fund." George quirked his eyebrow as though to suggest this wasn't to be sniffed at. "They'll be able to afford a new hall, all right."

Henry didn't tell you because Henry didn't know. But Henry covered his surprise with a smile. He tipped his head to one side, doing his best sympathetic gaze for Tabitha. He could almost hear the plaintive piano music which, had this conversation been filmed, would now be building in the background into a strident orchestral sweep, while some chap warbled incoherently over guitars to the crescendo.

"It's the only way, Tabitha, for a rural community like Longley Parva..." He patted George's shoulder. "Selfless generosity, that's what we have to rely on."

Tabitha nodded. Henry was fairly sure she had tears in her eyes. She looked away, toward the humble, shabby village hall.

"Wow. You two. My goodness. Henry — those eyes of yours are *dangerous*. You nearly had me reaching for my bank app to make a transfer!"

"All donations gratefully received, Tabitha." What had Henry become? Was it George's fault? But no — it felt good. Shameless, yes — but bloody good.

"Take no more than you need and all that, Tab." George looked to Henry and smiled. "And yes, I know it's easy to say that when you have *much* more than you need, which is why it won't be in the script."

"Of course, of course." Tabitha nodded toward one of the posters advertising the next fundraising event. "Now — this 1940s dance next week. We're all set for filming, yes? Let's get a small camera crew down."

Henry shoved his hands into his pocket. "Mrs. Dalrymple's organizing it — I'll pop in and speak to her if you like?"

"I very much *would* like!"

"One thing, Tab, because I promised Fitz." George took his sunglasses from his pocket and cleaned them casually on the bottom of his cricket sweater. "I know I had a bit of a joke about it, but I don't want to make the village something to laugh at. And if anyone *doesn't* want to be on camera — I have a feeling Fitz will be one of them — we're not going to be the pushy telly folk. I'm going to be living here, and I don't want to be burned in a giant wicker cricket bat."

"Who *doesn't* want to be on the telly?" Tabitha tipped back her head and laughed. "I mean, I don't, of course. But — all right. We've got release forms and the like, and the dreaded face-shaped oval of blur! Then we'll avoid shooting anyone who doesn't want to be involved."

"Good." Henry grinned at her. "By the way, if you think it would help the village if I was on screen for a bit, I don't mind, you know. I am the lord of the manor, after all. It would be a bit odd if I wasn't in it. I'd hate for people to think that I was some dreadful curmudgeon."

Tabitha grabbed Henry's arms. "Lovey, you *have* to be."

"But make me look idiotic..." Henry wagged his finger. A long line of Justices of the Peace awoke in his blood. "And I'll put you in the ducking stool over the village pond."

"Fitz, you don't have to—" George frowned and quickly put his sunglasses on, concealing his eyes. Then he patted Jez's neck and walked on, murmuring to the foal as it trotted beside him.

"You still have a ducking stool?" Tabitha grinned. "And stocks, too? We could put George in them, couldn't we?"

There had been a time when Henry would have agreed and been the first in the queue with a cabbage to lob, but he had to laugh.

"The stocks and the stool are in a museum now, I'm afraid. I was only joshing!"

He didn't feel any humor in his own joke, though. What had he said to make George retreat? Didn't he want everyone in the village to be in his program?

"To the pub, I think!" Tabitha struggled on the gravel road in her kitten heels, so Henry took her arm in gallant fashion and led her toward The Green Man.

"Be prepared to watch George get swamped in the pub garden!" Henry led the way toward the motley collection of wooden picnic tables and wonky sun umbrellas advertising obsolete drinks. The sun-dappled garden was already busy and Henry was proven right as a swarm of well-wishers descended like excitable wasps, leaving George and Jez in the middle of them, the little horse proving as popular as his guardian.

Out came the beer mats and the Biros, the phones and the smiles, and George did his duty with that bright, never-fading smile.

"He's so good at this." Tabitha smiled indulgently at George. "There's a lot of people I work with in TV who'd boot everyone out of the garden and hurl tables if anyone dared to come up and speak to them. But look at George — he loves it!"

It didn't annoy Henry now, even though it was barely a week since George had gatecrashed the Bonny Baby Contest. He took a seat and passed Tabitha a menu from another table.

"I can recommend the pie." Henry hoped she wouldn't notice the sharing platters.

"Pie? Oh, look—homemade Scotch eggs! How terribly rustic! With meat, I see—in London now, you're hard-pressed to find one that's not been hewn from an avocado." Tabitha laughed. "Your face, Henry! Hahahaha, yes, avocado."

"What a world we live in…"

Jez was first to arrive at the table, having dodged the fray in a moment when George was occupied by a smiling baby in the crook of either elbow. It was another couple of minutes before he could make good his escape and join the trio, bringing with him a solitary small boy who left only when George had written *exactly* the right inscription on his proffered beer mat.

"I think everyone's probably got an autograph now," George said with an exaggerated puff of air. "They'll get sick of me soon enough when they realize I'm living here."

"Scotch eggs made from avocado, George, that's what they eat in London. Can you imagine?" Henry's eyes were wide with horror. "Have *you* ever eaten one?"

"I don't think so." George shook his head and glanced around before lowering his voice. "Look, I don't want you to think you have to agree to appearing on TV because— Well, I don't want you to do anything because you think you *have* to."

Under the concealing safety of the table, Henry tapped George's knee.

"It's all right, really. I'd like to. It's for the sake of the village, after all. A chap's got to do his duty and all that." He rested his hand on his chin. "You never know, it might even be rather fun."

"Don't think you have to change." George smiled, momentarily touching his hand to Henry's beneath the table. "You're perfect as you are."

Jez, seemingly as happy with his fans as George was, turned and trotted away across the garden, his tail swishing. George watched with a lazy smile as assorted children followed in his wake, calling for him to wait.

Then George's smile faltered, his face darkening with concentration.

"Is this wishful thinking, Fitz, or does Jez's limp look a bit easier to you?"

"In my expert opinion, do you mean? Yes, I think it does. Wonder how much exercise he was getting at Ed's stables? Probably shut the poor sod away and hoped he'd disappear." Henry heard a shocked intake of breath from George. He patted his hand quickly. "But you took him away from that, so… You've given him a snug little house and a garden to roam about in, and he goes off on walks and it's the exercise that's helping him. As well as —" Henry didn't want to cause a scene in the beer garden, even if he wanted to twine his fingers with George's. He cleared his throat. "As well as love. And maybe that's the most important thing of all."

"If that's what he needs, then he'll be winning the Derby this time next year." George laughed, but even behind the sunglasses Henry could feel the warmth in his gaze. "No, Jez's life is all cuddles and fun now, no racing, no hassle, just kids telling him how cute he is. He'll probably end up being the star of the doc!"

"He'll be on kids' TV in no time. The face of a thousand lunchboxes!" Tabitha put down the menu that she had been pretending to be absorbed by.

"Right, who wants what? I'm going for the famed steak and ale pie," George decided. "Full-on rural pub grub!"

"I will too." Tabitha rubbed her hands together with relish. "Made with your local ale, too, I see. You're all over their menu, Captain George!"

Henry winked at his boyfriend.

"Comes with George's face airbrushed onto the crust!"

It apparently took Tabitha a moment to realize that he was joking.

"Pie, Fitz?" George stood. "Keep an eye on Jez for me?"

And he was gone again, just in time to miss the roar of the Ferrari as it raced into the pub car park in a cloud of dust. Ed Belcher emerged from the car's air-conditioned confines, resplendent in a black shirt that was open just a *little* too far and jeans that were just a *little* too tight. He called, "Is that my old nag? Tired of it already, has he?"

Henry whispered to Tabitha, "Here we go—the delightful Ed Belcher has arrived." He got up and stroked Jez, eyeing Ed carefully. It wouldn't do to be antagonistic, but Henry was tired of being polite to the man who wanted to make him homeless.

"Ed! You'll be on the lemonade, then. Don't drink and drive."

"I'm not staying, Henry, but when I saw Foal 12 here abandoned in the beer garden, how could I drive by?" He boomed a laugh, barely glancing at Tabitha. "I told Standish-Brookes it was a cripple but he's a sentimental old bugger. Too squeamish to have it shot, was he? Thought he'd foist it off onto the pub instead?"

"He has a name, Ed. And a loving home with George. And it just so happens that Jez has a fan club among the locals to rival George's. He likes coming to the pub garden."

Henry was aware of Tabitha's scrutiny, and wondered if this was how psychics felt, because he knew exactly what she was thinking. *This'll make great telly!*

Ed turned slightly, putting his back to Tabitha so he could ask in a leering whisper, "Who's the bird? Bit long in the tooth, Fitzwalter, is she rich?"

For a crazed second, Henry wondered if he could get away with saying that Tabitha was his property lawyer. But truth was easier to maintain than a lie.

"This is Tabitha Shakespeare, George's television chum. Tabitha, this is Ed. He's…" *An arsehole.* "The descendent of that chap who may or may not have been killed in a duel."

Tabitha revealed her teeth to him. Her fake smile was almost convincing.

"Nice to meet you." She obviously met shits like Ed all the time in the world of telly.

"Ms. Shakespeare!" Ed was practically bowing. "I bet George's told you all about me, hasn't he? I imagine you'll be wanting my card to talk about how we can help each other?"

He pulled out his fat wallet and opened it to remove a business card. It was gold, and embossed in silver, and he held it out with a look of pride. Jez shied away from Ed, nearly standing on Henry's foot as he stepped sideways, trying to evade the man who would have sanctioned his death. No wonder the foal was flourishing away from Ed. It was a wonder that anything could avoid withering within a five-mile radius of the man.

But what business did George have, talking to Ed about the documentary? Unless it was a wind-up. Maybe so. Maybe George was going to cast Ed as the baddie, and he didn't know.

"Thank you." Again Tabitha's fake smile as she took the card from Ed and tucked it into her leather phone case. She made no attempt, Henry noticed, to offer her own card in response.

"Call me." Ed pointed what he probably thought was a commanding finger. "Let's talk turkey."

He gave Henry a swift look up and down and turned, the sunlight catching the enormous silver dollar symbol on his belt buckle as he strode away.

Tabitha grimaced. "What a revolting individual! *Let's talk turkey*, for heaven's sake—does he think he's on *Howard's Way*?"

Henry thought it best not to make his partisanship too obvious.

You never know whose ears might be flapping in The Green Man's beer garden.

"That's our Ed, a bit of local color for you. Ball-breaking stock exchange type. Went to school with George and me. Married my ex, in fact."

"Your ex? Oh, I didn't realize he was—"

Perhaps Tabitha had noticed how Henry dropped his chin to his chest, awkwardly fascinated by the sight of his own shoes. She grinned kindly at him.

"Ah, I see. It's all right, Henry."

Ed honked the Ferrari horn in an approximation of George's trademark *toot-toot*, but it sounded different coming from the supercar. It wasn't friendly, the promise of approaching silliness, but an aggressive, demanding sound that bellowed *look at me, world*! No, he couldn't see Ed Belcher ever replacing Standy-Bee in the public's affections, no matter how fickle.

At the sound Jez lifted his head and looked up at the car. He gave a whinny and tossed his mane in a gesture that might, if one were being fanciful, be taken as a show of a rather defiant attitude. It might also be taken as *very* Standy-Bee, the same look George had given when he'd showed up to the school disco wearing mascara. Ed and his cronies had laughed but George hadn't cared because George had *known* he could get away with it, that he was as close as a rural Sussex private school would ever get to seeing David Bowie.

And those long, dark eyelashes had framed George's eyes beautifully.

Henry turned toward the horse, pressing his face to its mane. How were he and George to keep this a secret? Would they have to move away? And yet, the Reverend and the Squire had kept their love a secret for years. So, then, could Henry and George.

When he returned, George was carrying a tray on which were two pints of Spitfire and a cool-looking glass of white wine. Jez trotted over to welcome him and together they walked over to the table. George put down the tray and took his seat opposite Henry with a broad smile.

"You remembered!" Tabitha took the wine. "Cheers, you two!"

"I'm not about to forget, Tabs." George laughed. "I've bought you a few in my time!"

Henry saw movement from the corner of his eye and noticed Lil Dalrymple approaching Jez. The foal whinnied a greeting and she affectionately rubbed his nose, pouting her shiny lips at him.

George peered up at her and slowly slid his sunglasses down his nose. He cocked his head to one side before asking, "Lil, is it fair to say that you know as much about makeup as you do about horses?"

Lil grinned at their local celebrity. "Makeup? I don't wear makeup! I'm entirely *au naturel*, I'll have you know?"

"That's a shame." He shrugged good-naturedly. "I was going to ask if you fancied giving me a bit of a one-to-one later, but I'll have to keep looking for the right girl."

Lil's jaw dropped. She clutched at her collar like a surprised society dame clutching at her pearls.

"Oh, well, actually — I mean, I do know a lot? I gave a contouring demo to the Girl Guides the other week, actually? Yes, so, actually, I am *just* the right girl for you? Erm…actually?"

Henry reined in his urge to chuckle.

"Could you spare an hour this afternoon to show a chap how to put on a face?" He silenced Tabitha, who was no doubt about to remind him of the extensive *professional* makeup artists at their disposal. "I don't want to look like a drag queen, I want to look like this is just what I do."

"That would, like, be the most amazing thing that I've ever actually, like, done?"

"Good stuff, and I'll bung you a few quid to say thanks. When can you come over?" He smiled his most winsome smile and told Tabitha, "Lil is the only person I'd trust to babysit Jez, other than Fitz, obviously. She's going to be *very* big in the horse world."

"Or the makeup world, actually? I can come over when you're finished here?"

"Walk back up with us after lunch if you like?" He looked to Tabitha and asked, "Think of it, Tabs, local talent behind the scenes too?"

"Oh, I like it!" Tabitha dropped her sunglasses onto her nose and took an enormous glug of wine. The food arrived along with a generous bowl of water for Jez and there, in the early summer sun, George's next venture began to take shape.

Chapter Nineteen

A sudden shaft of sunlight struck the metal blade as Henry worked his way through the brambles. He had taken the papers concerning Rupert the goat with him when he'd left George's cottage earlier and was now searching for his two-hundred-year-old resting place.

Where would an eccentric Georgian vicar bury his pet goat? Somewhere in the garden of the manor. But that was not so straightforward as it might at first have appeared because Henry's back garden was measured in acres, rather than in meters.

Yet among the papers there was a clue.

All our days are gone
But the sun shall not set on Rupert
And The Seven shall watch over his sleeping place.

Would there be a headstone for the creature that the Reverend had so doted on? But if he had had only a wooden marker, it would have rotted to dust years before. George so wanted to pay his respects that Henry felt honor-bound to tackle the overgrown garden, even though it seemed a Herculean task. His mother had been a great one for the garden, but she had died from a wasp sting when Henry was a boy. His father had neglected the garden, as if he blamed the natural world for his loss and enjoyed watching it helplessly tangle in on itself.

A stream ran through part of the manor's grounds, which curved round to feed the lake. In one corner, far from the house, the banks were very high, and Henry had been forbidden from venturing there as a boy. Being the sort of child who always did as he was told, he had never transgressed the order.

Until now. For George.

Because Henry had a hunch as to who 'The Seven' were.

Despite the heat of the day, it was cool and shady near the stream, the moss along the bank bright emerald green. The brambles had grown up around a grove of tall trees that Henry's father had called The Seven Grandfathers. Why, Henry had never known. But if they were The Seven from the goat's eulogy, then that name and the trees must be old indeed.

Much of the bramble was dead, despite the ready source of water from the stream, so clearing it away in gauntlets was not as hard as Henry had feared. As he worked, a breeze rocked the high branches of the Grandfathers, and Henry had the strangest notion that he was not alone here.

A hand fell onto his shoulder.

Who on earth – ?

But when he turned, it was only a branch that had caught his shirt.

"Show me, then, Billy — if that's you."

The breeze stirred the trees again and sighed like a voice that Henry couldn't quite decipher.

He tutted to himself. What a superstitious fool he was. He took up the scythe and swept forward again through the bramble.

His scythe struck stone with a clang.

This was surely it — the headstone for a goat.

Henry flung the scythe down to fall where it would and, with renewed energy, heaved away the brambles.

But what rose up from the floor of the grove to greet him was not a tombstone. At least, not a conventional one.

Because, of course, the Reverend and the Squire had not been conventional people.

Chapter Twenty

Are you out vetting? J and I sunbathing at the lake with a beer, got a treat to show you! Love you xxx

It was a couple of hot, hard-working hours later that George's text arrived. Whatever he had spent his afternoon doing, however, George had not been hacking back a century's worth of bramble. Instead he was sunbathing, because he was George.

Henry knew he must look a sight. His hair was stuck down with sweat, his plaid shirt was torn, his arms and face were scratched, his stained gauntlets bulged in his trouser pockets and he was carrying the scythe over his shoulder like a sinister fashion accessory.

But George was in his cargo shorts and nothing else besides a pair of Wayfarers. And as Henry got nearer — *makeup?*

He'd left it on?

"My *God.*" At Henry's approach, George pushed himself to sit up on the grass. He slid his sunglasses up into his hair to reveal not only that white powdered face and rouged red lips but a perfectly outlined eye. And there, on his chiseled cheekbone, a small, black heart. "Fitz, you look— You're bloody gorgeous!"

Henry gave him a lopsided grin but couldn't tear his eyes from the transformation before him.

"You—you look just like… It's like seeing a ghost. Except it's a ghost in cargo pants! I can't quite— George, you look amazing!"

Henry crouched to put the scythe down on the ground, checking that Jez hadn't taken an interest in it, then hurried to George. He reached toward his face then brought his hand back, wanting to touch but restrained by George's otherworldly beauty.

"I don't look like Joan Crawford, then?"

"No—not at all! You look just like Lady Georgina. The very image of her, as if she'd just stepped out of her portrait! And for some reason, decided to wear cargo pants and lounge about on my lawn."

As Henry stared, a thought occurred to him. "So— you walked from Lil's—with your face like that?" He looked away, nervous suddenly, toward the curve of the driveway. "Did anyone see you? Did they see you heading up my driveway? Maybe no one would think—would assume—but…"

Henry dropped to his knees beside his lover. He stroked George's bare shoulder, the skin warm from the sun.

"I'm not scolding, George—please don't think that. At the risk of stating the obvious, we must be careful, darling."

"I told her the truth, that it was for the program. Fitz, I'm not about to out us to the village." He blinked, peering up at Henry. "You look very… Well, you look very physical."

Henry pinched his sweaty shirt away from his chest and puffed out his cheeks.

"I look—and unfortunately smell—like a man who's been wrestling with brambles on a hot day! And has found what seems to be your goat's last resting place. And not only that, but the last resting place of a dog called Nimrod as well."

George's perfectly shadowed eyes widened, his mascaraed lashes falling in a shocked blink. "You've found our ancestors' faithful friends?"

"Would appear so!" Henry slid his hand from George's shoulder to his neck and toyed with the warm hair at his nape. "Over on the other side of the garden, in a grove of trees. And it's not just any old headstone, either—it's a sundial with a brass goat on top. Do you see? *The sun shall not set on Rupert.* And around the plinth, there's a huge brass dog's collar, with *Nimrod Fitzwalter* etched into it. It's in very good nick—I suppose the trees and then the brambles sheltered the memorial from the worst of the elements over the years. They were quite a pair, our ancestors!"

George glanced over his shoulder then caught Henry's hand and drew him closer for a kiss. His skin smelled of perfume and his rouged lips were soft against Henry's own.

"So the only question is whether we swim first," George gave a casual smile, "or pay our respects to the boys in full slap?"

"*We* swim?"

Henry couldn't remember the last time he'd swum in the lake. But it had been with George, that much was certain. Before all that business with the dratted Longley Parva Cup. A day in late summer when they'd stood on the jetty by the boathouse and taken a run up to jump as far as they could into the lake. They'd had a good-natured tussle in the water over who had jumped out the farthest. But a swim, now? He didn't even have swimwear anymore. Not since Steph had laughed at his Bermuda shorts on their last caravanning holiday, when it had done nothing for a week but rain.

"Let's go and look at the sundial, m' lady." Henry began to stand, helping Lady Georgina to his feet. "We can follow the stream from the end of the lake."

George curtsied as he rose and, with Jez trotting over to join them, slipped his arm through Henry's.

"Last night was wonderful, Fitz," he murmured.

"I never dared hope to be as happy as I am now, George—Lady Georgina?"

It was said that Bad Billy's uncle had been rather partial to Lady Georgina. Had they walked here, where now George and Henry wandered, winding their way beside the route of the stream to The Seven Grandfathers? Billy and Toby most certainly had.

Henry smiled. "Just think—Billy and Toby walking here, like us. Off to commemorate their animal chums. I'm not sure if Billy was all sweaty or if Toby had made-up like his mum, but!" They passed a rosebush and Henry snapped off a pink, petal-heavy head, offering it to George's nose. "For Rupert and Nimrod."

George inhaled the scent, his eyes closing for a moment before he whispered, "I don't think I'll ever want to leave here again, Fitz."

Could it really be that the man who had seen the world, had climbed to the highest peaks and dived into the deepest oceans, might have been so bewitched by the place he had known longer than anywhere? Had Captain George Standish-Brookes, hero of the Household Cavalry, savior of helpless children and wide-eyed foals, come home to stay? Henry held George's arm more tightly, resting his cheek against his.

"If you stayed, I'd make you happy, George—I swear it. I'd never let you be sad for even a second."

"You wouldn't cricket bat me if I left the lid off the toothpaste?"

"No—but I might tickle you!"

"I could live with that." George stepped in front of Henry and slipped his arms around his waist, meeting his gaze. For a few seconds he was silent, studying Henry's face, then he whispered, "I'll always look after you, even if— I'm sorry this has to be a secret."

"I understand, darling—honestly, I do. It's not something I can go shouting about either. We're in a bit of a bind—but we have each other now. And I can bear anything if I have you, even in secret."

"You *could*, Fitz, that's why I feel so dreadful. I'm stopping *you* being who you are, and—" George let his forehead rest against Henry's. "You understand now, but one day— I don't ever want you to think that it's anything about you, it's this stupid bloody career thing."

"*I've* stopped myself from being who I am. I love this village, but how would they react? And there's Dad as well—he's not the most understanding of people. I'm not angry. What a splendid secret to share. *Us.*"

A breeze from high above moved through the branches of the monkey puzzle tree and stirred the warm air. Jez flicked his tail.

"If those two reprobate grandads of ours kept their secret for two hundred years, then so can we." Henry's lips brushed against George's.

"Let's go and lay this on our boys' graves," George told him tenderly, touching his fingertips to the rose. "They've been forgotten for too long."

Henry took Lady Georgina's arm again and they wandered along the path of the stream, beside the pink and blue hydrangeas and the waxy-leaved rhododendrons with their purple blooms, past the mallows and the foxgloves and the lavender buzzing with bees. They went farther and farther into the reaches of the garden, until Henry gestured toward the grove of trees before them. The branches stretched up to form a green lattice ceiling overhead.

"See, George—it's The Seven. Although more accurately The Five, now, thanks to that hurricane when we were little. The sundial is right in the middle. Can you see it? I cleared away as much of the bramble as I could."

But George was already on his way to the sundial, towing Henry along behind him into the shelter of The Five. George picked his way closer to the monument, the trainers on his feet crushing the remaining bramble cuttings beneath them.

"They stood here, Fitz," George said with wonder in his voice. "Billy and Tobias stood right here, just like us, and remembered."

"And I doubt anyone else has been here since. Because who would look at a sundial where the trees obscure the sun? Even back then, these trees would've been quite tall."

Henry bowed his head. His voice took on the soft quality it always assumed when he spoke of other people's pets. "I hope Nimrod was a good friend to Rupert."

"The best."

"I wish I still had my dog. Then he could've been Jez's friend."

"He was a lovely old boy." George smiled. "If you wanted to look for another dog— Well, I'll be in the village working on my next book, so I could dog-sit if you needed it."

"That'd be very kind—George, you're going to stay, aren't you? In Longley Parva, I mean."

George nodded. "The job will take me off from time to time but I want to really buckle down to Georgie's bio, and I can do that here. I owe my publisher at least two books, so they'll be happy, and I've a feeling there're a lot of *Secret Histories* to be told here in the good old British Isles!"

He took the rose and, with a reverence Henry had rarely seen George display, put it down atop the sundial. Then he closed his eyes and bowed his head as though engaged in a silent prayer for the two faithful companions who rested here, hidden away from the world.

Henry held his breath while George paid his respects. *He's going to stay!* Surely George would be able to hear how loudly Henry's heart was beating in the quiet of the grove? He wanted to jump into the air and click his heels together and shout *Hooray!* But that seemed somewhat undignified. He lowered his head, thinking of Rupert, and Nimrod and the late faithful Dave, Border Collie extraordinaire, who had been buried under a camellia when Henry was eighteen.

If he could save the manor, then he would ask George to live here with him. But not yet. Because if his home was wrenched from him, then where would he go? The wind sighed above them again and the branch tapped his shoulder. Henry turned to brush it away, but there was no branch there. Only a shimmer on the air that fast disappeared before his eyes.

"I think I'm going mad in this heat. I could've sworn —" But there was no one there besides a vet, a television personality and a gangly-legged foal.

Must be the heat, Henry decided, and he put his arm around George's waist, resting his head against his lover's.

"I think," George's voice was still quiet, but rich with mischief in place of contemplation, "that Rupert, Nimrod and Dave the magnificent dog are having a hell of a time somewhere."

He turned his head to capture Henry's mouth with his own, leaving yet more of Georgina's rouge on his lips.

"Come for a swim? Let's leave Tobe and Billy to pay *their* respects?"

Henry stared at George in amazement as they began to walk away. Whispering, to avoid disturbing the other visitors to the sundial, Henry asked, "So you felt it too?'

His answer was to shrug and comment casually, "Why would anybody want to leave? They love it here as much as we do."

"Then we have to save the manor, don't we? We can't let Ed get his mitts on it."

"I've got a fair bit of cash going spare and it's yours if you need it, but I'm nowhere near Ed levels of green." George clicked his tongue, clearly musing on the problem. "But you leave it with old Georgie, he'll sort it. Don't ask *how*, just know that I will."

"I still haven't hired a property lawyer — if you could lend me the money for that, it would be brilliant."

Henry nudged his friend. "*Lend*, that is—I will most definitely pay you back. Whatever happens."

They blinked as they emerged from the shady half of the garden back into the sunlight where the lake glittered before them.

"Now, enough of lawyers and money and worrying, swimming awaits!" George pecked Henry's cheek and untangled their arms. He stepped out of his trainers and moved to unfasten his shorts, leaving Henry to assume that his companion must be wearing trunks. Not so, for the shorts fell away to reveal boxers, then George's hands were on the waistband, clearly about to shed what remained of his clothing.

"Erm—hang on there, George!" Henry turned quickly to look at the driveway. It was empty. The heat of the day hung silent and heavy over the quietened village. "What if someone turns up? What if they see?"

"They'll see the straightest man on telly and the straightest man in Sussex swimming?"

"In the nude!"

"Do people just call by unannounced often?" As he awaited the response, George dropped his boxers and stepped out of them. Then he set his sunglasses and watch down atop his discarded clothes, shedding the very last remnants of the world.

"N-no one ever calls." Henry knew it was rude to stare, but George, standing there stark naked beside the lake, muscled and masculine from toes to neck, feminine in the face, was the most erotic sight Henry had ever seen. He couldn't look away. A noise escaped his mouth. It might have been "Oh my God," but Henry wasn't entirely sure.

"Are you coming in?" George held out his hand. "You look terribly hot and bothered, it'll be nice."

Swim? Without swimming trunks, without a towel – without a bloody care in the world!

"If a chap can't swim naked in his own bloody lake, then what, I ask you, is the world coming to?" Had Henry just said that? He appeared to have done. And it was Henry who was untying his shoes as fast as he could and had his shirt off before he could remember his scar, pulling it over his head to save time unbuttoning it. Once he had dropped his trousers, it became obvious that his boxer shorts could do very little to conceal his appreciation at the sight of George's nudity, so he took a deep breath and asked, "Should I? Or am I too indecent to go naked?"

"You're the most marvelous sight I've ever seen." George's gaze swept over Henry's naked body, the sunlight leaving him with no hope of hiding the scar, but there was nothing in those green eyes but love and – there was no avoiding it – *passion.*

Who would ever have thought it?

"Come on then, you can't go swimming in your underwear, after all." George put his hands on his hips and affected a stern look. "It's not *British*, old boy!"

Henry gave him a lopsided grin and swept his hand through his hair. "All right. I'll do it. We always used to dare each other – we haven't changed so much!"

Henry dropped his boxer shorts and kicked them away. He stood there in his own garden, by his own bloody lake, the warm sun on his skin and the light breeze ruffling his hair.

"I feel free!" Henry punched the air, then ran down to the lake's edge, where he flung himself at the water in an enthusiastic but clumsy dive.

"Go on!" George gave a cry of encouragement and ran down after him, tucking his knees into his chest as he bombed down into the water just as he always had done in boyhood. The bigger surprise came when Jez followed them down to the edge and touched the surface of the lake with his velvety muzzle. He drew back a little and walked a few more feet, occasionally brushing the surface until, with a small, tentative movement, he stepped down into the water. It wasn't deep here, rising to just above Jez's knees, and he stood happily, swishing his tail and surveying this new, unexpected world.

Henry moved his arms in figure-of-eights to keep afloat, then kicked his way through the water over to George.

"Jez seems to like the lake as much as his dad does!"

"*Dads*, Fitz." He looped his arms around Henry's neck. "If you don't mind?"

"I would love to be Jez's dad." Henry pecked a kiss to George's mouth. Miraculously, despite his dive-bombing, George's makeup had stayed put. It was like swimming with a very sexy Georgian water nymph. "What a handsome son we have!"

"And don't think I've forgotten that you *must* have a dog!"

"You'll have to help me choose one. A fresh-faced puppy? Or some poor old loveable sod with one eye and a broken tail?"

"We don't need to stop at one, do we? Whatever, though, let's make it a rescue like Jez?"

"I wouldn't have anything else."

As Henry kissed George again, holding him close, enjoying the sensation of their wet skin touching, he wondered just how much swimming they would get done. The kiss went on and on, their bodies tight together as the water soothed him after the rigors of the afternoon.

A horse, dogs, George staying in the village — everything was perfect. The only fly in the ointment drove a Ferrari and wore tasteless belts. But at this moment, Henry didn't want that odious man anywhere near his thoughts. He kissed his lover with renewed passion, to push away the unwanted thoughts that would otherwise crowd in on him. Their legs tangled, and they rose and fell in the water as they held on to each other. Henry ran his fingertips down George's spine to the dimple just above his pert bottom and circled it there.

A soft moan of approval escaped George's lips into the kiss and Henry felt his lover's hands come to rest on his own bottom in a firm, rather determined grip. He certainly wouldn't get swept away, that was for certain. George's breath seemed to be coming quicker than ever with each second that passed and he shifted his hips, his erection pressing against Henry's.

Between kisses, Henry whispered, "I owe you for yesterday evening. Don't like to be in a gentleman's debt."

Under the water, he closed his hand around George's erection. His strokes were slowed by the weight of the water, the sensations all the keener as he felt every contour of his lover's cock in his hand. In reply, George took Henry's erection in his palm, echoing his movements. His grip was firm and sure, his kisses deeper than ever. What magic had George worked on him? A week ago he had been grumping about alone, buttoned tightly in tweed. Now he was naked in the lake, in the arms of the man he loved. And on this perfect summer afternoon, they were making plans for the future. *Their* future.

"I'll never hurt you," George whispered, nuzzling Henry's jaw. "I swear it."

"I know you won't. And I'll never hurt you."

George's hand tightened on Henry, the strokes faster. Henry increased his efforts in response, his hips bucking against George's hand as he moaned with the pleasure George gave him. He felt George's other hand slide across his buttocks, caressing and stroking beneath the surface of the water and all the time those soft, erotic groans in his throat, a sound of utter abandon.

George's wonderful racket filled Henry's ears, the water rippling and splashing around them as they brought each other to pleasure. They kissed deeply, tongues sliding together. Henry's moans turned into a cry of joy as his hips jerked forward and he came in his lover's arms. He shivered as his orgasm trembled on, dutifully bringing George higher and higher, the groans in George's throat singing of love and lust.

"Fitz!" Henry's name — the name *George* called him — was torn from his lover in a cry of delight. His hips moved hard against Henry's hand, then he sank against him, his climax playing itself out in soft moans and gentle thrusts.

They embraced, drifting in the lake, gazing at each other with happy, lazy smiles.

Henry rested his lips against George's ear. "You looked so beautiful when you came. If I hadn't felt your skin against mine, I wouldn't have believed you were real."

"I'm real and I'm yours." George stroked his face. "Always."

They kissed slowly, the water lapping against them. Henry felt the bottom of the lake against the soles of his feet as they moved into the shallows.

"We'll never make the Olympic team if we swim like that, Captain George! Although there might be an opening in a very *specialized* synchronized event."

"Look at Jez."

The horse had ventured out farther and was merrily paddling up to his knees, tossing his mane with delight. George let his chin rest on Henry's shoulder and watched with a soft smile, the foal seemingly oblivious to anything other than the delightful coolness of the lake.

Chapter Twenty-One

Steph's satin dress, hand-picked by an expert from a vintage shop in Paris, hung on the back of the wardrobe door. When she had tried it on, Steph had been ecstatic to discover that it clung in all the right places, with a neckline that plunged as low as it could without leading to arrest.

She glanced at the dress over her shoulder as she brushed her hair.

"Captain George'll be putty in my hands, Ed-babes."

"He better bloody be, Stephy, because that damned vet seems to hang on his every word, from what I've heard." Ed tipped his golf clubs onto the bed and sat beside them, a cleaning cloth in his hand. "You want to watch that. You sure Brookes isn't pally with him again?"

"Henry chased George out of his garden. Does that sound like someone being *pally* to you?"

"He's going to have to get bloody pally sharpish, though, isn't he? Because he's the only person Henry ever listened to!" He scowled at a clod of mud on the end of an expensive five iron. "I want a contract for the TV series and I want Brookes leaning heavily on the bloody vet to hand over the house."

"Hasn't that old woman rung you yet, the one you gave your card to?" Steph had visions of enormous television cameras rolling away from her, out of reach. No series on the telly for her thanks to her useless husband. "Anyway, it's a careful balance. George is still nostalgic for our childhoods—at least that's the impression I got. And I'll work it in our favor. I'm a master manipulator, Ed-babes—I'm always playing people off against each other. Just you wait and see."

Yes, just you wait and see, Ed-babes, when the divorce papers land on your desk and your ex-wife whisks George off to the Maldives for a wedding that will grace the pages of Hello!

Steph wiped a cotton pad across her face, trying to remove her triumphant smirk. But Ed hadn't looked up from his golf clubs.

"He still hasn't replied to the lawyer's letter—I reckon he's going to cave, Steph." Ed laughed. "That lad who went mental with the cricket bat way back when wouldn't cave, but timid old Henry the vet will. He's not got two pennies to rub together. I just need to lean on him a little bit more and he'll give up the manor to us. And then good ol' Randy will find out that he's not the only one who drives a hard bargain."

Ed chipped at the mud, affecting a New York accent. "Fifty million for a shitty flea-bitten house, Mr. Belcher?"

"Why yes, Mr. Cheese," he was himself again, "or there'll be no Cheese Acres Golf Resort. You play Ed Belcher, you're gonna lose. Cheese or no Cheese, this is *my* land, and I'm the only one who pisses on it!"

Steph tittered, imagining Ed as he picked up that copy of *Hello!*, his ex-wife with her new husband posing for the cameras, smiling while Ed was utterly crushed. "You should go up there now and piss in that precious lake! He always banged on about the newts — but then he has a lot in common with them. Little and slithery, slinking about in the dark."

"You know what I *should* do? I'm going to nail him where no man can resist." He stood and mimed a swing with the club. "I'm going to offer him half a mill cash right there on his doorstep, and he'll kiss my feet. He's all high morals now, but wait until he's staring down a five hundred-k gun barrel, Stephanie."

Steph giggled inanely, but behind her rictus grin was the horrible thought — *if Ed resolved the issue of the manor now, then what about George?*

There was still the TV contract, of course. Surely Ed would allow her to continue her flirtation for the sake of that?

"He's a miserable skinflint, is Henry." Steph sniffed. "I bet he's got fifty-pound notes stuffing his mattresses. He's probably far richer than any of us can imagine. He'll laugh at your half a mil. Go on — offer him three-quarters!"

Steph eyed Ed carefully in the mirror. She enjoyed watching the kaleidoscope of colors that his face changed through whenever he was on the precipice, about to part with more money than he intended. From white, to puce, to blushing pink, to a worrying purple that signaled the early signs of a coronary. If only she were an artist and could capture the colors on canvas.

"No," he decided eventually. "It's half or nothing. He says no, you need to flash the flesh at Brookes and Brookes needs to lean on his mate. If that doesn't work, it's court and I'll bankrupt the fucker. Either way, I'm getting that house and holding a gun to Mr. Billionaire Cheese's head."

He put his fingers to his temple and mimed pulling the trigger, then laughed.

"I'd say you should shag Fitzwanker and get the house that way, but I don't reckon he fucks *anything*, let alone the sexiest girl in Sussex. Eh, Stephy, eh? Only one man puts it to you and it's not Fitztwat. Brookes too. He can touch as much as he likes, but he's not putting his cock anywhere it shouldn't go, right?" He assumed a high-pitched voice, obscene and wheedling. "*Ooh, Georgie, you can give Stephy one after you've convinced Henry that he'd be better off without his house. Stephy'll be waiting in her best knickers as soon as the papers are signed!*"

Steph pushed back the velvet-upholstered stool at the dressing table and stalked toward her delightful husband. She walked him back toward the bed and pushed him down with one nudge of the shoulder. Parting her silk dressing gown to reveal her tan, bare legs, she straddled his hips.

"Well, darling, I *am* a monumental prick-tease." She smiled as Ed chuckled between her legs. "There wasn't any sex for my Ed-babes until our wedding night, was there? And no sex at all for television's George Standish-Brookes — as my darling husband wishes."

Until the moment the divorce comes through.

Steph brought down Ed's zip and lightly dug her manicured nails into his testicles.

"Not now, Stephy," he told her. "I'm thinking about money. Get your arse over to the safe and pull out half a mill, I'm off to have a fucking laugh at Fitzwanker."

She dug her nails in a little more.

"We're going to get that manor, and we're going to do whatever it takes, aren't we, Ed-babes? But just remember, darling, your Stephy-Steph is easily upset sometimes. You have to let your Stephy-Steph have her treats."

"You've got your credit cards," he told her snappily. "Now get over there and fetch the cash. Are you coming to watch the show?"

Steph trotted through the thick, spongy carpet toward the enormous oil painting of their daughter. It was attached to the wall with a hinge, and Steph swung it outward to open the safe. She pressed her lips tightly together as she counted out the wads of notes.

Ed picked up his club again, swinging merrily at the air.

"I'm going to be the next Cheese, bigger than Sugar, bigger than Trump, big as a big fucking fat pair of swinging balls!" Ed declared. "Lord and Lady Belcher!"

You'll be as small and shriveled as your own dick by the time I've got my dues from the prenup.

"Lady Steph has a certain ring to it, doesn't it!" *As does Sir George.* She clanked the safe shut and swung the oil painting back. For a moment, her unfortunate daughter grinned back at her.

Why did the poor girl have to resemble her father? It's so very difficult to love the child.

Steph slunk back to the bed and chucked the money onto the shiny duvet.

"There you are! And I'm not coming—I'll stay here and buff my toenails."

How long would her husband be gone? Half an hour, perhaps. She'd text George.

No – Snapchat him. A smiley, friendly face and a bit of cleavage. Get him in the mood for tomorrow's dance.

Chapter Twenty-Two

The past few days had drifted by as if Henry and George were floating along a river, hands dangling in the water as they traveled it together. They had met every evening, and shared a meal, laughed and kissed, and slept through the night in each other's arms. *'We're still courting,'* they told each other, so held back from *that moment*, the intimate bodily connection that they both yearned for. But it would happen. *'It'll be very special if we wait.'* Although Henry wasn't sure he could wait all that much longer.

This evening, George had been at the village hall with the production crew, getting everything ready for the dance tomorrow. Like a groom hidden from the wedding preparations, George had insisted Henry stay at home — with the promise that George would come to the manor as soon as they were set up.

Henry was waiting with a brandy in his armchair, looking through a list of potential pets that he'd picked up from their nearest dog shelter. It was so hard to choose when he would willingly have given all of them a home.

A knock sounded loud and heavy on the front door. It didn't sound like George, but even so — *Ed Belcher*.

Bloody hell.

"Henry!" Belcher held a closed briefcase. "I've been thinking and I've not done right, putting pressure on you over your old house. It's not the way old school mates should do business."

"Good. Then that means you'll sod off and stop blathering on about some old bet between a gang of drunken hoorays two hundred years ago." Henry made to push the door shut, but Ed interposed himself.

"I've got a cool half mil here in used notes. Let's shake hands here and now and do the deal."

"Are you high, Ed? Are you hallucinating? Can you see an estate agent's *for sale* board in my front garden that is otherwise invisible to every other living soul? What part of *my house is not for sale* do you find so hard to understand?"

"A grand an *hour*, that's what you're looking at for the sort of lawyer who can see off my people." Ed sneered. "One. Thousand. Pounds. Per. Hour. What can you afford, Fitzwanker? Thirty minutes, maybe? Take the money, buy a little place, sit back and pay a girl to lick caviar off your balls. Let Eddie Belcher take this money pit off your hands."

Why had Steph chosen to marry such a grotesque bully?

Bad Billy Fitzwalter would've fought tooth and nail for his home, and so would Henry. Until he had nothing left, he would fight — for the house he had grown up in, for the lake that he and George had loved in, for the grove of trees where the centuries collapsed in on themselves and the dead still walked.

"Take that shiny little briefcase of yours and shove it, *mate*. Because I'm not being bought and I'm not being bullied. You're not having my house. *My* house—*not* yours. My lawyer will be in touch! Go on, Ed—shove off!" Henry gripped Ed's shoulder. He found his hand mainly full of foam padding, but he forced Ed to turn ninety degrees anyway. "There you go—there's the gate. That's where you came in at, and that's where you're sodding off to. Bye-ee!"

"Don't ever say that I didn't try and do this the right way, Fitzwanker. I'll ruin you!" Ed walked back to the Ferrari, the case swinging in his hand. On reaching the supercar he opened the door and hurled the case inside, then he turned to remind Henry, "And don't forget, company accounts are public record, Fitzprick! I know *exactly* how much your business is pulling down and it's not buying you an hour with Judge Judy, I can tell you that much!"

He climbed into the sports car, gunned the engine and roared off down the drive, his hand slammed hard against the horn as he went.

Henry pulled his cricket bat out of the umbrella stand. Its heft felt good in his hands. As much as he would've enjoyed ramming the bat between Ed's legs, the only balls Henry was going to hit that evening were cricket balls. Shouldering his bat, he sauntered down his driveway, headed for the practice nets at the cricket club—an hour walloping leather against willow would be a perfect end to the day.

And tomorrow, they would be dancing.

Chapter Twenty-Three

It was a pleasant evening for a walk so, back in his best, freshly dry-cleaned tweeds, Henry made his way to the village hall. A flow of people drifted from their cottages along the street toward the dance in their best approximation of 1940s costumes. Some appeared to have hired their outfits from fancy dress shops, while others had cobbled them together from the backs of their wardrobes.

"Love the costume, vet'n'ry!"

Henry waved politely. Smokers and vapers were lounging about the car park and a large white van signaled the presence of the television crew. He couldn't see George's car. George, who had insisted Henry get ready at the manor, because he had *'things to do'*.

If only he and George could dance together. Music was already spilling from the opened doors of the hall. Henry wasn't too bad a dancer, really, having been sent to classes by his mother, thinking it would cure him of his clumsiness. It hadn't worked, but at least he could dance.

He nearly tripped over a cable as soon as he came in through the door. Mrs. Dalrymple pressed a drink into his hand, patting her hair as a compact television camera swooped by.

"Orange squash!"

"Perfect!" *Oh, for something stronger.*

The lights were low and Henry gazed about the room at the decorations. Reproduction posters declared 'Dig for Victory', 'Loose Lips Sink Ships', 'We Can Do It!' and 'Look Out in the Blackout'. Bunting and paper chains and balloons looped around the room. Someone in a gas mask was chasing small children dressed in home-knitted tank tops and cotton frocks. The camera followed them. It wasn't George in the gas mask, was it? It seemed like a very George thing to do. But the figure in the half-light pulled off the mask—it was the vicar. Henry laughed and took a swig of his orange juice. There was so much sugar in it, it made his teeth rattle.

The camera operator moved toward Henry, so Henry raised his hand and waved. Then, remembering that people in documentaries often behaved as if the camera was invisible to them, he assumed an air of gravitas. He lifted his chin, put one hand in his pocket and stared away across the room, toward the 1970s brocade curtains that hung in front of the stage. He held his pose until he was aware of the camera moving away again, and just as he was about to turn, he saw a figure by the piano on the far side of the hall.

Captain George Standish-Brookes of the Household Cavalry was leaning rakishly, one elbow atop the piano, and gazing at him.

Oh God.

Henry remembered now the gleaming buttons George had been polishing, lounging across his chair in cricket whites, a bright-red mess jacket in his lap. Now he wore that mess jacket with its gold buttons and trousers the color of midnight, a row of medals gleaming across his chest and, in pride of place, the DSO. He was at the center of a crowd of admirers and holding court as ably as ever, but his eyes were fixed on Henry, a mischievous light dancing there. He looked as though he had stepped out of the past, from a cinema screen sometime in the 1940s, and for all those admiring young ladies who flocked to surround him, George Standish-Brookes, *the hero*, was Henry's.

And Henry was his.

Then, lazily, perfectly beautifully, he gave a casual salute.

What a vision. Henry forced himself not to gape, not to make it obvious. Everyone would see it in his face — not just the Parvans in the village hall, but it would be beamed into front rooms and streamed onto computers across the country. The vet gazing with longing and love at the handsome soldier. Even so, Henry's feet decided for him and he took a step forward. Nothing wrong with bidding the fellow good evening, after all.

A sharp elbow in his side stopped him.

Steph. And she was headed straight for George.

From what Henry could see of her as she shoved by, she had spruced up well, but everything about her screamed *expensive*, everything about her outfit was obscene compared to the make-do and mend costumes of the Parvans. She barged aside the girls who were talking to George and with an expression that Henry couldn't read, George's eyes shifted to Steph. George smiled and moved forward to kiss her on both cheeks. The camera focus moved to catch them. It was almost imperceptible but Henry saw it—the television would love this glamorous lady of the manor.

She will dance with George.

What were they saying to each other? If only Henry could hear. Maybe George was just being polite. They'd all been at school together, after all, and it wasn't as if he could give her the cold shoulder in this crowded room, with television cameras ready to capture everything and with very un-1940s mobile phones snapping away.

But why was Ed grinning? Ed, standing under a poster of a cartoon Hitler with airplanes raining bombs down on him. Ed who had come done-up as a slightly slimmer Churchill, complete with unlit cigar. Didn't Ed mind that his wife was leading George out onto the dance floor? Didn't that bother him at all?

Trumpets blared out *In the Mood* and Henry had to drag his attention away from George and Steph as they whirled across the dance floor, Steph's eyes wide and unblinking like a shark's.

"Henry!" Churchill raised his hat to Henry. "You didn't have to worry about fancy dress, eh?"

Henry raised Churchill his own V-salute in reply and swallowed down his orange squash. Too late he realized that the camera, now at the far end of the room, had managed to capture George and Steph dancing as well as Henry in the background, on the edge of the dance floor, sticking two fingers up at his tormentor.

Mrs. Dalrymple grabbed Henry by the arm. She took the empty paper cup from his hand, and although "A dance, Mr. Fitzwalter?" was phrased like a question, it was, clearly, an order. Henry let her take him onto the floor. He put his hand on her comfortable hip, his other on her shoulder.

The camera hove into view again, catching Henry's smooth footwork as he glided Mrs. Dalrymple around the hall. She seemed to be enjoying herself, her rouged cheeks reminding Henry of the last time he'd seen the Munchkins in *The Wizard of Oz*. Her hand was somewhat mobile across Henry's broad back, and he noticed her throwing out the occasional beaming smile at her friends, who waved back at her.

Henry felt someone's gaze on him and realized it was George's.

That bloody jacket.

Henry thought back once again, as he had many times over the years, to that moment when George had swung open the changing room curtain and appeared there before him in that jacket—the gold buttons, the braid, the bright-red fabric. He had looked so handsome back as a teenager, but now, as a man, it knocked Henry sideways to see him in it.

But he had to keep dancing. Couldn't gape. It really wouldn't do.

Look away, George, for God's sake, look away.

Henry swallowed and smiled down at Mrs. Dalrymple.

"Did you like Captain George's makeup?" Lil called the question as she glided past in the arms of her boyfriend. She was a land girl, he a squaddie. Once again it seemed as though time in Longley Parva were standing still.

"Yes!" Henry called to her over the music. *He had looked beautiful.* "Historically accurate, I thought."

"My turn now!" Mrs. Arbuthnott, in green dungarees and wellingtons—not far removed from her usual get-up—tried to peel Mrs. Dalrymple out of Henry's arms. "You can't have the vet all to yourself."

"Goodness—it's all right—I don't mind—" Henry glanced round in time to notice that the camera was on him again. Of course it was, a man in tweed was being fought over by the two leading lights of the WI.

"Let's share him, Mrs. A.!"

"Oooh, a threesome!" Mrs. Arbuthnott giggled and slotted herself in.

Bloody hell.

Henry kept going, not quite sure how he managed it, the television camera following. In his mind, he could hear Tabitha. *'This'll make brilliant telly.'*

And all the while, red and gold flashed in the corner of his eye. George. His George. And he couldn't dance with him.

You Do Something to Me began to play, and Henry felt his heart squeeze. Oh, why couldn't he dance with George, in the village hall, in front of everyone? Why was he forced to hide how he felt? It was like being in a wartime film about furtive homosexuals in the blackout. Surely the world had moved on from that?

Apparently not. Because George was so charming, smiling as he danced Steph right through Henry's path. Steph, her bosom pert, her teeth bared, her eyes wide.

Henry and his harem had to divert their path and went flying straight into the folding chairs.

"Oh, Christ, my bloody knee!"

It had all been captured on camera, of course. Gripping his leg, Henry hobbled about, resurrecting the scattered furniture. He looked over his shoulder at George and Steph, all laughs and smiles, dancing with their arms around each other, and Henry realized that he couldn't bear to spend another moment in this room.

He politely shoved his way out of the village hall and strode across the lane. Resting on the stile, he stared out across the empty field.

"What the devil was that display, soldier?" A figure leaned on the fence beside him, the early evening sunlight shining from buttons and medals, each one a tiny flame. "Running out on a lady or four?"

"Display?" Henry rounded on him. Why did George have to be so bloody attractive? He would've brought him into his arms if it hadn't been for the smokers in the car park. Or the entire population of Longley Parva being only meters away in the village hall. With a film crew. "I've hurt my bloody leg—I need some air."

"I'm sorry you've hurt your leg, Fitz." George patted his elbow and smiled. "Because I was hoping you'd do me the honor of a dance."

"A-a dance? With you—with all the village here? And the cameras? George—what will people say?"

"I'll ask the crew not to film it and the locals will think it's just Fitz and Standy-Bee having a lark." He shrugged. "But your leg's not good, so—"

Henry grabbed George's hand, but promptly let it go.

"It was only a knock—I can still dance." Henry leaned in and whispered, "I'll probably have a bruise, but you'll kiss it better, won't you?"

"Every bit of you, darling," he purred.

Henry shoved his hands into his pockets, the only reliable way to prevent himself from reaching for his lover.

He lowered his voice as they walked back to the hall. "Careful, or we'll be dancing horizontally over the refreshments table…"

"Or in a four-poster." Then, for a man who seemed so protective of his heterosexual image, George seemed to throw caution to the wind. His hand shot out with the same speed with which it had almost amputated Ed Belcher's ear, but this time, his fingers closed around nothing more delicate than Henry's tie. Then he turned on the heel of one mirror-shined boot and, with Henry's tie still gripped over his shoulder, marched his *private* back into the hall.

Henry was certain that the residents of this most quintessential English village had never seen anything quite like the sight of Captain George Standish-Brookes in full, uniformed flight, a captive vet following *very* close behind, and it was a sight that few would forget in a hurry. With a quick wave to the camera operator that clearly meant this wasn't to be filmed, George cut a dash through the near-swooning ladies.

Henry didn't care anymore. *Sod it, sod it all.* He followed Captain George onto the dance floor, where they laid their hands very properly on each other at waist and shoulder. Not a hint of impropriety could be seen. This was two chaps having a lark. But still, they had their arms around each other in public, and instead of scandal and horror, there was no reaction from the Parvans other than laughter and smiles.

Mrs. Dalrymple and Mrs. Arbuthnott appeared beside them, dancing cheek-to-cheek, with smiles broader than the time that Mrs. Arbuthnott's champion marrow had won first prize at the summer fête.

"Ladies." George gave a very polite nod. "You dance marvelously together."

Henry let his lips brush George's neck, a fleeting movement that could have been an accident — but wasn't.

George closed his eyes and whispered, "I am *so* bloody happy, Fitz."

"As am I, Standy-Bee."

"You're the belle of the ball." George laughed as they moved through the cheering crowd, their dance as elegant as it was joyous.

"No, no, that's you—you never look more handsome than when you're in this get-up."

"Well, I thought a night like this called for mess dress. No doubt they'll want a few pick-up shots of me actually putting it on but—" He tossed his head and assumed a diva attitude. "The things one does for one's art!"

"You always were a show-off," Henry whispered affectionately.

The good-natured laughter of the Parvans was disturbed by the hooting, mocking laughter of Winston Churchill and his satin-clad floozy.

"Has Ed spiked the orange squashes? What's he finding so funny?" Henry danced himself and George out of range of the Belchers' guffaws. His partner's response was to shrug as though it was nothing, and perhaps it wasn't. Henry had a lawyer now and he had George and maybe that would be enough to see off Ed Belcher's threat to the manor.

"Jez is having a sleepover party with Lil's donkeys," George told him. "He's visiting friends whilst his parents go dancing!"

"I'm glad our son is making friends in the village." Henry could've easily kissed George there and then, but he pressed his lips together in a tight line to stave off temptation.

A flash went off on someone's camera phone. Henry squinted in the bright light. He heard giggling. Another flash fired.

"Your fan club are in tonight, George!"

George shrugged and said, "Television's straightest man having a lark!"

Henry grinned. He felt naughty. Reckless. Bad Billy Fitzwalter was twitching their shared DNA. "What would you do, though, George, if they guessed?"

"Tabs and Howard — my agent — they seem to think it would be an amazing career move." George frowned and shook his head. "I don't know, though, my image isn't really that, is it? I worry I'd end up — Do you think I'd ever work again?"

"Because you love a man? Why would that stop you from ripping off your shirt and climbing up a mountain?"

"*Fitz!*" George's voice was a warning whisper and he widened his eyes, clearly intending to indicate that walls have ears. "I remember how it was in the Army. You didn't ask and you *definitely* didn't tell."

"But if people found out that I'm — I'd get some joshing, I bet, but —" Henry swallowed. "Perhaps you're right. I don't know anything about showbiz. Look — perhaps you should dance with one of the ladies again. Keep everyone from guessing."

But it hurt. That the sight of them dancing together was a joke, and that George wanted to keep their love secret. What else could he do, though, when George was the only man he had ever wanted? The only *person*. And surely showbiz was one world where it *didn't* matter? If anything, wouldn't it just *widen* George's fan club? But what did a provincial vet know?

The song drew to an end and George asked him, "Are you going to take off, Fitz? You look a bit — Are you all right?"

"I'm fine." Henry's abrupt, tight-lipped reply was, he hoped, enough to let George know that he wasn't. But not enough to cause a scene. Not enough for anyone to know, or guess, that television's straightest man had, that very morning, enjoyed mutual hand jobs with him against the Aga in the kitchen of Longley Parva Manor. Heaven forbid that anyone knew *that*.

"I have my own fan club, thank you, George. Small and select though it is, I shan't be short of dance partners."

"And later?" His gaze searched Henry's, no longer impish, but filled with concern. "Will we see each other tonight? Don't be angry with me, Fitz."

If only all the bloody people would clear the room and allow Henry to say what really needed to be said. Even a reassuring pat on the arm was impossible. Over the noise of music and conversation, Henry had to lean close to George's ear.

"Your place or mine?"

"That depends if you want a ride in the Jaguar first."

"Pleasant evening for a spin — why not?"

"Why not indeed?" George's green eyes gleamed with happiness. "I'll even take the top down."

"Makes a change from the top *off*." Henry gave him two matey slaps to his cheek. "Meet you after the raffle? Let's squire the ladies about for an hour or two, like the red-blooded heterosexuals we are."

"I'm drawing the ticket." George stepped away from Henry. "I hope you win something!"

Henry tried not to laugh at the prizes arranged on the stage. "That Thermos flask could come in useful, but I'm not too sure about the basket of lady's bubble baths."

"I've got a couple of hundred tickets in the barrel!" Ed slapped his hand down on Henry's shoulder. "Might be a Belcher landslide!"

"All those tickets for charity, and you might win a car blanket or a sharing platter for two at The Green Man?" Henry smiled falsely. "You're the soul of generosity, aren't you, Ed?"

"That's the general idea, mate." Ed smiled toward the camera. "Can't take my millions with me, after all!"

Realizing the camera was on him again, Henry assumed the mantle of phony bonhomie and laughed, patting Ed's shoulder.

"How true that is! The whole lot could be gone tomorrow in a stock market crash! Ha ha! Imagine!" Henry inclined his face toward Ed's, which was struck by a fleeting, nervy look. "*Imagine.*"

"Let's just say that I've taken that into account," the millionaire assured him. "And that's *all* I'll say — I'm sure you follow."

Henry turned away and saw Barney, son of one of the farmers, talking animatedly to George. He had gussied up for the occasion, his hair an elegant plume. Henry had roped Barney in to help on numerous occasions when he needed a hand wrestling uncooperative livestock on the farm. He was a good lad.

What Henry hadn't quite expected was that Barney would talk George into dancing with him, but that was exactly what he had managed to do. And just as another camera flash went off, realization struck Henry. Barney was, possibly, gay. How had he never noticed? Perhaps seeing Henry and George whirl across the dance floor together had made Barney brave enough to seek a dance with a man himself.

"Mr. Fitzwalter?" There was a gentle pull at his sleeve and there, standing beside him, was Polly, the small, wide-eyed child of the village's underworked constable. He had last seen this little girl when she'd pronounced him a real-life wizard for saving the life of her Yorkshire terrier puppy after an overzealous leap from a high wall had nearly done for the little chap. She held up the little dog and said, "Will you hold Nancy so I can dance for a bit? I was going to ask Mum but Nancy wanted to hang out with the wizard again."

Henry chuckled, thinking of George's idea of playing their local wizard in the nip. "Yes, of course, let me hold him."

But just as Polly skipped away to her friends, there was another tug at Henry's arm.

"Mrs. Tanvir—how are you?"

"Very well. Nice dog! Now how about a dance?"

Henry looked about for someone to hold the dog for him, but with no one forthcoming, he slipped her into his large jacket pocket. "As long as you don't mind a third coming along for a ride?"

"Not at all!"

The camera operator appeared in Henry's face again, but he didn't mind. Yes, to the rest of the world, it probably would look a bit eccentric but, he realized, maybe it was endearing. He half-turned to the camera, giving his best angle. Not that he'd practiced in the mirror, of course. Heaven forbid.

And on and on they danced, Henry with his own fan club, George with anyone that asked, regardless of age or gender. The cameras whirred and flashes flashed and even Ed and Steph took a turn, though her grin wasn't half as bright as it had been for the village's favorite soldier. Nancy peeked out from Henry's tweed pocket, seemingly having the finest time any dog had ever had and attracting a fair few admiring glances herself.

George, a man who had never really *left* the 1940s in a lot of ways, had seen none of his fan club disappointed. The heroic Captain Standish-Brookes had earned his place among the pantheon of WI greats tonight, lending that most particular charm of his to any who hoped for a little glimpse of the fabled *twinkle* that had made many a duchess and even a couple of dukes flutter their eyelashes.

The closing bars of *We'll Meet Again* ended the evening. The Parvans flowed from the doors of the village hall into the gloaming, arms filled with raffle prizes. Even Ed had won a prize, though he looked far from happy with his basket of fungal foot powder treatments. Henry was a winner too, taking home an enormous poster of none other than George in full WWII RAF gear posing beside a Spitfire. Across it, in bold silver pen, he had written, 'Toot-Toot, George S-B xxx'.

Henry rolled his poster into a baton and tucked it under his arm. He lurked about in the car park, waiting for George to disentangle himself from his adoring public. Would it be odd if he hung the poster over his bed? Maybe put it up in the surgery somewhere? It would make a change from pharmaceutical adverts warning of fly strike and kennel cough.

"Fitz!" George emerged from the crowd at the door to the village hall and trotted over to where Henry waited. "I hoped I'd catch you. Can we have a quick couple of minutes about Jez? I can run you home while we talk if you like."

"Yes, yes — of course. Doing well, your little chap, I hope?"

"Splendidly." George strolled on, his hands behind his back. "And did I see you with a terrier in your pocket or was it something in the punch?"

"Oh — that. Yes. One of my patients! Seemed to enjoy it."

"Good, good." They ambled on in innocent silence for a minute or so, the twilight deepening around them. George's pale pink cottage was not hard to miss and with TV's famed Jaguar parked outside it with the top already lowered and its owner clad in the immaculate mess dress of his regiment, it was a promo calendar just waiting to happen. George unlocked the door and opened it for Henry, who put the poster behind the seat as he climbed in.

When George slipped into the driver's seat he turned to look at Henry and asked, "Did I look all right tonight? Would you let this dashing soldier sweep you off your feet?"

"Did you look all right?" Henry laughed and gently slapped his palm against George's thigh. "I had to remind myself to breathe, for heaven's sake! That jacket — it does things to me. All I can say is, I'm bloody relieved these trousers are loose-fitting! You handsome bloody bastard, Captain George."

"This old thing?" George blinked his long eyelashes. He reached to the top of the dozens of buttons of the tunic and unfastened a few, just enough to give a glimpse of the skin beneath. "Would you like me to keep going, Fitz?"

Henry squeezed George's firm, uniform-clad thigh. Barely opening his mouth, he groaned his answer.

"Yes. For God's sake, *yes*."

George glanced over his shoulder at the empty road, the few stragglers who remained from the dance having scattered to the winds and fast-arriving night. Then, with deliberate, delicious slowness, he unfastened the buttons of the mess jacket, revealing the body that was so familiar to Henry now. He felt as though he knew every contour of that muscled chest, every inch of the skin that he had kissed and teased and loved, but this was like seeing it afresh all over again, tan and forbidden beneath the immaculate uniform.

"Bloody hell, Captain George." Henry's voice was thick was desire. He sat forward in his seat, gazing at his lover. Gazing, but unable to draw any nearer. "I can't touch you, can I, here? Take me home."

George's movements were lazy as he reached to turn the ignition key, but the rise and fall of his chest betrayed his own need. When the Jaguar pulled away from the cottage it was at a *slightly* impatient speed, the lights falling on the tarmac as they peeled out into the empty road that would take them between fields and around the twisting lane that led to Longley Parva Manor.

The gates of the manor had rusted open long ago, so George entered the driveway unimpeded, heading up past the lake to Henry's front door. The trees were dark with the advancing night, birds looping across distant clouds, heading home to roost.

As soon as the engine was turned off, Henry had his arms around George, pressing his lips to his. All those people had crowded around his lover at the dance, clamoring for him, but it was Henry who was kissing him, Henry who was running his fingertips light and teasing down George's skin, exposed by the opened jacket.

"Dancing with you," George whispered, "was the most perfect thing."

"Would you like to dance with me again? *Without* an audience."

"I would love to," was the purred reply.

Henry combed his fingers through George's previously immaculate hair.

"Captain Standish-Brookes, would you do me the honor of accompanying me to the bedroom?"

"Mr. Fitzwalter, it would be my pleasure." George kissed Henry's lips softly. "Lead the way."

Henry proudly took George into Longley Parva Manor. A quick detour to the kitchen to collect a bottle of wine and glasses and they headed upstairs, kissing on every step.

The staircase still had portraits of Henry's family on it, but pale squares on the decrepit wallpaper showed where his father had sold the older, more valuable artworks. The landing above was silvered by the moon, which shone through the cracked glass of the skylight. It illuminated the way for the two lovers as they went along the corridor's worn and faded carpet.

"I haven't any music to dance to," Henry said, "so we'll just have to make up our own."

The door opened with little pressure as the handle had repeatedly dropped off and now served only as an ornament. Beyond, Henry's bedroom had blue wallpaper, over a century old, with a design of large paisley swirls across it. Henry put the bottle and glasses down on the bedside table and loosened his tie. George, already unbuttoned and rather ruffled, opened the bottle and filled the glasses. He held one out to Henry and said, "A toast?"

Henry took the glass.

"Yes, a toast. To us!"

They clinked their glasses together then, entwining their arms, drank deeply. This would be *their* home, Henry knew, because life was finally going right.

Henry put aside his glass and made a neat bow. "May I have this dance?" Henry tipped his head toward the roosting birds, who were calling in the trees outside the window. "The orchestra have struck up my favorite tune."

"What the hell did I do to deserve a man like you? I must've been a saint in a past life." George's words were a whisper. "I love you, Fitz."

"George, shush, you're making me blush."

And he was, too, because in the spotted mirror over the cracked washbasin, Henry caught sight of his face. He was reddening like a sunset.

"I like it when you blush." George smiled, taking another drink. "And what would you have this soldier do for you?"

"Dance with me." Henry looked from George's handsome face to that bare torso that peeped out from his unfastened mess jacket. His eyes settled on George's adoring gaze and he swallowed. "Then make love to me."

George put his glass down and took Henry in his arms. Then he drew their bodies together as they swayed to the melodic birdsong outside. They kissed softly, tenderly, the taste of wine in each other's mouths. Henry sank his hands into George's thick hair, bringing their faces closer, deepening their kiss. He loved this man so much — he wanted to possess and be possessed by him. George's arm was around his waist, pulling Henry ever closer to him, as if he would never let him go.

"Don't ever change, darling," George whispered against Henry's lips. Henry breathed in the scent of him, the exotic cologne and the fragrance of his skin, the indefinable *something* that he had fallen in love with decades ago. He had never believed himself to be much of a dancer but here, in the dim light, safe in his lover's arms, he could be anything.

"George, will you do something for me?" Henry laid his palm flat against George's exposed chest and stroked gently up and down the firm, warm skin, the brocaded edges of the jacket brushing Henry's hand.

"Anything."

"Now, far be it for me to kick up a fuss about you going topless on television. Nor will I complain if they film you in this splendid jacket of yours. But...when it's like this...half-on and half-off, your chest and your stomach peeking out — will you keep that just for us?"

Henry felt embarrassed even asking, let alone wanting such a thing. He bit his lip, watching George's glittering eyes. They lit up with love at the words and George nodded, promising, "It's ours, Fitz, I swear it."

"Thank you." Henry's reply was breathless as he returned to kissing George, sliding his other hand to the small of George's back. He could feel George's erection against his own, the heat that coursed through Henry's veins growing even warmer when his lover's hand crept down to rest on his bottom, stroking tenderly. "I want you, George, I mean it."

"Don't ever stop." Then they were kissing again and the hand on his bottom was still caressing, their dance having taken on a *very* slow, sensual pace by now.

"Help me out of this jacket, won't you?" Henry reluctantly brought his hands away from George so that he could pull his arms out of his tweed. With another kiss, George slid the jacket down from Henry's shoulders and it fell heavily onto the floor, but George was already nimbly unknotting Henry's tie. With a flamboyant gesture he threw it aside, the movement causing the medals at his chest to add their metallic percussion to the birdsong.

Henry ran his finger over the medals. He didn't want to turn them into a fetish, but he loved his courageous George.

"You've taught me to be brave," Henry whispered. "You didn't even intend to, but you have."

"No—" George's reply was a murmur. "You've always been the finest man I know."

Henry guided George's hand to his shirt buttons, their fingers moving together as they unbuttoned him, the soft rasp of fabric accompanied by Henry's sighs as George kissed each inch of skin as it became exposed. It seemed absurd now to think that he had ever worried what George might think of his body, because there was only love and the heat of passion in each touch. He slid the shirt off then they embraced, the smooth fabric and coolness of the medals pressing against Henry's bare skin. They tangled their fingers in each other's hair, gasping as they kissed, hips circling just a little where their erections pressed together.

"So," George teased as his hand slid round to press against Henry's trousers, "uniform on or off?"

"Is it exceptionally saucy of me to want you to keep the jacket on? Your trousers are fabulous too, but…I fear they might get in the way."

"Whatever my chap wants." He beamed.

Henry slipped his hand inside the waistband of George's trousers, sliding it down as far as he could before the immaculately tailored fabric stopped him.

"Imagine if we'd danced like *this* in the middle of the village hall!"

"They might've cried foul when you won that poster!"

"I had my eye on that. Glad I won it." Henry winked and stroked George's chest. "And I shall put it above my bed and kiss it every night before I go to sleep."

"What about the real me?" He pouted. "I'll be *in* your bed waiting to be kissed!"

"Every night?" Henry brought his hand round to the front of George's trousers and cupped his erection.

"Sorry, Fitz, rather cheekily moved myself in there, didn't I?" He smiled, bashful. "Bit full-on?"

"I wanted to ask you the other day, when you said you were going to look for somewhere." Henry lowered George's zip as he kissed his lover's ear. "But I didn't because I felt like such an idiot over all this business with the house. I can't ask you to move in and then I lose dear old Parvy Manor. But we'll be together whatever, won't we? We'll find somewhere."

"You're not going to lose this place, I gave you my word," George told him. "No matter what it costs, you won't lose it."

"I hope not — because I started clearing out one of the stables for Jez!" Henry paused, about to lower George's trousers down his hips. Was this an awkward moment to mention their equine son? George, however, kissed him again and unfastened Henry's belt and the button beneath. He slid his hand inside, beneath the waistband of his lover's boxers, until he could take Henry's erection in his palm. Henry tipped back his head and George kissed his way around his neck. It took Henry a moment to recover his senses enough to continue stripping George. The fabric susurrated as Henry skimmed George's trousers and boxer shorts down from his waist, freeing his erection. Henry sighed as he closed his hand around its firm heft.

"So if you're moving in—we're past the courting stage, aren't we?"

"First we'll send Ed packing, then we'll sort out the bedrooms." George's breath caught as his eyes closed at Henry's touch. "But we're definitely past courting."

"I'd say we're doing a capital job of sorting out this bedroom! If by that you mean wanton debauchery." Henry's hips moved against George's hand, stroking George's erection in time with his own thrusts. "And I'm so bloody glad we're past courting."

George kicked his boots off and stepped out of his pooled trousers, leaving him naked save for the bright-red jacket with its impressive array of decoration, and asked, "Shall we go to bed?"

"Yes—for heaven's sake, yes!"

George made short work of the few clothes that Henry still wore and, amid kisses and caresses, they were soon tumbling down onto the bed in each other's arms. He wasn't sure if he had expected George to agree to keep the jacket on, but the fact that he *had*— Well, it seemed like the most erotic thing Henry could imagine as he ran his hands from the rich fabric to the bare skin beneath it.

He gazed into George's dancing eyes and danced his finger from George's mouth, down his neck to his chest and farther down still until he ran it along George's cock.

"What is the captain's pleasure this evening?"

"To please the squire."

Henry kissed George's jaw, then caught his glance again. "That jacket melts me. When I first saw you in it,

I was so close to asking you, then and there, to pinion me against the wall and to just…just…" Henry sighed at the memory of it, aware that his cock had twitched in George's hand. "Ravish me."

"Do I get another medal for that?" George smiled a smile that might charm the devil up from hell, one eyebrow quirking. Then he dropped his head to Henry's chest and drew his tongue from his throat to his nipple, teasing and tempting.

Henry responded with an abandoned moan, the kind that, only a couple of weeks ago, he hadn't known he was capable of making.

"I would have, you know," George whispered against his skin. "Right there in the changing room, you and I."

"I've thought about it so often, I've lain here and imagined it and wished I'd said something. Wished so many things—" Henry stopped. *Wished I'd never accused you of stealing that bloody trophy.* He laughed because George was smiling and Henry suspected that he was thinking exactly the same thing.

"Doesn't matter now, because here we are." Then, his lips still tracing gentle patterns across Henry's torso, George admitted, "I've got medals but I don't have condoms. Tell me you planned ahead, darling?"

Henry beamed at him. "Of course I've got johnnies— I bought them the other day. And lube. No chap wants to get caught short like that, do they? Most inconvenient."

George's reply was to go lower still, drawing his tongue down Henry's erection. His hand, meanwhile, slipped around Henry's waist and over his bottom but this time—was Henry mistaken or was there the suggestion of a finger teasing just between his buttocks?

Henry sighed his lover's name.

And that finger slipped a little deeper, easing inside him. Now George's mouth was on his chest again, licking and kissing, his teeth grazing Henry's nipple. Soft sounds of pleasure rose in his throat and George responded by moving his finger, encouraging his lover on.

George's erection pressed against Henry's thigh. It promised so much pleasure, bliss that Henry had dared himself to think about over the years but had never hoped to experience. Henry stretched toward the bedside table and gathered up a box and a tube with one hand.

"George... Shall I do the honors?"

"God yes," George gasped. "Please."

Henry unwrapped the cellophane from the box and took out a condom. His hands were shaking with building pleasure as he tore the packet open with his teeth—a skill he had learned not from nights of wild sex in Brighton, for he had never had any, but from working as a vet all these years.

He slid the condom onto George with the gentle precision he used on his patients, then flipped open the tube. He slicked lubricant over George's sheathed cock, watching the joy in his lover's face at his touch and the anticipation of what was to follow.

Henry panted. "George—give me your fingers."

He was quick to obey, his lips falling to Henry's neck again, gentle groans in his throat sending soft tremors over his skin. Getting carried away, Henry squeezed the lubricant across George's fingers and the excess dropped onto his skin. But fortunately, not on the jacket.

"Whoops — making a mess!"

"One or two of these medals have pointy bits," George told him playfully, his hand returning once more to Henry's bottom. "Do say if they catch you?"

"I rather like the idea of — oooh! — that."

"You saucy sort," was the teasing reply. George had introduced another finger — stretching Henry, preparing him, he knew.

And was it obvious to George that Henry had never done this before? Or would he have to take a deep breath and announce, "George, I'm a virgin — as far as — you know — my bottom is concerned."

And he'd said it.

"We'll go slowly." George lifted his head to meet Henry's gaze. His green eyes were so full of love that Henry's breath was almost stolen from his body. "Everything's on your terms, darling."

"I love you, dear old Captain Standy-Bee — you know that, don't you?" Henry was so happy that he was sure he'd cry. But he didn't. He smiled instead and pulled George to him, into a kiss. It went on and on, the medals warm against his skin now, but not as warm as George's lips on Henry's, and still George's fingers were moving, deeper than ever.

Henry broke from the kiss for long enough to sigh a question. "Am I ready, darling?"

George gave a sound of acknowledgment that was caught in their kiss and slipped his leg between Henry's. He withdrew his finger, then his hands were on Henry's hips, urging him to lift them a little higher. Henry obeyed on instinct, feeling the hardness of

George's erection against him, the softness of the fabric under his fingers, the heat of their touching skin.

As George entered Henry, Henry knew some essence of himself had entered George. Their bodies were linked in the most intimate way they could be, with a tenderness that made Henry ache for the unreachable part of himself and George that, in those sweet moments, had at last become tangible.

George didn't rush, and Henry knew it was for his benefit, that he wasn't allowing himself to get carried away. Slowly, slowly, he nudged his way inside and retreated again, then advanced once more, deeper. He took his time, with gentle thrusts, gradually building until, with one final push of his hips, he had entered his lover entirely.

Henry lay underneath him, his fingers twining with George's where he held his hips, barely blinking as he gazed into the green eyes that blazed down at him with love and passion, all the secrets of his soul laid bare. George's beautiful body, the perfect muscular planes of his chest, the toned stomach, were all revealed to Henry through the unbuttoned jacket, without shame, without fear. Only with love, and the need to connect.

George's movements were slow but sure, gentle despite the hardness of his body, and he kept a steady pace with each thrust, coaxing Henry further along the path of pleasure. He lowered his head to dot exquisite, tender kisses to his lover's lips, his tongue exploring as though this were their very first kiss.

His fingers still entwined with Henry's, George lifted his hand to take Henry's erection in his grip. Their joined palms stroked and caressed, teasing out every moment of delicious ecstasy.

Henry could feel the might in George's body, the tensing of the muscles in his torso, in his legs, with each delicious thrust. Could George feel Henry's body, his hips moving of their own accord, following George's rhythm in perfect time? It was a wonder that something so intense could be so gentle, and moments, minutes stretched out, time forgotten even as their hearts beat out the seconds of the day against each other's body. Henry grasped George's thick hair with his free hand, holding him close, enjoying him, tasting him, two lovers wrapped about each other, entering into bliss.

George, of course, wasn't quiet — when was he ever — but the sounds were soft, each gentle moan against Henry's lips sending a new erotic thrill through their kisses. His arm slid around Henry's waist, lifting his hips even higher until George was as deep as he could be, and Henry felt as though they had truly become one.

"I love you," he gasped, catching Henry's lip very softly with his teeth. "My beautiful Fitz…"

"My darling George! My handsome captain."

Henry groaned — the pleasure, the closeness, the tender infinity that they had plunged into, the glory of their bodies combining. Wanting and being wanted, loving and being loved.

"Together." George gasped the promise, his muscles tensing against Henry's body again as he drew out their lovemaking. "Always…"

"Always," Henry sighed. He brought his leg up to embrace George's waist. "*Together…*" he breathed.

George's hand tightened just a little against Henry's cock in response, his kisses growing hungrier as they tumbled toward bliss in a tangle of limbs and sighs, utterly united.

A tremble ran through Henry, beginning like the touch of feathers in his toes and fingertips. It grew into a shudder, as if a renewal of life itself were rushing through his veins, uncontrollable and unafraid. He clung to it, resisting the urge to surrender himself, drawing more sweetness from the intensity.

Ecstasy shuddered through him. His lover was the only thought in his head, the only sensation he could feel. He tried to say his name, but the only sound that spilled from his throat was a deep cry of joy.

And there was George with him, both of them soaring into that light, making it brighter with their kisses, more dazzling with every sigh of pleasure. There didn't seem to be an end to their bliss, as if forever on into the future they would be together, embracing, cocooned in an aurora of love.

George sank down onto Henry, holding him close, the medals pressed against Henry's bare skin. His head rested on his lover's shoulder, that thick, dark hair tickling his face, and together they stayed there, unmoving, locked in each other's arms.

Henry felt peace, stillness, and a viscous silence that flowed around them as sure and soft as the sea. His bed had become an island, solely for himself and George — and in one moment plucked from many, they had finally found the love that had ever eluded them.

Chapter Twenty-Four

Lil opened the front door before George had time to knock. She must have been waiting behind the curtain. Her eyes were large with astonishment and at first Henry wondered if something had happened to Jez overnight. But he dismissed the thought because it was all too obvious—Lil was trying to hide a broad grin.

"You're, like, famous?" Was there any need to tell George that? Henry put his hand over his mouth to stifle a laugh, but realized it wasn't only George that she was addressing. "No—you're, like, trending online? Hashtag mystery man?"

"You're going to have to say that in English." George laughed. "My agent does all that stuff, I just talk about history."

"On, like, social media? My friend Gemma took a photo? Of you two, like, dancing? And put it online?" Lil grinned as she swiped her phone's screen. "And now everyone's sharing it and going like *hashtag gsb mystery man* and like *hashtag I want to find a man who looks at me like that* and *hashtag gorgeous George's gorgeous guy?* It's been shared like two thousand times since last night?"

"What?" George's tone was shell-shocked, and he glanced at Henry. "Are you serious?"

Nervous laughter tickled Henry's throat. George laughed too, but it sounded forced, and Henry could see from the tightening of his lover's jaw that he was desperate to know more. He couldn't ask, though, could he, because then she might start to wonder, and what would George do then? Yet would it be the end of the world in the twenty-first century? Hardly, Henry was sure, and he felt a nudge of *something*, a wish that George wasn't so troubled by it.

"How's my boy?" George's voice was cheery again. "Had a good night?"

Lil put her phone in her pocket and visibly changed gears, her face moving from awed-to-be-in-celebrity-presence to friendly rural girl.

"He's had a well massive time with the donkeys."

Henry marveled at what this meant. Had they danced about with glow sticks at some sort of animal rave?

"Let's go and have a look at him?" George took his hand from behind his back and held out the bunch of vibrant flowers he had been concealing. "For you, Miss Lil, to say thanks for looking after my little fellow so well."

"Oh wow! They're so beautiful!"

Lil, nursing the flowers in her arms, took them round to the large garden at the back of the modest cottage, to a simple stable where Jez had had his *'well massive time'*. There the foal was pottering with his two new donkey friends, the three of them happy in their own little world. At the sight of his pa, however, Jez threw back his head in a cheerful whinny and cantered across to butt George's chest in welcome. The limp that had been so pronounced was now virtually gone, Henry realized, smiling as George threw his arms around Jez's neck and snuggled him, cooing about what a happy, handsome lad he was.

"He should so be on social media. He's a babe." Lil grinned, glancing from George to Henry. "*Gorgeous George's gorgeous guy.*"

A mischievous light shone in Lil's eyes. And in that moment, Henry knew without a doubt—Lil could see that he and George were a couple. Henry passed his hand through his hair and, out of sight of George, gave Lil a conspiratorial wink.

"Righty-ho, we'll be off, then." Henry patted George on the shoulder.

"Lil." George looked to the young woman, his arm still around Jez's neck. "Online...are people saying really rotten things?"

"Don't think so? Didn't see anything? Only some blokes who said they're bored of seeing your chest all the time? Hang on—I'll show you."

Lil put the flowers down and grabbed her phone from her back pocket. She tapped at the screen and held it out to George.

Someone had announced to the world—

At least he's got his top on for once! #whataposer #gsbmysteryman

Henry couldn't resist and raised his eyebrow. "George did do a good job of keeping his jacket on last night."

Someone else had written—

Top bants — #gsb is the Archbishop of Banterbury! #gsbmysteryman #ladsontour

"Lads on tour — was that laddy, was it, dancing?" Henry could feel himself about to laugh again. Although he had no idea what 'bants' were.

"I still appear to have a career, which is good since the England cricket team are arriving next week," George said archly. He chewed at his lip, though, a hint of anxiety beneath his bonhomie. "I don't think I'm very laddish really."

"You were in the Army, though? I know loads of lads who are fans of yours, George — they were well jealous when I said I look after your horse."

"So if this were true, you wouldn't have a problem?" George peered at Lil. "And your mates wouldn't?"

"What — if you two were boyfriends? Why would anyone care? You looked well cute when you were dancing."

"I wouldn't wish that on Fitz!" George laughed and rubbed his hand against the back of his neck, too casual to *be* casual. Once again Lil gave Henry that *men* look.

George's phone beeped with an incoming message. He glanced at it, his brow furrowing, then thrust it back into his pocket.

"Got a message from Tabs?" Henry asked him.

"PPI or something." He shrugged. "Let's get Jez home, give Lil her house back!"

"Bye, Lil!" Henry raised his hand to her in farewell.

She waved them off, holding the paddock gate open for the men and horse. George was preoccupied, though, clearly troubled by the online speculation that had put this most private of private lives at the very top of the weekend gossip columns.

Once they were out in the lane, Henry whispered, "Won't people find it boring when your 'mystery man' turns out to be just a countryside vet! They'll soon find something else to talk about. And we were only dancing—it's not as if it's a photo of us having a kiss."

"My dad died of a heart attack, Fitz," George reminded him. "I was eight years old and the last thing he said to me was *you're a fairy*. And now the world's going to say it, and they're going to say it to you, too."

"Jesus, George—you never told me that before." Henry was about to reach for George's hand when he stopped. *Imagine what would happen if someone saw?* "But do you think I've never heard that myself? *My* dad's said it to me often enough. I ended up with this scar on my stomach trying to prove that I wasn't a sissy, or all the other things he's called me. And do you know what? I should never have bothered. Because there's plenty enough people in the world who honestly don't care one way or the other. We have each other, George. We won't be coming out alone. Maybe I'm a little bit frightened, but you know what? I'm excited. And, more than anything else, bloody well relieved!"

George said nothing, though, his gaze fixed on the horizon, his teeth worrying at his lip again. This wasn't a man who was excited or relieved or anything other than deeply upset, and that was upsetting in turn.

"I need to talk to my agent," he eventually decided. "See what the damage is."

"*Damage?* Did you see the look on Barney's face, that lad you danced with? You're a hero to him. He saw two men dance together, and—that's not damage, George. You've just shown a youngster that there's nothing wrong with being who he is. That it's okay."

But it wasn't okay. Henry could feel waves of *not-okay* emanating from his boyfriend, and he hadn't the words to put it right, nor even the vaguest clue of how to fix things.

"It's okay for you, isn't it? I've never— I keep myself *private*, not hung out on the bloody Internet to be picked at!" George closed his eyes and ran his hand over Jez's mane. "Are you coming back with us or—?"

Henry shoved his hands into his pockets. He scuffed a stone with the toe of his shoe.

"Do you want me to? Or shall I let you get on and talk to your agent?" Henry shook his head. "I don't know what to say with you. One minute you're moving in with me, the next you're panicking because a photo of us dancing ends up on the Internet. *Dancing*, for heaven's sake. What the hell would you do if a photo of a removal van parked up outside my house got online? Everyone'd know then, wouldn't they? But before you think any further about moving in, perhaps you should run that past your agent, too. Just in case."

Henry sidled toward the other side of the lane, staring down at the silhouettes of dried, squashed frogs in the gutter.

"I'm sorry, Fitz, for being in the public eye and for worrying what this means and for not being as loud and proud as you've become!" His phone beeped again but this time George ignored it. "Want me to scoop up a little lad and drag him away from a primed grenade? Done. Be a human shield while the shrapnel rains down over an innocent kid? No problem. Tell me to let the world know that I'm gay? That's a *lot* tougher for me. What if people say what my dad said?"

"And?" Henry blinked at him. "Maybe some people will. But who cares what fuckwits like that think? Are you going to live your life in the shadows because you're scared of what someone you don't even know may or may not say? But then I'm not in showbiz, I'm not a celebrity. I'm just a boring vet, who—well, perhaps this is closer to the truth—you're embarrassed to be seen with."

"How can you—" George shook his head. "That's what you think of me?"

Henry tipped back his head and stared up at the patches of blue sky between the overarching branches of the trees. He had walked so many times along this lane, all those years ago with George. Before he was famous, before he had his career. And now they were having a row. After last night, this should have been the best of days. It should've been the first day in a whole heap of best days.

"Maybe I just don't suit your 'brand'. Is that what your agent will say?"

"I've got the whole England team and half the BBC here next week, what do you want me to do?" He threw his arms aloft as the phone went off again. "You really think I'm embarrassed by you? Welcome to my world, Fitz. One photo online and the phone doesn't stop!"

"Do? What should you *do?*" Henry came to a halt, the dust skidding up around his feet. "Decide what the hell you want, *that's* what you should do. Move in with me, and everyone will know that television's Captain George is attracted to men. Or, don't move in, and go on pretending you're the straightest man on television. And then I'll know where I stand. I can carry on living all on my tod—I'm used to it! Lucky old me!"

"That's it, is it? I either move in or we're done?"

In exasperation, Henry dragged his hand through his hair and sighed.

"That's not what I said—I'm not giving you an ultimatum. But I want you to *think*. What sort of future is there for us? Last night, it was you who suggested moving in, and I was so happy at the thought of it! And now, now I can see very clearly that you never would move in, because *people would find out*. I don't somehow think in the twenty-first century it would wash, George, would it—*oh yeah, me and Henry, we live together in the same house, but we're just really good mates, it's not like we're lovers or anything like that*. Don't raise my hopes and dash them. It's not fair."

"It's not what you *said*, but it's implied. Move in or *I stay living on my tod*. I'm paying for your lawyer, I'm pulling every string I've got, don't you make out that I don't care." He looked down at Jez as the phone rang again, The Beach Boys ringtone ludicrously cheery right now. George pulled it from his pocket and turned it off. "This is too much, all right? I just wanted to come home for the summer!"

"If you decide to read things into my words that I didn't even say, then—" Henry shrugged. "What can I do? Of course I'm grateful to you for helping me. Of course I am! What sort of a git would I be if I wasn't? But that's it, isn't it—you were only ever going to come here for the summer. Squeeze what you could out of the village for the furthering of your precious bloody career and sod off again—*toot-toot!* Move in with me? What a bloody joke! And what a titting idiot I am to have ever believed a word that's come out of your mouth since the day you turned up here!"

Henry began to walk away. His hands were shaking and he battled with himself not to cry. He hadn't meant what he'd said—he hadn't, not a word of it. But he couldn't stop, because his heart had shattered and every broken sliver of it hurt.

Putting his foot on the stile, Henry paused just before he pushed himself over. "Oh, and so you can't accuse me of taking advantage of you, just so no one thinks I was after your money, I'll make sure you get every penny back that you've spent on the lawyer." He leaped over the stile and brushed his hands as he began to retreat. "With interest."

"I've never lied to you and I don't care about the money." George's voice was quiet. "But if that's what you really think of me — I have to be here for the cricket next week but apart from that, I'll keep out of your way."

He patted Jez's head and gave a click of his tongue, which urged the horse to walk. With a last glance at Henry, George and Jez turned away and made their way along the lane.

Chapter Twenty-Five

So that was that, just as George had always suspected it would be one day, because Henry was far too good for the likes of him. Henry wasn't timid and cowardly, he was brave and proud and he deserved a better man than George Standish-Brookes. *A fairy*, as his father had angrily raged after another school report mentioning George's love of dress-up and theater. And that night Major Standish-Brookes had gone to bed and didn't wake up, and at eight years old, wide-eyed and lanky as the foal he had rescued, George had decided that he would never be a fairy again.

Because *being a fairy* had given his father a heart attack.

It hadn't, of course, and he knew that now, but when he'd seen that photo online, read the speculation in the press, on social media, he'd felt that same cold chill. What happens now? What happens to boys when people find out that they're *a fairy*? He imagined the work falling away, the rejection of the world and the end of everything he had ever worked to achieve yet it seemed to be far from the case. When he finally dared speak to Howard, his agent told him that the phone had been ringing off the hook and Tabs, bless her, was full of similar stories.

"Hot property, boy-o." She'd beamed.

It didn't matter. He could have the brightest and best career the world had ever known, shelves full of awards and the respect of his peers from now to his dying day, but it meant nothing without Henry. Henry who thought he was a liar, who had looked at him with love this morning then, just an hour later, with bitter disappointment.

'What a bloody idiot I am to have ever believed a word that's come out of your mouth…'

Yet they were true. Not scripted or edited, just *him*, just a George that the rest of the world wasn't ever allowed to see.

And I should've guessed that he wouldn't believe me.

It wasn't good enough, even though every single word was true. So he had to go, because how could he stay in this tiny village where Henry's house was just a short stroll away, where everywhere he looked held memories? The cricket pitch, the tree from which he had tumbled, the village hall where they had danced? He couldn't bear it.

Back to London, to a place to hide courtesy of Princess Eleanor, the friend who owed him one, to a place for Jez to continue his recuperation and to a place that would give both George and Henry time to forget. He could use the excuse of preparing for next week's cricket match and the filming, of course, and that was what he intended to do. A week away, a couple of days back in the village to make the program and away they would run again, Jez and George looking for their next adventure.

"Keep saying it, Standy-Bee, you might start believing it." George addressed his own reflection, sure that he looked the part of friendly yet formal, a man who wouldn't be messed with. Henry might not love him and his efforts to sweet talk Steph into leaving his lover alone might not have worked, but he had one last card to play. Ed Belcher loved money and George made plenty of it, so if a quick dip in the pool hadn't been enough to convince Steph that her husband's plan should be consigned to the scrap heap, hard cash might be.

Then he'd be a *real* hero, wouldn't he?

Save the house of the man whose heart you broke and never even tell him you did it? Save the house of the man you'll always love?

That would be worth more than any number of BAFTAs.

* * * *

Jez was happily munching in his stable when George left the house. George ambled down the path and across the green, toward the towering gates of the Belcher mansion. Perhaps he should have phoned first to check that Ed was there, but that would have given his adversary a warning and he needed Ed to be caught off guard — he would only get one chance at this, after all. George pressed the intercom and waited, composing his cheeriest tones when he heard Steph answer.

"Hello, Longley Parva Old Hall?"

"Hey, Steph, it's George. Is Ed around?"

"George! He's gone to London. Won't be back until lunchtime tomorrow. Did you need to speak to him, or were you," her voice assumed a theatrical whisper, "wondering if the coast was clear? For a swim, that is." She attempted a seductive giggle, but only sounded like she was afflicted with hiccups.

He felt a pang of shame at the memory of their encounter beside the pool. How stupid could one man get? How arrogant to have believed that a bit of a peacock show would convince a woman like Steph to give up the truth behind her husband's plans for the manor, or even see her telling Ed to leave Henry, *his Fitz*, to enjoy a peaceful life.

Just be honest, he told himself. *She's human, after all.*

"Can you spare me five minutes, Steph?"

"I can spare you more than that, Georgie!" The gate clanked and she buzzed him in. His heart hammered as he walked up the driveway, his mouth dry with the thought of what was at stake.

Fitz's home. The place where Billy and Tobias had been happy with their pets, the place where braver men than him had lived and loved. He arrived at the front door and knocked, the image of the sundial fresh in his mind.

He heard the click of high heels over marble and the door opened. Steph's lips were fresh with gloss, her eyelashes heavy with mascara. She stretched her arm up against the doorjamb, her blouse unbuttoned just enough to reveal a hint of cleavage.

"Come for another dance?"

Had she seen the speculation online?

Probably.

"I've come to ask a massive favor," he admitted. "And hope you're feeling kind."

Steph pouted and lowered her eyelashes. "I can be as kind as you like, Captain George."

"Can I come in?" He told himself that she wasn't attempting to look seductive, that it was just something Steph *did*. It was easier to believe that, after all, than to speculate about what price she might demand in return for her help, and even George wasn't so self-confident as to expect *that*.

"We're not going to get very far if you don't." She batted her eyelashes at him and gestured inside. "Come on in — there's some Pinot chilling in my wine fridge."

"I'm off back to London tomorrow," he told her, as though the decision hadn't been made in the last hour or so. George concentrated instead on the sound of their feet on the marble floor because it was the easiest thing to think about. "Back next week for the return of the LP Single Wicket with the England lads and a brand-new trophy, of course!"

At the words *England lads*, Steph's eyes widened. She kept her gaze on George as she took glasses from the cupboard and brought the wine out of the fridge.

"The national squad, coming to little old Parvy?"

"Yeah, most of the village've signed up for a go against them. Minimum fiver a punt, all proceeds to the village hall fund!" George smiled, safe in talk of such things. "And it'll be the backbone of my Christmas doc."

Steph grinned at him as she poured the wine. "So are you bringing the cameras up here next week too? Like you said? Because if so, I'll need to get booked in for a deep-clean. The house, I mean — not me!"

She tipped her head back and launched into the world's most grating laugh.

"Yup, next weekend!" He nodded. "And I haven't forgotten that *we* discussed putting the Belchers in the show. That's really why I'm here, to ask that favor."

"Ooooh!" Steph drummed her heels against the marble floor and grinned like a bratty child. "Here's your wine. Now ask away!"

"This house business. The problem is, you chaps coming after the manor is going to make you look like the villains of the village." He pouted a *poor you* pout. "If you're really set on dragging Fitz through the courts, there's no way the Beeb'll risk putting you front and center, Steph. They're going to want an assurance that you've called off the lawyers."

Steph pursed her lips. Her nostrils twitched as if she had detected a bad smell.

"I can't—it's not really my decision to make, George. And after all, the manor *does* belong to Ed's family. Henry's a squatter."

"No, no, it doesn't. And we both know that no court is going to rule in Ed's favor—he's counting on bankrupting Fitz before the judge has a chance to sling the case out, Steph, then he can take the house for peanuts."

He saw her eyes flash and knew that he had hit the nail right on the head. It was the land, of course, not the house, because there was no way Ed would want the manor. Ed loved all things modern, so whatever his plans were for the manor, George had no doubt that it was down to acreage, the simple matter of land and cash.

"Now, I don't know *why* he's so desperate to get the place, but it's Fitz's home," George implored. "Tell me how much you want to back off and I'll pay it. He loves that house, it'll break his heart if you keep this up."

"And you care about that, do you? Breaking his heart?" Steph snorted. The clickity-click of her acrylic nails tapping on the granite worktop sounded like the advance of an army of cockroaches. "All that pissing about last night, dancing with him – a big joke! But it's all over the news this morning – *Captain George's mystery man*. Except he's not a mystery in Longley Parva, is he? Oh, yes, I can see it now. That's the only reason you came round here in the first place, tarting about in my pool – for your boyfriend! That hopeless old bore. How long have you two been shagging?"

It was like a slap in the face, the disgust in her voice, because that was *exactly* what he had been waiting for. She was the first, but she wouldn't be the last, and he was going to cut it off now.

"Shagging?" George laughed, but the revulsion that jolted through him wasn't for Steph or for Henry, it was for himself. This was how low he got, then? Henry was right – he was a liar after all. "You believe that?"

'Nothing worse than being a fairy, George,' he heard his father say darkly. *'Nothing more disgraceful than that.'*

"Remember how long I suffered going out with Henry? That revolting scar on his stomach – and he was dreadful in bed. Never spent any of his money on me. When I saw all those people speculating over a photo of my ex-boyfriend and *you* together, I suddenly saw it – I'd been taken for an utter fool by a pair of poofters!"

George stared at her, his mouth opening with what was intended to be a denial, but no sound came out and for a few seconds he was simply *there*, not quite able to believe what he was hearing. *Is this the moment*, he dimly wondered, *when I stand on the precipice, on the edge of the Rubicon, with the future shrouded before me?*

Is this the moment father prepared me for?

'Nothing worse than a fairy.'

You're wrong, Pa, he told himself. *Because I'm looking at something far, far worse.*

Who knew the face of hate could be so glamorous?

"I was stupid enough, Steph, to think that you were basically all right. A bit shallow, ambitious, terrible taste in husbands but essentially decent, and — this is even better — stuck with Ed." He frowned and cocked his head to one side. "So yeah, I took my shirt off and had a bit of a swim and flashed the skin because I thought it'd make you happy and that you, being decent and nice and caring, would tell your husband, *Fitz's a good bloke, leave him be.* Except I was wrong, you're not basically okay but a bit shallow, you're just perfectly suited to Ed Belcher."

"You have no idea — no idea — what my life is like!" Steph flung her arm out toward him, her nails like talons pointing toward George's face. "What girl wouldn't have her head turned by Ed after suffering a pathetic plonker like Henry? Ed has money, connections, he can give a girl the lifestyle. Look at this house, and the pool, look at this tan — this came from a holiday, you know, not out of a bottle! And I tied Ed up by the balls with a prenup, just to make sure that that money, that lifestyle — it's mine. Forever."

Steph's face flashed with triumph, but her jubilation faded as quickly as it had appeared.

"But then — I have to live as Ed's wife. With an ugly child. Ed's even worse in bed than Henry. And at least Henry pretended to be affectionate. Ed's not even here half the time. And you come along, ripping off your shirt — what was I to think? Is that your stock in trade, is it, teasing lonely housewives? And what was I to say, about Henry's bloody rathole of a house? Not just to Ed, but to a man like Randy Cheese, who — "

A gurgle escaped Steph's mouth, like a waste disposal unit that was trying to digest a bag of nails. She tried to cover her face with her hands, as if that could hide the name she had just revealed.

But it was too late.

Randy Cheese? What the hell does Randy Cheese have to do with any of this? George knew the billionaire with the odd oil slick of hair from the media, the whole *world* did thanks to his reality shows and skyscrapers and steak clubs and mineral water and wives and scandals and — Well, the list never ended. Yet what did a man who lived atop a tower of gold in the center of Manhattan have to do with Longley Parva?

Something was afoot, and George knew that there was no hope he would get anything further out of Steph Belcher. She had gone white as milk beneath her tan and her eyes were wide as she stared at him.

"You're lonely for a reason, Steph," he told her. "But at least you're rich, eh?"

Then he strolled out of the kitchen, his heart hammering in his breast. *Hopefully Steph isn't the type to come at a chap with a carving knife when his back's turned.* His hands were trembling slightly when he pulled open the front door and stepped out into the night. Then he took his phone from his pocket and called Tabitha, praying that she would answer.

"Well, wow-ee, if it's not Gorgeous George!" Tabitha laughed down the phone. A background noise of conversation and the clank of cutlery and glasses indicated that she certainly wasn't alone. "Why the hell are you ringing me when you should be with your *hashtag mystery man*?"

"I'm coming to London tomorrow," he told her. "Eleanor's sorting a place for me and Jez and before you have a go, I know I'm running away but— Look, you know you always said you know *everybody*, is that really true?"

"Yeah, it is—but—" Rustling on the phone, footsteps, the sudden echo of tiles and a creaking door told George that Tabitha had gone somewhere private to take the call. A toilet cubicle, glamorously enough. "Oh, George, what can have happened between you and your dashing vet in less than a day? Everyone's cooing with delight over that photo of the two of you. It looks like the first dance at a wedding reception!"

"Please, Tabs, can we not talk about that?" *Because he hates me, because he thinks I'm a liar, because I screwed it up for the sake of a father who was never the most reasonable chap on a good day.* "I'm going to make some calls of my own, but can you just get the word around to anyone in business, law, *anything*, who might be able to connect Randy Cheese to Longley Parva?"

"Randy—? Ahem." Tabitha, George was well aware, had worked in this business for long enough to know that, as the poster said, *Loose Lips Sink Ships.* "I'll see what I can find out. Wasn't he stopped from building some massive golf resort up in Scotland when he said he'd only locate it there if they took down the wind farm. And the mountain?"

"Was he? I spent the last year sailing around the world, Tab, so I probably missed it. Look, I'm back in London tomorrow so I'll give you a shout?" He managed a smile even though she couldn't see him, and it made his face ache. "And before you ask, it won't be at Kensington Palace, sorry."

"That's all right, darling. You and me should have a night out on the razzle — we'll sort out Randy, then I'll fill you with Cava and you can tell me all about what happened with your chap."

"I'm not good company right now," he admitted. "You enjoy your night."

"Thank you, darling. Gosh, I don't like hearing my lovely George all sad." Tabitha had adopted her Girl Guide pack leader voice. "But don't worry, Auntie Tabs will look after you!"

"Randy Cheese," he reminded her. "And I'll owe you one *again*!"

Chapter Twenty-Six

Henry spent his every spare moment in the practice nets at the cricket club. It was better than sitting about in the manor on his own, remembering George in every room. He couldn't even sleep in his own bed anymore and had taken to kipping on a musty camp bed in the lounge, with Bad Billy's portrait looking down on him.

But that hadn't helped much. Because Henry, in his hunt for paperwork that might save his home, had taken the portrait down, to see if there was anything hidden behind it. There wasn't, but seeing the portrait up close, he'd realized that Billy was holding a silver oval in his hand. It must have been the miniature of himself and his lover, and their entwined locks of hair. They had lived in this house for years and died within days of each other.

My dear, loving friend.

But at the cricket club, he could forget everything. Find a willing youth to lob balls at him and knock them as far as he could. All that knotted despair in his body had a vent.

He could forget the words he'd hurled at George, words he hadn't meant. He had only wanted George to see that his career wasn't everything. They had love. Still did, because Henry hadn't stopped loving him.

Even though George had gone.

Each evening, when Henry came back from the cricket club, he would stand in his garden looking out toward the cottage. It was always in darkness. Because George had chosen his career over love. Perhaps that was sensible, in a way—love wouldn't pay the rent. But surely there was some way that they could be together and George could go on pootling about on television in that bloody car and whipping off his shirt.

Whipping off his shirt. An obvious signal to the entire viewing public that Captain George Standish-Brookes might not be entirely straight. Not one person had been surprised by the photograph of the formerly straightest man on television dancing with a man.

But it wouldn't do to dwell. Because Henry had handled the whole thing very badly. Even if he was hurt, George hadn't meant to wound. If they'd had time, Henry knew that George would've come round. Would have dealt with it. But thanks to that bloody photo, they hadn't had a chance.

The media had descended on Longley Parva and the hunt was on for the mystery man. To save George his blushes, Henry had stood on the gravel car park outside his surgery and told the world, "George and I are old friends, just having a laugh, nothing wrong with that, eh? Two grown men dancing, enjoying each other's company. Anyway, things to do, thank you, ladies and gentlemen of the press."

And each night, in the practice nets, after Henry had knocked the ball flying, it would always be brought back to him by his new friend.

No one knew the name of the dog who had started to hang around the cricket club, so Henry called him Nimrod. A large, shaggy stray, with a sore on its side and a bend in its tail. A mix of Border Collie and god knew what else, with a Husky's ice-blue eyes. After the third night of it hanging about the practice nets, drawn to Henry as if it somehow knew him, the vet took him home.

Nimrod lay on the floor beside Henry's camp bed, and as Henry endured through the sleepless hours of the night into morning, he was comforted by the snuffling of his dog. Not the dog that he had chosen, but the dog that had chosen him.

Everyone in the village was abuzz about the Single Wicket match, but Henry kept himself aloof. So many questions from people about *'your friend George'*, and Henry could only shrug. *No, I don't know why he's not in the village. No, I don't know if there's any tickets left. No, I don't know when the footage of the dance will be shown on television.* Would they never stop pestering him?

But there was still the issue of the house. Another solicitor's letter, this time from his own lawyer, explaining some fees that Ed Belcher was demanding. Henry had screwed the letter into a ball and hurled it across the garden as far as he could. It had landed on the undisturbed surface of the lake and floated for a moment before it capsized and sank.

On the night before the match, Henry came home from the nets with Nimrod. The dog had been pampered at the surgery — shampooed, de-fleaed and bandaged up. He even had a microchip now, in case he should wander again. But the dog didn't seem inclined to leave Henry's side.

That's one friend, at least.

Until Nimrod came to realize that Henry was a curmudgeonly, misanthropic, miserable old bastard and ran off like—

Nimrod whisked his mended tail in an enthusiastic circle, tipped back his head to unleash a bark that could split eardrums at thirty paces and yanked his lead so hard that it slipped out of Henry's surprised grip before he could stop him.

"Nimrod!"

The enormous dog hurtled across the garden with Henry in pursuit. Just as Henry registered that the lights were back on in George's house, Nimrod took the fence in one effortless bound into the meadow, heading toward the cottage.

Well, everyone was drawn to their local celebrity.

Henry faffed with the bolt on his gate and managed to get it open, calling to Nimrod as he tried to follow him.

Of all the bloody awkward things.

He could hear the dog's massive paws padding over the dry earth, the grasses swishing as he swept through the meadow, the swoop of that metronome tail back and forth and Nimrod's regular, rhythmic panting. But he couldn't see the damn creature in the rapidly failing light.

"Nimrod, come back here, where do you think you're going—bad dog! Nimrod!"

Henry followed Nimrod as far as he could, until he came up against George's garden fence. The dog was nowhere to be seen or heard. Henry was about to cup his hands around his mouth to call for his dog once again, when he dropped his arms to his side.

One really can't bellow across another chap's garden.

The kitchen door was open, a soft light shining out across the twilit lawn. From inside, Jez appeared, trotting out to stand beside the pond. He looked at Henry, his head on one side, then meandered happily over to greet him, whinnying a delighted welcome at his *other* pa.

As Jez nuzzled at Henry over the fence, thoughts of the stable at home came into his mind. Henry closed his eyes and allowed himself a short reverie, of the jet-black foal in the stable yard at the manor, swishing his tail. That could've been theirs, they could've been a family. But circumstance had decided otherwise.

Henry whispered into his mane, "I'm so sorry, Jez."

"Your ma and pa are going to be fretting!" George's voice was full of enthusiasm as he stepped out into the garden and turned back to address Nimrod, who was chasing him from the house. "Where do you live, boy, eh?"

Surprised and embarrassed that his dog had gone uninvited into someone else's house, and George's cottage at that, Henry leaned over the gate and called to the human occupant. "Good lord, George—I'm sorry! That's my dog!"

"Fitz!" George spun on his bare feet and looked at Henry as though he was the most unexpected sight in the world. He glanced down at Nimrod then back at Henry and smiled. "He and Jez were trying to steal my chips."

"He's been at the surgery all day—he's the most well-fed, pampered dog in the South Downs. Bad Nimrod—bad boy! Stealing this nice man's chips. Bad dog."

Nimrod tipped his head to one side, considering Henry as he wagged his tail from side to side. The dog was in no hurry to abandon his new friends at the cottage.

"Sorry about that, George. He's a stray. Been hanging about the practice nets. I've tried to find his owners, but... Well, he decided to adopt me, so there wasn't all that much I could do."

"Nimrod?" George beamed, but the smile didn't quite reach his eyes. Instead he looked...tired, Henry thought, as tired as Henry felt, and his cheer sounded forced. "So, tomorrow... I hope you're ready to defend your Single Wicket record? We've got a brand-new trophy, which I hope nobody will steal!"

"The dog seemed to know me. I had this strange fancy that—" Henry shrugged. Canine reincarnation was not a subject for a vet to entertain. "Anyway, he needed a name, and that seemed as good a one as any. And—yes, I've been in the nets all week after work. I'm in fine fettle! And you? I do hope you'll at least hit the ball this time!"

The old jovial rivalry of youth was back in Henry's tone.

"Can we—" George swallowed whatever the question was, though, and instead held out his hand. "Bearing in mind that you'll have a cricket bat in your hand tomorrow, can we at least call a truce?"

Henry reached for George's hand and shook. He didn't want to let go, and looked away as their hands dropped apart. "I'm past walloping people with cricket bats. Although if Ed Belcher's there tomorrow, I might be tempted!"

"And I'm sorry you thought I lied to you." George's voice was quieter. "I'm sorry for all of it."

"I said a lot of things, George. I didn't mean—I keep thinking it over, and I don't... I was all over the place. I'm sorry if I hurt you. I didn't mean to. I just wanted you to— Nimrod, stop that!"

The dog's paws were on the fence, slathering Henry's face with his long tongue.

"Nimrod, you ill-mannered cur!" Henry managed to maneuver his dog off the fence and wiped the slobber away with his handkerchief. George laughed and for a moment, they could be back where they were, about to fall into each other's arms. That was then, though, wasn't it, before those angry words had been exchanged?

"Jez has been staying with royalty." George smiled. "But he prefers LP, so we're back for a couple of days and then— Georgie gave me a very dirty look when I arrived today. I think she missed me!"

Henry smiled at the man he'd once held in his arms. Was there the slightest chance that they could salvage something from the rubble?

"Are you—are you going to stay? For a spell?"

"Ma's back next week." He shrugged. "I love her, but the thought of sharing the yoga temple...no thanks!"

"I just hope Nimrod doesn't slip his lead again, although I can't imagine he's the sort of chap to be interested in your mum's lentil casserole." Henry gazed at George, at what he could see of his face in the darkness, where the light from the house cast a glow over him. He tried not to stare, and looked down at his shoes as he knocked the toes lightly against the fence.

He glanced up at George.

"Did I do the right thing? When those reporters turned up in the village? I thought first of all that I'd ignore them, and then I thought, damn it, they'll keep pestering me at the surgery and at home, so I thought, I'll just go on camera and say my piece. Was — was that the right thing to do?"

"I didn't want them on your doorstep. I'm sorry for that too." George gave a rueful smile. "Turns out my dad was wrong — nobody hates me for being gay. In fact, people don't seem very surprised at all."

"You can't apologize for the reporters. I didn't mind, really." Henry lowered his head. His eyes fell somewhere at the level of George's chest. He dropped his head again and returned to staring at his toes. "I…I did it for you."

From inside the cottage the phone rang, splitting the idyllic night. George glanced back, clearly torn when he said, "I'm really sorry, I've got to answer that."

"It's okay. I'd better drag this reprobate home before he causes any further havoc. Come on, Nimrod!"

Henry clicked his fingers and the dog jumped over the fence into the meadow.

"See you tomorrow then, George." Henry waved as he turned to go.

"Bye, Fitz, nice to meet you, Nimrod," George called, and Jez whinnied his farewell.

Back through the meadow, Nimrod trotting at his side, Henry wanted to look back over his shoulder at the cottage where he and George had been so happy. But instead he pressed on, making his way through the darkness in his cricket whites.

Have I turned into a ghost?

Chapter Twenty-Seven

The following morning, George drained the last of his tea, slipped on his sunglasses and made his way out into the garden. The day had dawned bright and warm, the cricket team were safely billeted in a very pleasant country house hotel just half an hour down the road and the BBC were already here, filming the setting up of the cricket field and talking to the very characterful elderly chaps who served as volunteer groundskeepers. Tabitha adored them, of course, and they were more than happy to provide a bit of local color.

He had lain awake all night thinking about the conversation with Henry, wishing he had found the courage to speak up, to ask if they might try again. Yet George couldn't summon the words because he already knew that the answer would be no, and that would be too much to bear. Even so, his mind turned again and again to Nimrod and Fitz, to the stable his lover had started clearing, to the sundial and the double miniature, to Billy and Tobias, Nimrod and Rupert and all that he had run away from. Their ancestors had risked everything to be together and he — Well, it was a mistake he would regret for the rest of his life. He would never know a love like that again, and it felt like losing a part of his soul.

"Don't look at me like that," he told Georgie's portrait as she looked at him accusingly. "He wouldn't want me now anyway."

George's run that morning had taken him around the village where he had grown up and where, for a few weeks in a glorious summer, he had been loved. It was like something from a time long since lost even now, with bunting fluttering in the soft breeze and every garden at its best. The streets were empty yet by lunchtime they would be full, and the village hall fund would be a lot better off by the time the sun set tonight. Where George would go when filming was finished he didn't know, but he knew that it couldn't be here, because property in Longley Parva came up for sale once in a very blue moon. Besides, it wouldn't be fair on Henry to hang around, the proverbial thorn in his side.

George caught his reflection in the window as he passed. In whites and his regimental cricket sweater he looked every inch *TV's George Standish-Brookes* — unflappable, chappish and full of banter. Today it felt like the heaviest mask he had ever worn.

Keep smiling and don't think about what you've lost, about the man you love.

Just do you.

He walked to the kitchen door and looked out at the garden, where Lil was plaiting Jez's black mane. The horse's tail swished this way and that happily and George called, "He looks *very* snazzy, Lil!"

"Best-groomed horse in the village?" Lil slapped Jez's side and grinned at George. "I should open a horse beauty parlor."

"You'd make a mint!"

She reached in her bag for something. "For under your eyes."

"What's that?" He wandered out to join her. "Are you saying I need to slap up again, Miss Dalrymple?"

"Not, like, full makeup? But just a dab of Touche Éclat. Covers the shadows?" She inclined her head in a knowing fashion, blinking.

"They'll sort all that in the wagon," he assured her warmly, though it was the confirmation that he looked as exhausted as he felt. "Do I look dreadful?"

Lil turned her head just slightly in the direction of the manor, then looked back at George and shook her head.

"No?"

Even a yes or no answer from Lil elucidated nothing. He followed the path of her gaze to the manor, thinking that at least he could keep one promise to Henry. Today Longley Parva Manor would be saved. With that thought, George glanced at his watch, mindful that it wouldn't do to be late for the illustrious guest who was due in Longley Parva today. After all, it wasn't often that a billionaire came to the village.

Chapter Twenty-Eight

Ed Belcher, successful millionaire, golfing enthusiast, stock exchange badass, mover and shaker and ball-breaker, all-round affable bastard, husband and father, arrived at Longley Parva cricket club with a spring in his step.

Another deal had been made. Another yacht had been bought. Another Lambo in the garage. And, today, yawn bloody yawn, Ed bloody Belcher would be lensing more TV.

Just another day in the successful life of Ed Belcher. Livin' la vida Belcher.

Not that Ed had any time for cricket. But one stuck one's slightly doctored nose in. Especially when the Beeb were set up at the old cricket pav, waiting for Mr. Longley Parva himself. Cricket jumper in Sussex colors draped around shoulders, limited-edition Oakley sunglasses just *so* on mussed yet perfect hair, here was Ed — *cock o' the bloody walk*.

"Cap'n George!" Ed clapped his hand across the back of their local celebrity. It made a good hollow noise, like an old tree. "Marvelous shit. Love it."

"Ed." George smiled, because George was George and there were cameras in the vicinity. For some reason he had that crippled, useless foal with him, its mane plaited as though it was as much a nancy as its owner. "Have you met the England boys yet? They're down at the nets with the kids. Your little Sapphire was there with her nanny."

"Was she?" *Who knows what that child gets up to?* "Better go and press the flesh with the England lads, eh? You all ready for the off? Thrash old Fitzwanker's arse, eh?"

George laughed, showing teeth that were infuriatingly white even without the help of veneers. Not as white as Ed's, of course, but they probably didn't take as much upkeep either.

"Don't go far, Ed, I've got a special surprise for you," George told him brightly. He always was a gullible bastard, Ed reflected, just as dumb now as he had been when he'd pranced around the school disco in eyeshadow and a dog's collar. "I promised I'd make you a star, and I intend to keep my word."

"You better, Brookesy!" Ed wagged his finger at George. He started to laugh, realizing he had stumbled over a rich seam of humor. "Talking of thrashing Fitzwanker's arse—that's something you do quite often, so I've heard! Ha ha! Eh? His arse! It's funny because you're a pair of gaylords!"

George grinned, clearly seeing the joke, which surprised Ed, who had long been of the opinion that his sort didn't have much of a sense of humor. Alternative comedy, maybe, but not actually funny stuff, not honest-to-God straight-up laughs like Ed enjoyed after a round of golf with the boys from the exchange. George turned away and addressed a young woman with a clipboard and a headset, who seemed to be the go-to for anyone who needed anything.

"Can we grab people and get them around the podium?" he asked. "Ed's waiting for his big moment, aren't you, Eddie-boy?"

"Too bloody right I am!" Ed rubbed his hands together. The dry skin did rasp a bit, but it was better than having a moist handshake.

There were more cameras here than at the dance. Ed made sure to grin at each one, then held his head up, teeth bared in his best version of a smile. With a 'Thanks' from George the clipboard girl hurried away, then Ed had his undivided attention once more.

"By the way, Ed, one last go." George laid his hand on Ed's shoulder. "Are you going to let Fitz keep his house?"

"You pulling my plonker, mate? No, I'm fucking not. Your bumchum can sod off."

"I suppose it'd take billions to fight you in the courts. Wish I knew a billionaire." He shrugged and shook his head. "Ah well, Fitz's problem. Grab Steph, Ed, and I'll get set to kick things off at the mic."

Ed looked across to the crowd of locals. There she was, the Ice Queen, face like a slapped arse, perched on a plastic chair.

"Darling!" Ed hurried toward his wife and yanked her up to her feet.

"You've been eating pickled eggs again, haven't you? Your breath smells—like you've been farting out of your mouth."

"Do shut up!" Ed locked his teeth into a grin, flashing it to camera and crowd alike. "This way, hot stuff! Television beckons!"

Chapter Twenty-Nine

"Nimrod — bad dog! Drop the ball!"

The red ball, shiny with Nimrod's plentiful saliva, dropped from the dog's jaws to the ground. Henry picked it up and laughed over his shoulder to the Parvan kids and the England squad.

"Sorry — he's very keen. This way to the — "

As they rounded the corner of the pavilion, Henry could see George, immaculate in his cricket whites, holding a microphone. He was saying something to a woman with a clipboard.

George was effortlessly handsome, debonair and lovely, and Henry had utterly blown it. Without thinking, Henry brushed his hand against his chest where George's medals had imprinted on his skin when they had —

"Don't dribble on my shoe, Nimrod."

It seemed as though everyone in the village was here, and a good many hundreds besides. In fact, so many people had tried to enter the village to witness Standy-Bee's cricketing extravaganza that the police had been drafted in to ensure that numbers didn't get out of hand. The plan had been presented to the parish council as a *fait accompli*, all taken care of by the unflappable Tabitha Shakespeare. So far, Henry reflected, she had certainly ensured that this illustrious event ran as smoothly as even the most simple jam sale.

George was still talking to the young woman, his hand resting on Jez's mane as though the foal were a lapdog, and soon, Henry knew, both the hero and his horse would be gone. But Henry wouldn't go back to how he had been before George's return. No more hiding away from everyone. He would be honest about who he was. He had lost too much already, too much time and too much love.

"All right, Mr. Fitzwalter?"

"Barney! How are you?" Henry ruffled the boy's hair in avuncular fashion.

"Great. It's nice Captain George has come back, isn't he? He's fab!"

Henry nodded, smiling gently. "Yes, he certainly is."

There was no chance that the new Longley Parva Single Wicket trophy might be stolen, placed as it was in full view of the cameras and spectators atop a podium so grand it might have been found at the Olympic Games. This new cup was a long way from the modest vase that disappeared fifteen years ago, a great construction of gleaming silver on which was engraved three wickets, a bat leaning against them. It would look wonderful in the manor, but not as wonderful as that photo of George and Henry that he kept beside the bed.

"Can everyone gather in!" The clipboard woman waved her arms as she called the instruction. "We've got a speech and a guest, we need everyone to pull in, look happy, enthused, glad to be here!"

Looking around, Henry decided that little prompting was needed. Every face he could see was lit with excitement and happiness. He came forward, gripping Nimrod's collar, his bat under his arm. Barney followed, stroking Nimrod's wide head.

A guest? It's not David Gower, is it?

George climbed up onto the podium and Jez clambered nimbly up beside him. The pair seemed effortlessly at ease in front of the cameras and phones were raised aloft, snapping picture after picture.

From the corner of his eye, Henry spotted Ed and Steph, smug as ever in pole position at the front of the crowd. They were half-turned toward the hordes who had come, not to see Longley Parva's richest, meanest couple, but television's Captain George and the England cricket team. As the crowd cheered for George, Ed and Steph smiled and nodded as if the applause was for them. *Typical.*

George waited for the applause to reach a natural lull, then rested his hand on Jez's mane again and said, "Thank you to all of you for coming to Longley Parva today for the return of the hotly contested Longley Parva Single Wicket!"

A deafening cheer went up from the Parvans, mobile phones and hands waving in the air as the camera panned and swooped, catching the lively villagers. Someone in the crowd shouted, "Take your top off!", which George greeted with a raised eyebrow, the gesture enough to win him another cheer. Steph glanced round, and despite her smile, Henry saw no joy in her eyes, only cold uninterest.

"I've traveled the world," George went on, "and now I'm home. Thanks for welcoming me back."

Another roar of approval went up, more shouts and whistles directed at the stage by the livelier attendees.

"To Tabs, to the England boys and to every single one of you, Jez and I owe a massive debt. We're batting for glory, for the roof of the Longley Parva Village Hall and for the magnificent *new* Single Wicket Trophy. Mr. Fitzwalter, the record is currently yours — can you hold onto it?"

Henry stared about in surprise. Everyone, and all the cameras, had turned to him. Realizing his mouth was hanging open, he quickly pressed his lips together and, folding his arms, replied with a firm, confident nod.

Even if he wasn't feeling quite as confident as he may have looked.

"This won't be in the documentary," George told the crowd. "But you all know that my private life and that of the man I love became public property overnight last week and almost every single one of you rallied round. To say thanks for that and for all this village has done for its resident shirtless historian, if there's any shortfall on the roof fund, I'll make it up out of my own pocket."

While everyone cheered, Henry only stared in silence. Had George really just said what he thought he'd heard? *'The man I love'?*

Captain George Standish-Brookes had just come out.

And everyone was cheering.

"And I need to say something to that man!" George had to raise his voice to be heard above the crowd. "Thank you for showing me what it *actually* means to be a hero. Whoever spends their life with you will be the luckiest chap alive!"

Forgetting that the entire village was there, Henry hurried up to the podium, Nimrod at his heels.

"My darling George! Won't *you* spend your life with me?" Henry almost tripped in his haste as he rushed up the steps. "*You* taught me how to be brave — and I adore you, Standy-Bee!"

George caught Henry's hand and pulled him into his arms. They clung to each other as though caught in a tide and George pressed his mouth to Henry's ear and whispered, "Marry me, Fitz?"

"Yes — bloody hell, yes!"

Henry ran his fingers through George's hair and, trying not to laugh as a swelling 'oooh!' rose from the crowd, drew his lips to George's in the most tender of kisses. There could be no doubt what George thought now as the kiss went on and on until someone, probably the woman with the clipboard, began spiritedly clearing her throat.

There was a schedule to follow, after all.

Ed, jabbing at his watch, had grabbed one of the camera operators by the arm.

"Look, I'm an important guy, can't hang about here all day while those two whatsits play tonsil-tennis!"

"Cool down, mate," the cameraman told him. "It's a weekend!"

"Important people like me don't do weekends, we don't do holidays and we don't do lunch hours!" Ed's face was purpling to an alarming shade. "I'm an important man and my time costs serious turkey. So just get my close-up ready, Sonny Jim, or I'll have you sacked!"

"Ed, let's have you and Steph together!" George called happily into the microphone, his arm tight around Henry's waist. He beckoned them with a flamboyant wave. "Come on where we can see you, chum!"

"Come on, Stephy-Steph! That's it." Ed gripped Steph's shoulders. She grimaced at the crowd, her head at an uncomfortable angle as Ed pulled her toward him. "Up on the podium with the gayboys, is that there where you want us, George?"

Henry glared at him. "For someone who's so fond of grabbing testicles —"

A squeak of feedback from the microphone told Henry that his aside to George had been broadcast to the entire audience. And the audience roared with laughter. *Once again, I mess it up...* Henry realized they weren't laughing at him, but with him. How many other unfortunate men had been grabbed at the crotch by Ed Belcher? Quite a few, judging by the pained expressions on several faces in the crowd. Even the vicar's.

"Hello, Steph." George sounded so happy, but was there a sly edge to his smile. "You're certainly looking the part!"

Steph pouted from under the brim of her wide sunhat. Her cold eyes settled on Henry, her teeth clenched. She flared her nostrils as she snapped her head away.

"Shall we get on?" George addressed Henry then turned to the crowd. "Who's ready for a bit of history?"

A cheer went up, and a jocular wag shouted, "Toot-toot!" The crowd laughed then settled, waiting for their resident television historian to speak.

"Six hundred years ago, the Fitzwalter family built Longley Parva Manor, and from that day to this, there has been a Fitz here in the village. A raven in the tower, if you will." He looked to Henry, his expression nothing short of adoring. "But some members of the family were a little flighty and two hundred years ago the hall was wagered in a game of cricket between Bad Billy Fitzwalter and Octavius Belcher. The umpire was a certain Reverend Standish, and, though he managed to mislay the score sheet, the general drunken consensus was that the victory belonged to Billy."

George looked to Ed with that same smile and went on. "But Octavius Belcher left some convenient papers, as such chaps are wont to do, in which he alleged dark deeds. The vicar must be in the pay of the squire, said he, and that meant the hall was his. Now, our Ed found them and rather than say, *what an interesting bit of family history*, instead he told Fitz here, *via a lawyer*, that he was going to lose his home."

Henry lowered his gaze from the crowd. He felt the tightening in his stomach that visited him whenever an official-looking letter arrived through the post. There had been many of late.

Bloody Ed bloody Belcher.

"Booo!"

"Hissss!"

The crowd came alive, as if they were once again in the village hall for the Longley Parva Christmas panto.

"Now, now, George!" Ed fiddled with his sunglasses, the swagger ebbing from his tone. "You make me sound like the baddie of the piece! Ha ha! I'm just a man who's been denied his birthright—you tell the Parvans *that!*"

"Because all Ed wants is to live in Longley Parva Manor, isn't that right?" George blinked innocently. "Or might your scheme have been rather more...*ambitious* than that?"

"I want the bloody manor! It should be mine!" Ed clenched his fist, his words spittle-flecked. "What— what scheme? What a lot of rot!"

Someone in the crowd managed an extremely loud belch and Ed swung round to look at them. "Which one of you clod-hopping yokels did *that?*"

A cameraman hurried across the grass toward him, capturing Ed in close-up, the stockbroker's face turning a deeper hue of purple.

"But Ed's plan was bigger than that." George slipped his arm matily through Ed's, holding him in place. "Ed was going to bully Fitz's house out from under him by tying him up in legal tape until he had no choice. You, ladies and gentlemen, are looking at the man who was going to sell Longley Parva so a billionaire could turn our village into a golf course!"

Ed's eyes bulged liked the pickled eggs he was so fond of, his mouth hanging open as he tried to stutter a denial. But he was caught staring into the face of a crowd that was beginning to advance on him, arms aloft, cricket bats swinging, dog leads whirling. They coined a chant and it grew louder as they came ever nearer.

"No ifs, no buts, we'll kick him in the nuts!"

Over and over and over again, building and swelling, menace and hate climbing.

A small, blonde-haired child came running from the crowd. A pretty little girl in an expensive blue dress, clapping her hands and laughing. And joining in with the chant.

Ed's own child, Sapphire.

"This is a cricket match, not a lynch mob." George held up his hands. "Ed, Steph, Mr. Randy Cheese is in the pavilion and he's keen to make the Belchers *very* famous. Don't keep him waiting. Ladies and gentlemen, Mr. and Mrs. Ed and Steph Belcher. A round of applause for our happy couple, and let's get on with some cricket!"

The crowd were happy with this outcome, clapping and cheering with glee once more. Mrs. Dalrymple heaved Sapphire up onto her hip and carried her off to watch the game. Ed and Steph, however, looked like a couple on their way to face the executioner. How George had uncovered the scheme and convinced one of the world's richest men to sit in a cricket pavilion would remain a mystery for now, but Henry knew that this could only mean one thing — Captain George had kept his promise. He had saved Longley Parva Manor, just as he'd sworn he would.

Before George could hop down from the podium, Henry caught him in his arms.

"My hero, Standy-Bee! Thank you, darling — I don't know how I can ever repay you, other than by kissing you a thousand times. Would that suffice?"

"I've put you in to bat last," George whispered. "Just you versus the whole England team fielding, Fitz. Make it a walkover?"

Henry laughed. "You're not making this easy, are you? Right — let's play cricket!"

The England cricket team took up fielding positions, each with a member of the youth team shadowing them. One by one the Parvans went up to bat or bowl, and the England team did their best not to catch anyone out on their first go, no matter how easy a catch they were.

There were some impressive reaches into the nineties for runs, but Henry's record of one-thirty stood unbeaten. Then lunch was called.

Henry and George trotted to the pavilion, arms loosely about each other's waists. The spectators cheered more loudly for them than they did the visiting cricketers.

A figure had appeared on the veranda, vaguely familiar to Henry, though he couldn't say why. He wondered if it was a pharmaceutical salesman who'd visited his surgery.

But once they drew nearer, Henry realized who it was.

"You Fitzwalter?" Randy Cheese took an enormous cigar from between his teeth and gestured toward Henry. "You're the laird of the manor?"

Henry blinked at the man he'd only ever seen on television, and occasionally in newspapers, stepping down from private jets. And now he was on the veranda of Longley Parva's cricket club.

"Strictly speaking, the lord of the manor, but—you're Mr. Cheese, of course." Henry extended his hand to shake. Randy Cheese seized it in a bear's paw and pumped hard, staring fiercely at Henry.

"This is a man who can make things happen," he told Henry, gesturing toward George. "Belcher's a double-crossing bastard but I'm a man of honor, so let's make this a deal between men. I'm still looking to put Cheese Acres Golf and Resort right here in Soo-sex and I'm offering you fifty million dollars to secure your house, Mr. Fitzwalter. What do you say?"

All of Henry's breath escaped his body in one go, then he recovered and laughed.

"I won't give up Longley Parva Manor—the only home I've ever had and ever want—for *anything!*"

"What if I were to say to you," Cheese raised his eyebrow, "name your price?"

"Mr. Cheese, I tell you kindly, sir—my house is *not* for sale."

"You're a man of honor too, Mr. Fitzwalter. You passed the test!" Cheese laughed. "I'm gonna build my *own* British village out in Vegas. Eighteen holes, a Tudor palace, baseball pavilions and a good old British tavern. Cheese Acres, Nevada, opening 2020!"

"Maybe we'll visit, but that'll depend on Nim and Jez!" George shook Cheese's hand. "I don't know *how* Tab convinced you out of Manhattan, but welcome to Longley Parva!"

"She's a hell of a woman," Cheese told them as he turned and gave a nod of acknowledgement to Tabitha. "I'd hate to be married to her."

Tabitha raised what look like a vase to Cheese in salute. Henry looked again and realized it was a particularly large glass of wine.

"To the lunch, George—I've got a surprise for you!"

"I like the sound of that!" George kissed his cheek. "It's a day for them!"

Henry held his hand. They might be in public, but it really didn't matter.

"This way, this way...this way to— Oh, there's hardly any left."

An old china cake stand dug out from a crockery cabinet somewhere in the manor stood on the refreshments table, covered mainly in crumbs. Henry rescued the last remaining slice and put it on a plate for George.

"You said you wanted me to make you a chocolate cake, so I did."

"Oh, Fitz!" George rested his head on Henry's shoulder. "I think my inner Reverend approves."

"I'll make you lots more, I promise. But now—ah, cucumber sandwiches!"

They took their loaded plates outside and sat next to each other, their animals beside them. Henry was aware of a camera shifting about in the corner of his eye and saw Tabitha wave them away. Nimrod made short work of a pork pie and immediately headed off to hunt down more from other plates. He returned with crumbs in his whiskers and found a patch of shade, where he lay down to sleep.

Dark clouds threatened the game immediately after lunch, but they rolled away toward the coast and the Parvans went back to their match. Still no one got a century, and still the England team fielded kindly. Then it was Captain George Standish-Brookes' turn to bat, and Henry's turn to bowl.

"The last time I did this, I scored a big zero," George told the assembled audience. "And the man who is now my fiancé tried to brain me with a cricket bat. Let's hope I do rather better today!"

Henry flushed and scraped his fingers through his hair as he went to his position. When he turned, the rapt attention of all the spectators and the players was on them. Several television cameras had readied themselves for the big moment. Television's Captain George Standish-Brookes, challenging the Single Wicket record.

"Ready, darling?" Henry backed away so that he could get a good run-up, rubbing the ball up and down his thigh. George blinked, his gaze fixed on the movement of Henry's hand. He tapped the bat on the grass, glanced to where Jez watched, safe in the care of Lil, and winked.

"Ready!"

Excited chatter rippled through the spectators, followed by several admonishing shushes. There was silence. Even Nimrod's snores had quietened.

Henry ran on long powerful legs which, day to day, carried him through muddy fields, over stiles and fences, up hillsides. Solid, muscular legs that gripped farm animals to keep them still, that saved him — these days — from advancing, angry animals. Firm legs, that had gripped George around the waist while they made love.

Henry's overarm was perfect, the ball bouncing once two-thirds of the way along the pitch, rising into the air at the perfect height for George to hit.

And, just as he had fifteen years earlier, George missed.

In fact, he didn't only miss, he didn't even try.

When a cry of surprised sympathy rose up from the crowd George seemed to come back to life. He blinked and looked around before announcing, "Falling in love is *very* bad for my cricket score."

Henry dragged both his hands back through his hair, laughing.

"Oh, George, what shall I do with you?"

"Break your record, Fitz." George kissed his cheek as they passed each other. "If I don't bowl you out first!"

Here's the moment, then.

Henry puffed out his cheeks. With his bat, he poked down the uneven ground where the turf had been torn by the game. Perhaps it was unwise to challenge oneself as a youth. Where was the energy of that young man? Or perhaps, in the intervening years, had Henry matured, like a fine wine, or maybe a wheel of cheese? He might not have the energy he'd once had, but all the silly anger had gone.

Yet George's routine hadn't changed. He stood back and gave that same casual salute that said to Henry, *may the best man triumph*. Then he polished the ball on his jumper a few times until his head dipped and, just as he always did, hitched the leg of his whites a little. Up came his hand again, ruffling his hair, touching his lips, then he tossed the ball into his palm and ran, bowling it at Henry with a flourish.

Henry saw nothing, heard nothing, save that ball coming toward him through the air. He lifted his bat and it met the advancing ball with a satisfying slap. It arched up, but its trajectory didn't quite match what the younger Henry had been capable of. It plummeted too early and hit the ground just inside the boundary. It rolled over the white rope, three of the England team running after it, and scored Henry a four.

But still, it was a four.

The spectators clapped politely.

One of the fielders hurled the ball toward George. He caught it and off they went again, setting the pattern for what promised to be a very entertaining innings for the final batsman, Longley Parva's finest ever wielder of the willow.

After the initial good but not brilliant attempt, Henry imagined himself back in the practice nets with the friendly stray at his heels, and hit a six with the second ball. The England team gave him a round of applause and Henry bowed awkwardly to each of them, acknowledging their praise.

On the game went, George's ritual never changing. Henry had to avoid meeting George's glance or risk distraction, but the spectators did their best to put him off. Nimrod barked and ran around in circles, apparently helping the fielders to collect the cricket ball. Ed wandered into Henry's eyeline, barking into his mobile phone. Someone popped a champagne cork. A small child squealed and ran onto the field.

Henry reached his century, but not as quickly as he had done before. He paused to stand up straight, stretching out his arms and his back. Then they continued.

The sight of Ed, wandering into his eyeline yet again, made Henry clench his jaw. The bloody man had lost, yet he was still there, an irritant determined to rob Henry of his triumph. Not that it mattered now, because Henry had bested all the other batsmen who had played in the tournament today—but he had that hot-headed youth of fifteen years ago still to challenge.

On and on they went, Henry's record creeping closer, the crowd cheering louder and louder, the sense that they were witnessing a moment for the ages seizing hold of the Parvans. That infamous score of one-thirty had never been bettered but today, with Henry standing at the wicket with one hundred and twenty-five runs to his name, the record might be broken by the very man who already held it.

The numbers were stark on the scoreboard, shouting to everyone present, *Just hit a bloody six, Henry!*

"This one for the record *and* the new trophy," George called. "Make it a good one, Fitz."

"Wait a minute—wait a bloody minute!"

"Oh, Christ." Henry paused and leaned against his bat, feet crossed.

Bloody Ed Belcher.

He was smiling a particularly fake sort of smile. Once he'd barreled onto the pitch, Ed declared, "I should get this go. Seeing as at the last match I couldn't even play after I fell out of a helicopter! Only fair I bowl now!"

Tom Golding had started to jog onto the field after Ed. He waved to Henry and George.

Henry bit his lip in thought. He could very easily — and very gladly — tell Ed to sod off. It was George's ball to bowl. And if Ed threw some terrible, confusing ball that went haywire and knocked off the stumps, or didn't land solidly enough and was an easy catch, then Henry's attempt at breaking his own record was finished.

But.

Henry had beaten everyone else who'd played today. And he'd got within touching distance of his record. The hot-headed boy he'd been would've gone after Ed with his bat. But this was the older, more mature Henry.

A gentleman.

And on this day, two hundred years ago, Ed's ancestor had played with Henry's ancestor, while George's had kept the score.

History was pushing in on Henry, guiding his hand.

"Well — okay, Ed. You can have your go!" Henry waved back to Tom and gave him a thumbs-up. He grinned. *Still not all that mature.* "Make it a good one, or I'll brain you with my cricket bat!"

"Hang on, old man!" George waved his hand. "Fitz, can I have a minute?"

"Yes?" He jogged across to meet George at the center of the pitch. George's expression was a frown, his eyes darkened with concern, and when he spoke again his voice was a whisper.

"Do you think it's wise to let 'orrible Ed bowl such an important ball?" George blinked. "I'm all for an independent bowler so people don't say I gave you an easy time, but — *Ed?*"

"You do remember what happened two hundred years ago today, on this very spot?"

"Then I wish you the very best of British." George kissed his cheek. He turned and gently bowled the ball to Ed, who caught it with a look that said, *just you wait.* "Knock it into next week, Fitz."

"That's exactly what I intend to do." Henry smiled as he walked back to his position by the stumps. George wandered across to join the spectators and sank down onto the grass beside Jez, resting his head against the horse's leg.

"I'm not beaten yet." Ed drew himself up and weighed the ball in his hand. "But *you're* about to be. You've crossed me one too many times."

Henry shone his sweetest grin on Ed and tapped his bat against the ground. The dry, hollow earth echoed like a drum.

"Really? Says the man who grabbed me by the balls and tried to steal my house. The man who was going to have a bolt put through the brain of a perfectly healthy animal that just needed love."

The man who married my ex-girlfriend, who – No, Henry was too much of a gentleman to mention it. Knowing that Ed now had Sussex's least enthusiastic bedfellow beside him every night was enough.

"Here it comes, Fitzwanker." He looked at George and bellowed, "Stick this on television, nancy boy!"

Ed took his run and let the ball fly. The bodyline bowl was just suited to Ed's way of life and it hurtled toward Henry at a hell of a speed, daring him to miss and endure the agony of a cricket ball *somewhere* he didn't want it. Clearly already sensing victory as it left his hand, Ed made a fist and pumped the air, shouting, "Come on then!"

Henry's shoulders burned, sore from the length of his innings. All he was aware of was bringing his bat forward with such speed that he barely saw the ball connect with the willow. But it had done—there was now a massive red mark on the bat, with a nick in the varnish to show where it had hit.

But where the hell was the bloody ball?

He turned, as had everyone else, in the direction the ball had gone. To the pavilion.

Was someone hurt? He hadn't hit a spectator, had he? There was commotion, a scream, followed by shouting, then laughter. Tom running with a ladder.

Had he hit the ball into the gutter?

But no. Tom was climbing higher than the gutter, and a collection of film crew and spectators held the ladder steady as he went onto the roof.

To a hole smashed through the tiles.

"Oh Jesus bloody hell! I've wrecked the pavilion!"

Applause. Cheering.

Henry rubbed his shoulder, staring at the hole in the pavilion roof that stared back him like a dark, unblinking eye.

He felt George's arm encircle his waist and Nimrod licking his hand as the cheers grew louder and someone, possibly the captain of the England team, called, "Six! One three one!"

"I've beaten my own record, George! I've also destroyed a roof—but—I did it!" Henry held George as tightly as he could, tears of relief and joy staining George's cheek.

When he looked up from their embrace, Henry saw the pavilion again, Tom climbing down from the ladder with something in his hands. Not the ball, no. A surprised gasp ran through the spectators as each of them realized what it was.

It can't be.

"The Longley Parva Cup," George whispered as Tom reached the ground. Then he turned and held up the willow pattern vase by both of its handles, as though he had just won the Grand Prix. Yet this willow pattern wasn't a scene of chinoiserie, but of Sussex life, and nobody had seen it for fifteen years.

All that time spent searching, turning the village over, and it had been there all along, hidden in the corner of the cricket pavilion's cobweb-strewn loft space.

George and Henry looked at each other and George said impishly, "Not guilty, Fitz."

Henry nuzzled his face to his fiancé's neck, laughing softly. "Dear old George! But — how the heck did it get up there? It didn't fly!"

"Hahahahahaaaa!" It was the laughter of a madman, of Rumpelstiltskin stamping on the floor, of Ed Belcher standing at the wicket, his hands on his hips. "We got you, Pops and I! We took your trophy that day and hid it because your *fucking* family was always getting one over on us! No trophy for you, Fitzwanker, and all of you stupid inbreds crawling all over the village. And it was there all along, what a bloody prank! And because of that, you couple of queers didn't get to bum each other for fifteen years! Hahahahaaaa!"

Henry and George stared at him. Everyone on the field, all the spectators, stared at him. The television cameras swooped nearer.

"*You* hid the Longley Parva Cup?" Henry gaped in disgusted surprise. "You stood there and saw me accuse George and you — You are not a gentleman, sir!"

"Not a— At least I'm not a bloody bumchum!" Ed wrenched the stump out of the ground and hurtled toward Henry with a cry of, "Bloody Fitzwanker!"

Henry's heart thudded in terror and he raised his bat, knowing that if he hit Ed with it, when he was running at him, he could fracture his skull. And yet, the sharp end of that stump—

"So help me God, Ed—don't you—"

A flash of black and white and sandy fur shot across the cricket field and Ed yowled as he went flying to the ground.

Nimrod stood with his front paws on Ed's chest, fabric ripped from the crotch of Ed's trousers in his teeth.

"No lasting damage, Ed?" Not getting any other reply than a dismayed moan, Henry threw aside his bat and grabbed Nimrod by the collar. "Nimrod, bad dog!"

He didn't hear Tom's shout of surprise, or wonder at the sound of shattered china.

"Oh, Fitz." George's voice was very quiet and the crowd, so loud a moment ago, was suddenly silent. There in Tom's hands were the handles and attached narrow neck of the recently rediscovered Longley Parva vase while, in a hundred pieces at his feet, lay the remains of the lost trophy. Atop them, like an X marking the spot, was Henry Fitzwalter's discarded cricket bat.

Tom looked down, then up, then down again. With a soft whisper, a scroll of yellow paper slid from the shattered end of the neck and dropped down onto the mound of broken china.

George moved first, every camera pointed at him as he crouched and scooped up the scroll. It was tied with a red ribbon that Henry recognized from the papers of

Reverend Standish and he met George's gaze as his lover slowly unfastened the bow. Like a court page he unrolled the scroll and cleared his throat.

"I, Reverend Tobias Standish, do bear witness that a game of cricket was played on this eve between Messrs Octavius Belcher, Esquire, and William Fitzwalter, Esquire, both of Longley Parva. The stakes are decided upon thus."

He raised his eyebrow, teasing the spectators as he unrolled the scroll further. Henry tried to catch George's eye, shaking his head very slightly, mouthing *Don't read it!* But George was in character. Despite the absence of a cassock and a shovel hat, this was verily Reverend Standish before them. Henry took a deep breath. He was a gentleman, and he must accept the outcome.

Maybe he would, after all, lose the manor.

"Should the victor of the game be named as Mr. Fitzwalter, Mr. Belcher agrees to grant the said Mr. Fitzwalter deed and title to his Sussex estates in perpetuity." He looked at Henry, then at Ed. "Should the victor of this game be named as Mr. Belcher, Mr. Fitzwalter agrees to grant the said Mr. Belcher deed and title to Longley Parva Manor in perpetuity."

"Bloody fucking right!" Ed called from his place on the floor. He was silenced by Nimrod's bared teeth, a low growl vibrating in his throat.

"Let all present here agree that the score of Messrs Belcher and Fitzwalter as recorded in The Green Man, witnessed and dated by those signed below, is inscribed herein."

This was the moment that would decide their fate, yet George paused to milk it. He stroked his hand over Jez's mane and slowly revealed to himself alone the numbers written there by Tobias two hundred years ago.

"Mr. Octavius Belcher, Esquire, one hundred and seventeen runs." He glanced at Ed, who pumped his fist in the air, clearly smelling victory. George's poker face was unreadable until he met Henry's eye and gave a broad, delighted grin. "Mr. William Fitzwalter, Esquire, one hundred and thirty-one runs. Let all present agree that Mr. William Fitzwalter, Esquire, is the victor!"

He turned the scroll to face his audience, letting them see the same flamboyant handwriting that had neatly recorded the daily comings and goings of Rupert Standish's life in the goat's packet of papers. Beneath the declaration was an assortment of signatures, each attesting to the veracity of the document and score recorded on it. There, alongside that of the Reverend and Billy, was the tightly written signature of Octavius Belcher, accepting once and for all that he had lost.

"Huzzah!" Henry bounced into the air, and on landing almost managed to execute a cartwheel. "Bad Billy, you were a reckless twit, but bloody hell—one-thirty-one! Ha! *Ha!* Hear that Ed? Octavius *lost!* Lost!"

Henry ran to George and they embraced tightly. He would never get bored of hugging him. The two men were in the midst of a rapidly growing crowd as the spectators gravitated toward them.

"It all came right in the end, then!"

"It always does when you're in love." George laughed, pressing his lips to Henry's. "Most of the time. Usually."

"Although this isn't the end—not really. We're right at the beginning."

"A new adventure for the Standish-Brookes-Fitzwalters." George drew back just a little, his arms around Henry's waist. "With Billy, Tobias, Rupes and Nimrod keeping an eye on us? And maybe giving the odd cricket bat a helping hand?"

"As long as they don't keep an eye on us *all* the time." Henry whispered, "Chaps need a little privacy every so often!"

"Especially newlyweds."

"Let's go, dear old George — to the home you saved."

"Jez and I were saying just last night how much we'd love to live in the manor...if the offer still stands?"

"Of course! The stable's ready and the lake is perfect for a swim this time of year."

"Don't you want to collect your trophy first?" George glanced toward the podium. "I'd hate to drag you away before your big moment."

"*You're* my prize, I don't need anything else."

But Henry didn't have a choice. The surging crowd of Longley Parva residents hoisted him onto their shoulders and carried him. When he looked over his shoulder, he saw that George was being carried across the cricket field in identical fashion. With Jez and Nimrod trotting alongside they were borne to the podium and there, surrounded by the villagers of Longley Parva and the national cricket team, Henry finally received his trophy as Ed Belcher, with his wife and Randy Cheese's lawyers in hot pursuit, slunk away.

There were photos to take and interviews to give and champagne to drink but finally the little family was winding its way through the lanes and home to Longley Parva Manor. The scroll was safe inside the cup and this time, George promised, he *wouldn't* forget where he had put it. This time, there would be no question who was the winner.

The house wore a different face now all anxiety had melted away. Permanence, not decay.

Everything that had been lost was now recovered.

"Fancy an evening stroll in the grounds, dear?" Henry linked his arm through George's, the cup swinging from his other hand. George responded with a nod and a smile of pure contentment as he drew in a deep breath of fresh evening air. The day had been more than a success. It was the start of a new life for both of them and here, in the manor where their ancestors had fallen in love, Henry and his captain would continue the story.

The breeze shivered the high branches, whispering like the voices of ghosts. In the half-light, Henry could almost swear that there were figures in the grove of trees, watching. Two men and their animal companions, out for a stroll in the balmy summer night.

George and Henry looked to the grove as one, though neither seemed to want to be the first to speak. It was George who broke the silence with a playful murmur of, "It's a big enough house for everybody."

Then they kissed again, little caring *who* might see.

Want to see more from these authors?
Here's a taster for you to enjoy!

Captivating Captains:
The Captain and the Theatrical
Catherine Curzon & Eleanor Harkstead

Excerpt

Summer 1817

As Captain Ambrose Pendleton strode through the gates of Vauxhall Gardens, he didn't see the crush of people or the lights in the trees, or hear the music. He was thinking only of seeing his friend Orsini once again.

But first there was the show, which Orsini had raved about in his letter. Cosima was from his stable of talent, and Orsini had been insistent that his friend watch the most remarkable, exquisite and well-formed young lady to grace the continental stage.

And her adorable performing parrot!

Ambrose entered the pavilion where Cosima was to perform. He took his seat and, as he waited for the show to begin, found himself enjoying the hubbub of ordinary people around him. How nice it was to be back among the throng of humanity, without the smell of gunpowder or the roar of cannon or the parade-ground shout. He glanced about the audience, wondering if his friend was there, but Orsini was nowhere to be seen.

The quartet struck a note, and applause rang through the pavilion as the velvet curtain was drawn back. The woman who emerged was tall and slender but, as Orsini had promised, well-formed. Here in a summer London, her diaphanous gown and tumbling curls transported Ambrose instantly back to his youth in Italy, to a world of classical myth and striking women, yet none that he could recall were as striking as the creature who now tripped across the stage, one slender arm outstretched for the bright blue parrot that perched upon her pale wrist, the yellow and red feathers beneath its wings and at its breast shimmering.

A woman in Roman dress and a parrot… It was very Orsini, if nothing else.

There was likely nothing else quite like it in London that night as the magnificent Cosima ran through her repertoire of silly stories—just the right side of bawdy—and Italian songs, sometimes accompanied for the sake of comedy by the bird and sometimes, for the sake of entertainment, by the quartet. Every man in the audience was enraptured by her, enchanted by each flick of her auburn curls, each sly aside, and every woman became a confidante, laughing behind ladylike hands at some wry comment from the performer on the stage.

Wherever had Orsini found her? Ambrose wondered, though he knew instinctively that some of this material must belong to his friend, for it had that same devilish mischief so beloved by Amadeo Orsini. They claimed that she was his sister but Ambrose knew better, for he had met Orsini's numerous siblings and none of them were La Cosima.

Yet she certainly could have been family.

The show ended with rapturous applause, Cosima curtseying to her admiring audience as the parrot took a small, proper bow. Reluctantly, Ambrose followed the crowd out of the pavilion and back into the balmy summer air. He would happily have watched Cosima and her parrot perform all evening, if not for his promised reunion with Orsini.

Off he went toward the Cascade, where they had arranged to meet. But he couldn't see Orsini anywhere. Where was the young man Ambrose remembered, always decked out in silks? He certainly would have noticed him among the crowd — unless, and Ambrose thought it most unlikely, the great impresario had adopted a somber guise.

But wouldn't he notice Orsini's dancing eyes, and his knowing smile, and his — what the devil?

"Now, madam, please stop that!" Ambrose laughed politely — as politely as a man could with a woman's hands over his eyes. He could smell her perfume and feel the lace of her gloves and hear her giggle. "You must have confused me for your husband, or your sweetheart!" *Or a paying customer*, but Ambrose thought it best not to voice that.

"Captain Pendleton," came the singsong-voiced reply from close to his ear. "The great Orsini begs your indulgence, but, alas, he is detained by matters feminine. He asks that I escort you to supper tonight!"

Ambrose clenched his jaw. Matters feminine? Was Orsini involved in some sort of intrigue with a lady?

And why did he recognize the woman's voice — but of course!

"Cosima!"

He turned quickly and took her hands as they fell from his face. There she was, standing before him, the leading lady of Orsini's show, a dazzlingly red shawl wrapped around her narrow shoulders. As much as he'd longed to see his friend, what an honor it was to be favored by such a performer—and the parrot too, who perched on her shoulder like a little admiral.

"How excited I am to make your acquaintance!" Ambrose bent to kiss her gloved hand. "I very much enjoyed your show this evening."

The parrot administered a sharp peck to Ambrose's hair and Cosima exclaimed, "Pagolo! Captain, forgive my little chaperone, he is so very protective of his Cosima and his applause!"

"I enjoyed your performance too, Pagolo, of course." Ambrose grinned as he gave the imperious parrot a bow. "How very remiss that I did not congratulate you, as well."

"His career has been long and celebrated." Cosima tapped her finger gently against the parrot's beak and he cocked his head to one side. "He might teach all of us how to improve our performances, he thinks! Now, sir, what delights might the gardens offer an innocent Italian girl and her escort?"

"We are stood before the marvel of the gardens, dear lady. The Cascade! Now watch carefully, for I think it is due a performance." Ambrose offered Cosima his arm as the crowd swelled around them.

He couldn't hold back his smile as the curtain lifted and Cosima's elegant fingers gripped his sleeve, her mouth falling open in an expression of perfect wonder. Before them the night lit up bright as fireworks illuminated the heavens and the gasps and appreciative murmurs of the audience greeted the scene of bucolic splendor. As the artificial metallic water cascaded down, a mill wheel gently turned, the intricately rendered bridge in the center crossed first by a coach and horses, then a whole troop of soldiers, strolling ladies and ambling gentleman. It was magnificent, Ambrose knew, but he took more pleasure in his companion's wonder than the mechanical marvel he had seen a dozen or more times.

"How is it done?" Cosima laughed, shaking her head in utter wonder. "What a thing engineering must be, it is all sorcery to me!"

Ambrose knew, but only because his father had told him, for he had an acquaintance who had known the fellow who had devised it. Even so, it still didn't make much sense to Ambrose, which gave him pause — how would he ever follow his father's wishes and turn industrialist now that he had left the Army?

"Cogs and wheels, I believe. Gears and pulleys." Ambrose wafted his hand, as if it was all thoroughly familiar to him and actually rather dull. "And such things of that nature. Now, may I offer you a refreshment? You must be in need of one after your performance."

"Cogs and wheels," Pagolo agreed, pecking at Ambrose's hair again. "Cogs! Wheels!"

"You should not pay him any heed." Cosima slipped her arm opportunely through Ambrose's own. "I confess, sir, I am of a mind to dance!"

A dance with such a lady as Cosima? Ambrose nodded, quite unable to form a coherent reply. His evening was not turning out quite as he had expected, but how lovely to lead Cosima toward the first dance floor that presented itself, and witness at close hand the glee leaping in her eyes.

"See? Is not Vauxhall Gardens the most splendid of places, Cosima? Have you ever known the like?" They stood, arms linked, on the edge of the dance floor and watched the couples in the set.

"Cogs," decided Pagolo somewhat archly, earning himself a sharp look from his mistress. She turned her gaze back to the dancers, tapping one silk-slippered foot lightly in time to the music as she twirled an auburn curl around her finger.

With Cosima absorbed by the dancers, Ambrose had a chance to see her unobserved. She was a dazzling lady, quite unlike the women Ambrose was used to, the daughters of ambitious parents keen to see their charge wed to a captain of industry's son. None of those girls had Cosima's grace, or her easy elegance, and certainly none of them could have put on a show such as Cosima had that evening.

The more Ambrose looked, the more he saw something oddly familiar about her. The large hazel eyes, for one, but perhaps that was not unusual among Italians. The rather prominent nose, but it wasn't shaped quite the same as Orsini's. Even so...

"Gosh, I hope you shan't think me an impertinent sort of fellow, but are you not—tell me now, if my dear friend Orsini had a sister, would she be you?"

"Alas, he does not have a sister, though the world thinks it is so." Cosima turned her head just a little, then dropped her voice to a whisper and asked, "Wasn't that a riotous night in Florence, Pen? You and that saucy old creature in the wimple, your eyes nearly popped out of your head!"

Ambrose Pendleton's eyes nearly burst from their sockets again as he realized his error. Unless Cosima was an exceptional mimic, but—

"Orsini! My dear friend!" He clapped the elegant lady on the back and pumped her arm up and down with eager enthusiasm. "As I live and breathe!"

They were now the object of some amusement, for what sort of a gentleman behaved like that to—as far as anyone else knew — a lady? Ambrose felt a blush rise to his face and the parrot glared at him from his perch on Cosima's shoulder.

"Unhand me, sir," Orsini — for it was he — teased in that delicate voice, the pretty young man of just a few years ago barely visible beneath the construct of Cosima. "Did you really not know your old friend? I take that as an exceptionally fine review of my work!"

"I own that I did not!" Ambrose offered Cosima — Orsini — it was confusing — his arm again. "I had thought there was something familiar about Cosima. Her humor on the stage, for one. And —" Ambrose cleared his throat. He tore his gaze from his friend and watched the dancers skip by instead. "And her eyes."

"Amadeo Orsini was simply one more pretty young actor in a sea of pretty young actors." Cosima pouted softly. "Cosima was merely intended as a party piece and yet her star soon eclipsed mine, and I could never hold back a beautiful young lady!"

"When you wrote and told me you'd given up the stage for the role of impresario, I had no idea that —" Entranced, Ambrose found himself gazing once more into the large hazel eyes of his friend. "My goodness, but you do make a very pretty lady."

"I have devoted myself instead to producing and managing the career of the dear, mysterious Cosima," he told Ambrose. "It allows me to see two rather different views of the world, I can assure you!"

"I'm not surprised!" Ambrose smiled to himself, rather pleased to have Cosima on his arm. "And I wager there must be quite a fight for your hand from king and emperor alike."

"All remain disappointed, for Cosima has yet to find the fellow who might claim her heart." He blinked, long eyelashes batting as he teased, "Perhaps that has changed tonight, kind sir!"

Heavens, what a thought!

"That depends — I have no title, but I do have a very wealthy father!" Ambrose patted Cosima's hand. A note of sadness came into his voice. "Alas, I believe that Father has found a wife for me — not that he has told me so, but what else can I assume when a young lady is so frequent a visitor to our house?"

"Oh!" Orsini sounded genuinely surprised by that revelation. "Tell, Pen. Who and what?"

"There is an industrialist, by the name of Mr. Tarbottom —"

Orsini opened his eyes very wide, then blinked as though he had something in his eye, the blinks growing more frequent until, with a hoot of noise, he broke into a fit of hilarity. He patted Ambrose's arm daintily and threw back his head, his laughter filling the air as Pagolo joined in for good measure.

"Yes, really — Mr. Tarbottom." Ambrose tried to narrow his lips in disapproval at his friend's reaction, but the gray cloud that had followed him in recent weeks began to dissolve in the face of such unbridled laughter. "Where was I? Yes — Mr. Tarbottom is an American industrialist, and he happens to have both an open position in his mines and a daughter of marriageable age. If I know my father, he will believe my fortune is set."

"A position?" Orsini nodded, his smile fading a little. "He must have mines in England then, yes? I am to remain here for a time, Pen, so I shall visit your mines and entertain the workers if you wish!"

"If only that were so." Ambrose's gaze passed slowly over the revelers and the pavilions, the garlanded trees and the musicians and dancers and tumblers. "I very much doubt I shall ever return, alas. The position Mr. Tarbottom would offer me is in America."

Orsini's chin dipped, his gaze falling away to the floor. He said nothing for a few moments, but gave Ambrose's arm a little squeeze. "You must be very excited, Pen."

PUBLISHING

Sign up for our newsletter and find out about all our romance book releases, eBook sales and promotions, sneak peeks and FREE romance books!

About the Authors

Catherine Curzon

Catherine Curzon is a royal historian who writes on all matters of 18th century. Her work has been featured on many platforms and Catherine has also spoken at various venues including the Royal Pavilion, Brighton, and Dr Johnson's House.

Catherine holds a Master's degree in Film and when not dodging the furies of the guillotine, writes fiction set deep in the underbelly of Georgian London.

She lives in Yorkshire atop a ludicrously steep hill.

Eleanor Harkstead

Eleanor Harkstead often dashes about in nineteenth-century costume, in bonnet or cravat as the mood takes her. She can occasionally be found wandering old graveyards, and is especially fond of the ones in Edinburgh. Eleanor is very fond of chocolate, wine, tweed waistcoats and nice pens. She has a large collection of vintage hats, and once played guitar in a band. Originally from the south-east, Eleanor now lives somewhere in the Midlands with a large ginger cat who resembles a Viking.

Catherine and Eleanor love to hear from readers. You can find their contact information, website and author biographies at https://www.pride-publishing.com.

Club Sixxes
Another Pretty Face
Another Curvy Body
Another Sweet Smile

Clandestine Classics
The Phantom of the Opera

Anthologies
Treble: Savin' Me
Boots, Chaps and Cowboy Hats: Between Us

Collections
Naughty or Nice?: Wrapped in Red and Green
Heart Attack: Over My Head
Haunted By You: Miss Me Baby
Wanton Witches: Candlelit Magic
Jolly Rogered: Ruined by the Pirate
Hot Bite: Summer Sizzle
Falsely, Madly, Deeply: From Fake to Forever